THE ORC WAR CAMPAIGNS

A SWORD OF DRAGONS STORY

Jon Wasik

ISBN: 1537688278
ISBN-13: 978-1537688275

For you, the fans of Sword of Dragons, for inspiring and encouraging me!

Also by Jon Wasik

Rise of the Forgotten – The Sword of Dragons Book 1
Burning Skies – The Sword of Dragons Book 2

CONTENTS

ACKNOWLEDGMENTS

First and foremost, I want to thank the fans! I began this anthology purely to give something new and exciting to you all, and it spiraled into this much grander and highly enjoyable project. Your support and excitement has inspired me!

Thank you to my amazing wife, Beck, for helping me hone all of my crafts related to writing, and for always encouraging me to keep going! You continually challenge me to do better, and your creative eye has been invaluable in making the best novel that I possibly could.

Thank you to my parents for always believing in me and supporting me, regardless of how crazy my writing endeavors have been.

I also want to thank Wayne Adams of VtW Productions for your incredible insights and advice. You've been a huge help over the years, and this novel largely became a reality due to your advice!

And as always, a huge thank you to Nick and Natalie Welts, for always beta reading and giving vital feedback to me. Especially Nick, my best friend for two decades! I couldn't have done this without you.

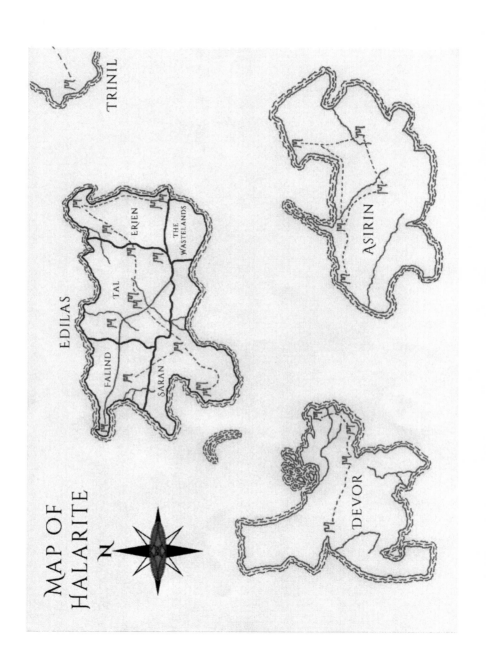

MAP OF
HALARITE

N

TRINIL

EDILAS

FALIND

TAL

ERJEN

SARAN

THE
WASTELANDS

ASIRIN

DEVOR

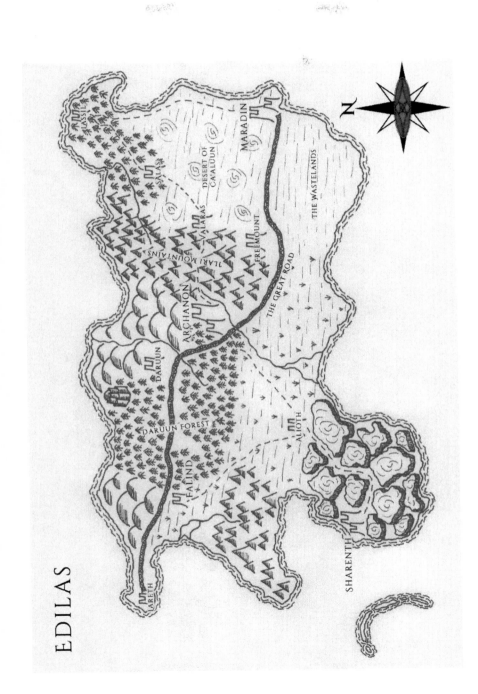

EDILAS

KASSIL

MARADIN

DESERT OF
CAALUUN

VALAS

VALARAS

ILARI MOUNTAINS

FREEMOUNT

THE WASTELANDS

ARCHANON

THE GREAT ROAD

DARUUN

DARUUN FOREST

FALIND

ALIOTH

ARETH

SHARENTH

Episode 1

INVASION

Zerek Betanil wanted to escape! Escape the mines, flee his father's shadow, just plain run away. And he wasn't afraid to let the whole world know it.

"I don't care!" he shouted at his father, his voice echoing within the mine chamber. The two other workers present had long stopped their work to watch the argument. "I'm never going to live a good life here, so who cares?"

His father, Tegeth, tried to draw himself to his full height, but bumped his steel helmet against the ceiling. It almost always made Zerek laugh. Almost.

"I care!" his father bellowed back in his deep voice. "I care about your safety, and the safety of every man and woman here."

Seeing red, even in the low candle and torch light, Zerek tore his helmet from his head and flung it down, sending it skipping back towards the chamber exit. "Like a stupid helmet is going to keep me safe from a cave-in."

One of the other miners behind his father, Elina, wiped dirt from her face and shook her head. "Listen to your Dad, kid. There's…"

Tegeth reeled and pointed a finger at her, "Stay out of this!"

She looked taken aback, but then just rolled her eyes and turned to hide her embarrassment. Zerek had never seen his father openly yell at Elina. She was small for a miner, smaller than even Zerek, but she was strong and never seemed to run out of energy. She was his father's favorite. More so than Zerek ever was.

He ran his gloved hand through his mussed up black hair and clenched the back of his neck. "Dad, look…"

His father turned back to Zerek, and despite the fact that he couldn't stand up straight, he finally looked intimidating. "I'm done fighting over this. You want to make it in the Miner's Guild, you follow my rules. It's as simple as that."

Zerek wanted to shout back that he didn't care if he made it in the Guild. He didn't *want* to be in the Guild. Not *that* Guild, anyway. But those born to miners rarely got to choose their life, not unless they were born with magic. Then, and only then, they got to choose a Warrior's life.

He had no power. No power over magic, and no power over his life. And his father never missed an opportunity to remind him of that.

Tegeth took two steps towards Zerek, forcing him back up into the wall. He felt the cold rock and iron ore on his bare arms and through his dirty, stained, tattered work shirt. "And you *will* stop mocking this life, do understand? You're a sight better off than a lot of those homeless kids in the city."

"That's a matter of opinion," Zerek muttered under his breath, and then immediately felt his stomach drop.

The wide-eyed glare his father gave him made him gulp. "Get out of my mine," Tegeth roared, flailing his hand towards the exit tunnel.

"Fine," Zerek yelled back and stomped past his father.

"And pick up your helmet!"

Zerek stopped when the helmet was at his feet, and was sorely tempted to kick it out of his way, not caring how much it might hurt. But no, that might actually earn him a smack across the face, a rare punishment since his mother's death. Knowing how hard his father could strike, he scooped the helmet back up, stuck the cumbersome thing on his head, and stormed off.

It took fifteen minutes to make his way out of the mine, and he had to pass through several other chambers that were actively being mined before he made it to open air and clear skies. Normally he reveled in the freedom from the mines, and after each shift he would stop and take a moment to stare up at the sky, usually nightfall by the time he was allowed to leave.

This time, it was not yet sunset. The sky was just starting to show signs of the coming reds and purples, and that should have comforted him, but he was still boiling inside. As he passed by other miners loading up a cart with fresh ore, they asked him what was wrong, but all he could manage was a snide, "Nothing."

The one thing he *did* take the time to do was tear his helmet back off. He passed into the tree line, clenching the helmet, wishing he had the strength to smash it.

The Relkin Mine was in the far south of the Ilari Mountains, not far from the Wastelands, but still far enough north that trees grew tall, and the underbrush thrived.

So he found solitude in the trees, away from his father. Away from the dark, dank, deep mines.

When he felt like he was far enough away, Zerek screamed up into the trees, and threw his helmet as hard as he could against a boulder. He hoped to have broken the ridiculous thing, but it clanged and bounced off of the boulder harmlessly.

He felt pressure build up in every part of his body, like he was ready to explode. To no one in particular, he screamed, "I don't want this life! I don't want to be stuck underground for the rest of my life. Why can't you just let me find my own way?"

His own way. That's what he wanted. At that moment, he looked out straight ahead, further into the forest, towards the center of the vast mountain range. That could be his freedom. All he had to do was keep walking. Keep walking and finally be free of everything he hated.

Free to do what he wanted, when he wanted. Go where he wanted. Go...go where?

To Archanon? Where he would be lost in the streets, another homeless child? Or to another country? No, he couldn't leave Tal.

What could he even do to survive? He was too old to join the Warriors. He had nothing to offer them, anyway. What about one of the other Guilds? No, they wouldn't take him. Why would any of them need a boy who only knew how to work the mines?

That was the truth of it. He had no other skills worth bartering for. He was born into a mining family, and he would always be a miner. Always trapped underground.

Feeling defeated, just like always after an argument, he slouched down onto the boulder, drew his legs up, and covered his face. His gloves smelled of leather and dirt, and that did little to help his mood.

Before he could stop them, the tears streamed out, and the dirt and dried sweat around his eyes stung. The void in his stomach grew only deeper and darker, made worse by how empty his stomach actually was.

If only it had been his mother that had lived. She always understood, even if she didn't know how to help him. At least she had understood.

So did someone else. "Hey, kid," Elina's voice startled him. He looked up, saw her walking towards him with her helmet in her hand, and he tried to sniff away the tears.

"Hey," he choked out. She saw his helmet on the ground and tossed hers next to it.

"Don't let him get to you," she said, sidling up next to him. He knew she wanted to put her arm around him, but she knew he never liked that after an argument with his father. Not anymore. It only made him miss his mother.

"He shouldn't have yelled at you like that," Zerek croaked, clenching his hands into fists. "What's wrong with him?"

She looked back towards the mine and shrugged. "He worries. About everyone, but…" She glanced at him and sighed. "You more than anyone. You really scared him today."

The argument had started when part of the newest tunnel collapsed near where Zerek was working. He had set his helmet aside before it happened, so when his father rushed into the chamber and saw Zerek without his helmet on, he exploded in rage.

Now that he felt less angry, Zerek did realize how stupid he was. It was less about the cave-ins than about the low ceiling and jagged rocks and ore that jutted out. Someone could easily split their head open if they stood up too fast without a helmet on. Plus Zerek once saw a helmet save someone from an errant pick axe.

He shook his head slowly, realizing all too well the stupid dangers that came with being a miner. If he was to die, he would rather die fighting an enemy Warrior or bandit. Not from a rock slide or a cave-in.

4

"I just don't want to do this anymore," he sighed and buried his face in his hands again. He kept the tears back this time, but just barely.

"I know, kiddo," Elina spoke softly. "I know."

For a long time, they sat in the diminishing light silently. After a while, Zerek raised his face just enough to look into the forest, towards the mine. The shift would end very soon, and he'd have to face his father back in their tent. Either that or sleep out in the cold.

But then they heard it. At first, it was nothing more than a low rumble. Zerek figured that someone had accidentally dumped an ore cart. Then the shouting started, and the rumbling grew louder.

And then they both heard the inhuman roar. Zerek's heart leapt into his throat and he and Elina leapt to their feet. "What in the name of the Six was that," she breathed.

Another roar, and another. The shouts from the miners turned to terrified screams. His skin turned cold, as did the pit of his stomach. They both took off at a run towards the mine.

It was a short distance back to the clearing, but in that time, Zerek's mind ran through countless possibilities.

Bandits?

Nope, not with that kind of roar.

Wolves?

Not even close.

Bears?

He'd heard bears roar, he knew what they sounded like, and that wasn't what he kept hearing.

Cresting over a small hill at the tree line, they finally saw what was happening, but neither could believe it. Neither wanted to believe it.

Monsters! There were real monsters, and they were attacking the camp! And not just a few, either, but a whole horde of them.

No, not a horde. As a wave of dozens of the hideous, long-armed, muscular, armored creatures poured out of the forest and overran the miners, there was only one word that was right.

It was an army.

Some wore leather skins for armor, others wore rusted, battered iron. One he saw in particular wore blackened metal plate armor. That one monster pointed its blackened sword towards a group of miners clustered together, and suddenly a blast of fire shot out from its tip. The fire engulfed the miners, men and women that Zerek had known all of his life. Their anguished screams made him jump.

Neither he nor Elina could speak, or move, or do anything. They stood frozen and watched as the horrific scene played out before them. The monsters continued to overrun the miners, burning and destroying the tents, slaughtering everyone not working the mines. They even struck down the children that tried to flee.

And then the miners rushed out to see what was happening, just as the orcs reached the entrance.

Zerek's father was the first to emerge and face the beasts. When the first came upon him, Tegeth drew himself up to his full height and swung his pick axe right down into the charging monster's head. A sickly black-red blood oozed from the wound, and the monster fell aside, tearing the pick axe from his father's hands.

The other miners tried to fight too, and some managed to kill or wound a few of the blood-thirsty brutes. But their victories were short lived, and they were quickly overrun. One miner fell, and another. One of the monsters leapt onto the back of one of Zerek's friends, Doren, and sliced his throat. Zerek felt his throat catch, a scream withheld by fear.

Until he watched a sword jab straight into his father's stomach. He never remembered screaming, "No!" He never remembered what happened next. He just remembered the rusted iron blade running straight through his father's gut, out his back, and the look of rage on his father's face.

The next thing he remembered was running through the forest as fast as he and Elina could. He heard the sound of rushing feet behind, and he glanced back to find three of the monsters chasing them. All three wore leather, two held haphazardly-forged daggers, and one held a rusted iron short sword.

Worse still, the long-legged monsters were faster than them, and were gaining fast. Terrified, Zerek looked ahead and tried to run faster. Elina was just ahead of him, and glanced back, but the terror on her face told him he didn't want to look again. That was when he noticed a dagger in her hand, the one he knew she always carried. It was rare, but sometimes bandits attacked the miners' camp, and the more experienced miners knew that they needed to be able to defend themselves.

She glanced at Zerek. And then she stopped. He ran past before he realized what was happening, and he too stopped. Elina turned and faced the orcs. There was no way she could beat them!

But that didn't stop her from trying. The first one leapt on top of her, but she stuck her dagger straight into its chest, the sharp steel blade easily piercing leather. They tumbled to the ground together, and she worked to pull the blade from its chest. The others were right behind their now-dead companion, but suddenly stopped, realizing probably for the first time that they were alone, and that the woman before them would not go down without a fight.

She faced them, and then screamed in rage, "Well come on!"

The beasts glanced at one another, but only the one with the sword was brave enough to attack. It jabbed its weapon towards her, and she managed to dodge it before she thrust her dagger at it. She missed. Then she started swinging her blade wildly, but it merely stayed back.

As their fight took them away from the other monster's body, Zerek saw his chance. He didn't know how to handle a weapon, not really, but he had played with wooden ones when he was a kid. So he rushed to the dead creature and pried its weapon from its still-warm hands. The handle was just as shoddy as the irregular blade, covered in what looked like lizard skins.

Elina had drawn the monster so that the third one faced away from Zerek. In a blind rage, he ran at it and stabbed it in the back. It screamed in surprise and agony, and batted Zerek away with its giant arms. Zerek's torso exploded in pain, and the wind was knocked out of him when he landed several feet away.

Its scream distracted the other one, which allowed Elina to push in and stick her finely-crafted dagger right in its throat. It coughed, and whatever strength it had quickly disappeared. After only a moment of clutching at its throat, it fell to its knees.

The one Zerek had stabbed turned towards the fight again. Elina tore her dagger free and rushed at the last one. She let out an enraged cry, and jabbed her blade straight into it

From where Zerek lay, he couldn't see where she had stabbed it, but it was enough to stop it dead in its tracks. For a moment, they stood staring at each other, the monster's face one of shock and pain. Then Zerek saw that Elina had the same look on her face.

It had jabbed its blade straight into Elina's side. Bright red blood began to seep into her dirt-ridden white tunic. Together, they fell to the ground. Elina pushed the creature's hand away and tried to pull the dagger from her side, but then yelled out in pain.

Feeling too weak to stand, Zerek crawled over to her. "Elina," he cried.

He made it to her side. The monster next to her was also still alive, squirming in pain as the life drained from it.

"Zerek," she managed to say. She reached her bloody hand towards his cheek. He clasped it firmly against his face, not caring about the blood.

"No, please," he shook his head, and felt his eyes sting from renewed tears.

"You must..." She coughed blood, and gulped. "You must tell Archanon." He clenched her hand in his, not wanting to let her go. "Find...someone. Orcs." The word froze his heart. That's what those monsters were. "The orcs are back."

Before she could say more, her eyes grew distant. Her hand slackened in his, and her head eased back. She exhaled her last breath, and was gone.

He wasn't sure how long he sat there, her hand in his. He stared at her beautiful, blue eyes. The last time he would ever see them.

It was night fall by the time he recovered. He eased her hand onto her chest, and let it rest there. Both of the moons were out, one nearly full, the other only half, but enough of the pale light broke through the trees that he could see everything around him.

The final orc was long dead, but it had managed to roll over and reveal Elina's dagger, planted right where a human heart would be. Clearly it was a good place to stab an orc, too, whether there was a heart there or not. He crawled around Elina, and then grasped the dagger's handle. It did not want to come out, so he struggled at first, but finally yanked it free. Through his stuffed nose, he caught the stench of the orc, and felt himself gag.

Then he actually threw up, even though he hadn't eaten since lunch.

When he finished retching, he sat back, feeling weaker than ever. After several minutes, he wiped his mouth clean, and then looked down at the dagger. Unlike the orc's, this one was very well-crafted steel, with a light leather cover on the handle, and a usually shiny hilt and pommel, both of which were now stained with the monster's blood.

He used his dirty shirt to clean the blade as best he could. But he could not see it well enough, so he knew he had to find an open space to get better moonlight. He looked up, had no idea where he was, but knew he couldn't stay. So he stumbled up onto his feet and started to walk away. Away from the carnage. Away from his family.

***

Lieutenant Amaya Kenla marched through the corridors of Archanon Castle with her head held high and her posture tall and strong. Or at least as strong as it could be in shackles.

She strained against the restraints in a vain attempt to pull her arms to their sides, chaffing her wrists. Her black hair, dirty and unkempt, kept getting in front of her eyes, and she had to jerk her head to one side to try to get the errant, dirt-clumped locks out of the way.

It was a point of pride for her, that even as a prisoner, she was composed and resolute. Two months in the Archanon dungeons would not destroy her, nor would she show weakness in front of her Warriors.

She and her six Warriors trudged through the stone halls of Archanon castle towards the throne room, escorted by several city guards. A room she had never stood in before, and one she had never expected to be led to as a prisoner.

Tal was, after all, the very kingdom she had served all of her life. She was a Warrior of Tal, but she was betrayed. Betrayed by one man that had been closer to her than anyone else. And betrayed by royalty.

But as they approached the throne room, she smiled. Today would finally be their vindication.

Word had spread quickly amongst the countless other prisoners. King Beredis had recovered from his mysterious illness, and he had rescinded all of the Prince's new laws. All prisoners arrested as a direct result of the Prince's laws were to be brought before the King for a review of their crimes, and to determine if they would be pardoned or not.

She and her Warriors were not guilty of any crime, as far as she was concerned. Now she had to make the King believe it.

The two soldiers in front of her reached the throne room doors and led the way in, the doors already opened from within by the

King's personal guards.

It was a sight she would not soon forget. Several statues of past kings and queens set in stone stared down upon them as they walked through the long, great hall. The throne room had long, long ago served as a vast mead hall, housing dozens of citizens in the early days of Archanon. A great red carpet was set from the main entrance right up to the steps that led to the throne, where the King sat proudly as he awaited their arrival.

Beside his throne stood the Prince, and it was all Amaya could do not to look at the brat with hostility. At the foot of the stairs, she recognized Draegus Kataar, one of the King's personal guards and, so she had heard, father of the man who now possessed the powerful Sword of Dragons. He was a former Warrior himself, but had resigned his commission to join the King's Guard. Instead of a Warrior's tabard, he bore over his armor a tabard of Tal Kingdom, a black cloth with silver embroidery of a mountain guarded by two crossing longswords.

King Beredis gave them his full attention. She felt hope at seeing him, and a little out of her element. Never before had she earned the right to have an audience with him. Now she felt shameful that her first and probably only audience with him was in shackles and rags. Idly she pulled the chain tight.

Once they reached the foot of the stairs, her Warriors lined up behind her, and the guards in front of them stepped to the side. Knowing all too well that her life, and the lives of those she once commanded, were now on the line, she knelt and bowed her head, her Warriors following suit.

With only a moment of dramatic pause, the King slowly stood up and descended the stairs. The Prince remained by the throne, upon which he rested his hand. "You may rise," King Beredis spoke in his deep, powerful voice.

When she stood, she noted that the King's skin was a touch darker than his son's. His age and wisdom showed powerfully in and around his brown eyes, and somehow she knew he was a good man.

When he was at her level, she suddenly felt very self conscious. They had been doused in water before leaving the dungeons to help with the smell, but it couldn't hide the fact that she wore the same rags they were given two months ago. The King, on the other hand, wore very finely-threaded clothes beneath his black and white-trimmed robe. The bejeweled crown upon his head was made of gold, and showed none of its three thousand year age.

"You are Lieutenant Amaya Kenla," he said. It was not a question.

Never-the-less, she stood up as straight as she could and nodded. "Yes, sire."

He nodded to the men and women behind her, "And these are the Warriors that were under your command when you were sent to raid the bandit camp."

She craned her head back to look at them. Six men and women under her command, the ones she knew had been the most skilled in her unit, the ones she had personally chosen for the assignment.

Each of them nodded to her encouragingly. It was a sign of the utmost trust and respect — it was her orders that had doomed them all to prison, but their loyalty to her was resolute.

When she turned back to the King, she knew she could not fail them again. She *must* not. "Yes, sire. They acted under my orders alone."

The King's stern look surprised her. "I doubt that very much, Lieutenant. General Artula provided me with the full report." He looked up at his son, who did not dare look into the eyes of his father. He turned his head down and away, which only added to his image as a spoiled child.

"Never-the-less," King Beredis returned his gaze to her, "the law under which your orders were issued has since been rescinded."

She really wanted to add more, and she almost gave into that impulse. Etiquette demanded that she remain as silent as possible, and only defend herself fully if given leeway to. So she held her tongue, and did not tell her King why she was justified in disobeying orders.

He seemed to understand her desire, since he remained silent for a moment and looked at her expectantly. What was he thinking? She believed that he was a truly good, moral man, so why would he even hesitate to dismiss her case and free her and her Warriors?

Warriors…they weren't even that any more. Neither was she. That title was stripped from them, likely forever.

The King's next words echoed her thoughts. "You do not believe you can return to the Guild, do you?"

Taking that as giving her some leeway to speak, she shook her head curtly, "No, my Lord. No matter your decision today, we disobeyed orders. I do not believe the General would take us back into the Guild. And even if he did…"

She hesitated and felt a well of pain and anger inside of her chest. It took every ounce of control she had not to give in to her desire to turn on the Prince. All of her anger was ready to burst out, directed not at the man before her, but at the Prince and Commander Din, the Warrior that had ordered her to wipe out the entire camp. Wipe out every single one of them.

Even when their scout discovered children living in the camp.

Never before had her emotions boiled like they did now. Never had she needed a moment to compose herself. Certainly not before a superior.

"I understand your anger, Lieutenant," the King turned and walked to the foot of the steps. There he stood, his eyes fixed on his son, who continued to look away. This, she suddenly realized, was his punishment. It was also meant to teach him that his actions could have dire consequences on the people under his rule.

She balked at being used as an object lesson for the little devil. Wasn't she worth more than that to the King?

After another moment of barely controlled rage, the King turned to her again. "As you know, I have no tolerance for criminal activity. However," he clasped his hands behind his back and shook his head, "that does not mean we should slaughter their families. Your former commander's orders were out of line, and I have conveyed my disapproval of said orders to General Artula."

She respected the General, but somehow she had the feeling little would be done. Too many lives were lost in the recent war against Kailar and Klaralin. The General would be hard-pressed to find adequate replacements for every Commander and Lieutenant that had blindly followed, or even reveled in, the Prince's laws.

The sympathy in the King's eyes told her he knew this as well. "Lieutenant." He paused, and seemed to realize that she no longer held that rank. "Miss Kenla. It is with my deepest apologies for your hardship that I hereby acquit you of all criminal charges." Despite their uncertain future, she felt the jubilation of her Warriors, their cheers shattering the quiet of the throne room.

The King raised an eyebrow at their outburst, which instantly silenced them. Then he looked her squarely in the eye. She didn't care what came next. Nothing could be worse than the two months they had spent in the dungeon.

She could feel more than hear the jibing and excited nudges the men and women behind her were giving each other, and as she often did, she wished she could join them. But it wasn't appropriate for her to do so. Not yet. Not so long as she stood as their leader before the King.

Soon, she would have such freedom. Unless she decided to enlist in the Guild again.

Would she?

Could she?

The hint of a smile cracked on the King's face, revealing his humanity. It was that humanity, which he kept in check only when needed, that made him so popular, so beloved by the people of Tal.

She had lost her faith in the throne thanks to the Prince. And for as long as the Prince remained the successor to the throne, she would always feel doubt. But for now, she could at least have faith in the King.

A frown crossed the King's face when he suddenly looked over her shoulder. She followed his gaze and was surprised to see one of the King's guards escorting a young man in. The boy looked even more disheveled than she felt. Still a teenager, she thought that his tunic and trousers appeared to belong to a miner, but those clothes were soiled with what looked like dried blood, some of which looked far more black than red.

Orc blood, she thought, never having seen it herself but having learned about it in training.

The King immediately recognized that there was a far more urgent matter at hand. Whatever apologies he meant to offer next, or questions, or words of encouragement, she would not get to hear it.

"My apologies," he nodded to them. "You are dismissed. You two," he nodded to the soldiers that had preceded them in, "Release them. See to it that they are given clean clothes. Take them from my personal wardrobe if necessary," he smiled warmly at them. "And give them a gold piece each to start out with."

It wasn't much, but it was more than she could have ever expected. The guards looked at each other in astonishment, and then at her and her company. "Yes, my Lord," one spoke, and then motioned for them to exit through one of the side doors.

As they walked out, she glanced one more time at the young man. His gaze was distant, and she suspected he hardly knew where he was. She was shocked to see a fine looking steel dagger clutched in his hands. Civilians weren't generally allowed before royalty while armed.

Something terrible had happened to him.

As they were led out, her freedom suddenly was at the back of her mind, even if only for the moment. That was dried orc blood on his tunic and covering his hands. It could not be coincidence that this came mere weeks after an attempted orc invasion of Archanon.

Something was coming.

***

Cardin Kataar pulled his fingerless leather gloves on with a feeling of both trepidation and excitement. It had been nearly a month since the Battle of Archanon, and in that time, he had spent every spare moment training with his newest friend, the Wizard Dalin.

The training was meant to help him understand and control the powers he had gained from the Sword of Dragons. When he finished pulling the gloves on, he absently reached back to grasp the black handle of the Sword, strapped to his back in an enchanted scabbard, and pulled it against his back. The weapon was as light as a dagger, so pulling on it helped reassure him that he hadn't lost it.

Despite the light weight, there was no denying the incredible burden he felt from carrying it. He could never allow another to hold it, never allow another to take it, or he would fail his oath to protect it.

He was ready, observing his armor rack to ensure he hadn't missed anything. Running his fingers through his cropped black hair, he took in a deep breath to brace himself.

At least the leather armor felt comfortable on him, and for the moment, he felt at peace. The house itself was still in the same dilapidated state it had been before the Sword of Dragons came into his life, but no longer because he could not afford repairs.

Rather it was still in disrepair because he never had the time to repair it himself. He hadn't even had time to look for and hire someone to do it for him. He, along with his friends Sira and Reis, had spent much of the past month helping to rebuild Archanon, the Southwest quarter of it having been demolished by Klaralin's attack.

When he wasn't working on repairs, he trained with Dalin.

All of that was about to end. The days of training were over, at least for the moment. Orcs had attacked the Relkin Mining Camp, and he and his friends had been tasked with scouting the incursion.

With that thought, the peace was shattered, so he turned and quickly left. The sun was shining, it was a hot late-summer day, and suddenly his armor felt stifling.

As he made his way towards the Warriors' Guild complex on the western side of the city, he felt a pang of guilt for his earlier excitement. Men and women had lost their lives in the orc attack. He had to remember that, remember what was at stake. The message that had been brought to them only a half an hour ago, brought to Daruun quickly by way of a Wizard's portal, had said that the lone survivor reported hundreds of orcs. If that was true, it meant that the orcs were still assembled as an army, even without Klaralin's leadership.

He wasn't sure he liked the implications of that fact.

The energetic bounce in his step turned to determination. He wouldn't let anything happen to anyone else. No more loss of innocent life.

Cardin quickly arrived at the complex, and wasn't surprised to find that he was the last one to the party. Dalin, dressed in his usual dark-blue robes and wielding his oak staff, stood in the center of the courtyard, and watched Cardin silently. In appearance, Dalin was in his late twenties or early thirties. But all one had to do was look into his eyes to know he was far older, and in fact Cardin knew that he was over 250 years old, which explained the streaks of gray in his hair. Still young for a Wizard.

On either side of him were Cardin's oldest friends, Reis Kalind and Sira Reinar. Both wore light leather armor, prepared for a scouting mission rather than battle. Reis had the usual smirk on his face, though somewhat subdued today, and his long brown hair was pulled back into a tight pony tail. Sira, on the other hand, let her short almost-white hair hang loose around her ears. They faced away from him, but turned as Cardin entered.

"About time," Reis sighed, tapping his foot mockingly.

Cardin stopped next to him and shrugged, "Hey, I'm here, that's what counts. And I'm ready to take down some orcs."

Sira raised her eyebrows, and rather curtly retorted, "That's not why we're going, Cardin. The Allied Council decided to send you, send *us,* because of the obvious advantage you have in case we are caught." She shook her head, looked at the others, and then back at him. "Don't try to engage them."

He nodded, and then smiled. "Yes, ma'am."

She didn't look amused, nor did the others. His smile faded, and suddenly he felt embarrassed. It was only then that he realized his attempt at humor was actually disrespectful towards Sira, and he felt his face grow warm.

Sira looked very curtly at Cardin. "When the Council asked if you could work with us, specifically with me as your commanding officer, you said there would be no problem. Can I still count on you to be true to your word?"

His face burned even hotter, and he gulped, feeling for the first time in over a decade like a raw trainee again.

"Of course," he nodded, his gaze fixed on her eyes to let her know that he truly meant it. "I'll follow your orders, I promise. You're in charge."

For what felt like forever, she stared with even, stolid eyes at him. Then her hard exterior cracked, and her face blossomed into a smile. "Yeah, I am. So here's an object lesson in that fact." She nodded to Reis, "Smack him for me."

Cardin felt his jaw drop, and he felt too shocked to react as Reis sidled up next to him and slapped the back of his head.

"Hey!" He held where Reis had hit him, and then glared at his friend.

Barely containing a chuckle, Reis shrugged and pointed at Sira, "Don't blame me."

Sira chortled, and Cardin readied a rebuke. But then Dalin cleared his throat and stepped forward. "I believe this is hardly an appropriate attitude, considering what has happened."

Once again, Cardin had to sober himself up. He felt only minor comfort in the fact that it wasn't just him that had to be reminded.

"Sorry." Sira dropped her hands to her side, took in a deep breath, and exhaled slowly. "You're right, of course. It's just…"

After a pause, Reis finished for her. "We're excited to all be working together again, the three of us," Reis motioned to himself, Cardin, and Sira. "Almost like old times. Except this time, we have our friendly Wizard with us."

Even Dalin couldn't keep a smile from crossing his face at that remark. "Quite," he nodded.

With the smile still on her face, Sira put her hands on her hips and nodded. "Alright, let's move out." She looked at Cardin and motioned her head towards their Wizard friend, "Dalin and I already picked out a location about a half mile away from the camp to portal into. You ready?"

Cardin reached back to grasp the Sword and willed the enchanted scabbard out of existence. Pulling the unusually long weapon before him, he mentally thanked the Wizards again. He promised himself he would never take that gift for granted.

"I'm ready," he nodded.

With a nod from Sira, Dalin turned and planted his staff firmly into the ground. The sudden rush of magic released a clap of thunder, the gem in Dalin's staff glowing bright blue. Cardin felt the Wizard direct that power in front of him, and it burst forth into a cascade of light. Moments later, the portal to the deep south of Tal Kingdom was before them.

Reis and Sira drew their longswords and prepared to step through the portal.

Feeling overly protective, he stepped in front of them and faced the portal. Dalin, as the creator of the portal, would have to pass through last. But given the danger ahead of them, Cardin would not let his friends go first.

With only a cursory glance back at Sira, who nodded her approval, he stepped through the sheet of white light.

The moment he passed through to the other side, he was relieved to find the forest clear of orcs. He stepped further away from the portal, and then took a moment to get his bearings.

The forest was a mix of pine and aspen trees, many of them stretching high into the deep blue sky. The sound of rushing hooves startled him, but he relaxed when he realized it was a nearby deer, startled into bolting away.

Sira and Reis quickly followed him, ready for battle, but they too relaxed after a quick survey of their surroundings. Once Dalin was through, the portal closed behind him.

Their arrival had gone unnoticed.

Using only hand motions, Sira ordered them to stay low and make their way east. The forest was so dense that Cardin couldn't see the nearby mountain peak. However, through the currents of magic, he was able to instantly get his cardinal bearings, and knew which way to go.

He was about to go ahead of the others, but then remembered he was *with* others. Years of being alone had created hard habits to break. Looking to Sira, he let her lead the way, even if he stayed right with her.

At first, their trek was uneventful. There were no orcs on patrol, not this far out. But it wasn't long before Cardin, being their most skilled tracker, noticed signs of recent tracks.

He stopped the group by reaching out and placing a hand on Sira's shoulder. They crouched down, a position he noted that Dalin appeared unaccustomed to and uncomfortable with. As quietly as he could, he pointed to where he had spotted the tracks and whispered, "Looks like a regular patrol."

She looked to where he pointed, and then she nodded. "Not surprising," she whispered back. Reis looked around, but the bushes and low branches throughout the dense forest meant that they could not see very far, so the patrol could come upon them at any second with little notice.

"Maybe we should wait for nightfall," Cardin suggested.

"Not a bad idea," Sira nodded. "I told the messenger to go back and tell the Council we would report within a day."

Only a day. So much had changed with the return of the Wizards. Before, messenger travel between Daruun and Archanon took a minimum of four days. Now they could send messages in a matter of minutes. And a scouting mission that normally would have taken weeks could be accomplished in a day.

"Well I'm the best scout," Reis shrugged. "Let me go on ahead, see what I can see."

At first Cardin wanted to object. Reis was always good at sneaking around, but this wasn't a childhood game.

Then again, Cardin realized that Reis had had plenty of time since they were kids to improve his game. Plus it was Sira's mission, Sira's call, so he remained silent.

"Alright," she whispered. "But if you think there's any chance of being caught, come back immediately. We'll fall back a hundred paces. And Reis," she placed a hand on his shoulder. "Be swift."

Without waiting a moment longer, Reis took off further east.

Within moments, he disappeared into the underbrush, amazingly silent.

***

What in the blazes is wrong with me, Reis thought to himself. Sure, he was a scout, but volunteering for this was insane! Sneaking up on a mining camp that might have hundreds of armed, crazy orcs in it?!

Of course, there was no turning back now. He could never admit to being afraid, even to his friends.

He hoped his plan would pan out. Trying to sneak up on the camp from the west was suicide, and wouldn't give him much of a view. No, he needed a birds-eye view. And while the trees in general were tall, he needed to see *over* the majority of them, so climbing just any tree wouldn't do.

So he circled north to climb the base of the mountain. He didn't know if he was as good of a tracker as Cardin, but he could still readily see the regular paths of the orc patrols. Each time he found one, he hid in the underbrush, and waited and listened.

Only once had a pair of orcs passed while he waited. Their stench wasn't any better than he remembered, and he almost gave away his position with a gag. One thing was for sure, orcs would never be able to sneak up on them, not unless they were downwind. And it'd have to be a very strong wind.

Even as far north of the camp as he was, the grunts and growls of their enemy, the sound of hammers, and of pick axes smashing into rock, it was obvious that there were a lot of orcs.

At one point, he snuck in close enough, and there was enough of a break in the forest underbrush so that he could just barely see movement down the tree-covered mountain side. It wasn't enough, he couldn't see clearly, but he didn't dare go closer. So he searched for a tree nearby that he could climb up.

Of course, none of the ones right near him were suitable. So he moved as quietly as he could to find a better tree, and ended up moving further away from the camp before he found one with branches low enough that he could get a start.

Knowing it would be impossible to climb with his sword, he unstrapped the sheath, laid it down on the ground, and brushed fallen leaves and branches over it.

He paused to look around for any errant orcs, his pulse

quickening. What he was about to do might be considered stupid and dangerous. No, scratch that, it *was* stupid and dangerous. But he had to do it. He had to contribute to the mission.

When he could neither see nor hear any approaching orcs, he leapt up to the branch, grabbed hold, and used his legs on another branch to leverage himself up.

As a young teen, he'd spent a lot of time with Cardin and Sira in the edge of the Daruun forest, even though their parents forbade it. In that time, he had climbed many, many trees. He was a bit rusty now, and almost fell out twice, but somehow managed to keep the broad trunk of the tree between him and the camp.

Then he froze when he realized that they might be able to see the tree swaying. He looked up at the top, and saw that the top of the tree was, indeed, beginning to sway more the higher up he went.

He peeked around the trunk, and saw that the tops of the trees further downhill were just barely blocking his view. "Great," he whispered to himself.

Then the wind came, a strong blast from the mountain down towards the camp. He held on as the tree rocked back and forth and groaned beneath his grasp. "No, no, no, please don't blow me off," he mumbled, clutching the trunk and hoping it wasn't an oncoming storm.

Almost too afraid to look, he craned his neck around to look up the mountain, but there were no signs of storm clouds. It was just a blast of wind.

It was also his chance! Every tree moved, concealing the evidence of his climb. As fast as he dared, he scrambled up higher. Finally, he reached a point where the branches were too small and started to bend in his grasp, and the trunk of the tree was growing too narrow.

Then he looked down.

Oh gods, he thought, clenching his eyes shut. *Damn you and your need to prove yourself, Reis.*

Forcing his eyes open, he stared face-to-face with the trunk. It was now or never.

The wind blew again, sending a fresh surge of panic through his body.

Slowly, as carefully as he could, he maneuvered so that he could start to peak around the trunk southward. And then his veins turned to ice.

The boy's description was wrong, very wrong. It wasn't just a couple hundred orcs. It wasn't a single unit of their enemy. It was an army.

The human camp was gone, the tents and few wooden structures erased.

The forge was the only thing left. The orcs had trampled, torn apart, and generally destroyed everything else, and had begun constructing their own camp. Only this one was surrounded by a wall. It was a good thing Reis hadn't come from the western side. The orcs actively cut down trees to the west and were carving them up for construction material. They also had begun construction on several makeshift huts. Through sheer number of workers, their progress was terrifying.

There were at least a thousand. Two thousand. Off to the south, their ranks stretched far into the tree line. Campfires blazed, the smoke filtered through the tree tops, creating a gray-white haze above. If the wind had blown in the opposite direction, Reis had no doubt he would have choked on the smoke.

He noticed that while most of the orcs he saw wore makeshift leather armor, and those that were still armed had poorly-constructed weapons, there were pockets of them that wore the same dark metal armor as the army that had attacked Archanon recently. The longer he watched, the more he suspected that those orcs led the others.

It was an invasion. Thousands of orcs. Maybe more, who knew how far into the forest they occupied. This *was* the closest mine to the Wastelands. If they were going to invade Tal, this would be where they would start.

Not to mention an iron mine gave them materials to forge more weapons of war.

Reis took in a deep breath, and then slowly let it out. He had to report back. Archanon had to know this. The new Allied Council had to hear about it.

Going as fast as he could, he climbed down, no longer caring about the swaying of the tree. With that many orcs bumbling about, there was no telling how far they might decide to explore west. They might run into Sira and the others soon.

He didn't even let himself get to the bottom branch, he jumped down from as high as he dared, and then grunted loudly on impact, his stomach jostling.

A surprised grunt followed. And he knew it hadn't come from himself.

Slowly, he looked up to see a small group of orcs just ahead of him. And they stared right at him. They didn't move at first, probably too stunned. So was he. But then he remembered he didn't have his sword. It was only a foot away from his right hand. Of course, he knew that the moment he reached for it, they would charge.

One, two, three…seven orcs. Nope, no way he could take them on by himself. No matter what, they were going to attack. So he needed to move. Now.

As quickly as he could, he hopped over and grabbed the buried handle of his sword. And the orcs roared.

***

Dalin felt it before he heard it. A stir of magic not far off, a disruption in the flow of energy that he knew came from enchanted weapons. Cardin's head snapped in the direction that Dalin felt it from.

Forgetting Cardin's growing power for the moment, he stood up. Sira whispered loudly, "Get down!"

Then they all heard the roars, and shortly after heard and *felt* the pounding feet coming towards them. Sira and Cardin both stood up as well, and looked east.

Cardin shook his head. "Great…"

As if on cue, Reis came barreling out of the underbrush, scratching his face on a branch as he did so. It wasn't the only scratch he had.

The moment he saw them, he waved his free hand, the other carrying his sword, covered in black-red blood. "Go!" he shouted. "Get a portal open, now!"

There was no time. Reis was on top of them, and a moment later, several orcs burst into view. Followed by more. And more.

"Run," Dalin said, quietly at first. When Reis flew past them, he shouted, "Run!" and followed after. Sira turned and dashed into a full run. Dalin felt a sudden surge of power, and knew that Cardin fired a blast of pure energy at the orcs.

Reis outran Dalin. His feet were quick, and he seemed to have no trouble navigating through the forest.

The Wizard needed at least a couple of seconds to spare, and a small clearing for a portal. Right now if he stopped, the orcs would overtake them before everyone could get through the portal.

"Back to the clearing," he shouted ahead to Reis. The Warrior stopped only a moment to get his bearings, then only had to turn a little left before he sprinted ahead again.

Dalin felt and saw shards of ice fly all around them suddenly, impaling trees or glancing off of their trunks. He realized that even if they made it to the clearing, there simply wouldn't be enough time. Was he powerful enough to both raise a shield and create a portal? He'd never done that before. The portal alone would be difficult under the circumstances, he had to concentrate hard to make one.

It didn't take them long to backtrack, and soon they burst out into the clearing. The sun still shone bright, but was creeping behind the trees as evening approached.

Reis stopped and turned, and Dalin very nearly plowed over him before he too stopped. Cardin and Sira were right behind them.

Two more shards of ice whistled by their ears. Dalin pushed Cardin aside, and then pointed his staff in the direction of the orcs. A moment later, another ice shard shattered against his hastily-erected shield. He felt the impacts as much as he saw them, barely straining his concentration for the moment.

Then he turned around, keeping at least part of his mind focused on the shield. He planted his staff firmly in the grass, and quickly summoned as much energy as she could and focused it through his crystal and into the world before them. His mind was focused on the canyon west of Archanon.

Normally he could summon a portal in a couple of seconds. But with the strain of the orc attacks, it took him longer to focus the needed amount of energy, and he immediately felt fatigued.

Finally, he did it. The portal flashed open before them.

Without needing to be told, Reis jumped through. Sira and Cardin maneuvered around Dalin, who felt a greater strain as several more blasts of ice shattered against his shield. It was about to fail, if he wanted to keep the portal open.

They both turned to look behind Dalin, who likewise craned his neck around. The orcs burst out of the forest, and were about to overtake the shield. He could not keep it up against a physical attack *and* the ice attacks.

He turned and shouted at them, "Go now!"

They glanced at each other, and then fled through, one after another.

The shield failed from another ice attack. Dalin felt his heart pounding in his chest, his head suddenly spinning. The portal fluctuated, and the flow of power through him began to wane.

He stumbled forward, leaning heavily on his staff. The portal was only a couple feet away, he had to get through it. It almost winked out of existence.

And then he was through. He nearly collapsed on the other side, but he immediately felt the release of his hold on the portal, and it closed behind him. Sira and Cardin caught him with their free hands and helped steady him.

He turned to where the portal had been, and sighed. Not one orc had made it through after them.

With a huge sigh of relief, he stood up tall and nodded for Cardin and Sira to release him. When he looked ahead, he saw the gates of Archanon, welcoming them in.

Then he glared at Reis. "Did you really have to bring their entire army down upon us?"

Reis used a cloth to clean the blackened blood from his sword. He glanced at the Wizard and shrugged. "What? It's not my fault."

Dalin rolled his eyes, and mumbled, "Best scout, indeed."

Cardin and Sira sheathed their weapons, and then turned to Reis. "Well?" Sira asked. "What did you see?"

The innocent grin on Reis's face faded, and for the first time since Dalin had met the Warrior, he looked completely serious. "It's worse than we feared." He looked at each of them, and then focused again on Sira. "There are thousands of them. It's an invasion."

Dalin felt his heart sink. He exchanged worried looks with both Cardin and Sira. She grimaced and looked at the city. "Then they are in the perfect position to march upon Archanon."

Cardin nodded. "It sounds like a new Orc War is about to start."

***

Amaya hefted her new backpack onto her shoulder, and grimaced at how heavy it felt. She had tried to keep up her strength while imprisoned, but they hadn't been fed well, and she could feel that she was weaker. It was going to take a lot of time and hard work to regain all of her strength.

She and her former team stood at the western gate of Archanon, checking their supplies one last time to make sure they could hike home safely.

Known as the First City, Archanon was easily the largest home of people on all of Halarite. The outer wall, at almost fifty feet tall, encircled almost the entire city, broken only by the cliffs it ran into in one small section. For over five miles the city stretched east of the main gate.

Although they were allowed to stay in castle guest quarters last night, it was now time for them to head home, to Everlin.

As soon as the first shops opened, they had each purchased packs and supplies for the three day journey.

As they approached the western gate, the iron doors began to slowly creak open, right on schedule as the sun edged over the mountain peaks to the east.

Beside her strode one of her former teammates, Elic Morgin, while the others walked behind them, everyone silent. Her former team was excited that they could go home and see their friends, and for most of her unit, their families. However, it would be a bittersweet reunion. None of them had made a decision yet whether they would try to regain entry into the Warriors' Guild. She also suspected that Din still commanded her hometown's Guild. He would not be kind to them.

She wasn't particularly excited, either. She didn't have anywhere to go in Everlin, and had considered staying in Archanon to find work. But she couldn't let her team make this last journey together without her. She would at least go back with them once, and then figure out where to go from there.

Everlin had been her home all of her life. It was where she had lived, trained, and fought. Her promotion to Lieutenant had been the proudest day of her life.

Had it all been for nothing? Was her life up to this point meaningless?

She shook her head, and then looked out at the road beyond the gates. It didn't matter. What mattered today was the journey.

But before they reached the gates, a familiar figure stepped out from a guard post to block their path. They stopped and stared at Draegus Kataar.

Amaya exchanged glances with Elic, and then looked at the King's guard again. "Is there something we can help you with, sir?"

Draegus nodded. "I know you are anxious to leave for home," he stepped a little closer, "But I have a message from the King for all of you, if you'll permit me a moment of your time."

She raised her eyebrows in surprise, and then crossed her arms in front of her. "Oh? Something you couldn't have told us yesterday?"

Draegus eyed her curiously, and she wondered if she had been a bit too harsh. He wasn't a Warrior, not anymore, and he had never served under Din. However, for all she knew, he had served the Prince as loyally as he had the King.

"His Majesty the King wished to speak to you about it in the throne room yesterday," Draegus continued evenly. "However, the appearance of that young man took precedent, especially once we found out what had happened."

She nodded once and said, "Orcs."

Surprise crossed his face. "Yes. How did you…?"

"The blood on his tunic and his hands," Elic replied before she could. His voice was strong and steady, a characteristic she had always counted on. "We all saw it."

"Yeah, I guess that is a give away," Draegus nodded thoughtfully. "What you don't know is that we sent scouts to that boy's mining camp. What no one else knows," he stopped and looked around to make sure no one else was close enough to listen. He stepped closer, and the rest of her team crowded in to hear.

"The King will be making the announcement shortly, and the Allied Council is convening today in an emergency session," he spoke quietly. "It wasn't just a small band of orcs that attacked his camp, it was an invasion army."

She felt her stomach twist. Even though she had never fought an orc before, she had read all about them, knew more than she ever wanted to know about them. She had heard stories of how even now, the city of Freemount, which stood at the borders of Tal Kingdom, Saran Kingdom, the Wastelands, and the Desert of Ca'aluun, often fought off small orc raids on caravans.

They were vicious, monstrous, terrifying, strong, and she had hoped never to have to face them in battle.

"Which means," Draegus said a little louder after a dramatic pause, "we're about to go to war, again. Only this time, they won't have a central leader like Klaralin through which we can defeat them. We'll need Warriors. And we'll need soldiers. That means that what the King was about to offer you in sincerity he now also asks for in earnest."

Draegus took a moment to look at each of them before he spoke again. "His Majesty would like you to join his personal guard. As would I."

She immediately balked at the idea. "Guards?" She laughed and exchanged similar looks with her companions. "We are not guards, sir. We are Warriors. We belong on the front lines, not protecting the King and his," she scowled, "son."

"You don't understand," Draegus shook his head "I do not mean as a protector of the throne. I mean as a member of the Tal elite. I know you have heard rumor of what I speak."

Her feelings of insult suddenly gave way to surprise, shock even. "Are you saying the Guardians are real?"

Nodding once, he continued, "These are unusual circumstances. We normally do not speak of them in public, even though they are well known by all leaders of the kingdom." He hesitated a moment longer, and then nodded. "You and your team would serve as a special unit that reports directly to the King. The assignments you will be given may be highly dangerous, but," he shook his head, "I think that is something your team would revel in."

She looked back at the others, men and women she had commanded for only a few years, but were the ones she could always count on. They were the best that Everlin had produced, and their imprisonment, she had no doubt, was to the detriment of the Everlin Warriors.

They looked at her, but none of them seemed certain about the orders. Had their spirit been broken in the dungeons? Had hers?

She had no weapons, no armor. Suddenly she also realized that, without a spouse to take ownership, her home in Everlin would have been sold. After all, she had been charged with treason.

There was no reason for her to go back.

The rest of her team, however, was another matter. Elic had a wife, Idalia had a husband, and Peren had a daughter. And she knew Vin had parents in Everlin, though he hadn't spoken to them in years. She couldn't ask them to stay away, she certainly couldn't order them to.

So it would be up to each of them. There was no unit without them, but it was their decision to make. "What do you all think?"

At first, none of them replied. They looked to one another, and she felt her heart beat hard in her chest.

She wanted it. It was a way for her to continue to serve, to put her skills to use, but was she alone in her desire?

Vin was the first to speak up, a surprise to them all since he was usually the quiet one. He was a good Warrior, strong with a sword and shield, but he often preferred daggers, and he was quick on his feet. "Can we at least have a chance to go tell our families we're safe? Or, well," he blushed and corrected himself, "at least that we aren't prisoners anymore?"

Draegus hesitated. "It would be up to the King, and time is short, now that war is upon us." Then a look of realization crossed his face, and a grin followed. "However, we *are* allies with the Wizards. We could possibly arrange a portal to take you."

Idalia asked, "What about weapons? Armor? Ours were all taken from us." Her voice was strong and determined, and she sounded willing, even anxious. Especially if they would be issued new weapons.

"That too will be provided," Draegus replied. "You will want for nothing, except perhaps rest."

Amaya felt her face start to blossom into a smile. They were thinking about it. All of them were considering actually doing it.

Elic glanced at her, and then did a double-take. "Well I think we know where your heart lies."

Her stomach leapt, and she gulped and nodded. "Well, yes. But I don't have families to go back to. You all do."

They grew silent at that, and nodded to one another. All except Gell, the only other member of their team who had no family back in Everlin. He just looked down at the ground and remained silent.

Then something she did not expect happened. Peren looked up, and asked, "Why are we even having to think about this? Orcs are invading. That puts all of our families in danger." The look of realization on everyone's face, including Amaya's, was almost amusing.

After only another short pause, Elic nodded. "He's right. This will give us the chance to protect them."

Everyone nodded in agreement. However, even though she heard no dissent, she wanted to be sure. "Let's make certain that we're all clear about this. This means that we only get to go home this one time, and even that is not a certainty. After that, we're here, under the King's command, doing what needs to be done. So without any question or hesitation, each of you say yes, or no."

She started with Elic, and went down the line. Not one of them hesitated, every one of them said yes. And so it came down to her. Even though she was not their leader, they still looked to her as such.

With a united team behind her, she turned back to Draegus. "We'll do it," she nodded.

Smiling with relief, Draegus Kataar nodded. "I'm glad to hear that. Now come," he stepped past them, "The King is waiting for you."

As the others turned to leave, Amaya looked out of the open gates, out into the world beyond. Very briefly she wondered if she had just made a mistake. Out there was her freedom.

Then she remembered that she was a soldier, she always had been. This was the life she had always wanted. Fighting to protect her kingdom.

This was her purpose.

Episode 2

COUNTERSTRIKE

The world was a jumbled mess. Zerek Betanil hardly was aware of anything around him, choosing to ignore everything and just let everyone else guide him around the castle.

Choose. What did he choose? What was his choice? Did he have a choice?

That's when he realized that he would never have a choice in life as long as he let everyone around him decide where he went and what he did. It wasn't so long ago that he was angry for not having a choice in life. Maybe that meant he should choose to pay attention now, to start making a choice now.

It wasn't easy. It was safe, closed up inside of his mind. Safe when he could close his eyes and see his mother, smiling down upon him. Sometimes, that image made him cry uncontrollably. Sometimes, it made him feel happier than he ever remembered being.

Safe. He was safe in his mind. But would he stay safe in there?

Not likely. So he decided he needed to return to the real world.

As the world around him cleared, he saw that he was in a stone-walled corridor. A man dressed in black and red, loose-fitting clothes walked beside him, lightly guiding him with a hand on his shoulder. Lightly, not firmly. As if to let him know that he was not trapped.

They walked towards a set of closed heavy wooden doors at an intersection, bracketed by a pair of guards wearing what was clearly ceremonial armor, and black tabards with the symbol of the Tal kingdom embroidered into them in silver.

He must be in the capitol city's castle! A rush of excitement coursed through him at that thought, but then he tried to remember how he got there.

Terrifying images flashed before his eyes, and he almost ran away, ran back into his thoughts.

Zerek looked again to the man guiding him and realized that it was a member of the Order of the Ages. Based on his black tunic, trimmed in red, he was a cleric. The symbol of the Order, six lines that expanded outward from a central space, was embroidered in red on a patch on his left breast.

The cleric noticed Zerek staring at him, and he looked over with a completely fake smile. "Welcome back, young man," he spoke with false kindness. "We feared you would not be able to speak before the Council today."

Zerek asked, "What Council?" But then the guards ahead opened the doors, and they entered a very crowded room. Kings and a Queen, members of the Covenant, and so many others crowded into one room. There were six simple wooden tables arranged to face the center, and extra seats lined the outer wall of the room. He felt his heart begin to thunder in his chest, threatening to break out and run away, like the rest of him wanted to do.

He looked down and dared not meet the gaze of any as they all stared at him. Gently, the cleric guided him into the center, and stood there, his hand a bit firmer on Zerek's shoulder. Somehow he must have known that Zerek wanted to flee.

The cleric spoke, but Zerek didn't hear a word. Zerek was the center of attention for some reason, and the only reason he could think of was something he never wanted to think about again.

After a while, the cleric stopped speaking. Were they all waiting for him to say something? He wouldn't. He couldn't. That would give them a chance to break him open, make him spill out everything he bottled up inside. It would all break forth into his mind, and he couldn't face all of that.

Then an elderly man at one of the tables stood up and approached. Zerek started to back away, but suddenly the cleric's grasp became iron. He was trapped, he couldn't escape. They were coming for him. They would always come for him, because he had survived when no one else had. He was alone, trapped, and then...

And then, without any warning, the world became a brighter place. The dark weight, the shadow that pressed upon his chest, the one he didn't even realize was there before, lifted. His eyes cleared, his heart cleared, everything became so much clearer.

Before him stood a tall, ancient man, dressed in golden-trimmed white robes. In his left hand, he held an equally white staff with an amber gem at the top. The gem glowed warmly, and Zerek found himself staring longingly into it. He wanted to be there, to be inside of it, where it was warm and bright and nothing could harm him.

As if reading his thoughts, the white-robed man smiled and said, "Do not be afraid, my young friend. You are safe here. No one can hurt you." He leaned forward a bit and added, "I won't let them." He winked ever so slightly, which made Zerek smile.

Smile. When was the last time he'd smiled?

After several moments, the old man asked, "Will you be okay?"

At first, Zerek's voice cracked, like he hadn't spoken in days. Maybe he hadn't. "Yes. Yes, I think so."

The old man's smile warmed, and he started to move away. Zerek reached for him, "Wait!"

He didn't need to say anything more. The old man came back and stood beside him. "Very well. I shall stand with you." The cleric stood by as well, but Zerek moved closer to the white-robed figure. "I will take care of the boy."

At first, the cleric was hesitant. Then he nodded and bowed, "As you wish, Master Wizard."

A Wizard? Here? So it was true, they *had* returned to Halarite. Zerek looked at the table that the white Wizard had come from and saw three other Wizards, each wearing a different colored robe.

After the cleric was gone, another man wearing dark violet robes and a golden crown stood up and addressed everyone in a powerful voice. "This is the survivor I spoke of. Though he has not spoken since, the Warriors who found him said that he gave his name as Zerek, and that he said that orcs destroyed the Relkin Mining Camp."

It took a moment for Zerek to realize that the man speaking was

King Beredis of Tal. Slowly he began to look around and get his bearings. At three other tables sat someone with a crown upon their head. At another sat three members of the Covenant of the Order of the Ages. And then there was the Wizards' Table.

The Council. That's what the cleric had meant. A council of the four kingdoms, the Covenant, and the Wizards. Suddenly he felt sick to his stomach. So many important people, all to see him?

"Young man," King Beredis addressed him directly. "I know you have been through so much, and it is unfair of us to ask you this, but we must. Tell us what you saw. What happened? We know orcs attacked the mine, and our scouts have confirmed that they occupy the camp now." The camp. The face of the monsters suddenly flashed in his mind, and he started to back away as a sick, sinking feeling overtook his stomach.

Then the Wizard's hand rested on his shoulder, and unlike when the cleric had held him in place, warmth washed over his body, giving him goose bumps, but otherwise making him feel so much better. The face of the orcs suddenly didn't scare him.

Zerek looked up at the Wizard, who looked down at him with piercing, dark eyes, and nodded once. "You can do this. I know you can."

Nodding once, Zerek turned back to King Beredis. "There was no warning. I…" His voice cracked a little, but the Wizard's reassuring hand never left his shoulder. "I wasn't there when it happened, not at first. But then I saw it. They just attacked. No reason, no warning. They overran the camp, killing…" A lump formed in his throat as the images seared across his imagination. "Killing everyone who stood in their way. Destroying everything. And some even had magic."

"What sort of magic," one of the other kings asked. Tall and broad-shouldered, that king flicked his blonde hair out of his eyes and looked very interested in what Zerek had to say.

"From their weapons, like a Mage." Zerek frowned and gulped. "But not Mage magic. Fire. Some ice, too, but lots of fire."

The Wizard beside him frowned, and looked at him curiously. "Did you see what the magic ones wore? Or what their weapons looked like?"

Another sensation of warmth from the Wizard's hand. Somehow it seemed to clarify the images in his head. "Yes. Yeah, I did. They wore very dark armor. Almost black. Same with their weapons." He shook his head, wondering how he could recall that detail now.

This time the only woman monarch, whom he knew to be Queen Leian of Erien, asked a question. "But not all of the attackers wore such armor?"

"Very few," Zerek nodded. "They stood out, there were so few of them." Where was this calm feeling coming from? It grew stronger the longer the Wizard held his hand on Zerek's shoulder.

"That's a relief," another man next to King Beredis spoke up. He wore a very large sword sheathed on his back, and was one of the very few armed persons in the room.

"Is it," the Wizard next to Zerek asked. "We know that several hundred orcs survived the attack on Archanon." Rumors had spread through the mining camp a few days before the orc attack. Rumors of an attack on Archanon. *So that was true, too,* Zerek thought. "If these are indeed orcs from that battle, and if they are leading the attack, where are the rest of the survivors?"

The blonde King scoffed. "Do not attempt to make the situation seem worse than it already is." He shook his head. "The Tal scout reported that he could scarcely see the extent of the army. They were likely all hidden from view in the forest, with the rest of the orc army."

"None-the-less," Beredis clasped his hands behind his back, "There is an army of thousands of orcs. Even if they are the only army opposing us, this represents a perfect opportunity for us to collaborate as an alliance. If we strike with a combined force, we can defeat them quickly with minimal casualties."

"I agree," the white Wizard nodded. "We can assist with quickly mobilizing your armies and to strike at the camp."

Zerek felt completely out of place. They were speaking of grand battle plans, invasion tactics. He should have been excited, he had always dreamt of becoming a Warrior. Instead, he felt afraid, and overwhelmed, and he wanted to get out.

His anxiety once again diminished when he felt warmth course out of the Wizard's hand. How did he do that? Still, he looked at the Wizard, who at first was too intent on the conversation to notice. When he did, he looked at Zerek with a frown. Then that frown turned to a look of understanding.

While he didn't want the calming effect of the Wizard's firm grip to go away, his desire to escape steadily grew stronger. So the Wizard motioned for the cleric to come back. The conversation around them continued, and the Wizard piped back in when the cleric nudged Zerek towards the same doors they had entered through.

The moment the Wizard's hand broke contact, he felt a void form in his stomach. But surprisingly, the full weight of everything did not come crashing down inside of him. He was okay. Somehow, he was okay. For now, anyway.

As they left, he overheard them speak of increasing patrols along the Wastelands. He wondered how long he would be safe. The orcs were invading. Maybe none of them would be okay for long.

Maybe he'd get to see his mother again soon.

***

Amaya Kenla had argued against returning home with her team after their hasty induction into the Guardians. Now that she had a purpose again, she had no desire to return. She had no family there, and no friends outside of her team to visit with. More than that, she didn't want to risk running into her former Commander.

When her mind had been set, and she went to wish them a good journey, they all reacted in unison and practically begged her to go with. She tried to pull the 'I'm the commanding officer, I don't fraternize with my subordinates' hand, but they wouldn't hear anything of it. They weren't Warriors anymore. Neither was she.

After she tried using every excuse she could think of, they finally wore her down, and she agreed to go with.

It was only for a day, right? She would be okay. What could possibly go wrong in one day? And she could avoid Din for a day.

Fortunately, their journey to Everlin would be by Wizard's Portal. Their journey with a Wizard served a dual purpose – the Allied Council decided to mobilize the Warriors as quickly as possible. They would be accompanied by General Artula, who would command the Everlin Warriors to prepare for war. While Amaya's team enjoyed a day with their family, Artula and the Wizard would continue on to other towns and villages. Later, they would return to retrieve her and her companions.

Their journey was a unique experience. They had all read about Wizards and portals in their lessons during training, but she quickly realized how inaccurate those lessons were.

The first surprise was the Wizard they travelled with. Nia was relatively young, and wasn't the pompous, arrogant old hag that books would have everyone believe. Nor was she warm and inviting. The best way to describe her was polite and sincere.

When the General arrived, he was very quiet, and barely spoke two words to them. Amaya wondered if he knew who she was and what her team had been accused of, or if he had only been told that they were merely travelers taking advantage of the convenience of their journey by portal. Either way, she didn't speak to him except for the formal 'hello' and, after their journey through the portal, a formal 'farewell.'

The trip through the portal was another surprise, and could hardly be considered a trip. One moment, they stood just outside of Archanon, and the next, just outside of Everlin, as simple as stepping through a doorway.

That was when her whole attitude changed. The moment they arrived, she wanted to turn around and run back through, even though she knew that she could not. She didn't want to be in Everlin. She didn't want to be anywhere near the Guild, near Din.

She wanted to run.

And then Elic was beside her. Somehow, his presence instilled a calm in her, made her take a deep breath and refocus her mind. There was no danger. She would not see Commander Din tonight. He would not be invited to their festivities.

That had been a topic of much debate amongst them all. Where should they go? Should they all visit their friends and family separately, or should they celebrate together?

The answer turned out to be self-evident – after everything they had been through together, their time in the dungeons together, they had grown so accustomed to one another that they couldn't imagine celebrating separately.

So they would go their separate ways to say their initial hellos, and explain what had happened, and then meet for dinner and drinks at their favorite tavern.

Except that Amaya still didn't want to go. She watched as Peren, Idalia, Nerina, Vin, Elic and Gell walked towards the town, leaving her alone on the edge. She looked with nervous eyes upon the town, and her hands felt numb. Idly she rubbed the small Guardian logo that had been branded into the inside of her left wrist, as if the constant ache mirrored how her own heart felt. Everlin had once been a place she loved so dearly, and swore she would protect with her life for as long as she lived.

Now she was terrified of it. Amaya, once a brave Lieutenant in the Warriors' Guild, a powerful Mage, terrified of her hometown.

She was ready to turn and run, to leave them all and find safety in the wilderness.

Everlin wasn't large, but it was protected by a stone wall built by the Guild centuries ago. She watched with a void in her stomach as her team passed through the gates. Just as they were about to turn a corner and leave her sight, Elic stopped and looked back at her. His eyes bore into her, and she wondered if he knew why she couldn't go in.

Not likely. Nor could she explain it to him.

Somehow Elic got the message. He merely nodded solemnly, and then disappeared, leaving her to her thoughts.

Knowing that they weren't supposed to meet Nia and General Artula again until early morning, she would have to find some place to sleep for the night. There was only one choice, a very small lumber community up-river. It would take her a couple of hours to walk there, but right now that prospect was so much better than passing through those gates.

Not to mention stretching her legs would be a welcome reprieve from months in the dungeon. When she thought of that, a great smile stretched across her face, and she started jogging.

At first it felt strange, like a sensation she had long forgotten. But the further she ran, the more familiar it became, and the more energized she felt. Faster and faster she ran, her heart racing until it thundered in her ears.

It didn't matter how much her legs burned or how hard he heart beat – the further she was from Everlin, and from Din, the more she felt free.

***

The Wizard had done something to Zerek. He wasn't sure what, but he was both angry and relieved for what he had done. The world was no longer a haze around him, he felt fully aware and no longer terrified of being a part of it.

However, there was a part of him that still wanted to retreat back into himself. To ignore everyone around him, and to just pretend that his mother was still there to comfort him.

Unfortunately, the Wizard's trick also made him realize just how childish that desire was. He was fifteen, not five. So as much as he wanted to hide, he wouldn't let himself.

Of course, that meant facing another reality. He had no family left. Not that he knew of, anyway. No siblings, no parents, and if he had aunts or uncles, he had never known about them.

He was an orphan.

Now he sat in an empty hallway on a bench, staring at the wall across from him, contemplating what he could possibly do next in life. Find another mining camp? He knew the trade, there was no getting around that. It would be the easiest thing for him to do.

Easiest, but not what he wanted. He wanted to be a Warrior. He thought about the dagger he had taken from Elina's hands. It was wrapped in cloth and tucked under his belt now. They had tried to take it away from him, but he wouldn't let them. He would never, ever let it out of his sight.

He had dreamt of becoming a Warrior for as long as he could remember. But could he? Warriors trained from childhood, so was he too old? Probably.

Maybe that dream was another part of his childhood that he would have to leave behind now. He would have to become an adult, take care of himself, make his own way in life. That meant doing what was necessary, not what he wanted.

Yet the thought of ever going back underground again, of ever seeing another mine, terrified him. His hands turned clammy and his heart raced just from imagining walking into the mouth of a tunnel, hard hat on, pick axe resting on his shoulder. Like being swallowed into a giant mouth.

"So," he jumped when the cleric suddenly spoke. Zerek forgot that the fake man still sat with him. Why were they still just sitting there, waiting? Hadn't the Council meeting been hours ago?

The Cleric finished his thought, "Have you given any thought to where you will go from here?"

Zerek shuddered. It was like the cleric could read his thoughts. He could see out of the corner of his eye that the cleric didn't look at him, he just stared ahead at the castle wall, like Zerek did. "I don't know," he slouched and looked down.

There was a long pause, and he wondered why the cleric had asked that. The man just seemed so *fake*, and it made Zerek uneasy. He was supposed to be a kind, caring man. Yet his kindness didn't seem real, and his smiles always seemed completely off.

"You could always join the Order of the Ages," the cleric looked at him. He didn't dare match the man's look. "Every child of the Six has a place waiting for them in the Order."

He considered that offer, but only for a brief moment. The gods hadn't saved his family, after all. More than that, he just didn't want to have to stick around the creepy cleric.

Not all clerics were like this one. Several had visited the mining camps often, as part of their missions to spread the truth of the Cronal to every corner of the world. Those clerics had all been genuine. This one...there was just something wrong about him.

So Zerek shook his head. "No, I don't think so." He glanced at the cleric, but quickly looked away again. "Thank you."

The cleric did not reply for some time, and Zerek felt even more uncomfortable by the silence. Finally, the man nodded, and stood. "As you wish. We will always be here, should you change your mind." Zerek glanced up again at him, wondering if he was going to leave him. He walked past Zerek and down the hallway. He wasn't sure if he should follow or not. Was he supposed to stay with the man until someone else came along?

Or was that it? Was he now free to go do whatever he wanted?

Not that he knew yet what he wanted.

Just as the cleric was about to turn down the hallway, a woman's voice spoke from the other direction, "I understand that you have no family to claim you."

Zerek turned to find a tall, skinny woman with sharp facial features and hard eyes. She stared down her nose at him, and began to look at every inch of his body, as if assessing a piece of clothing.

"That's right," he nodded and frowned. "Who are you?"

She narrowed her eyes. "I am the house steward, Kai Loric. Your name is Zerek, yes?"

Was she angry? Her features and mannerism confused him. "Umm, yes," he replied. "Zerek Betanil."

She raised one eyebrow. "Well, stand up, let me get a look at you."

He frowned at her, but somehow felt compelled to obey her. She didn't look like someone you said no to, for any reason. So he stood up and faced her, trying to find his courage. A Warrior wouldn't shy away from her, right?

After a moment of looking him up and down, she nodded with satisfaction. "Yes, you are a strong young lad." He had no idea what a 'lad' was, but it seemed like she had just given him a compliment. "His Majesty, the King, has commanded me to ask you to remain within the castle as a servant. You are by no means required to," she raised her right eyebrow, "but it would seem you have little other choice at the moment."

Zerek's face burned red when she said that, and he wanted to tell her 'no' out of spite. Maybe the Order wouldn't be so bad.

However, another thought occurred to him. A servant in the castle. That would mean he'd be around castle guards. Perhaps he could find a way to impress them and they'd ask him to join their ranks. It wasn't as glorious as becoming a Warrior, but it would be better than any alternative he could think of.

"What job would I be doing," he asked.

She rested her hands on her hips and huffed a sigh. "Well, let's see. We have need in several areas. How fast on your feet are you?"

The memory of running from the orcs briefly passed through his mind, but for some reason it didn't seem to hurt or scare him as much as it had before. He felt stronger now.

"I don't know," he shrugged. "Fast."

Kai rolled her eyes. "That's descriptive." She folded her arms in front of her and narrowed her eyes appraisingly at him. "Well, if you are indeed as fast as you appear to be, we have need of a delivery boy. Someone to take or retrieve letters or supplies throughout the city. Do you think you are up to this challenge?"

He didn't know the city at all, but he was a quick learner. Plus mines often became mazes of branching tunnels, and he had learned to navigate them. How difficult could it be to navigate open streets?

"Yeah, I think I can," he grinned and nodded.

"Good." She sighed and shook her head. "First, we will teach you proper etiquette. Come along," she turned and walked away. He was too stunned at first to follow, but then realized he did not want to cross her, so he took off in a jog after her.

It probably wasn't going to be a fun job, but anything was better than the mines.

***

Over the past several weeks, Cardin Kataar's free time had mostly been spent with his Wizard friend Dalin, learning everything he could about the new powers he had gained from the Sword of Dragons.

Which hadn't been much. And that frustrated him to no end. Sure, initially his powers had grown considerably in the first few days, and his strength and speed were far greater than he thought possible for a person, but he'd learned little more than that.

He hadn't learned how to make portals. Kailar had learned how to within minutes of picking up the Sword, but somehow he hadn't, and he had to grudgingly rely on Dalin or other Wizards for portals.

As a result, his daily lessons with Dalin had grown more and more frustrating, and he wasn't looking forward to today's. He and the Wizard, who was clad in his usual blue robes, strode through Archanon towards the Southeast Quarter of the city, still under heavy construction in the wake of the battle against Klaralin and the orcs.

The Wizard was being unusually cryptic about the lesson for today and why they couldn't accomplish it in the castle courtyard. Cardin eyed the Wizard suspiciously, who noticed almost immediately and smiled ironically at him.

That's when Cardin stopped and folded his arms in front of him. "Alright, I'll bite. What has you in such a cheerful mood today?" Cheerful despite the renewed war against the orcs. It was usually Dalin who had to remind *him* of the dire events at hand, not the other way around.

Dalin had walked past him before he stopped and turned to face him. He placed both hands on his staff and glanced at the gem. "I am smiling because today I feel that you are ready for the next level."

With a raised eyebrow, a personal quirk he had picked up from his Wizard friend, Cardin replied, "Next level? I haven't learned any new powers from the Sword. Are you saying there is something you can do to change that?"

A part of him was ready to pounce on Dalin's next words if he said 'yes.' Cardin had made his frustration well known, and if Dalin held back key information he needed to unlock new powers, he would not forgive the Wizard easily.

"Perhaps," Dalin shrugged, "but not directly. I do not believe you truly appreciate how much your power has grown, nor the deeper connection to the universe that this has provided you."

Dalin began to pace back and forth. It was a habit that annoyed Cardin, mostly because it reminded him of some of his teachers from Warrior training. "The Wizards are not just powerful, my friend," he spoke slowly, not looking at Cardin directly. "We have learned to control and harness the power we have access to through knowledge, through understanding. Your connection to the magic around you has increased dramatically, and I believe we must begin to teach you to have a more refined understanding of that power."

"You're kind of repeating yourself," Cardin grit his teeth. "What's your point?"

Dalin stopped pacing and smiled at Cardin. "Have you ever felt a connection to someone through magic? Have you ever formed a link where you can feel their very essence, and they yours? Even pick each other out in a crowd just from that feeling."

Cardin immediately thought of Sira, and felt his face grow warm. "Yeah, I have. It was...well, it was magical, to use exactly the right word."

Dalin nodded. "It was with someone you were already close to, was it not?" He continued without waiting for Cardin to answer. "That connection you felt, whether you were in proximity to her or not, is a perfect example of what I am going to teach you today. Come along," he turned and continued towards the Southeast Quarter. Cardin quickly caught up and fell into step beside him.

As they strode deeper into the quarter, Cardin noted a considerable increase in activity. More men and women building or rebuilding homes, shops, storage houses. It was a hive of activity.

It was beginning to look like a city again. While some buildings were just getting started, most were in the final stages of being rebuilt, and several were already completed. Cardin and his friends had helped with that effort in the beginning, but it wasn't long before there had been an incident with his new powers, and the decision had been made for him to focus more on honing those abilities.

Dalin began to search around, but for what, Cardin couldn't begin to guess. After only a short walk, the Wizard smiled and led him over to a house that, at least on the outside, was not being worked on. At the front of the building was a freshly-built wooden bench large enough to seat three. "This will do," he nodded and sat on one side. He motioned to the other side and nodded to Cardin, "Please, sit."

This was a surprise. Most of Cardin's previous lessons had been combat-based. Lots of running, jumping, attacking dummy targets or, in the case of when he used his enhanced Mage powers, lots of boulders to be pulverized. He reached back and grasped the Sword – the scabbard vanished at his mental command – before he sat down and rested the Sword in his lap.

Dalin sat back and looked out into the activity around them. "Now, first take a look around you. Look at all of the men and women, working hard, moving everywhere like a swarm of ants."

Uncertain of the end goal, Cardin did as he was told. At first he just generally stared at the movement, like he would ants. The movement was almost mesmerizing, a blur of little and big motions all mixed into one. Arms moved back and forth with every stroke of a hammer or pull and push of a saw. Little movement of legs as their owners finished a task and moved just a few inches over to do the next task. People walked between buildings and jobs, runners rushed back and forth to fetch supplies to help keep the workers busy.

The runners. He focused in on them. He didn't know why, but he watched each individual as they ran about. Then he focused in on one of the women hammering away on a board. Then another man who was cutting a board for that same woman.

Individuals, working as a whole to achieve a common goal, but still individuals.

"Good," Dalin said. "I already can feel your spirit focusing."

Cardin felt his eyebrows rise up, "It is?"

He focused inward to see if he could feel it, too, but Dalin quickly said, "No, no, do not look inside yourself. Keep your focus out in the crowd, on the individuals. Each one, a piece or part of the moving whole, independent and yet linked at the same time."

Cardin felt himself blush, and then refocused his attention. After another moment of getting a general sense of the individuals working, Dalin continued on. "Now close your eyes, but keep your focus outward."

A part of him began to suspect what Dalin was trying to help him accomplish, but another part told him 'no, that's impossible.'

However, without further hesitation, he did as he was told and closed his eyes.

"Can you feel it yet," the young Wizard asked. Dalin said nor asked anything more, so Cardin felt himself frown as he tried to focus. He could feel the currents of magic around him, far easier than he had been able to when he was just another Mage, but that was it.

On the other hand, there had to be a point to this lesson.

The people. The purpose was in all of the workers scurrying about their tasks. So he imagined them before him, the same kind of mesmerizing blur of movement.

Then, he finally began to see it. That imagined view of motion began to sync up, quite of its own accord, with the pulse and throb of energy that he felt all around him. Like the flow of a river, where in some places it flowed fiercely, and in others sedately.

At first it was just a general sense, but then he recalled what had happened when his eyes were open, and how Dalin had said his spirit began to focus. So he began to try to make out individual collections of energy within that sea of movement. It wasn't easy, not at first. After all, how do you follow a specific part of a river as it flows?

You throw a stick in and watch it float with the current, he thought to himself. *So I need something unique to focus on and follow.*

There it was! Someone, he didn't know who, walked by, and he caught onto the ever-so-slightly unique feel of the energy within that person and how it flowed around them. He felt the person walk by like someone felt a breeze - gentle, but distinct.

That was the key. He didn't know how, but somehow he began to pick up on the minor differences. This pulse of energy throbbed at a certain rhythm. One was stronger than the others around it. And another one had a warmth to it that the others did not.

They were all different, every single one of them. The points of energy were as unique as each individual they belonged to. Before long, Cardin began to wonder how he'd never noticed it before, how he had never felt or seen the obvious differences.

Suddenly it was no longer an indistinct river of energy ebbing and flowing. Now he felt *them*, their energy, every single one of them. And he could see them, too, through closed eyes as if they were all spirits of an unimaginable array of colors, shapes, and sizes. They were twinkling stars against the dull backdrop of the world.

People were made of magic.

His stomach tingled at his excitement. He opened his eyes and beamed at Dalin. "That's...that's fantastic!"

Dalin grinned and nodded. "Yes, it is."

Cardin gazed about the worksites and realized that the sensation remained. Though he could no longer see the lights, he could still feel them, feel their energy tugging or pushing against him. He knew which ones were Mages now, too. They shined like beacons amongst the others, their intensity strong and mesmerizing.

"This is how you see the world," he breathed.

"Always," Dalin nodded. "You have barely scratched the surface, my friend. There is more, so much more to what you have learned."

As the Wizard spoke, Cardin watched as a platoon of Warriors marched by in formation, headed for the Southeast Gate. The two in the lead were Mages, the rest were not. He noticed something about how they felt, like they shone with a sharper clarity. He closed his eyes and allowed his senses to remain extended, and sure enough, that was how they appeared in his mind's eye.

He again focused on the workers rebuilding the city, and began to suspect why their colors were all a little duller than the Warriors that had just marched by.

"They are tired," he turned his head towards Dalin. Unsurprisingly, Dalin's light shone brighter than the brightest star, and with an intensity that almost overwhelmed him. He opened his eyes, and saw a curious frown on the Wizard's face. "The workers. I can feel it, they are exhausted."

Dalin's eyes widened just a little bit, almost imperceptibly. He turned to look outward and closed his eyes. Cardin felt the energies around them shift a little as the Wizard flexed his powers to perceive the world. After several moments of silence, he frowned and shook his head. "I do not feel any such indications."

"I can't really explain it," Cardin looked back out at the workers. Then he noticed that many of them moved a bit sluggishly, little cues he probably could only physically notice because of what he had learned about tracking in the wild. The signs were there, so he knew his perception was correct. "But I can see it now, too. Look at how they move, how they walk."

The young Wizard opened his eyes and looked carefully at them. After several more moments of silence, he turned and looked at

Cardin, his mouth hung open slightly. "I have heard," he said quietly, "that the very wisest of Master Wizards can perceive such nuances within each individual, and more. Never would I have thought it possible for you to pick up such ability in a matter of moments."

Cardin felt his face flush, and then he looked down at the Sword, almost forgotten in his lap. He lifted the near-weightless weapon and examined it as if the answer lay within its core.

Before he could say anything more, he felt a surge of energy from the center of the city. He turned to see Sira and Reis approaching, both clearly in a hurry, and both wearing full armor. That wasn't the surge of energy Cardin felt, but he knew they were linked to it. "Something is happening," he said as he stood up.

Dalin joined him a moment later, and they greeted their friends ever so briefly. "We've been recalled," Sira stated, an edge in her voice that told him this was no exercise or war game. "The Council has decided to attack the mining camp now, with as many Warriors as we can muster."

He exchanged confused glances with Dalin, and replied, "I thought the plan was to mobilize our entire force before we attacked. They have superior numbers."

"That's the concern," Reis replied. "Some general from Erien brought up the point. So many orcs in one place can't stay long, there isn't enough food and water in the area for them."

Sira nodded, "General Zilan. He believes the majority of the orcs are going to move on for other targets as soon as the mining camp's fortifications are up."

Realization dawned on Cardin. "The longer we wait, the more likely they'll attack somewhere else."

"Exactly," Reis said. "Come on, we're mobilizing now."

Cardin placed the Sword on his back and willed the sheath back into existence. He realized that the wait was over.

The war was starting today.

***

Amaya had run as fast and as far as she could, but even with the freedom it had given her, she ran less than a mile before she had to slow down. Her legs had burned, her chest had heaved, until she could stand it no more, and she nearly collapsed on the trail.

No matter how much she had tried to remain fit in the dungeons, the fact was there wasn't room to run down there.

Now, after only a couple of hours of walking, she approached the lumber community, known as Ironwood Lumber Mill, at a leisurely pace. She had entered the southernmost tip of the massive Daruun forest, which stretched from here, far in the south, almost all the way up to the northern shores of Edilas.

Ironwood was a community she knew quite well. More than once, she and her Warriors had been asked to fend off bandits or wild animals, even some fairly strange and dangerous creatures.

When Din had only been a Captain, she had even once helped him fend off what was now assumed to be the last werewolf to ever terrorize the forest. That was when he had first gained her trust.

She shook her head to dispel the memory, and continued on. Just one more hill to crest, and she would be able to rest.

It was only then that the hairs on the back of her neck stood up. She stopped, not entirely sure why, except that something felt off. The magic around her felt wrong, like something was missing from it.

Birds. She heard no birds. No wildlife at all. No insects. Not one single frog.

Where were all of the animals? It was as if the area ahead and around her had become a void of wildlife. Not just in sounds, but in energy.

No. Not a void. There was...*something* out there.

She reached for her sword, only to remember that they hadn't issued her one yet. All she had was a dagger she had purchased on their first day of freedom, sheathed horizontally at the small of her back. Slowly, quietly, she pulled the long, slender steel blade out, and then moved right off of the path.

The forest was never this quiet, except when something was terribly wrong. Unfortunately, the part of the forest she was in was not dense with foliage, so there was very little for her to hide in, but she did find a large tree to duck behind.

Expecting *something* to come from the camp, she waited with bated breath. Her pack would become cumbersome if she had to fight, so as slowly and quietly as she could, she shrugged it off of her shoulders and set it down beside her.

Moments passed. Minutes passed. But nothing came into view over the hill. Yet with each passing moment, the feeling that something horrible was on the other side grew stronger.

When it felt like she had waited an eternity, and she was about to step out from behind the tree, she began to hear it. Low grumbles and grunts from countless sources. Talking. The grinding of saws and the reverberating thumps of axes chopping.

It was what she would have expected to hear from a lumber mill. Shortly thereafter, she began to hear the sound of the pulley-driven large saw at the actual mill, designed to slice trees in half length-wise.

Yet there still were no animal or insect sounds, and the feeling that something was wrong did not abate.

She had to see what was wrong. She had to know. It would have been very easy for her to just turn around and go back to Everlin. Or would it?

If she went back to that town, with that wretched human being, it would have to be for a very good reason. So she crouched low, and edged out from the cover of her tree. No one was on the path, but she was not foolish enough to take it any further.

She wore no armor, but that only made her task of remaining quiet easier. With the greatest care, she moved further away from the path towards the ridgeline. It took her longer than she would have liked to reach the top of that ridge, but she dared not move any faster.

Fearing detection if she remained in the open, she approached a tree at the crest, and then began to edge her face around it to peak at what lay ahead.

Only to feel her breath catch. From the ridge onward, the way was clear, with the majority of the trees having been cut down for the mill. That gave her an unhindered line of sight to those who worked at the mill.

Orcs. They were here! And judging by the pile of human corpses that had just been set on fire, they had recently slaughtered every member of the community. Unlike the reports of the Relkin Mine, however, the lumber mill had been left completely intact. It was now under the control of the orcs.

She didn't know how they could have made it so far into Tal undetected, or why they had made such a bold move, but it turned her veins to ice when she realized what it meant. If they were at Ironwood, they could have made it even further into Tal.

The mines hadn't just been a one-off attack to gain a foothold. It was part of a larger, coordinated attack, very unlike what they had come to expect from orcs.

They were organized, and more dangerous than ever.

Quietly, she eased backwards, and crawled away from the ridgeline. She feared her hammering heart would give away her position. There had been dozens of orcs working the mill, and there was no way she could defeat all of them by herself. She needed help.

She needed her team.

***

It wasn't the largest force they had assembled, not nearly as large as what they had defended Archanon with, but Cardin still found himself in awe. Before this year, he had never found himself in a war. Now he was in his second.

West of the First City, a small army of Tal and Erien Warriors had assembled, as quickly as could be mobilized with the help of the Wizards. As he, Sira, Reis, and Dalin hurried out of the western gate, he felt a rush.

However, it wasn't his own inner excitement that energized him. It was what he felt from his new ability. He could see and *feel* the Warriors, the Mages, the Wizards, a mix of powers, abilities, and colors, all gathered together. Is this what it would have felt like just before the Battle for Archanon?

They had not been given the time to return to Daruun to collect their heavy armor, and supplies in the city were still scarce. Cardin worried for his two friends, especially Reis, who had neither a magical or physical shield, and wore borrowed armor from the castle armory.

His friend had always insisted that he had the ability to keep up with any Mage in battle, and to be fair, he had proven that fact not two months ago on the Great Road between Daruun and Falind. As the Daruun Warriors had been decimated by the entire Falind army, his quirky, prankster friend had held his own against two Mages.

Cardin wore a simple suit of leather armor, the same one he had worn when they scouted the Relkin Mine. He did not need as much protection now, not with the powers he had gained from the Sword.

Of the four of them, Dalin looked the least protected, wearing nothing but his blue robes and wielding his oak staff. Yet of the four, he was easily the most powerful.

Today, all of their skills would be tested. Orcs were not generally intelligent, and based on the young boy's description, most of them were armed only with rudimentary weapons. But there was no discounting the strength of orcs, or their viciousness.

Together Cardin and the others rushed to the front line, where they knew the Keeper was needed most. Among his many new abilities, he had learned to expand his shield, much like a Wizard, and could protect large numbers from archers or other ranged attacks.

Unfortunately, General Artula was still out, travelling from city to city to mobilize the Tal army, and the Allied Council had decided he was best left to complete that task. That left them with General Zilan, Erien's lead Warrior, to take them into battle.

"Keeper," the General used Cardin's new title. He wore very pristine, well kept steel and chain armor, which was dyed a navy blue and white, his country's colors. "We have awaited your arrival." Was that his politically correct way of voicing his annoyance at his and his friends' tardiness?

"Then the army is ready," Sira asked.

"Let us find out," he stepped away from them and turned to address the forces. "Captains, report readiness!"

His voice was stronger when he needed to command attention. Cardin's initial impression had been of a simple political pundit, not an experienced leader. Now, however, the crowd of a couple hundred Warriors and Wizards grew quiet, and the various Captains assigned to lead the dozen units reported that all was ready.

Zilan nodded, and then seemed to consider his next words carefully. There were legends of the General's speeches, always inspiring, but always with the hint of a political agenda. Would he give such a speech now?

"Today we stand united once again," he began, using some of his Mage abilities to enhance the volume of his voice. It was usually a skill only politicians learned. "Tal and Erien Warriors, as it always was and always should be, shoulder to shoulder."

That was why there were no Falind or Saran Warriors. Zilan *was* making a statement. Unfortunately, it was the opposite statement than what King Beredis wanted. The idea was to unite all four kingdoms, not break down into their previous alliances.

"While far outnumbered, we stand with over fifty Wizards in our ranks today, our newest allies in our continuing struggle to maintain peace and security in the East." He placed his fists on his hips, and Cardin had to actually stifle a chuckle. Was he attempting to look heroic? "No matter what happens, no matter what odds we face, stand together, stand united as we always have." He drew his longsword and pointed it into the sky. "March with me! March to victory, and the destruction of the orcs!"

The Warriors all drew their weapons and raised them into the air, and cheered along with him. "To victory!"

Cardin, Sira, and Reis joined with him, and then steeled themselves for what came next.

"Wizards," Zilan addressed Master Syrn, charged with leading the Wizard contingent. "The time is now. Take us to war."

As one, a dozen Wizards stepped forward, including Syrn, and planted their staves in the ground. Cardin felt a torrent of energy suddenly rush into the area, and in a matter of moments, twelve blue-white walls of light, portals to predetermined locations near the Relkin Mining Camp, came to life.

Now it was Cardin's turn. He and the remaining Wizards would all pass through together, so he stepped up next to Syrn, and felt as much as saw the other Wizards fill in the spaces between the portal summoners. It was the same strategy employed by the Wizards and Tal Warriors to defeat the Falind Warriors to great effect.

He hoped it would be just as effective now. It *had* to work.

"Now!" Zilan shouted.

Heart thundering in his ears, with the Sword of Dragons in hand, Cardin led the charge ahead of the Wizards, and passed through the nearest portal.

Only to run into a wall of orcs.

He hadn't expected instant battle, but his instincts took over, and he swung the Sword in a wide arc that sent a destructive wave of energy out. The group of orcs before him smashed into one another and into the forest, hopefully dead.

It had merely been an unfortunate circumstance. They were a patrol of orcs just outside of the mining camp, and thankfully no others appeared in the immediate vicinity. He was in a small clearing in the forest, not far from the camp. The sun was closing in on the horizon, but there was still more than enough light for them to fight, and would be for at least another hour or two.

Knowing he had to make way for others to pass through the

portal, Cardin did not stop. He pushed forward towards the camp, looking for any more orcs that could threaten the portal. He glanced back and saw Dalin pass through. "Come on," he beckoned, and charged forward alone.

"Wait," the Wizard pleaded, but Cardin didn't listen.

His heart raced, and he felt magic flowing through him like it never had before. He felt like he could take anything on.

Passing by the orcs he had first encountered, he continued on, finding more orcs that were rushing towards the intruders. The Sword was as light as a dagger, so he swung it with confidence and ease, charging the blade with ethereal power that allowed it to cleave right through the orcs' weapons and armor. He tore through them, slaying them one by one, moving closer and closer to the camp.

Unfortunately, his forward momentum quickly came to a stop when he encountered the first enemy armed in darkened steel. It was not so easily defeated.

When the Sword met the orc's blade, the clang echoed off of the trees and rang in his ears. The darkened steel sword had not broken.

And then the orc went on the offensive. It was stronger than the others, faster, and its moves were much more calculated. Cardin attempted to parry and strike, but the orc anticipated his attack and turned the tables back against Cardin.

Back and forth they struggled, one trying to take the advantage over the other, their swords flying with a furious speed. Cardin was relieved when they paused for a moment and he noticed deep gouges and nicks within his opponent's blade.

Then he noticed that several other orcs were charging to their companion's aid. He could not keep this orc at bay and take on the others by himself. He had to think of something fast.

Suddenly the leading orc was struck by a bolt of lightning. Then another was impaled by a shard of ice.

Cardin turned, and saw Dalin, Sira, Reis, and the rest of their unit rushing to him. They had all come through the portal and were ready to advance.

His opponent tried to take advantage of the distraction and swung from overhead, but Cardin was too fast. He stepped aside, spun around, and jabbed into the orc's abdomen, though the armor prevented him from cutting very deep.

It was a great blow to his opponent, but the orc did not give up.

It released its weapon with one hand, clenched it into a fist, and punched Cardin hard on his cheekbone. Stars exploded in his vision, and he stumbled backwards, jerking the Sword free of his opponent's body as he nearly fell over, fighting against a spinning world.

The wounded orc pulled a small knife from its boot and moved to strike Cardin down, but a pinpoint precision blast of energy struck it in the chest, flinging it violently to the forest floor. A moment later, Sira was there to steady Cardin. He looked at her and saw that she spoke, but at first her voice did not register. A flurry of Warriors and Wizards rushed past them to meet the charging orcs from the camp.

"Are you okay?" she repeated.

"Yeah," he tenderly touched his bruised cheek, the ringing in his ears subsiding.

"What's the matter," Reis smirked, "never taken a punch to the face?"

"Hey," he frowned at his friend, "you try getting punched by one of them."

The sounds of clashing weapons, shouts, and roars erupted throughout the surrounding forest, not just from their battle, but from everywhere. With the help of the Wizards, the army had instantly surrounded the camp from all directions except from the mountain.

"Cardin Kataar!" Zilan roared. The General had taken up the rear. Definitely nothing like Artula. "You were to cover the portal, not run off into a one-man war."

"Yes sir," Cardin looked at the General, barely able to contain his annoyance. "But I had the initiative, and I was able to keep them back."

"Do not stray from your unit again, Keeper," Zilan warned, jabbing a finger into Cardin's chest. "I cannot afford to fight the orcs while trying to control you."

Already annoyed with the conversation, Cardin backed away from the General and said, "Then let's get back to the battle."

Without waiting for further orders or reprimand, Cardin turned and, finally regaining his bearings, rushed into the fray of the battle.

As their unit made their way to the camp, Cardin found himself surprised at how few orcs there were. Reis's report had suggested many, many more, thousands, perhaps tens of thousands. However, all twelve units made it into the clearing around the camp in minutes, and before long, all of them had reached the wooden wall the orcs had hastily erected.

Dozens of orcs manned the walls with rudimentary bows, unleashing volleys of arrows. A few more of the dark-steel armored ones used their enchanted weapons to rain fire, ice, or lightning down upon the invading army, but the shields of the Wizards were more than adequate, so much so that Cardin didn't even need to raise a shield.

Far weaker than the Falind wall had been, the orc wall was breached in every quarter by simple blasts from individual Wizards. Even Cardin's own powers were strong enough that he blasted a gap large enough for one person at a time to squeeze through.

The camp itself wasn't as heavily guarded as he would have expected. More and more he began to suspect that they were too late. Zilan was right, the orcs had already spread out from the camp. It was their beachhead, and they were advancing.

Several dozen orcs began to stream out of the mine to join their failing forces. Cardin began to make his way there, knowing that if he could collapse the mine entrance, the Allies could then simply let the trapped orcs suffocate.

Cardin reached the entrance quickly, slaying a half-dozen orcs along the way. He began to gather magic into the Sword, ready to blast the mountainside, but then something he didn't expect happen.

One more enemy emerged from the mine, but it was not an ordinary orc. It was much taller than the others, at least a head and a half taller than Cardin. No, more, as it stood up straight now that it wasn't in the mine. Cardin also noted that it looked considerably stronger than its compatriots, vast muscles rippling under its mottled skin.

It also wore darkened steel armor, and wielded a large double-headed battle axe in both hands. Somehow it honed in on Cardin.

"By the gods," Cardin craned his neck to look up at the monster. "From what decadent swamp did they conjure you from?"

The orc smirked, sniffed, and shook his head. "You," he pointed the axe at Cardin. "You have no idea what has begun."

Cardin felt himself hesitate. The orc had not only spoken to him, but had done so in very clear, intelligent speech. That was not normal.

"I think I do," Cardin replied cautiously, stepping to the side. He still had a full charge gathered within the Sword, and wanted to take down the mine entrance. However, he noticed that no other orcs emerged from it. Perhaps the big one was the last of them. He looked again to the giant orc. "A war to wipe out your people."

The smirk on the orc's face vanished, replaced by rage. "You have no idea!" With incredible speed, the orc charged at Cardin. It was like a giant boulder coming down the mountain.

Cardin should have side stepped the monster, but he wanted to prove that his new powers were superior, so he stood his ground, enhanced his own strength by coursing magic into his muscles, and threw up a shield.

With a roar, the orc brought down his axe and shattered Cardin's magical shield. He did this while at a run, and he slammed into Cardin full force, plowing him back several dozen feet. Cardin gasped for air as he slid to a stop, clutching his chest and trying to gulp in air past the pain.

The orc didn't stop. With Cardin temporarily incapacitated, he began swinging his axe with deadly effect at the other Mages and Warriors around them, cutting them down left and right. One Mage managed to send a blast of magic at the orc, but the armor seemed to absorb it. Or the orc just didn't care or notice. Cardin believed that the latter was entirely possible.

The Sword! Cardin realized he'd lost his grip on the Sword. He struggled to sit up and looked around frantically. There it was, several feet away from him. And that was where the orc was headed. He wanted the Sword.

What terrible damage could an orc do with such power? Especially an orc as strong and apparently unstoppable as this one?

Cardin scrambled to get to his weapon, but the Orc just smirked, and sent a blast of fire at Cardin. He raised a magic shield to deflect the blast, but the heat still radiated through the barrier, and the blast of fire did not cease. Beads of sweat quickly collected on his face.

When Cardin felt like it was too hot to bear, he turned his head just in time to see Dalin launch a shard of ice at the giant orc.

He was surprisingly quick for his size, and managed to use his axe to deflect the shard, but it also stopped his advance on the Sword, and cut off the stream of fire. Dalin sent another shard, and another, but the orc managed to deflect each one.

"Puny Wizards," the orc shouted. "Do you truly believe ice can destroy me?"

Dalin paused, said, "As you wish," and then sent a half-dozen bolts of lightning all at once. The orc blocked these with the axe, but tendrils of the lightning played across the weapon and onto the orc's arms. He shouted in pain and stumbled backwards. He looked at his smoldering arm and bared his teeth.

"You overestimate yourself," Dalin retorted, and launched another barrage of lightning bolts. This was very effective in making the orc back off further. Finally, with a frightening glare, the monster turned away from the battle.

From somewhere in his armor, he produced a small vial filled with a lilac-colored fluid. He smashed the vial into the ground in front of him, and suddenly, with an unnatural rush of magic, a lilac-colored portal opened before the orc.

Before anyone could stop him, he disappeared into the wall of light, and moments later, it closed.

Cardin remained crouched down for a moment, staring after their enemy. Where had he come from? How was he so much stronger, so different from any other orc he'd ever encountered?

Finally, when it registered in his mind that he was safe, Cardin dispelled his shield and stood up. His back popped in several places as he did so, and he cringed.

Dalin approached him, and gently placed a hand on his shoulder. "That looked and sounded painful, my friend."

Cardin nodded in agreement, "Yeah. More my pride than anything else."

The Wizard chuckled. "This is why you should not run off on your own."

Feeling his face turn red, Cardin walked over to the Sword and carefully picked it up. It was the first time he had lost the Sword. The first time he had almost failed his mission.

Two months in and he was already close to failure...

That was when he realized how quiet their surroundings were. He turned back to the rest of the camp, and found that only a handful of orcs remained, and they were all surrounded. They didn't give up, however, and every single one of them fought to their very last breath.

The Allies had won.

Cardin returned to the Wizard's side and surveyed the battlefield.

There were countless orc corpses, maimed, burned, frozen, totally destroyed. As he looked closer, he saw that some Warriors were wounded, but were being tended to by their friends.

Against the regular orc army, they had suffered only wounds, no deaths. However, when Cardin looked back to where the giant orc had fought, he saw seven dead Warriors.

That one orc was going to be a major problem. And what if there were more like him?

How many had already left the camp before the Allies had arrived?

Cardin again looked to Dalin, and he commented, "Well no matter what I think about Zilan, he was right."

Dalin nodded thoughtfully. "The orcs have pushed further into Tal."

So much for a quick end to the war.

***

Pain. So much pain.

The orc General, Arkad, stood on the other side of the portal. He looked down at his smoldering arm and clenched his forearm muscles, shooting fresh currents of pain throughout his entire body. His grey skin was blackened in some parts, and even a little of his black-red blood seeped out. The Wizards were indeed a true threat. Just as his master had warned.

That didn't matter. Pain was temporary, and the Wizards were limited in number. Their power was great, but even they could not hold back tens of thousands of orcs. Nothing could stop his army.

In his other arm he held his enchanted double-axe firmly. It had served him well today. Many humans had been slain by his hand alone. With a satisfied smile, he looked up to find the Fortress of Nasara ahead of him.

The blackened fortress, a nightmare structure made of the black indigenous stones of the Wastelands, loomed ahead. Several of his brothers and sisters still worked on restoring its damaged exterior.

Summer in the wastelands was pleasantly hot and humid, and he inhaled a deep breath to take in all of the pungent scents. It was not his home, but it was close enough that he felt at least a little at ease.

With confidence undue for her rank, another orc approached him swiftly. She wore simple leather armor, blackened by fire in a pitiful attempt to match Arkad's dark-steel armor. "Arkad," she called out in clear, confident words. "Your return is premature."

He grunted at Orinda. "The humans attacked much sooner than expected." He began walking towards the entrance to the fortress. Several orcs stood guard, but as he approached, they parted, showing him all of the respect he deserved. "I must inform her."

Orinda placed a hand on his shoulder to stop him, and he nearly bit it off. She retracted her hand quickly, her face darkening in embarrassment.

"She already knows," Orinda stated. "She saw your failure and sent me out to meet with you."

He felt his own face grow warm. The master was sorely disappointed in him if she would not even see him. A broad smile crossed Orinda's face, showing off her long canines. She reveled in his failure and embarrassment.

"What are her orders," he asked through a clenched jaw.

She waved him off and began to walk away from the fortress. "Your failure is of no great consequence. It is but one of many."

He followed after her, clutching his axe with both hands, tightening his grip until he could hear the wood groan and crack. He could take her head off in one blow. It would be so easy with his strength and the axe's enchantments.

She moved towards an encampment of his warriors, all of whom began to stand up in honor of Arkad's approach. No doubt they could see the foul look on his face and knew that he would take *their* heads if they did not show their reverence.

Orinda stopped at the edge of the camp and looked at Arkad. "You will take this group to reinforce our armies in the mountains. Our master prepares another portal as we speak. Now that we know the humans are ready, we must reinforce our forces. They must complete their objective."

Arkad felt a broad smile cross his face, and felt even more pleased when Orinda flinched at the sight of his teeth. "I will not fail her again."

"Be sure you do not," Orinda lectured. "We need the supplies to arm the rest of our army."

He wanted so badly to take her head off of her shoulders, and he brandished his axe threateningly at her. Some fear showed on her face, but they both knew that he was unwilling to suffer the consequences of killing his master's favorite pet.

With a quick snuff, Orinda walked past him towards the fortress.

His anger at her boiled up again, but when he looked at the encampment of orcs, his anger turned to glee. His time was still at hand. He would lead his people to a victory that would ensure freedom for them all.

The humans would suffer for the indignities they had suffered upon his people. He would make sure of it.

Episode 3

ASSAULT AT IRONWOOD

Amaya Kenla almost barreled over from exhaustion when she finally reached the Everlin wall. Night had fallen, so the gate was closed.

She never intended to travel at night, and her dagger would have provided little defense against a group of bandits or dangerous animals. Let alone against the group of orcs she had found at Ironwood.

With barely any strength left, she pounded on the door inset into the thick ironwood gates. For a moment, no one responded, and she began to wonder if the city soldiers were asleep. Or perhaps she was too weak from running. Her muscles screamed in protest, but she pounded harder, until finally the wooden slat opened, and a pair of eyes lit by a torch glared out at her.

"What do you want?" a groggy male voice replied.

"Please," she breathed, leaning heavily against the door. "Let me in."

The eyes glanced around, life entering them at her condition. "Is something after you?" His voice was a bit stronger, clearer, and obviously worried.

"No," she shook her head, looking into the eyes, hoping she recognized the solider, or at the very least that he recognized her.

For a moment, she was about to tell the guard everything, about the orcs only a dozen miles into the forest. But then she realized he would be required to take her before the city Warriors, before Commander Din.

She couldn't bear that. "No," she repeated. "But it's dark out here, and I'm unarmed."

The man sighed in relief, and closed the slat. She heard him lift up the metal bar that secured the door, and then it opened before her. With her legs feeling weak, she gingerly stepped over the rim of the door. The moment she was inside, he slammed it shut and secured the door.

"Thank you, sir," she gulped a breath and nodded.

He turned to face her and started to ask, "What were you doing out there so…" Then he recognized her. "You."

Amaya felt her stomach drop. She didn't recognize the guard yet, but she saw that he wore only a regular soldier's armor, not a Warrior's. That was at least a relief.

"Do I know you?" she asked.

"I'm not surprised you don't remember me, but I do know you," he replied. "So the rumors are true, then. You were released. You and your team."

She nodded once, "Yes. Do you know where they are? They came here only a few hours ago." It was possible they were all at home, but it was more likely that they were still at the pub together.

"Barrowmen's Tavern," he pointed towards the center of the town. "I hear there's a big celebration."

Amaya nodded her thanks and turned to head that way, but the guard placed a hand on her shoulder to stop her, terrifying her for a brief moment. "Hey, just so you know…I think what you did was right. If the rumors are true." She turned to face him, surprised. "You are a true Warrior. The kind of Warrior we all aspired to be."

That's when she remembered him, and her cheeks warmed. He had trained alongside of her when they were teenagers, for a couple of years at least. And then he washed out.

"Kellan," she remembered his name as she spoke it. "I…"

He smiled when she said his name. "I'm glad I made some sort of impression."

There was no good response to give him. He had a good heart, and that was why she remembered him. But he was not built to be a

Warrior. In fact, she was quite surprised that he had even made the cut as a town soldier.

So instead, she nodded and smiled sheepishly. "I'm glad to see you found your way in life."

"Yes, I did." He nodded towards the center of town. "Be careful. I've also heard Commander Din is looking for you."

With a renewed grimace, she nodded her thanks and headed for the tavern. Her pulse still raced, but she wondered if that was from running or from the thought of seeing Din again. *By the gods,* she thought to herself. *Please don't let him be there.*

Everlin was the largest town in the Southwest corner of Tal, but it took only a few minutes to traverse the only stone-paved road into the center. Only a handful of residents still wandered the streets, leaving it empty and feeling peaceful.

That is, until she came close to the tavern. Normally it was dead this late, but tonight the first floor was alive with laughter and raised, jubilant voices.

She approached the two story structure cautiously, keeping to the shadows of the neighboring buildings. As expected, there were two figures seated at one of the outside tables. This time of year it was quite warm at night, so it normally wouldn't seem suspicious. Except that they did not converse with each other, and instead swiveled their heads constantly.

In fact, after only a minute or two of observation, she noticed a pattern. They would sweep the entire area with their eyes, take a sip of their drinks to keep up appearances, and then repeat. *Amateurs,* she thought.

The front door was the official way in, but it was not the *only* way in, and she absolutely did not want Din to know about her presence. With that in mind, she retraced her steps down to another cross street, and as quickly and quietly as she could, she circled around until she could come at the tavern from the back.

There was a small wooden gate that led to a small stable and chicken coop, from which the owner of the tavern pulled fresh eggs every morning. Keeping a wary eye out for anyone else who might be watching the rear, Amaya passed the stable, where she saw a single horse fast asleep, and up to the back door.

"Please be unlocked," she whispered, and tried the latch. It opened without protest, and she eased her way in. Right into the kitchen. Where a large man with a butcher's knife stood ready.

"Can I help you, miss," he asked with an edge in his voice. Then his face slackened and the knife lowered. "Amaya?"

"Jerec," she smiled, but didn't dare move another inch. "I'm sorry," she added hastily. "I know I shouldn't come in this way, but..."

"No, you shouldn't," he folded his arms, careful not to cut himself with the knife. "What in the name of the Six are you doing back here?"

"Avoiding Din's men," she grimaced. Would he side with her? She didn't actually know him that well, and had no idea if he was loyal to Din or not.

He motioned towards the front, "Those two out front?"

"Yes," she nodded, and glanced behind her. The longer she stood in the entrance, the more likely someone would see her. "Can I come in?"

For a long moment, Jerec regarded her with scrutiny. Her heart rate had slowed earlier, but now she felt it beating harder than ever. "Fine. Come on. But don't ever come in this way again."

With a heaving sigh of relief, Amaya quickly closed the door. Jerec reached past her and secured the lock. "Thank you, sir," she moved past him. Then she realized she didn't know her way around. "Which way...?"

Jerec pointed down one hallway out of the kitchen, "Straight through there. Tell your people it's time to get quiet."

Nodding her thanks once again, she swiftly moved through the kitchen, into the hallway, and out into the main tavern. Off to her left was the bar, where a young, sleepy looking boy tended. And occupying barstools were two of her team members, Gell and Vin, along with some of their friends and family. She surveyed the room further, and found Elic at the largest table next to his wife and two kids, along with Peren and his daughter.

Elic almost instantly spotted her, and was about to stand, but she shook her head and made her way over. Then Peren saw her, and almost shouted in surprise, "Amaya!"

That caught everyone's attention in the tavern, and all craned their necks around to look at her. She looked out the front window, but the two 'disguised' Warriors seemed not to have heard. Thankfully, the rest of everyone's surprised response at seeing her sounded like nothing more than the continued din of conversation and laughter she had heard from the street.

As she took an empty seat at the table, all of her team clamored around to greet her. Nerina was very clearly drunk, and she stumbled and almost spilled her ale on Amaya.

"I'm glad you came back," Elic said quietly, or as quietly as he could above the noise. When her eyes met his, however, he recognized the urgency in her. "Something happened."

"Yes," she replied, and again glanced out the window. She cursed when she realized the Warriors were gone. She would have to be quick.

"Do you know that lumber mill down the road," she asked him.

"You mean the Ironwood Mill?" Idalia asked.

"Yes," she nodded. "I went there to find a place to stay the night."

Before she could say more, Peren asked, "Why didn't you just come here with us?"

Her face burned with embarrassment, but she couldn't bring herself to tell him why. "It doesn't matter," she shook her head. "Orcs have overrun it."

Suddenly all background conversation ceased, and the entire tavern fell quiet. Somewhere in the back, she swore she heard Jerec sigh in relief. No one replied for a long time, and she gave them that moment to consider what she had just said.

It even sobered Nerina up a little, who was the first to reply. "Orcs? But how? There's no way they could have gotten this far into Tal. They're at Relkin still, all of them, remember?"

"I think this is bigger than anyone thought," Amaya shook her head. "Think about it. Every single Tal Warrior was mobilized last month to hunt for and defend against Kailar. Every single one of them left for Archanon to defend it. Everything has been in chaos ever since." She glanced out the window, half-expecting Din to have somehow already arrived.

Elic nodded thoughtfully. "Our patrols probably haven't all returned to our borders. They could have slipped through. How many did you see?"

She closed her eyes, doing a mental count one last time to ensure she wasn't wrong. "It looked like thirty or so."

"We should tell the Warriors," Gell suggested. "They can

overwhelm the orcs with ease."

"No," she said a little too quickly. Everyone stared at her. Elic's wife Denora seemed to comprehend what she wanted, her pained look clenching at Amaya's heart. "We should attack them."

Her heart went out to the woman when a terrible look of sadness and worry overcame her eyes. Denora had long ago accepted that her husband was a Warrior, but she always worried when he left on patrol. Now Amaya was asking him to attack an orc camp with just the seven of them.

"Are you kidding," Idalia's husband, Perth, burst out. He was a city soldier, but not because he had washed out like Kellan had. He had chosen it because of his desire to stay at home, to not have to leave Everlin on regular patrols. "Orcs aren't your common bandits, Amaya. Thirty will overwhelm you."

"Not if we attack at night," Vin Torik said. He rarely spoke, so when he did, it had the effect of ensuring everyone in the team listened. "If we leave now, we will reach them while they sleep. We can defeat them quietly."

Amaya nodded, grateful for the suggestion. Orcs were monsters, so she had no qualms about killing them in their sleep.

"What about weapons and armor," Gell asked. "We left Archanon before we were provisioned any."

She thought about that for a moment, not sure how to answer. She had her dagger, but she was used to fighting with a longsword. And even if they did catch the orcs by surprise, going without even the most basic armor would be suicide.

"I have my own daggers at home," Vin offered.

"Yeah," Nerina suddenly smirked. "And I have a mace at home." It was a weapon Nerina always liked, but the Warriors did not consider them to be traditional Warrior weapons. Usually only soldiers carried anything other than swords, mostly due to Guild tradition.

Each of her team nodded and spoke of weapons they could use. Elic had his own longsword that had been passed down by his father. Idalia's husband offered to let her use his duty sword. Peren had a bow and more than enough arrows, plus a short sword.

Everyone looked at Gell finally, who had yet to speak up about a hidden stash of weapons. He blushed and looked down. "Yeah. Well, I've always had a thing for battleaxes."

His reaction seemed suspicious, so she pressed him. "Gell?"

"Okay, so I have about a dozen of them," he flailed his arms about. "I like axes! Leave me alone."

She smirked, and as everyone around her laughed, she realized how much she missed that sound. Her team, laughing, enjoying each other's company. A couple months in a dungeon had a way of wearing thin fast.

She sighed and nodded. "Now all we need is armor."

It was Peren's daughter Taya who offered to help with that. "I work in a leatherworker's shop. I have a key, we could go in and…borrow some."

"Wouldn't we need chainmail for this," Idalia asked.

"No, not if we want to attack quietly," Amaya smiled. "I think leather armor will do nicely."

She slowly stood up from the table and looked at each of her team. "Well then. I cannot order you all to do this, as this is not one of the King's orders. If you are with me," she looked at each of her six companions, "speak now."

Nerina, Vin, and Gell voiced their support at once. That was easy, they had no families. Elic, Peren, and Idalia, however, did, and they each looked to their family members. Elic's wife Denora looked ready tell him to stay, but then she sighed and caressed his cheek ever so lightly. "You must go, my dear. This is who you are. The man I married."

He took her hand in his, squeezing it lightly, before he stood up and nodded. "I'm with you."

Peren looked to his daughter for her consent. His wife had died of disease several years ago, but his daughter was old enough to take care of herself, plus she had an uncle and aunt that lived in town. They remained quiet, and awaited Peren's decision.

Taya shrugged. "I already volunteered to help you get into the leather shop. You know I'm okay with it."

Peren laughed, stood, and also nodded his assent.

"I want to go with you," Perth said to Idalia. But then he sighed and shook his head. "But I'd just get in your way."

Idalia rolled her eyes. "You've never been in my way."

He nodded, "I know. But I'm not even half as skilled as you are. You go. We can't both use my sword, after all."

She smiled, and wrapped her arms around him. Then she looked at Amaya. "Let's do it."

Amaya smiled, realizing her entire team was still with her. That left only one last thing. She looked at Nerina with a raised eyebrow. "You sober enough to do this?"

Nerina looked at her drink, and then reached past Amaya to set it down on the table. "I will be by the time we get there."

"Excellent," Amaya nodded. She looked out the window, and swore she saw movement. Her heart leapt, and she felt her hands suddenly tingle.

When she turned to look at her team, they stared curiously. She shook her head to dissuade further questioning and said, "We need to get out of here. Taya," she looked to the young girl, "will you show us the way to your shop?"

With an energetic smile, Taya stood and began to lead the way out. "Yeah, come on."

Amaya liked her energy, but knew it would be a few more moments before they could leave. She stepped back and allowed those in her party to say their goodbyes. There were no tears, there were no sobs, just the mournful farewell that they were used to.

It took only moments, but they were precious moments. Once the farewells were said, they followed young Taya out into the darkness.

***

It hadn't taken long to reach the leatherworker's shop and for everyone to select and don their choice. None of it was made specifically for them, like their sets of Guild armor had been, but they fit well enough.

After that, everyone went their separate ways to pickup weapons. Amaya, knowing she had nowhere to go, was left with only the dagger she had bought in Archanon. The armor would help, but she longed for a sword.

At first she was hesitant to return to the gate right away. She felt guilty for the position they were about to put Kellan, the gate guard, into, and wanted to avoid the inevitable conversation with him. However, she also didn't want to leave her team waiting if she did not arrive before they did. Without further hesitation, she made her way to the eastern gate.

Knowing that Din was likely prowling the streets for her by now, she kept to the shadows, and avoided anyone who looked like they might be Warriors. Having to skulk about in her own home town left an unpleasant taste in her mouth, which was further exacerbated by the realization that she hadn't had anything to eat since lunch.

A rumbling, empty stomach would do nothing for her in combat, certainly not if they were going to rely on stealth. She rummaged around in her travel pack and found a small piece of bread still soft enough to eat. While still wary of her surroundings, she began to nibble on it as she walked.

Finally, she came to the square in front of the gate and stopped by a building. Kellan stood by the entrance, his arms folded and his head bowed down, as if he were thinking very hard about something.

Glancing around one last time, she began to walk out into the small square. About halfway across, Kellan heard her footsteps and looked up. Panic crossed his face, panic and regret, and she stopped cold in her tracks. "I'm so sorry," he hastened to speak.

Before she could ask what he was sorry about, she felt it more than anything else. A magic that she recognized, a familiarity that once elated her, but now made her stomach twist into a knot.

From the gatehouse emerged a tall figure, followed by two more flanking the first. The only man in the world she hoped to never, ever see again.

Uric Din.

"Hello, Amaya," he spoke, his voice soft and cold.

She said nothing. She couldn't. Her entire body felt numb. She wasn't sure if she should attack him, regardless of his two guards, or run away, or scream, or do anything. Or nothing.

He stepped closer to her, a towering figure that loomed over all. When he stepped further into torch light, she noticed that his hair was cut shorter than she remembered. It used to hang down to his shoulders, but now was only a couple of inches long and parted to one side. It gave him a charming, even dashing look. And even in the dim light, she could see his bright blue eyes staring at her.

Those eyes used to drive her wild. Now she wanted to rip them out of his skull.

"Nothing to say," he asked. He took another step towards her, but she jolted back. Her heart raced, and nothing she did to slow it worked.

"I...no," she shook her head, forcing herself to keep her hand away from her dagger. "I have nothing to say to you."

He looked genuinely saddened by her reaction, which made her frown and tilt her head to one side. Was he actually happy to see her? Did he actually feel saddened by her anger?

"I know we didn't part on good terms," he shook his head. "But you must understand, I had no choice but to arrest you."

"Arrest me?" she laughed. "You set me up, you son of a whore."

His face darkened. She felt herself smile, but then immediately felt guilty. Why did she say that?

"I had no idea what to expect at that camp," he shook his head, raising his hands up defensively. "I never meant to hurt you, dear. I trusted you to accomplish the mission, I gave it to you because I knew if anyone could do it, you could."

Backing up further, she shook her head. No, he hadn't trusted her. He had to have known the bandits had their families there. He wasn't an idiot, and he never sent his people into a situation without knowing what to expect. Never.

Right?

He took another step towards her, and she backed up. "Please. Don't come near me."

He stopped, and let his hands drop to his sides. "As you wish."

She shook her head, and then looked at the others. Could she say what she wanted to? Should she? She wasn't a Warrior anymore. But...wouldn't it still come back to hurt him? Why did she even care if she hurt him? She hated him, but she was afraid of hurting him.

"I'm glad you were released," he said.

Somehow that made her blood boil. "You lied to me! About everything."

"No," he shook his head furiously. "Not everything." He looked behind him, at his two guards, at Kellan. He took in a deep breath, and sighed. For a moment, he started to move towards her again, but then he caught himself and stopped. The contorted look on his face told her that he was wrestling with the same question she was – could he admit openly what she wanted to scream at him about?

Din looked at something behind her, and she heard the crunch of boot steps. She looked over her shoulder to see Elic coming up behind her. He had his hand on the hilt of his longsword, ready to defend her. He must have heard her shout.

JON WASIK

She looked again at Din. He shook his head, steeled himself, and then looked at her with an intense gaze. "My feelings for you weren't a lie."

Her jaw clenched, but she felt a tingling in her stomach. She wanted to punch him, and she wanted to kiss him. But she knew that she could do neither.

A lot of time had passed in the dungeon. Time to think back on her past. On the mistakes she had made. She wouldn't back down this time. She couldn't.

"Uric," she started, then stopped. It felt strange to say his first name out loud again. "Please. We've been pardoned. I can show you the papers if I have to, but you cannot detain me. So just leave me alone."

His head drooped and his shoulders slouched. She felt her heart ache for him, but she stood her ground. Finally, he nodded. "Very well. I will do as you ask. But," he looked up at her again. "I did bring you a gift. And seeing as how you're wearing armor, I think you may need it soon."

He motioned to one of his guards, who presented him with a sheathed longsword. She recognized it immediately as her former Guild weapon. Din held it in one of his strong hands and slowly set it down on the ground, knowing that she would never come close enough to take it from him.

"This was yours," he backed away from it. "So it shall be again, my dear." He heaved in a deep breath, and then smiled at her. "Farewell."

Without another word, he motioned to his guards to follow, and walked off into the night, in the opposite direction of where Amaya and Elic stood. She sensed more than saw Elic step up beside her. A part of her wanted to look at him, to see whether he judged her for what he had just learned, or if he sympathized with her. But she couldn't face him.

So she stepped away from him, towards her old weapon, her old friend. When she stood beside it, she almost couldn't bring herself to pick it up. Why had he kept it? Why hadn't it been destroyed? That's what usually happened to a disgraced Warrior's weapon, it was ceremoniously broken, and then melted down.

Finally, she crouched down and wrapped her fingers around the sheath. The weight felt familiar and brought countless memories to

70

the surface, all racing through her mind like flashes of lightning.

Grasping the grip, she slowly drew the sky-blue blade from its sheath. Even in the flickering torchlight of the streetlamps, there was no mistaking that color.

She did not pull it completely out, she merely stared at where the base of the blade met the guard. It held so many memories for her. So much happiness.

So much pain.

Could she keep it? Could she use something that hurt just to hold? The void in her chest told her she should just throw it away, and never look upon it again.

However, when she slid the blade back into its sheath, felt the comforting click when it locked into place, there was no turning back. It was as much a part of her as her arm was, and it felt right to have it back in her grasp.

It belonged with her.

Without another thought, she lashed the sheath to the right side of her belt, and gently rested her hand against it. A sense of warm familiarity coursed through her as she felt its weight on her hip again.

She looked over her shoulder at Elic, and saw the curiosity in his eyes, and the sympathy. When their eyes met, he slowly approached her. "Are you okay?"

A lump formed in her throat, and a part of her wanted to admit to him that, no, she wasn't okay. Not even remotely close to okay.

But she was his commander. And that kind of vulnerability had no place in their relationship. She was alone.

"Yes," she lied with a curt nod.

There was no mistaking the doubtful look he gave her, but she ignored it and turned back to Kellan. He looked terrified of her, but she knew it wasn't his fault. With a confidence in her step that she did not feel, she walked over to him and placed a hand on his shoulder. "It's okay." She squeezed lightly. "It wasn't your fault."

"I, umm, I didn't know, that is, I just couldn't, I mean…" He stammered, so she smiled and shook her head.

"Stop it," she patted his shoulder and then let her hands fall to her sides again. "Don't think on it anymore." She looked towards Din and his guards, now vanished into the night. "Just don't."

Before Kellan could say any more, she heard new boot steps echoing in the square. Everyone turned to see two more figures emerge into the square, Gell and Vin. A moment later, from another direction came Nerina.

Their troupe was gathering. And in just a couple hours time, they would face an enemy that none of them had ever fought before.

Then she could unleash her emotions.

***

Zerek was used to hard work, used to pushing himself to the breaking point almost every day. Not that he had ever wanted to, but his father had insisted he do so to build strength early in his life. Every day, he had worked at the mines, swinging pick axes, chipping away at the walls, hefting dirt and rock and iron and coal into carts, pushing those carts back and forth, into and out of the mines.

Today, and indeed since yesterday, he almost missed those days in the mines. The house steward, Madame Kai as she liked to be called, had made him sit and read. Thankfully he had learned how to read from Elina, when he was a kid. Before his life had ended.

The material was boring. Elina had taught him with stories, histories, tales of the Warriors of Tal and their adventures protecting the kingdom. With Kai, he read about how to address people properly, how to sit properly, how to stand properly. "Proper Etiquette" the Madame had called it.

Then she quizzed him with practical exercises. Exercises that he failed initially, after which she quite brusquely corrected him, shoving his lower back forward, tilting his chin up, and slapping his hand every time he spoke without 'proper respect.'

Suddenly he no longer wanted to stay in the castle. If this was what was required to serve royalty, to act pompous and haughty just to keep up appearances, he would have preferred living his days in the forests, or on the streets, almost anywhere else.

Worse still, tonight he would no longer be allowed to stay in his own room. As a new member of the serfs or servants or whatever they were called, he was required to stay in shared quarters, in a small building detached from the main castle structure.

It wasn't his first time there, most of his lessons had taken place in that building. However, Kai still insisted on leading him around until she was satisfied that he would not cause a ruckus or insult a royal. Her long dress swished about her, a dark plum color that was as colorful a dress as he imagined she ever wore. Whites, bright blues and reds, anything bright, and he imagined she would scoff at it and say "servants are never seen, it is not appropriate."

The sun had set long ago, and one of the moons was just cresting above the mountains. He used to enjoy nights like this when he was outdoors, back at the camp. Back home.

They entered the servant house and passed through a short corridor, until they came upon one of a few open doors from which candlelight poured out. She knocked on the door frame out of courtesy, but did not enter. When he walked in, he realized why – it was for boys, or men, only, not one single girl was in sight. Kai did not even look inside, but everyone looked at Zerek when he stopped just inside of the frame.

There were several bunk beds lined up along two walls, and the far wall had a wash basin and a few stalls surrounded by cloth where they could relieve themselves in privacy. There was no smell from those stalls, since all of Archanon had running water and a sewer system. The only city in the world with such a system, as far as he knew.

There were a couple of windows, both of which were open to let in the cooling night air. He could smell the warm spring air flow through the bedroom, but he grudgingly wondered what the room might smell like in the winter, when no windows could be opened. To the right of the entrance, he saw an unused fireplace, and was at least thankful they would be warm when winter came.

Zerek looked back to Kai, who looked down her nose at him and nodded. "This is where you will be staying for the foreseeable future. There should be a few open beds, just ask one of the boys to tell you which ones." She was very curt in how she spoke, almost stern, but he could tell she was weary. He could only imagine how busy she was from sunrise to sunset. It was apparent that she was always on the move, never able to stay on one task for too long before having to take care of something else.

Realizing as much, Zerek decided to show her his learned courtesy, and took a moment to bow to her. "Thank you for providing me with training today, Madame Kai." He stood up straight and gave her his best fake smile. "I very much appreciate your time."

The weariness and stern look in her eyes softened for just a moment, and she smiled. "That is much better. There is hope for you yet, young man." The smile disappeared, and the 'steward face,' as he was beginning to call it, returned. "Get to bed quickly. You have another full day ahead of you."

Again he bowed, "Yes, Madame Kai."

With another small grin, the steward turned with precision and marched off towards wherever she slept. That left Zerek by himself amongst a group of men he didn't know.

Most of them nodded or waved at him, a few even said, "Hello," but they all looked completely worn out, and most were in stark white night clothes and were getting into bed.

One young boy, who had to be the youngest of everyone present, walked over to him with a shy grin on his face. "Hi," he squeaked. The boy had short strawberry colored hair and a face full of freckles, and he seemed genuinely excited to meet Zerek.

"Uh, hello," Zerek replied awkwardly, not sure if he should continue to act proper or not. "I'm...I mean, my name is Zerek. Zerek Betanil." He extended a friendly hand, an act he had learned from his father.

"Endel Marric," the boy smiled, and took the offered hand. He tried to shake it gruffly, and had a fair bit of strength for someone so small. "You don't have to play all proper here," he shrugged, and retrieved his hand quickly. "We're all dirty here."

Zerek couldn't help but laugh at that statement, but then frowned when the boy appeared to be genuine. "I'm sorry," he shrugged. "I guess...I don't know. I'm just not used to all of this."

"Yeah, you're the one from the mines, huh?" Endel asked, almost bouncing with excitement. "I heard you saw orcs, even fought them! Killed a whole bunch all on your own, right?"

Again Zerek found himself laughing, and even felt embarrassed. "No, um. Just the one." He looked around the room nervously. He wanted to find an excuse to stop talking about it, but then Endel surprised him.

"That's so awesome!" He smiled from ear to ear. "I hear they are huge, and strong, and smell bad. Is it true? How did you kill it? Did you get hurt? Is their blood really black?"

The assault of questions made Zerek step back, and thankfully, that seemed to be a queue for the boy. He stopped, and the excitement on his face turned to fear, "Oh gods, I'm so sorry, I'm doing it again. It's just, not much excitement happens around servants, and I just wanted to hear about it all."

Feeling guilty for his reaction, Zerek rubbed his neck absently and shrugged. "I guess I could tell you about it. But, um, can we find a bed for me first?" He motioned towards the night clothes Endel wore, "And is there a set of those for me?"

"Yes. No. Sorry," Endel shook his head. "Yeah there's a bed, no there's no clothes, not yet." Endel grabbed Zerek's sleeve and tugged him along towards one of the bunks. "The bed above me is open, if you want."

Zerek wasn't sure if he was flattered or annoyed, but then he also wasn't sad to be on a top bunk. It would be less confining.

"Madame Kai will probably take you to the tailor tomorrow to get measured," Endel continued. They reached the bed, and Zerek had to pull his sleeve free of the boy's grip. "But the chest on the left side is yours, the right side is mine."

Endel sat down on the bottom bunk and beamed a smile up at Zerek. Suddenly he felt sad for the kid, and when the guys in the neighboring bunks groaned, he realized that the others probably didn't talk to Endel much. Could he tolerate the kid for long?

Despite the open window, it was still fairly warm in the bedroom, so Zerek decided to take his shirt off and stuff it in the empty chest. He then took the sheath off that held Elina's dagger. Kai had insisted he not keep the dagger with him, but when Zerek stoutly refused, she gave in and asked the quartermaster to find a 'decent' sheath for the weapon. It was a plain black sheath that had its own strap, doubling as a belt for him, and held the dagger almost perfectly.

He wouldn't put that in the chest. Never, ever would it leave his sight. He slowly pulled it out just enough to look at a sliver of the steel blade, and for what felt like an eternity, he stared at it and remembered the woman that it had once belonged to.

Only eternity was broken early. "Did you kill the orc with that?"

Zerek felt his face flush, and he pushed the blade back in. He was about to snap back at the kid, but the look of amazement and interest on Endel's face stopped him.

Something inside of him made him want to be Endel's friend. Maybe because Endel didn't seem to have many friends. Maybe.

In any case, he sighed and shook his head, "I know you want to know," he started hesitantly, "but I just can't talk about it." He shook his head and tried to force the pressure he felt in his chest back down. He wished he could see that white Wizard again. Maybe he could do that trick with his hand again to help Zerek feel better. "Not yet."

Endel clamped his mouth shut and looked sad. The pressure in Zerek's chest gave way to guilt, and he sighed. Slowly, he sat down beside Endel and said, "No, I didn't use this on an orc. But...it belonged to someone who did."

That night, neither Zerek nor Endel slept much. The last of the candles were blown out, and all of the other guys in the room slept, but he and Endel stayed up and talked quietly. More than once they were shushed when they, or rather Endel grew too loud.

When Zerek did finally crawl up to the top bunk, he felt completely exhausted, but more than that, he felt glad. Glad to have made a new friend.

To no longer be alone.

***

By the time Amaya and the others reached the Ironwood Mill, morning was only a couple of hours away. That wouldn't leave them much time, but it would leave them enough.

Vin, being the stealthiest of them all, led the group quietly in the night. One of the moons was nearly full, so even with the tree cover, they had enough light to navigate the forest without the aid of torches.

As before, the area around the mill was eerily quiet. Even the crickets had gone silent, and the moons could not penetrate the darkness that she felt. One by one, they each drew their weapons when the ridge came into sight. Though she knew these woods, a fear she had never felt before crept into her veins.

Vin came to a sudden stop and raised a hand for everyone else to follow suit. Amaya felt her heartbeat quicken and her skin crawl. There they remained in the dead quiet, her ears and eyes unable to pick up whatever had spooked Vin. She slowly stepped up next to him, but his eyes remained fixed straight ahead. When she followed his gaze, she saw only endless dark shadows amongst the trees.

Trusting her companion's instincts, she remained completely silent, and waited with trained patience.

Finally, he looked at her, and motioned with his hand for her and the others to stay put. She nodded, and crouched down to better hide her profile.

Vin also crouched low, and moved forward, somehow completely silent as he crossed over the bed of dead pine and ironwood needles from winters long past. His leather armor was a dark brown, so he blended very well into the shadows. At first she was able to track him by his movement, but every time he stopped for a moment, she lost him.

Before she could grow too nervous or curious, she saw a flurry of movement, and there came the sound of a muffled grunt, followed by a gurgling sound. Before long, the gurgling stopped, and Vin reappeared from the shadows.

"Come on," he whispered, and again led the way. A few dozen feet ahead, they came across a dead orc slouched against a tree. She surmised the orc was meant to be a sentry, but had fallen asleep. Vin had sliced its throat clean open.

This time they stayed on the path, as there was less underbrush or dead needles to give them away. No one would see them coming. Not yet, anyway.

When they crested the hill, they saw several small campfires still burning in the orc-occupied encampment. At first she was disheartened by the blazes. They would make it harder for them to sneak up on the orcs.

But then she realized that the ambient, low light would actually aid them when the encampment inevitably woke up from the sounds of battle. She stopped the group on the top of the hill, and they gathered into a small circle.

"Let's take out as many as we can silently." She nodded towards the cluster of campfires, "Idalia and I will hit the center. Vin and Nerina take the one to the left, and Gell and Elic take the right." She looked at Peren for a moment before she asked, "You still an expert shot?"

Peren grinned. "Always."

She smiled at him. "Good. Hang back and cover us as best as you can." Movement caught her eye and she looked down by the mill. An orc slowly walked along the length of the open-air mill platform, in front of the giant vertical saw. "Starting with the one that's awake."

Peren glanced down, and then shrugged. "With that much light, I could shoot a tick off of his shoulder."

Everyone rolled their eyes. Then Amaya looked at each of her companions, and smiled. "We can do this. I trust each and every one of you."

They returned her confident smile, and everyone gripped their weapons tightly. With nothing more to be said, she nodded, "Let's go."

As quietly as they could, everyone crept towards their assigned target, with Peren in the back, an arrow already set. Amaya's pulse raced and her hands began to shake. Had it really been so long since her last battle?

Knowing how outmatched they would be if they did not strike fast and effectively, she drew upon training from days long past and took long, controlled breaths. The closer they drew, the slower her heart beat became, and the easier she could hear even the smallest sounds, including Idalia's boot steps. Neither she nor her companion were as silent as Vin, but she hoped they would be able to get close.

A group of five orcs slept around the fire pit ahead, each sleeping in a different position, but all close to the fire. It was late summer and still warm at night, but she recalled that the orcs came from a much warmer climate. The Wastelands were always hot, or so she had read long ago, and the only thing that changed was whether it was humid or dry.

The orcs had stripped out of their varying types of armor, all of which lay nearby. She noted that one of the orcs apparently possessed the darkened metal armor that she had heard about.

As they drew closer to the fire, she kept glancing up at the orc on the mill platform. He was leaning against a post and looked ready to nod off. She felt disgusted by the sight of them all, their pale, hairless mottled skin looked creepy in the moonlight and firelight. Worse still, as they drew closer, she began to smell them.

Volumes of books could be written about that stench! Never before had she smelled anything quite like it.

They were close, scary close, and she readied her sword. The moment came when she was in range of the first sleeping orc – somehow they had drawn close enough without waking a single one. Idalia moved to the left to take out another, while Amaya prepared to plunge her blade deep into the closest orc's back.

Except that she hesitated. Slowly its chest rose and fell in its deep slumber. It slept soundly, as did the others. They were alive. Living creatures. And she was about to slaughter them in their sleep.

Why did that bother her? Weren't they monsters?

No sooner had she thought that than she had her answer. Killing defenseless sleeping creatures, regardless of what they were, was something Din would do.

She began to lower her sword, and considered for a moment what to do. Idalia raised her own sword and prepared to strike, but then stopped as well. After a long moment, she looked helplessly at Amaya, who looked back at her with a grim expression.

They would have to wake the orcs first, or leave the camp. No sooner had she thought that than she realized leaving was impossible. It was too risky, any one of them might hear their departure, or the orc on the platform might see them. They were here, now, and they had to do something.

Suddenly there was the snap of a dry twig to her right, from Elic and Gell's direction. A few of the orcs stirred but did not wake. Except for the one on the platform. It jumped, startled, and grunted loudly. Before it could even identify what had made the sound, an arrow whistled over their heads and struck the orc directly in its jugular, passing straight through and disappearing into the night.

The orc gurgled and clutched at its throat, then tumbled over the edge of the platform with a great crash. *That* was enough to startle every orc in the camp awake.

Amaya looked at the orc at her feet, who began to try to get up, picking up its dark-steel mace in the process.

It was now or never.

With a nearly automatic summoning of magic, she charged the blade of her sword with an ethereal energy, and swung with all of her might. The orc's head came clean off its shoulders.

The others struck their own targets, and another arrow whistled through the air to strike a target, Amaya didn't see which one. The other orcs roared and armed themselves.

Some of the magic in her blade was expended, but it took less than a heartbeat to recharge it, and she jabbed it at another orc charging at her. A blast of arcane magic shot out of the tip of her sword and blasted the orc back into another enemy. He was instantly dead, but his companion, knocked to the ground, scrambled to get up.

She hopped the distance between them and swung down, hoping to take him fast, but even in his groggy state, he was quick, and used his haphazardly crafted iron longsword to block her strike while he was still on his knees.

Faster than she could have imagined, he pushed her sword back and swung at her legs. Had she not unconsciously raised a magical shield, it would have cut right into her shins and ended her part in the battle immediately. Instead, the rusty blade was partly deflected, and she made her killing blow by impaling its chest, right where a human heart was.

It was not human. And her jab only angered it further. It grabbed hold of her blade, tight enough to cut his own hand, and stood up. She tried to pull her sword out, but somehow his grip was far stronger than she could have imagined.

With its free hand, it readied its sword and prepared to take her head off. Another whistle, and suddenly an arrow struck dead center in its temple, burying itself in the monster's skull. His grip loosened, she pulled her sword out, and he crumpled into a heap.

The orcs awoke and prepared for battle quickly, and combat was fierce and quick. Nevertheless, her companions were well trained, and their archer was still an expert. Within minutes, the battle was won. Several orcs, seeing they were defeated, fled into the woods. Most were picked off by Peren, but Amaya saw at least three escape.

Those three would be a problem later on, she had no doubt of that, but three were far less of a threat than thirty. Few battles were ever total victories, she reminded herself. Especially in war.

With the battle swiftly won, she took a moment to take stock. In the low firelight, she saw that all of her companions were unharmed, or at least none had any obvious wounds. Peren remained sentry on the hilltop, no doubt keeping an eye on as wide an area as possible to ensure that the three orcs did not return unexpectedly. The others rejoined Amaya in a circle, where they all stared at each other in the flickering firelight, their breathing fast, their pulses racing.

What she had felt before crept back into her heart, and she felt almost guilty for the easy victory her team had just won.

Until Gell brandished his two-handed mace and began to laugh. She didn't know what he laughed about, but suddenly the laughter broiled up within her as well. And before long, everyone joined in his jubilation.

It was then that she understood. They were back! Her team, her men and women, joined in battle together again, had won against a truly wicked enemy.

The dungeon was fresh in all of their minds, but on that night, the memory finally began to fade into the background. That night, they had done what no team of Warriors would have dreamt of doing. If they had told Din about the camp, he would have sent the entire battalion from Everlin to Ironwood. They were seven, and they had won!

That night, they had earned their new titles.

They were Guardians.

***

The morning after the battle at Relkin Mine, the battalion of Warriors and Wizards were just finishing rounding up the handful of surviving orcs, taking assessment of losses, and searching for any remaining orcs that hid and awaited a chance to inflict more casualties.

The Allies learned the hard way that the orcs, at least the ones using the low-quality weapons and armor, would hide and ambush unsuspecting Warriors whenever they could.

A pair of them had made the mistake of attempting to ambush Cardin and Sira during their evening patrol. Other than setting their nerves on edge, the ambush failed miserably.

Some orcs *were* captured during and after the battle. Seven of them, too wounded to fight on, were being cared for in a cordoned-off section of the camp, but only because the Allies needed them to live long enough to tell them about their plans.

None of the orcs bearing darkened steel survived or remained behind. In fact, few of them were among the dead. Based on everything Cardin had seen and heard, they were very different from the other orcs in skill and tactics, much smarter, much stronger, and far more dangerous.

Now, only an hour after sunrise, Cardin stood around a makeshift war table in one of the orc buildings, along with Sira, Master Syrn, and General Zilan. General Artula had just arrived at their camp, with news that greatly disturbed them all.

Wearing his gold-dyed plate armor, Geildein Artula was accompanied by a woman close to Cardin's age, one whom he did not recognize, and one whom did not wear Guild armor, but wore what was clearly a Guild-forged light-blue sword on her right hip.

"The orcs had clearly coordinated their attacks on the mine and the lumber mill," the General spoke in his clear, commanding voice. Even Zilan, pristine, prim and proper as he was, seemed a lesser man next to the General, and he listened intently.

Cardin shook his head. "That hardly makes sense." When all eyes turned on him, he felt his face grow warm. When everyone waited for him to continue, he said, "The mine I can understand, it's close to the Wastelands. But Ironwood? How could they have gotten so far into Tal undetected?"

No one replied. Who could? For so long, the four kingdoms had focused only on each other. On the Lesser Wars, and on the borders between each other. The orcs occasionally pressed the border of the Wastelands, but it was only ever a small clan here and there, looking to expand outward, and they were always easily defeated.

Now they were organized, and far stronger and more cunning than anyone could have predicted.

"If they could get to Ironwood," Sira spoke with a dire, quiet tone, "who knows where else they could be. In Saran, too," she shook her head.

"I agree," Zilan nodded curtly. "There is more going on here than I initially predicted."

"Than any of us did," Artula agreed. "Someone is organizing the orcs. Someone is controlling them."

Cardin raised his eyebrows. "That giant orc?" He felt his face grow warm again, but this time at the embarrassment he felt from defeat. He was stronger, and far more powerful than any Mage had ever been. How could one orc, even one so large, defeat him so easily?

He wouldn't let it happen again. He couldn't.

"I don't believe so," Master Syrn shook her head slowly. Cardin had only heard of Syrn before the battle, as the woman who had searched for and found the Star Dragons. She was much older than he had imagined, clearly one of the oldest Wizards in the Guild. She commanded almost as much respect as Master Valkere did by presence alone. "Though it is difficult to say based on your short encounter with him, I believe he is nothing more than a captain of the orc army." She gripped her blackwood staff and leaned heavily upon it. "I believe there is another entity at play, someone far more intelligent who commands these orcs." She stared evenly at General Artula.

The room remained quiet for a long moment, and Cardin felt the void of dread open up in his stomach. Someone worse than the giant?

"Klaralin is dead," General Artula stated resolutely. "Surely this time he is dead."

"Yes," Master Syrn nodded once. "I believe so. It is not a Wizard that I am thinking of. However, it must be one who wields magic." She then turned her eyes to Cardin, who felt her gaze penetrate into his soul.

His newfound ability to sense specific energies within magic allowed him to see how she focused more than just her eyes on him. She somehow probed him with magic, as if to ascertain what he was thinking through sheer willpower. "He escaped you and Dalin by throwing down a vial that then created a portal. Only a powerful practitioner and alchemist could have crafted such a potion."

The answer came to him almost immediately. "A shaman."

That caused quite a stir of movement in the room, but no one objected to the possibility. Not this time. It was the only thing that made sense.

The silence remained for some time, no one willing to speak. No one knowing what to say. They had heard of shamans, but one hadn't been seen in generations. They were known to be dangerous and cunning, far more intelligent than the other orcs.

If a shaman controlled all of the orcs of the Wastelands, with the help of the remnants of Klaralin's army, the Allies could be in for a bigger fight than any of them had expected.

The quiet was finally broken, but not by any of those present. Boot steps outside caught their attention, and they all turned to watch Reis and Dalin step just inside of the uneven door frame. Reis looked only slightly surprised to see General Artula, but otherwise the look on his face was one of defeat.

When Cardin and his friends first scouted the Relkin camp, Reis had seen battalions of orcs in encampments that stretched far into the forest. When the Allies attacked yesterday, the occupying force was considerably less. It wasn't long before they found tracks of an army marching northeast, into the mountains.

Reis and Dalin were sent late yesterday to track the orcs, and try to find out where they were so they could be stopped. The look on Reis's face, however, told Cardin that they had failed.

"What did you find?" General Zilan asked, his own face already grim.

"The tracks disappear into the mountains," Reis shook his head, folding his arms in from of him. "We tried to pick up their trail, but it almost looks like they scattered everywhere. The trail became indistinct, and we couldn't find a single one of them."

"I was afraid of that," Zilan placed his hands on his hips. "History books state that orcs are much faster than humans, able to travel great distances without rest."

"But the mountains stretch far into the north," Sira frowned at Reis. Cardin felt his stomach clench at her words, at the despair in her voice. "They can strike almost anywhere if we don't find them."

"I know," Reis threw his arms up in defeat, "but there's nothing else I can do. Not alone. We need to send a lot more scouts into those mountains to search for them."

"There's no guarantee we could ever find them," Artula shook his head. "The Ilari Mountains are vast, with so many perilous areas. I believe scouting the mountains would be a waste of time and supplies."

Cardin looked at him with shock and a little bit of anger. A waste of time? A massive army of orcs roamed freely behind their borders. Countless lives were now in danger. How could it be a waste?

"I think I know what you are suggesting," Syrn nodded, her face emotionless. "With the Wizards, we can send reinforcements to anywhere in a matter of minutes."

Artula smiled, "Exactly. Keep a Wizard or two at every village, every town, every city. With strict orders to send for reinforcements the moment they spot even a single orc."

"Indeed," the Master Wizard turned her head up. "Not the greatest task for a Wizard, but far more efficient than blindly searching every valley and mountaintop."

Cardin wanted to roll his eyes at the old Wizard's arrogance. He smirked when he noticed Dalin silently scoffed.

Artula nodded. "Then we should report back to the Allied

Council, with our recommended course of action. Master Syrn, will you do the honor of creating a portal back to Archanon?"

With barely a nod, Syrn stepped around the table and out of the exit, with everyone following. Cardin stayed back to allow everyone to step outside before him, his thoughts turning to what now lay ahead of them.

The war against Kailar and Klaralin was short and decisive. But this new war against the orcs? This would be drawn out, and their casualties would no doubt only increase.

However, while Master Syrn gathered power to open a portal, another thought occurred to him. The four kingdoms of Edilas were already coming together against the threat. This war wouldn't be Warrior against Warrior, kingdom against kingdom. For once, the armies of Edilas would stand united, together with the Wizards.

He couldn't help but smile when he thought of that. It was exactly what he had hoped for.

Maybe there was hope after all.

***

For the first time since Zerek came to Archanon, he was allowed to leave the castle grounds, and he reveled in that little bit of freedom, even if it was for an assignment.

He was shocked late in the morning when Madam Kai told him he was ready to go on his first errand into the city. However, much to his relief, she wanted someone who knew the city to go with. Seeing that Endel and Zerek had become friends overnight, she asked Endel to accompany him.

Now the two of them strolled down the main market street of the city, both happy for each other's company. Endel led one of the stable horses by a lead rope, while Zerek carried an envelope with an order for supplies that he and his young friend would bring back.

The street was overcrowded, but it didn't make Zerek uncomfortable, not like being in a crowded mine did. Endel explained to him that most people tried to get as much business out of the way as they could early in the cool morning during the hot summer months.

Zerek didn't care. His eyes were wide and his jaw stretched open as he gazed around at all of the people, the store shops, the vendor stalls opened in front of many of those shops. It was a hive of activity, full of people he had never seen. It was incredible.

In the past, he had travelled to smaller towns with his father to trade what they had mined for payment and supplies. The Mining Guild always made the arrangements for them through a rather efficient system of bartering with the Trader's Guild and Craftsmen's Guild, so time spent in those towns was short.

And none of those towns could compare to the vast city sprawled out around him. It stretched from east to west for several miles, and he couldn't fathom how many people lived within its walls. Ahead in the distance, he could see the main city gates, towering over the city, bracketed by cliffs that formed a partial natural barrier for the city.

The everlasting torches burned even in daylight along the street, providing no light, but their yellow-white color signified their district, as Endel explained.

"Every district has a distinct color," the young boy continued, his blue eyes darting around excitedly, looking for something new to point out to Zerek. "Yellow is for the trade district. Green for the farmer's district, though it isn't just farms in that part of the city. Plus there are way more farms outside of the city." He waved his free hand around and said, "The city is ginormous, but that also means too many people. There's always a need for more food." Zerek smiled as the kid continued on. "Blue is…was in the south east. It's where all of those homes were destroyed in the great Battle for Archanon."

"What was blue before then?" he asked, looking southeast, even though he knew he couldn't see it from the trade district.

"It was homes for those who worked in the other districts," Endel shook his head. "They say it once served a different purpose, but that changed as the number of people in the city grew and grew and grew. No one knows what its original purpose was, either. Maybe something to do with when the Wizards were still here. Then there's the red district, where the Warriors' Guild headquarters is. City guards. Barracks." He shrugged. "I've never actually been there, not yet. We only take care of the castle's horses, not theirs. They have their own stable boys and girls."

Zerek almost wanted to tell Endel to slow down, he was talking too fast and about too much. Thankfully, he didn't have to say anything. A commotion arose ahead, and someone shouted "Make way!"

The crowd began to part before them, revealing a small column of armed soldiers leading a group of people up from the gate and towards the castle.

"Come on!" Endel grabbed Zerek's grey shirt's sleeve and pulled him and the horse to one side. "It must be Warriors returning from the front," his friend about jittered with excitement. He stopped them and said "Let's stay on the street, see if we can catch a glimpse of them!"

Zerek felt his insides twist a little. Warriors from the front. Did that mean that whomever approached had fought orcs? Had they killed orcs? What about the mining camp? Were there survivors?

He knew he couldn't ask whomever it was. He was just an errand boy, nothing more. No one important. Not a Warrior himself.

A void filled in the pit of his stomach when he realized that he would never be anyone of consequence.

Drawing closer, he was able to see the faces and armor of those passing.

"No one get's such a big escort unless it's the General or the King," Endel hopped up and down to try to get a better look. "No, two generals! By the gods, it's General Artula *and* the Erien General!"

Zerek craned his neck. A few of the other bystanders in the crowded street got in his way, so he pushed around them to see. Suddenly the crowd surged closer to the Warriors. Everyone whispered about whom they saw, wondering what had happened in their first battle against the orcs. Some even began to cheer, a cheer that was taken up by more, and more, until the street was a roar of celebration for the returning heroes.

He didn't much care for being jostled around by everyone, but he wanted to see who else returned. He saw the bright blue of a Wizard's robes, could that white Wizard also be amongst them? Did he even go to the front?

Even a momentary glimpse of the Wizard would help him feel better, he knew it, so he tried to push closer. He was as tall as a fully grown man, so he didn't have an advantage, unlike Endel who could duck low and maneuver under arms to get closer.

Then he saw one man wearing nothing but light leather armor, with a giant sword strapped to his back. He recognized that man from when Zerek had stood before the Allied Council. In the days since that meeting, he had learned who that man was.

"It's the Keeper of the Sword," he heard more than a few shout in awe.

"Chosen by the dragons themselves."

"I know, I was there, I saw it happen!"

"He's so handsome…"

Zerek almost gagged at that last exclamation.

Most of the marching column were Warriors, wearing their battle armor proudly. He longed to wear such armor. To have his own longsword, dyed a special color unique to him. To have been trained to fight.

If he was a Warrior, he could avenge the death of everyone he had known and loved. Absently he reached down to where he kept the dagger sheathed on his belt.

It wasn't there!

Feeling a sudden panic, he looked down and saw that the sheath was completely missing, sliced off of the belt. He also noticed that the letter pouch strapped onto his belt was undone. He opened it, and saw that the sealed orders were gone.

"No!" His voice was lost in the cheering of the crowd. He looked frantically, trying to find who could have taken them. He couldn't have lost it, he just *couldn't* have.

Suddenly, he saw movement away from the street, away from the marching Warriors. Everyone else clambered to get closer, so why would someone walk away?

With his hands shaking, he tried to push through the crowd towards the offender. That had to be the thief. They wore a ragged-looking cloak with the hood up, so even when he caught a glimpse of the figure through the sea of people, he couldn't identify who or what it was.

People pushed and shoved, groaned and cursed at him, wouldn't let him by. The other person seemed to somehow just flow through the crowd without effort. How could anyone do that?

He was losing the thief. Sure, there was no way he could know that person had his dagger, nor the orders, but who else could it be?

The crowd thinned out as they approached the edge of the street and the lines of shops and vendor stalls. The stalls themselves were cleared out of patrons, to the obvious annoyance of the owners.

Most of the owners waited impatiently for the procession to pass by.

Now he could see the thief easier. They moved along in front of the shops casually, as if he or she didn't have a care in the world. The vendors tried in vain to get the thief to stop and look at their wares, but the thief ignored them.

Until she came across a stall of fresh fruit. It was a girl. He saw when she turned to look at the varying fruit, barely a glimpse of her face. He saw olive skin and locks of short, brown hair, but that's all he saw before she turned away and kept going. He nearly shouted in anger when he saw his dagger through a hole in her cloak, tucked under her belt.

What the shop keeper hadn't seen from his perspective was that she grabbed an apple from his stall while she had pointed to another basket of fruit. He would have missed it himself if he wasn't scrutinizing every detail about her. She was a thief, and a good one.

He moved as fast as he could, but some of the crowd occasionally stepped back and he was jostled about or tripped.

"Hey, watch it," someone shouted at him.

That must have caught the girl's attention. Without stopping, she turned around just enough to glimpse him. Their eyes connected for a split second, and he felt something tingle in his chest. She had beautiful almond-brown eyes!

At first she merely frowned at him, and then her features slackened in recognition. She knew that he was her latest victim.

Looking ahead, she walked faster. He started jogging and shouted, "Hey!"

Suddenly, she bolted to the left, between two stalls and down an alley between shops. It was a flash of movement, and had taken him so much by surprise that he didn't react right away. "Hey, get back here," he took off after her at a full run, nearly crashing into two more people as he did.

In an instant he was between the buildings, catching only a glimpse of her cloak fluttering behind her as she turned right down another street, headed towards the center of the city. He barreled around the corner, and almost smashed into another vendor's stall. Traffic was still heavy on this road, and was going to make chasing her a challenge.

Even at a full run, the girl somehow darted in between people without so much as brushing up against them. He marveled at her skill, but also hated that he was losing her. He was new to the city, and there was no way he was going to be able to keep up with her or find a way to cut her off.

So he did the only thing he could think of. "Stop that girl. Thief!"

Most everyone just gawked at him or the running girl without doing anything. But then a few people tried to grab her.

She was able to dodge their offending hands every time, but it did slow her down. He continued to call out after her, asking people for help, trying desperately to catch up.

"Please, stop," he finally pleaded desperately.

In that moment, her forward momentum slowed just a little, and she glanced back at him. Her hood fell down, and he finally had his first unobstructed view of her face. His heart fluttered when he saw her, and his face, already warm from running, grew hotter.

Despite her momentary distraction, she still dodged everyone who tried to stop her. He did, however, notice that she had slowed down even more, and never picked up the pace again. With great effort, he began to close to the distance, if ever so slowly.

Every few seconds, she glanced back at him again. Her cloak flowed behind her to reveal the dagger still on her belt, and he tried to focus in on that, determined to get it back. But he also couldn't help but look at her face every chance he could get. She was so beautiful!

The chase continued on, and he stopped shouting for help. It seemed like after he closed to a dozen feet of her, he couldn't catch up anymore, no matter how hard he tried. Was she toying with him?

After several minutes, his heart banged against his chest, and his legs started to feel weak. He was used to swinging a pick axe or chiseling away at rocks, using strength to get his job done. Running like this was something new to him, and he began to despair. She showed no signs of tiring, and he knew that he was going to lose her.

A part of him wanted to shout in rage. He couldn't lose that dagger!

Suddenly they ran out between two buildings to find a river before them. It was channeled into a canal running through the northeast quarter of the city. Endel had told him about that river too, last night. The river once flowed through the valley out where the western gate was, but millennia ago was redirected by human and

Wizard engineering. Now it twisted back around on itself, creating a small peninsula backed against the northeast wall, and entered and exited the city walls at points a few miles from each other.

The thief led him along the canal downriver, and Zerek saw that across the river, on the 'island' in the city, was the farm district. It took up the entire north east quarter, and only then did he begin to realize just how huge Archanon was.

They drew closer to a stone bridge, and he wondered if she meant to cross into the farm district. Then, quite suddenly, she stopped in her tracks and turned to face him.

He was so stunned by her move that, without even realizing what he was doing, he too stopped. Only a few feet separated them, but it may as well have been a mile, as fast as she was. She was panting a little, while his heart thundered in his chest and he struggled to slow his breathing.

Suddenly a little smirk came over her face, and she hopped over the low guard wall and down into the canal.

"No," he shouted, and looked over the edge. To his relief, she had landed on the bank of the river and hadn't disappeared into the water. The river was low enough that the muddy bank was about six inches wide.

She looked up at him, smiled and waved, and shouted in a strangely sweet and teasing voice, "Are you coming?"

With that, she turned and walked carefully along the muddy bank, disappearing into the shadows of the bridge.

Zerek frowned and glanced around, but no one was nearby. Across the river, he saw farmers tending to their fields and livestock, but no one was looking towards them. The rumble of the rushing river below had probably drowned out his earlier shout.

The drop down was only about five feet or so, and he could easily land that. Something else stirred inside of him. Something he hadn't really felt before, or at least he didn't remember feeling. Excitement and fear, all rolled into one jumbled emotion that caused his hands and feet to tingle.

After another moment of hesitation, he steeled himself, and hopped over the ledge. The mud was surprisingly hard, his feet barely sank, but he nearly lost his balance and fell into the river. He steadied himself on the canal wall, and then followed the thief's footsteps under the bridge.

There was an unpleasant smell in the shadows, like that of a back alley in the smaller towns, where people usually emptied their chamber pots.

Once his eyes adjusted to the darkness, he saw her leaning against the canal wall, arms crossed.

"You're a stubborn one, aren't you?"

He huffed, his breath still coming fast and ragged. "You have something that belongs to me."

"What, the orders?" she asked, pulling out the letter. She hadn't broken the seal yet. "Why would that matter so much that you would chase after me for so long? Orders can be rewritten."

Part of him wondered why she would even steal such a document if it was so unimportant, but he ignored that for the moment. He just wanted one thing. "I didn't chase you for the orders."

Then her face slackened into surprise. She stowed the orders, and then unclasped his dagger from her belt. "This thing?"

She looked very carefully at the sheath, and then partially unsheathed the blade. "Hey, careful with that," he raised a hand and took another step towards her. She backed up when he did, so he froze.

"It's just a dagger," she shrugged. "I mean, yeah, it's steel, and well crafted, but who cares. Get the castle to requisition you another one."

"It's not theirs. It's mine." He gulped in air, but was thankful that his breathing finally slowed and his heart no longer thundered in his ears. "It's all I have left."

Her surprise faded, and her lips drew into a thin line. "That's why you said please."

So that was it. That was why she let him keep up with her. Either out of curiosity or sympathy, his pleading had reached her heart.

He held out his hand, and looked at her with earnest eyes. "My family. That's all I have left of them."

For a long moment, she just looked from the dagger to his hand and back again. Until finally, she re-sheathed the blade and walked closer to him. He held out his hand further, willing her to give it back.

She hesitated for only a moment longer, and then placed it in his hand. The weight felt reassuring, and he pulled it in and clutched it tightly. A wave of relief washed over him, and he sighed and smiled.

"Thank you. Thank you so much."

Her eyes narrowed and she looked at him with great surprise. "Thank you? I stole it from you. You shouldn't be thanking me."

The warmth in his cheeks returned. He gazed into her amazing eyes, still beautiful even in the shadows. "You didn't have to give it back."

"Yeah, well," she backed away and averted her eyes. "I know what it's like to lose everything."

A long silence followed, and then she sighed and looked at him. "There's a place not far back that way," she pointed over his shoulder, "where you can climb up easily. I trust you can find your way back to the castle from here."

He didn't know how to reply. In fact, he couldn't think at all. "Umm," was all he managed.

At first she stared at him with a frown. Then she smiled awkwardly and stepped back a little more. "Go on, lover-boy," she motioned him away. "Get going before I steal something else."

He glanced behind him to see where she was talking about. About fifty feet back, there were several stone bricks jutting out of the canal wall. They could make a suspiciously easy ladder to climb up.

When he turned back to her, she was gone. His heart stopped for just a second, and he looked everywhere he could think. How could she have disappeared like that?

With a short laugh, he turned around and slowly made his way back. When he reached the jutting bricks, he stuffed the dagger into his belt and climbed up out of the canal.

He had lost the orders, which meant that he had failed his first job. But he didn't care. He looked back down under the bridge, and wondered about the girl he had just met.

There was nothing else for it, he would have to find her again.

Somehow, he had just fallen in love with a thief.

Episode 4

INTO THE FORGE

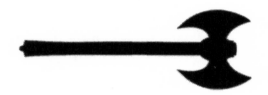

The Ilari Mountains smelled of pine, and of flowers still blooming against the coming fall. The air was warm, but not hot, not like Arkad preferred. Never the less, it reminded him of mountains remembered from a lifetime ago. Red skies, hot summer days, trekking through the same mountain paths since he was a boy.

He missed home. A great weight formed in his stomach, a familiar sensation when he thought of what he had lost. It wasn't so long ago, the wound was still achingly fresh. A sense of loss, not just of kin, but of birthright. Loss of identity.

Cold. That was what he had to look forward to now. The winter was coming, probably sooner than he expected, certainly sooner than he hoped. Winter in this wretched land.

The land that was now his people's only hope.

Tearing himself back to the present, he looked around at his warriors, scattered about in the mountain forests. Their army was at the eastern edge of the Ilari Mountains, scattered to help avoid detection. They could make no camps, make no fires, not without fear of detection by their enemy. They ate their hunted kills raw, and foraged any fruit that they could.

Stomach growling, Arkad rummaged in his travel pack for something to eat. There were still plenty of berries since he avoided eating them where he could. They were far too sweet for his palette, but he had already eaten the last of the mushrooms. Perhaps he could find something better. There were plenty of fresh kills to partake in throughout the scattered army, but he had ordered all of his soldiers to hold off on their main course until he decided if they would attack tonight or not.

He looked southeast, into the trees. Of course he could not see their destination, a city that the humans called Valaras. But he could smell it. They were upwind of the city, the breeze from the desert beyond pushing the human stench into the mountains. His nostrils flared, drinking in the smell in anticipation of what he would soon do.

Valaras was key to their conquest of the human lands. Many of the human mining camps sold their bounty to Valaras so that they could be forged into weapons and armor. Capturing Valaras would hinder the human war effort, and give the orcs new weapons, along forges to make more.

From what his master told him, the city was not well guarded and would be easy to take. Whether or not it was, he was confident in their ability to take it quickly.

His head shot up when he heard the sound of approaching footsteps. They were heavy and fast, so not human, but also two-legged, so not horses. Smiling, he momentarily abandoned his travel pack to stand up. Several other orcs around him likewise stood and looked east.

From amongst the trees, two of his kin, one clad in leathers skinned from the reptiles of the Wastelands, the other in dark-steel armor, burst out from the underbrush, and slowed to a jog. They did not look harried or worn, just determined, and both wore large grins upon their faces, their fangs gleaming in the sunlight.

When they saw General Arkad, they turned to approach him. He took two steps towards them, and then waited. His heart began to pump faster, his blood burning with anticipation.

"General," Kilack, the dark-steel orc, said as they came to a stop.

Arkad stood taller than any other orc in his army, and so he towered over his soldiers, which in and of itself demanded their honor and respect. He puffed out his chest and looked down at them. "You bring good news?"

"Yes, General," Kilack nodded and pulled a rolled-up skin out from his own travel pack. He unrolled it onto the ground before their leader, and knelt down. The skin had a crude drawing of the city on it. The city wall appeared to have six sides, all at uneven angles.

"From what we could see, the Warriors' Guild complex is here," Kilack pointed at the bottom of the map, "at the south end, not far from the main western gate. There is, however, two smaller entrances on the north and south ends. I believe we can breach one of them more easily with our qrishags."

Arkad smirked. If his master was correct, the humans still wouldn't know about the qrishags. He looked behind him at one of the great beasts several hundred feet away, under the cover of a large tree. With tusks and a single horn, and three times the size of a human's horse, they were terrifying beasts of the Wastelands. Beasts that the orcs of Halarite had never before used in war against the humans.

They hadn't known how to tame them before Arkad and his master had arrived.

The great, gray-scaled beast snuffed, blowing a cloud of dirt into the air. They were powerful, and would easily take down any wooden gates. Even ironwood would not hold up to them for long.

Arkad looked back to Kilack and asked, "Is the city well-defended?"

"No, General," the soldier puffed his chest out and smiled. "I do not believe they could have anticipated us travelling this far north. More likely they expected us to attack their capitol."

"Good," Arkad smiled and looked east. If they moved now, he had no doubt that they would capture the city by midnight.

"Tell everyone to feast on flesh now," he raised his voice, loud enough for all surrounding warriors to hear him. "We leave within the hour!"

***

With only a hint of a smile on her face, Amaya Kenla passed through the corridors of the old structure of Archanon Castle. Over the millennia, several wings were added and repaired countless times, but it was a point of pride for the kingdom that the original structure still stood ten thousand years later.

Pride was an emotion she was getting used to again, as her faith in the throne and in her king slowly returned.

Her destination was the throne room, and it would be the sixth time she had been summoned to it since she had become a Guardian. Every now and then she struggled with the castle layout, but the ancient central building was simple, and all paths led to it.

As a Guardian, she never used the grand entrance to the throne room. That was for dignitaries, peasants, or anyone else granted an official audience before King Beredis. She was one of his elite Guardians, and discretion was called for.

She rounded a corner to enter through one of the side passages, but came up short, and felt her heart skip a beat. Standing before her was the young Prince, Idrill Beredis. Her stomach soured when she realized that he was waiting for her.

"Ah yes," he spoke as bile built up in the back of her throat. "Ms. Kenla, my father's newest favorite pet."

It was her first time seeing the brat since her team was pardoned by the King. There was a part of her that had known she would eventually have to face him again, but did it have to be so soon?

Knowing how important it was to show him respect, regardless of her personal feelings, she bowed before him. "My Lord Prince." In her bow, she clasped her right hand against the sheath of her longsword, some distant part of her wishing she could draw it. It wasn't the two flanking guards that made her decide against it.

Hatred boiled inside, but she managed to contain it. Rising up to her full height again, which nearly matched the Prince's, she stared at him stolidly. She wanted to insult him, but she knew she could not speak further to him unless given permission.

The Prince stared at her with passive eyes at first, but disdain quickly filled his eyes. "Such manners for a criminal." Her blood boiled, and she squeezed the hilt of her sword like it was his neck. "You have begun to strut around this castle as if you belonged here, but mark my words," he raised his hand and pointed a finger at her nose, "you do not belong here. Criminals do not belong under the protection of this roof."

Jaw clenched, it took every ounce of strength she had in her not to reply. Something must have sparked in her eyes, however, since the Prince smirked. "I can see that you wish to reply. You wish to tell me exactly what you think." He scoffed and shook his head. "I give you leave to say whatever you wish to me."

In that instant, she nearly sealed her fate. She nearly did exactly what she wanted to. He was a spoiled brat, a would-be dictator whose selfish ambition would destroy their kingdom if the King allowed him to succeed his reign. An abysmal human, the lowest sort of pond scum, and a man she would never serve.

Instead, she forced her jaw to loosen, and replied coolly, "With respect, my Lord Prince, the King has decreed my team and I innocent of any wrongdoing or law breaking." Her voice was even, not betraying the rage within her.

The Prince's face soured and he placed his hands on his hips. "You broke the law," he spat out, "make no mistake about that. I do not care what ruling my father made. There will come a day when I ascend the throne again." He stood as tall as he could, as if his scrawny structure would frighten her. "When I do, your execution will come swiftly."

She almost reminded him that laws written at the end of Klaralin's reign three thousand years ago decreed that a King could choose his heir, it did not have to be his children. King Beredis was a good man, and he would choose an heir to the throne far more worthy than the Prince.

Wouldn't he?

Her courage faltered at that thought. Though there was no proof of it, many in the castle believed that the Prince had poisoned the King, and had it not been for the healing hand of a Master Wizard, the boy before her would already be king, and she would have been executed to honor his coronation.

"Step aside, whelp," the Prince commanded.

With only a moment of hesitation, she followed his order. He started to walk past her, but then stopped and leaned towards her to whisper, "I *will* have the throne some day. Of that, you may be certain."

She felt her cheeks burn when he said that, but he passed by after that, and left her fuming. The two guards flanking the entrance remained stolid, unmoving, but she wondered if they felt as she did. Or were they loyal to the Prince?

Several moments passed while she composed herself, taking in deep breaths and counting them out. When she finally felt calm enough, she turned to the entrance and nodded to the guards. One of them opened the door for her, and she passed through.

Amaya was dressed as a guard to save face when in the castle, allowing her to blend in with the countless other guards. If the King was in audience, it would appear as if just another guard had arrived, and no one would question her. The ceremonial guard armor was fine chainmail armor and a black tabard emblazoned with the kingdom's symbol in silver.

The only thing that could set her apart was if she drew her sword. Everyone would see that she held a Warriors' sword, a remnant from her past, but more a part of her today than ever before. The blade was sky-blue, and would forever remain her trademark.

The King was not in audience, and all of the guards were absent. She walked in as quietly as she could, but her armor gave her away instantly. The King, standing at the foot of the steps to his throne, turned towards her. Draegus Kataar was beside him, the man that she now knew to be the leader of the Guardians. He was perhaps one of two people in the entire kingdom who knew who each and every Guardian was.

The truth about the Guardians was not quite what she had expected. The common citizens, and especially the Warriors' Guild, knew of the rumors of their existence within Tal, but those rumors were of a completely secret group that operated without impunity for the King.

While there certainly was an element of truth to that, the Guardians were not as secret as she once believed. If no one in the Kingdom knew who they were and the authority that they bore, the Guardians would be largely useless.

As it turned out, everyone of influence, whether a mayor, a captain of the guard, or a Warrior Commander, knew about them. They knew that if anyone ever presented the seal of the Guardians, they worked with the full authority of the throne backing them.

Amaya bowed before the King. "Your Majesty."

King Beredis nodded, balancing his golden crown upon his head with ease. He wore black and silver robes today, and looked unusually concerned. "Amaya." He attempted to smile through his concern. She would never get used to being called by her first name by her King.

"Lieutenant," Draegus added his own nod. The King had granted her that rank amongst the guards, matching her former Guild rank and giving her needed authority to command her team.

"How may I serve you today, my Lord?" she asked, her face passive.

The King drew in a deep breath, held it as he glanced at Draegus, and then let it out slowly. "With something far more delicate than you are used to dealing with."

This was enough to worry her. The King was usually very direct with her. Her team had successfully completed two missions since Ironwood, both of which involved harrying orc encampments within the Kingdom. Every time, she and her six soldiers, plus the Wizard that now accompanied them, defeated the superior numbers and sent the orcs fleeing.

That, she assumed, was what it meant to be a Guardian. To fight the battles that no one else could. The armies of the Alliance were poised to strike the larger orc army the moment they showed themselves. They could not afford to spread their forces out for minor skirmishes.

"My mission for you today is not directly related to the war."

Now she really felt surprised. The war effort, and all preparations for the coming battles, consumed every city, town and village of Tal. Of every kingdom, for that matter. What could be so important that her elite unit would be torn away from that effort?

"My Lord?" She clasped her hands behind her back to hide her anxiety.

For a moment, the King stared at her with his endlessly dark eyes. She didn't know if she should continue to return his gaze or not, so she found herself nervously looking at his chest.

"Are you a devout follower of the Order," he finally asked.

Her mind turned blank for a moment, the unexpected question catching her off guard. "Sire?"

King Beredis frowned. "I believe the question was rather clear."

"I, um, yes," she fumbled with her words. "I mean no." She hesitated and considered her answer carefully. "I believe in the Order and the word of the Cronal, but I do not recall the last time I stepped foot in a sanctuary."

"I see," the King shook his head. "So you believe everything the

Order has told us."

Amaya grew suspicious of the conversation's strange direction. "For the most part."

Her King raised a curious eyebrow. "For the most part?"

Uncertain how best to continue, she nodded. "Yes, sire. However..." She trailed off and looked at her feet, her insides turning. "I find it difficult to reconcile what has been said about the Battle for Archanon."

Drawing his lips into a thin line, the King nodded. "Indeed. That is true for many throughout the four kingdoms. We tried to prevent word from spreading too quickly, but that just was not possible. By now, news of the battle has spread to every corner of Edilas. It won't be long before the colonies learn of it too, if they have not already."

She could only imagine how difficult the world would find the facts, and how close to panic everyone felt. Elves. Dragons. Both intelligent creatures. One elf had fought in the Battle for Archanon, alongside the Keeper of the Sword, helping defeat Kailar. And four dragons had disenchanted Klaralin's pendant, paving the way for his defeat.

For centuries, the Covenant was adamant that any apparent intelligent beings, especially any with superior intelligence, were actually demons. Evil spirits sent by Degrin to corrupt the followers of the Order of the Ages.

"If I may ask," she said after further thought, "what does this have to do with my team?"

Beredis looked at her with a stolid expression. "Many people within the kingdom have difficulty accepting these new truths. We have all been taught from birth to believe everything the Cronal says. Yet there is now proof that the Cronal is wrong. Many will not believe. Some will panic."

She felt a sinking sensation in her stomach when she began to suspect what their next mission might be. Never the less, she said, "We are yours to command, Sire. Please continue."

Beredis drew in a deep breath and sighed. "A group of zealots have begun to cause trouble in Valaras. They claim this war is the result of our sins, and have begun interfering or even sabotaging the smelters and forges."

"I see," she spoke slowly, the void within her growing into a gaping chasm. "And you wish for us to stop these people?"

"Yes," the King nodded. "Under normal circumstances, I would leave it to the Covenant to handle, or the local guards. However, today I received a report from a Wizard that these people took up arms and seized the Forge District. The Crafters' Guild is furious and is demanding action, and without a fresh supply of weapons and armor, we will lose this war."

Although she was not a strategic commander, even Amaya knew how disastrous it could be. The forges of Valaras weren't the only ones in Tal, but they were the key suppliers. In wartime, Valaras crafted more weapons and armor in a week than the rest of the kingdom combined did in a month.

However, the mission before her made her feel sick to her stomach. "Your Majesty, I..."

He raised a hand to stop her. "I believe I know your objections."

"Which is why," Draegus spoke up, "we have chosen you and your team for this mission."

She looked at her commander curiously. "Sir?"

"We don't want you to go in with swords drawn, ready to attack," Draegus said, shaking his head. "If it comes to that, we want it to be a last resort. These are citizens of Tal. Frightened, unable to cope with such an incredible paradigm shift. It also wouldn't surprise me if most of them are rallying behind only one or two leaders. If you can get those leaders to quiet down, the others might disperse on their own."

"With respect, your Majesty," she looked at her King, "I am not a politician or a negotiator."

"You are, however, a leader," the King looked at her confidently. "Which means you have charisma. I have also seen that you are reasonable, and you care about the lives of the innocent. I do not know if reason can sway these people, but we must try, and there is little time. Orcs could strike at any city at any time, including Valaras. We have to be ready. We need those forges up and running."

"Yes, Sire," she nodded, feeling wholly uncertain about the path before her. How could she convince terrified fanatics that they were wrong? Especially if they believed that the gods supported their actions!

"Let me be clear," the King stepped closer to her, a genuine look of regret on his face. The void within her threatened to grow larger, and she thought she knew exactly what he was going to say next. "Your mission must succeed. If they do not leave the forges willingly, the Guild will step in. I trust you know what that will mean."

She felt at least part of the weight on her shoulders lift, but only a part. For a moment, she thought that he would order *her* to clear them out by force. There was no possible way she could do that. These weren't bandits, they were simply frightened people who believed they were doing the right thing to earn their gods' forgiveness.

However, it still drove home the importance of the task ahead. If she didn't succeed, the Warriors would march in and force them to give up the forges. Only death could follow.

"Gather your team," Draegus nodded. "You leave immediately. Nia is already waiting for you outside of the western gate."

"I trust you are comfortable working with her again?" the King asked.

Amaya smirked, amusement filling some of the void within her chest. "Yes, Your Majesty. She seems to fit in well with my team." That was a lie. The young Wizard was barely out of apprenticeship, and didn't seem to understand the finer points of interpersonal relationships. That didn't stop Amaya from trying, and from doing her best to keep her team from ever taking jokes too far where Nia was concerned.

"Good luck, Amaya," the King smiled weakly. "I hope for everyone's sake that you succeed."

***

For three weeks, she was all that Zerek could think about. His heart beat faster when he imagined her face, and his entire body tingled in excitement. Some parts more than others. No matter what he did, she was always there in his thoughts. She was all that he wanted to think about.

The thief that had stolen his orders, his dagger, and his heart.

Gods, that sounded terrible even in his own head!

Of course, it didn't help that he was reminded of the event often. It had been his first assignment, and he had lost the orders, signed and sealed directly by the King. It wasn't just an embarrassment to him, it was to Kai Loric as well. She had trusted him and vouched for him, and in doing so, his failure became her failure.

His saving grace was that he was not the first of the King's messengers to become victims of thievery, and some of the other messengers were attacked when they tried to fight back.

Now he and another messenger, Chessick, stood face to face in the courtyard outside of the castle barracks, wooden short swords in hand, learning to defend themselves. A castle guard named Torick stood to the side, with Endel sitting on the cobblestone path next to Torick.

Chessick hadn't been kind to Zerek in the past few weeks. Taller than Zerek, Chessick's black hair was always pushed straight back, and he stared with founded confidence at Zerek.

"Now it's Zerek's turn," Torick commanded.

"Come on, Zerek!" Endel cheered, pumping his fist into the air. "Kick his butt!"

Chessick raised his eyebrow mockingly. "Yeah, come on kid. Show us what you've learned."

Zerek's nostrils flared with anger, and he charged at his adversary. He swung his sword in a fast circle to cut up from underneath, but his opponent easily blocked, as was expected. As his sword bounced off of Chessick's, he used its momentum to swing back around and continue his attack.

So the fight was supposed to go. Zerek was meant to use the momentum of his swings to keep the pressure on his opponent, and Chessick was supposed to only defend.

Of course, the session was just about over, and Chessick never missed a chance to humiliate Zerek. The next thing he knew, his sword hit thin air, and then the world exploded in pain when the flat of his enemy's sword smacked his face full-force. His head jerked to the side, and his face burned.

As did his temper. He turned back to face his opponent and his smug grin, and launched at Chessick.

Until Torick grabbed hold of his collar and yanked him back. Chessick burst into laughter, but this time he had taken it too far, and his own face caught the back of Torick's hand.

"That's enough!" Torick shouted. Zerek tried desperately to keep the smile off of his face when he saw how shocked and embarrassed Chessick was. Zerek's cheek burned just a little less. "I let you two continue to train together because I thought your rivalry would spur you to work harder." He pulled Zerek further away and then let go. "But neither of you are taking this seriously."

"Hey, it's not my fault he keeps playing games with me," Zerek defended. "I want to learn how to fight, I *need* to learn."

"You'll never learn, you little…"

Torick interrupted Chessick's insult with the threat of another backhand. It was enough to make Zerek's nemesis back down. For all of his bluster, not to mention his greater age, Chessick was still a coward when it came to actual pain.

With a great heave of a sigh, Torick crouched down between them, steadying himself with the tips of his fingers, and stared at the cobblestone for a while. Finally, he looked at Zerek. "Part of what I have been trying to teach you both is to know when to fight and when not to. I know it has only been a couple short weeks, but this is perhaps one of the most important lessons I can teach you."

He then turned to Chessick. "This also includes learning when not to instigate a fight in the first place. Never start one unless you know you're going to win-"

"I can beat him any time, any day," Chessick scoffed.

Torick paused, but this time he did not glare, he simply looked with a stolid, heavy face. "And unless you absolutely have to," he finally finished. "There is enough bloodshed, enough fighting in our world without needlessly shedding more."

With a laugh, Torick shook his head. "You two should never even be in such a position. You're messengers. You'll never find yourselves in the middle of a battlefield, or facing off against bandits in the wild. Just thieves in the alleys, and maybe an occasional mugger." He again looked at Chessick. "They will taunt you, they will try to goad you into going after them. Whatever these thieves want from the castle, they'll employ any number of tactics to get it. Like goading you into chasing them into a group of a dozen of them. Then what are you going to do?"

Even Chessick wasn't arrogant enough to think that he could take on a dozen thugs. He gave no response back, he simply folded his arms and sighed in defeat.

"Guile and deceit," Torick shook his head. "This is how thieves operate. While you're facing the biggest, baddest one in front of you," he held up his hand, fingers straight up in the air, "their sneakiest one will come from behind," he motioned with his other hand as if it were the stealthy assailant, "and take everything of value before you even realize it's a trap." Torick lowered his hands and shook his head. "Or worse."

Zerek knew what the 'or worse' was. Part of him didn't care if that happened. But then he realized if someone killed him, he wouldn't ever see the girl again. She had given him his dagger back. Hadn't hurt him. She had even allowed him to catch up to her. That could only mean that she wasn't like the other thugs in the city.

Thief. That was what he called her. What was her name? He *had* to find out. He *had* to find her.

Realizing their training was over, he began to feel impatient, and unconsciously began to fidget. Torick caught on quickly.

"Alright," he stood up. "That's it for today. Put your practice away and get out of here."

Chessick snuffed in Zerek's direction, and stalked off towards the rack where they kept their practice weapons. Endel leapt up off of the flagstone and walked over to Zerek, Torick sauntering off towards the guardhouse.

Impatiently, they waited for both Torick and Chessick to wander off. Then Zerek looked at his friend with a grin. "Come on," he hurried over to the rack, placing the well-used practice sword in its place next to Chessick's.

A moment later, they were off, not towards the servants' quarters like they should have, but towards the gate that led out into the rest of the city.

The gate guards, looking resplendent in their black and white tabards, hardly paid them any notice as they burst out and down the small hill. The castle and the elite of the city all lived on that small, flat hill at the center, the original borders of the ancient First City of Halarite.

Every now and then, Zerek gently touched his face, feeling the heat radiating off of where Chessick had hit him. He wondered how much of that heat was embarrassment. It wasn't like he had gone his whole life without injury, he'd worked in a mine. But somehow, this hurt worse than any rock falling on him or stubbing his toes or banging his shins.

"Where are we going to look today?" Endel asked. That was when Zerek realized that he hadn't been paying any attention to where they had been going.

Indeed, where could they search? The city was huge, and it would be impossible for him to search every street. Well, not impossible, it would just take a very long time.

After he had told Endel about why he had left the poor kid all alone in the Market, his friend had at first been saddened, perhaps even with a hint of jealousy. But then he had decided that he was going to help Zerek find the girl, no matter what.

They had started by going to the bridge by the farm district, where he had last seen her. They'd explored that part of the city, not crossing to the farms at first, but just looking around the homes and handful of shops near the river. All of this they did in the one or two hours they could get away from the castle, usually when on a delivery run.

At that rate, they would never find the thief. So they started asking those who lived or worked in the area about her, giving them a description and hoping they would recognize her. Olive colored smooth skin, short brown hair, almond eyes, tattered cloak, ragged trousers and tunic. Clearly she lived on the street.

To his dismay, no one they had talked to recognized her. Not one person.

Where else could they look? Across the river, in the farm district? Or deeper in the city, further away from the river?

He had to find her. So he looked at Endel with determination, hiding his doubts and the emptiness he began to feel inside, and said, "We just have to keep asking around. Let's go deeper into the city. *Someone* has to know who she is."

Endel shrugged and nodded, "Alright. Come on, we'll go closer to the red district this time."

Tugging on Zerek's sleeve, he took off into a run, Zerek right on his heels. They always ran to and from the castle district. That and his many errands outside of the city had started to build his stamina. He could run further, go faster, and not tire as easily. He knew that would come in handy if he had to chase her again.

It took them several minutes, but they finally got to the blue district again. He had begun to familiarize himself with the city's layout, and knew that they weren't far from the red district. It was a long walk to the river from here, so he questioned Endel's decision to stop there and begin asking around.

"It's like Torick said," he shrugged. "Thieves are about misdirection, right? Maybe she took you to the river so that you wouldn't have a clue where she actually spent her time."

Zerek considered it for a moment, and realized that his young friend was right. His heart fluttered with renewed hope. "Okay. So, what, start looking around here?" He looked west, towards the red district. During the day the everlasting torches that lined the streets weren't as easy to identify, but the borders between districts were still rather obvious. Especially the red district. Only military stayed there. City guards, Warriors, and their compounds and barracks and training grounds. Near the center of it was the actual Guild complex itself, with a stone-brick watch tower that rose up from the center.

"I kind of doubt a thief would hang around red," he looked at Endel, doubtful.

"Exactly," he smirked. "It's the last place anyone would think to look for a thief."

He sighed and nodded. "Alright. Why not, let's try it." The main streets of Archanon were all brick-laden or stone, and the one they stood upon now was no exception. It was busy with traffic, carts and horses, men and women, all going about their business. He often wondered about all of the people he saw every day, going about their business on the streets. So many people in one place, all with their own lives, with their own agendas, their own problems.

Having lived in mining camps all of his life, it was almost overwhelming.

Ignoring the fear he felt, he began to ask everyone that he could about the girl. Some ignored him completely, some were outright rude to him, but he was used to all of that. Every now and then, he came across a sympathetic ear, and he asked. But no one recognized her.

Just when he and Endel were about to give up and head back to the castle before they were missed, he found his first answer with an old lady at a bread stand.

"Excuse me, my lady," he put on his best charm.

Giving him a warm, albeit toothless smile, the old lady nodded. "Well hello there, young man. Come for some fresh bread?" She leaned in closer to him, which he found just a little uncomfortable. "I'll give you the freshest if you'll give me a handsome smile."

Feeling his cheeks grow warm, Zerek resisted the urge to back away. He didn't want to offend her, even if she didn't have any information for him.

"Uh, actually, no," he tried to smile for her. "No, I'm looking for someone."

"Oh, is that so?" The lady stood up straight, or as straight as she could. Folding her arms, she asked, "And just who might you be looking for?"

"I don't know her name, but I think she's someone who lives on the streets." He gave the description he had given a thousand times, adding in that the girl had the most mischievous, but beautiful, smile.

Zerek didn't expect the curious eyes the bread lady gave him. "Hmm. And why exactly do you want to find her?"

He'd never been asked that question before. Everyone just told him that no, they hadn't seen anyone like that on the streets. A spark of excitement ignited within him.

What should he say? Should he tell the old lady that the girl was a thief, but he was head over heels for her? No, that just sounded dumb. So what, then?

Endel came to the rescue, in a manner of speaking. "He's got a big crush on her," the kid chimed in. "Wants to find her and try to kiss her."

Zerek pushed at his friend, his cheeks burning in embarrassment. "Hey! I do not."

"You do too!" Endel stuck his tongue out at him.

Glaring and feeling completely beside himself, he was suddenly shocked to hear the old lady cackling. "Oh, I think your young friend is right," she beamed at him. He looked at her, but then turned his face down to try to hide his red cheeks. "Oh yes, you definitely do." She sighed heavily and leaned against her stall. "If only a man would pursue me with such fervor again. I tell you, in my day, I was quite the looker. If I had wanted to, I could have gone home with a different man every night."

Something turned in his stomach, making him ready to vomit. That was not a vision he wanted to imagine. The bread lady just stared off into the distance dreamily.

After what felt like hours, Zerek became impatient. "So, have you seen her?"

She snapped out of her reverie. "What? Oh. Yes, good lad, I have." She pointed around the corner, down a smaller street. "Go down there until you get to Freelance Square. Turn right down the very next alley. If you don't find her there, you'll find someone who knows her there."

With his excitement returning, Zerek smiled and started to jot away down the road she had pointed to. "Thanks, lady!"

"You better be nice to her, young man," she called after him, but he barely heard it. He barely was aware that Endel was rushing along side of him. All he could think about was finding the thief, seeing her again, and most importantly, finding out her name.

***

Amaya found her team already awaiting their new orders in the castle barracks. They had already cast aside their castle guard uniforms and were ready to deploy.

While they all wore castle guard uniforms when not on assignment, they had been given a great deal of freedom in what they wore and what weapons they wielded when on assignment, and that made for a very unique team.

Elic was a strong, steadfast Mage, so he chose to wear chainmail armor reinforced with steel spaulders, shin guards, and wrist guards. He also proudly wore the Tal tabard, black with silver rather than white lines, denoting his station as one of the King's elite. He also still wielded his father's steel longsword, passed down to him when his father, a city soldier, had been mortally wounded in battle.

Peren wore light leather armor and carried a pair of small daggers as backups to his ironwood bow. He was incredibly strong, making him one of the few people capable of using such a bow. He was also one of the most accurate archers she had ever served with. Archery was somewhat of a lost art due to the increased number of Mages born over the past century. Who needed archers when Mages could serve as ranged attackers?

She knew better.

Idalia wore only chainmail armor, preferring a balance between protection and mobility. She had returned her husband's duty sword after their battle in Ironwood, and had been provisioned one of Archanon's finest steel longswords from the armory.

Nerina, strong and brash, and often drunk when not on duty, wore full chainmail and plate armor, carried a one-handed steel mace, and a heavy spade-shaped shield bearing the kingdom's icon upon its face. It already bore several scratches and nicks.

Vin, the silent, nimble one, wore barely-adequate, blackened leather armor, and carried a pair of daggers and a number of throwing knives. When possible, he always preferred stealth and misdirection over direct combat.

And Gell, perhaps the craziest of her troupe, wore leather with only some chainmail reinforcements, and carried axes. Three to be precise. One was a larger, two-handed axe carried upon his back, another was a small one-handed axe on his hip, and an even smaller throwing axe was strapped to his left boot.

Amaya quickly briefed them, and after she had changed into her own armor of choice, they marched down the main avenue of the market district with a purpose and authority they had all easily adopted. She looked at her crew, and began to realize just how unique they each were.

The Warriors' Guild did not value uniqueness, she realized. Oh sure, you could dye your weapons and armor a unique color that suited your taste upon graduation, but she wondered if that was meant to mask the fact that a Warrior was part of a uniform machine. Everyone carried swords, no exception. Normal Warriors a short sword and shield, Mages a longsword. Most archers were approaching an elderly age, and had become subjects of ridicule in the Guild.

Now, as Guardians, she and her team could wear what befitted them best, and wield whatever weapon made them most comfortable. Maybe being forced out of the Guild wasn't so bad after all.

Amaya wore mostly leather armor, with hardened guards at her shins, hips, shoulders, and wrists. She had kept her sky-blue longsword, given to her by her former Commander, Uric Din, three weeks ago. Preserved by the one man she hated most, and given to her in a seemingly innocent and genuine display of kindness and affection. It should have been destroyed.

Yet she couldn't bring herself to get rid of it.

Once outside of the western gate, they came upon the Wizard Nia, waiting patiently outside of the magical enchantment that surrounded the city and prevented the creation of portals. She wore forest green robes, lightly embroidered with gold symbols that looked like they had meaning, but Amaya could not guess what. All Wizards seemed to wear the same kind of robe, and Amaya began to wonder if they ever changed clothes.

"Greetings, Lieutenant," Nia half-bowed to her, her pinewood staff remaining stationary beside her. "I have been briefed on the mission objective. We may depart as soon as you are ready."

It was like talking to a dead fish. And as they always did when seeing Nia after a few days, Gell and Nerina glanced at each other and snickered. Amaya shot them an icy glare, knowing exactly what they were thinking. Nia seemed to have little emotion, and they often chided her for that.

The one joke that recurred the most was that Wizards forgot to teach their children how to feel. Amaya didn't find it very funny. Less so when Nia seemed not to understand that it was meant as an insult.

"Go ahead, Nia," Amaya nodded once. "I take it you know where we are going?"

"Yes," Nia nodded, turning away from them and stamping her staff down, the jade stone embedded at the top flaring green. Amaya felt the sudden excitement of energy around them, her extremities tingling at the sensation. "We have negotiated portal entry points at every major city on Edilas."

Within moments, a blue-white wall of light opened up before Nia, and she waited patiently for them to precede her. Amaya glanced at her team, only to receive a mischievous smirk from Gell. She glared at him in warning, and then motioned for them to follow her.

Having grown accustomed to portal travel, she did not hesitate as she walked through the wall of light, and felt only a slight shift in temperature. Instantly she found herself standing in one corner of the courtyard at the Valaras Warriors' Guild complex. Her throat caught a little at that realization, but she quickly reminded herself that Din was nowhere nearby, and she was safe here.

She stepped away from the portal to allow her team through, and began to get her bearings. That was when it dawned on her, as her eyes fell upon the mountains the city was nestled up against. Mountains to the *west*, not the east. They were on the other side of the Ilari range, somewhere she had never been before, and never thought she would be. She knew that only a dozen miles east of the city, the land turned to white sands, the beginning of the Desert of Ca'aluun.

As the last of her team stepped through, they were greeted by an older Warrior she knew to be Commander Argus. His hair was shockingly white, his skin rough and dark red from years of too much sun. That didn't change his daunting demeanor.

He regarded her with a stoic, hard look, his eyes a sharp blue against his reddened flesh. She didn't know what he was thinking. Did he hate her because of her banishment from the Guild? It was considered to be a horrible dishonor, at least to Warriors. But if he thought less of her, he did not show it. He nodded to her, "Lieutenant Kenla." His voice was gruff and strong, the weight of decades of being a Warrior giving a slight edge to his words.

"Commander," she nodded back.

"I was notified to expect your arrival," he continued, regarding her assembled team. She still couldn't decipher what he thought about her, about her team. It was like conversing with a statue.

Deciding she needed an ally in the Guild, if that was even possible, she thought to appeal to his vanity. "I thought that might be the case. I could really use your advice in these matters, sir. Any chance you could brief us on the way to the Forge District?"

He looked at her and raised his eyebrows slightly, a hint of surprise and even admiration. Shrugging, he nodded and waved for them to walk with him. "Sure, why not?" Setting a brisk pace, they quickly made their way out of the Guild complex and into the streets of Valaras.

She was only partly surprised to find that, unlike most towns and villages, the streets were made of stone, similar to Archanon. No doubt that was due to Valaras's wealth as one of the key suppliers of refined ore, weapons, and armor in Tal. Not to mention their exports to Erien.

"Their leader is a man named Trebor Tem," he began, his voice still hard, but a purpose behind it. She noted he did not speak to her as if addressing a subordinate, but rather as if briefing a peer. That should have comforted her, but somehow it did not. She wondered about that fact, but focused her attention on his information. "He's a cook, runs one of the local taverns. Everyone in town knows him." Argus shook his head, "And I do mean everyone. That's how he was able to rally support."

With a frown, Amaya asked, "A cook? I almost expected it to be one of the clerics."

"Believe it or not, the Order is staying out of this," Argus shrugged. "I wish they'd condemn the man, he'd lose all support then. On the other hand," he looked at her, "It could be worse. If they publicly supported him, he'd have the whole city on his side. I don't have to tell you what happens then."

As they continued further into the city, she noticed how unusually desolate the streets were. Even small towns were usually busier than this, and Valaras wasn't small by any measure. She could only guess that with the forges and smelters shut down, the city had likewise shut down.

Moments later, she discovered she was partly right. They rounded a corner around a large three story building to find the famous Forge District of Valaras.

In most villages and towns, a blacksmith, whether their craft was weapons and armor, horseshoes, shovel spades, or any other number of metal pieces, had individual forges. Smelters were also often operated as single shops run by a family, with a single furnace for the smelting process.

Valaras was much more than that. She knew the history, anyone who served in the Tal Warriors' Guild knew it. Valaras had started like any other city, with individual forges. However, the eastern side of the Ilari Mountains was rich in ore, especially iron ore. This allowed for a greater number of smiths to work in the same area for a low price.

This began the slow, steady build up of forges and smiths in Valaras. Only a few centuries ago, it was already considered the center for weapon and armor smithing. Then a woman in Valaras discovered how to purify coal, allowing it to be used in smithing. With plentiful coal deposits in the mountains further to the north, Valaras boomed.

The first smiths forged business partnerships and combined their properties in town to build complexes with multiple forges and furnaces. This trend caught on, and before long, the entire central core of Valaras was made up of large, multi-forge buildings. When business was slow, they could shut down unneeded forges and furnaces. When a Lesser War started, every single one operated at capacity to produce the needed weapons and armor to fuel the kingdom's war machine.

It was why Tal had won so many of the Lesser Wars. Falind and

Saran often came to the negotiating table because they simply could not keep their Warriors and soldiers armed.

Though Amaya had never visited Valaras before, she could imagine the numerous streams of smoke pouring from the countless chimneys that broke up the skyline. What a sight it must be. Today, however, every single stack was cold.

And the streets leading into the Forge District were guarded by armed civilians.

Commander Argus led them up to a platoon of Warriors holding their own line fifty feet away from a mirrored line of civilians. There were only eight Warriors facing two dozen of the civilians. She noted that the civilians wore armor and carried weapons that no doubt came from the district, but even that would not give them the upper hand against the trained and seasoned Warriors.

Based on how nervous all of the civilians looked, they knew they were outmatched.

"Captain," Argus addressed one of the Warriors, a woman with bright red hair, steel plate armor, and a scarlet longsword that denoted her as a Mage.

"Yes, sir," she turned to Argus and stood at attention.

"Report," he ordered, looking past her at the line of civilians. They all shifted uneasily when he did that, and she began to wonder what his reputation in town was. Something inside of her was beginning to twist and turn the longer she was in his presence.

"No change, sir," she glanced over her shoulder. "No change in the guard, however, so I imagine they are getting tired."

Amaya could tell that was the case just by looking at the civilian line. They all had deep lines set under their eyes, and not one of them seemed able to stand up straight. One even leaned against one of the smithy buildings.

"Good," Argus smiled. "That'll make things easier."

He started to move past the Warriors, but Amaya grabbed his elbow to stop him. He did stop, but the icy glare he gave her was enough to freeze her stomach.

"To be clear, we're going to talk to them," she looked at him evenly. "Not attack."

At first he did not reply, he simply stared at her. The ice she saw before was still present, but beyond that, she still could not read any expression in his eyes, any emotion. It was then that she knew - if she didn't get the forges up and running again, a lot of people were going to die.

"Lieutenant," he emphasized her rank, "I will do whatever is necessary to ensure this kingdom is protected and ready to fight our enemies." She noted he said enemies, plural. She also knew he was a veteran of the last Lesser War.

"I understand that," she folded her arms. "But the King sent me to find a peaceful resolution to this situation, and you're going to give me a chance to do that."

Argus raised an eyebrow at her. "Oh? Peaceful?" He glanced over her shoulder, and then looked her in the eye. "Then why did he send you with your entire team?"

She stopped at that, knowing full why. In case she failed.

But there was also another reason. Her team created a more intimidating presence for her. Perhaps King Beredis thought it would give her an upper hand in negotiations.

That was when she realized that it would likely have the opposite effect. Looking again to the civilians, she saw how tired and overly nervous they were. They were ready to snap.

No, this wouldn't do.

So she looked back at Elic, and said, "Everyone stay back. I'll handle this alone."

Elic's eyes grew wide with surprise and concern, but he did not object. "Yes, ma'am."

She then turned to Argus and gave him a hard look. "We're giving peace a chance, Commander."

Narrowing his eyes at her, he shook his head. "You're not going in there alone."

"Yes I am." She felt her stomach flutter, a part of her still feeling nervous about standing up to a Guild Commander. It didn't matter that she had the King's full support backing her, a lifetime of training was hard to overcome. Wanting to help him save face in front of his Warriors, if that was even possible at this point, she added, "Consider it an order from the King, as communicated through me."

At first he simply continued to stare at her. Then he stepped closer to her, in a threatening enough manner that she felt and heard her team stir behind her. He leaned close enough to whisper in her ear, "Be cautious, *Guardian*." He said her title with disdain. "You do not want me as an enemy."

She stepped back from him and looked at him with determination. "Nor do you want me as yours, Commander," she spoke quietly. "Now my team will remain here, prepared to assist me if I call upon them. You will afford them every courtesy, is that understood?"

Her hands shook, her breath caught, and she felt like a young girl defying her parents. But she stood her ground.

"As you wish, Guardian," he nodded. "Be my guest. And when they kill you and string you up as an example, I shall tell the King you died through sheer stupidity."

With that, he turned his back to her, and stood staring at the civilian line. If it hadn't been for the seriousness of the situation, she would have laughed at his child-like antic. Instead, she turned back to her troupe.

"Be wary," she looked at each of them. "These sound like religious fanatics, and that is never a good start to negotiations."

She expected someone in the group to object to her going solo, but she did not expect it to be the Wizard. "Are you certain it is wise to go in alone?"

She looked deep into Nia's gray eyes, and slowly shook her head. "No. But if we go in looking like we're ready to destroy them, it'll immediately create a barrier in our discussion. They'll feel threatened and at a disadvantage, and will attempt to respond in greater strength."

"Then perhaps I should accompany, and no one else," Nia added, stepping forward and planting her staff next to her. "If the worst should occur, I can generate a portal for a quick escape."

It was a good thought, and for a moment Amaya considered it. Then she realized where it would go wrong. These were religious fanatics, reacting violently because everything they believed in was now in question. The Wizards, claiming to be a separate species from humans, were therefore considered heretical by many.

"I'm afraid this is something I must face alone," she shook her head. "But I thank you for your offer."

Nia opened her mouth to object, but then closed it and nodded ever so slightly, her face still unreadable. "As you wish."

Once again, Amaya looked to Elic, whose strength she had come to rely upon. "Keep them safe while I'm gone."

He smirked and nodded, "Of course. Lieutenant."

A smile crossed her face, the use of her rank a reminder to her that she was strong, and had earned her position as their leader. Her friend always knew what she needed to hear.

Though she still felt trepidation, she turned and faced the civilian line confidently. With her hands disarmingly at her sides, she walked past the disgruntled Commander Argus and into the neutral zone between enemies.

The distance was not great, but she swore she could feel an intense conflict of energy in the magic between the two sides, and it made the hairs on the back of her neck stand up. Resisting the urge to shudder, she quickly approached the line of civilians, all of whom readied weapons at her approach.

Stopping ten feet out, she addressed the closest civilian to her, "I am Amaya Kenla representing the King of Tal. I wish to speak to Trebor Tem."

***

Adrenaline surged through Arkad as his feet carried him swiftly through the pass between mountains. Here at the lowest point between the two monoliths, his army still had plenty of cover amongst the trees.

It was a well-travelled pass, and before they had even approached the summit, he had come across a small group of travelers taking an empty cart into the mountains. They hadn't stood a chance. He alone killed three of them, and Kilack had slaughtered the other two, leaving the rest of his army bloodthirsty and jealous of the first kills of the day.

That blood thirst would be their undoing someday, he knew that. Within himself and the others like him, the lust was strong, but under control. Those who had grown up in the Wastelands, however, could go into an uncontrollable rage. What little intelligence they retained was lost, and they became little more than animals.

Their fear of him is what kept them in check. What made them obey his orders no matter how strong that lust became. He could tear them all apart in an instant.

Or so they believed.

Running only a half dozen feet beside him, Kilack caught the same sight that Arkad did, a small break in the trees just big enough for them to see the city at the foothills of the mountains. "We made better time than anticipated, General," Kilack spoke. He was no more winded than Arkad, their run of dozens of miles barely fazing the orcs.

"I know," he replied, never faltering in his run. "We will reach the clearing long before sunset."

"Do we stop?" his Lieutenant asked.

He considered it. While he felt proud of his soldiers for running so fast without signs of tiring, he also knew that they were too close now. If they stopped to wait for the sun to set, it would increase their chances of being discovered. Thousands of orcs ran behind him, and as they further made their way down the slopes and the narrow pass opened up, they would begin to spread out in all directions, to eventually attack from their pre-designated flanks.

He had miscalculated, though he would never admit that to his troops. They had no choice but to go on. It would not matter. They would reach the city before reinforcements could arrive, regardless, and they would secure it quickly. Once they had the city, no force could overcome them.

"No," he replied, feeling the ground beginning to level out beneath them. Their pace would slow now that they no longer ran downhill, plus he would need to slow down to allow his troops to fan out to their flanks. "Keep going."

Then another thought occurred to him. "The humans I have known in the past were always overly cautious. It is not uncommon for them to build escape tunnels for their royalty and their rich."

"They are cowards," Kilack spat.

"Yes, but they are also industrious and intelligent," he glared warningly at the lieutenant. "Never underestimate humans. But we can use this to our advantage." Raising his voice, he shouted, "Pass the word to all units. On our approach to the city, raze all farms to the ground, and look for any hidden passages. If a unit should find one, enter it and take it into the city, in case we fail to breach the gates."

Immediately he heard his troops pass on the word, and Kilack looked at him with a twisted, toothy smile. "While they defend from without, we shall dismantle them from within."

Arkad smiled at the leap of logic. "Exactly."

He could almost taste it. The freedom and restoration of his people was at hand.

***

Freelance Square was like many of the other squares in Archanon, but that didn't mean Zerek didn't stop for a moment to marvel at it. So many people, walking in and around the various shops and stalls. Even in the blue district, there were so many stores, so many people, so much gold changing hands. It made him wonder how a city of its size could support itself. Did all of the shops survive, or did a lot of them close up shortly after opening?

In the center of the square was a fountain with a stone statue, and while there was no running water spouting out of the statue like he had already seen in several others, it was still an incredible effigy that towered several stories high. Set in a light gray rock, the statue was of a blacksmith pounding at an indistinct piece of metal on an anvil. He and Endel took a moment to approach the fountain and read the dedication upon it.

"In honor of the last true freelancer, Omerin Galatein," Endel read aloud. "Oh I know all about him!"

Zerek smiled at his over enthusiastic friend and looked back to the edge of the square, towards the alley that the bread lady had told him to go down. "Tell me about it," he said idly as he led his young friend towards that alley.

"He was the last smith standing," Endel smiled, "during the Freelance Revolution. All the other smiths, fletchers, everyone who crafted anything had been bribed or forced into joining the guilds. He refused, even when the Queen demanded he do so."

Crossing the square became difficult as a surge of patrons passed by, but Endel, being small and nimble, managed to stay near Zerek. He kept talking through the people. "When he was arrested, there was this public outcry, and all of the crafters of the city refused to work."

They finally pushed through, and stood at the entrance to the small alley. "Yeah?" Zerek looked at Endel. "How'd that work out for them?"

It was rare to see Endel's smile disappear. This was one of those moments, as a terribly sad grimace pulled the edges of his mouth down. "That was Queen Amaru."

That was a name everyone in Tal was familiar with, and Zerek felt his stomach sink. He knew what it meant. Mass arrests, executions, torture. She hadn't stopped until everyone did exactly as she ordered. And even then, she probably kept randomly arresting crafters just to remind them all just who they had defied. It had been centuries ago, but the memory was still fresh in their history. The one time Tal royalty had become worse than Klaralin.

Looking down the alley, Zerek drew in a deep breath, and turned his mind to what lay ahead. He hoped this wouldn't be quite so disastrous. "Come on," he smiled, and they entered.

More than once, Endel had warned him about going into alleys while he had any amount of money or valuables. Not *all* alleys were bad, he had said, but many were. Today, Zerek had no money on him what so ever. No orders, no valuables, except for his dagger, which he kept a hand on to ensure no pickpockets tried take it.

It was definitely more narrow than most of the streets he had stuck to, but not so narrow as to make him feel claustrophobic. It did, however, feel dirty, and several beggars sat or stood along its length, their rags of clothing reeking.

He didn't dare ask any of the homeless, and at first he was surprised that no one asked him for spare change. Then he realized that he and Endel were kids, and no one would guess they had change to spare.

Zerek didn't know whether to pity them or despise them. The city guards seemed to do a good job keeping them off of the main streets, so Zerek hadn't really seen any before now. He never would have guessed there were so *many* of them. Men and women, children, elderly. The elderly…they looked so frail, he wondered how they had survived the last winter, or how they could possibly survive the coming one.

He began to wonder why the old lady sent him here, but then he realized that the girl was clearly homeless. Only instead of eking out a living as a beggar, she stole what she needed to survive. So that meant he'd have to start asking them.

Scared that one might decide to mug him, like he had heard about, he wrapped his fingers around his dagger and prepared to draw it. Approaching a homeless boy that wasn't much older than Endel, he began, "Excuse me…"

The boy looked at him with sad, blue eyes. The look immediately pulled at his heart, and whatever trepidation he'd felt about the beggars before, it vanished. They were just people. Scared, lonely, frightened, more so than he was.

"Do you have any food," the boy asked, his voice weak and high-pitched.

"Um," he looked at Endel. "No, I'm sorry."

"Oh," the boy turned his head down and stared at the rags he'd wrapped his feet in.

"Look, I'm looking for someone. A girl. She's maybe my age, or older, I don't know." The boy didn't reply, he just continued to stare down. "Has a torn up gray cloak. Beautiful brown eyes…"

The boy frowned and looked up at him. "Go away. She doesn't want to see you."

When the kid turned to leave, Zerek reached a hand out to stop him, but his hand was snatched up by an adult man. The kid took off at a run, and the man held Zerek's hand so high it strained at his shoulder, and he squeezed hard enough to send jolts of pain into his wrist.

"Ouch!"

"Leave him alone," the man said, glaring down at him with blazing blue eyes. With black hair just past his shoulders, a shadow of a beard just starting, and decidedly nicer, albeit darker clothes than the beggars, the man was an intimidating sight.

"Hey, stop it," Endel charged the man and tried to jump up at his arm to pull it back down. The man shoved Endel away, who hit the wall and slid down onto his butt.

"Don't hurt him," Zerek kicked at the man's shins. The man hadn't been expecting that, and his grip loosened just enough for Zerek to break free and back away.

"Why you little," the man came at him, arms outreached.

Barely thinking about it, Zerek drew his dagger and sliced upwards, the tip of the blade catching the man's palm as he drew back. He looked at his palm, blood trickling down from the cut.

That was when Zerek realized the man was not alone. On either side of them, blocking both paths out of the alley, were pairs of darkly-clad muggers. It was exactly the kind of trap Chessick had warned him about.

One pair moved to restrain Zerek, but then blue-eyed man glanced at Endel, and then held up his wounded hand to stop them.

For a moment, the man stared at Zerek with searching eyes, his mouth slightly open in surprise. Zerek backed up to get closer to Endel, even though that effectively put him up against the wall. "You okay," Zerek asked his friend.

Endel whimpered a little, but nodded and pushed himself up, brushing off his trousers. "Yeah." He looked at the man and asked, "Why'd you do that?"

The man made a point to ignore Endel, and simply stared at Zerek.

"Hey," Zerek stepped closer to him, trying to act braver than he felt. "My friend asked you a question."

The man raised an eyebrow and grinned. "You've got a bit of a fight in you."

"Yeah, I do, and I've got nothing you can steal either," Zerek shifted the dagger in his hand to point the tip up and towards Blue-eyes. "So you best just move along."

Blue-eyes looked at his companions, and then bellowed out a laugh. "She's right. You do have spirit."

The tip of the dagger lowered a little, and Zerek narrowed his eyes, feeling his stomach leap into his throat. "Wait, you know her?"

"Yeah, of course I do," he shook his head. "And I know you've been looking for her. So does she."

Feeling excitement overcome his fear, he stepped even closer, lowering the dagger to his side. "Where is she? Who is she? I mean," he shook his head, "What's her name?"

The man shrugged. "It's not my place to say." He pointed at Zerek's waist, and added, "But you might want to see what it is that note says."

Zerek frowned and looked down to find a small piece of paper tucked into his belt. "How…"

Laughing, the man folded his arms in front of him and leaned back against the wall opposite of Zerek. "Go ahead, read it. We'll wait."

Not sure what to expect, almost fearing the paper, Zerek drew it from his belt and un-crumpled it. The handwriting was surprisingly neat, and easily readable.

It read, 'Top of the Warriors' Tower, midnight. Don't be late.'

The frown on his face must have spoke volumes to the man, who asked, "Not what you expected?"

Looking up at Blue-eyes, he shook his head. "How am I

supposed to get to the top of the Warriors' Tower?"

"If you can't figure that out," Blue-eyes pushed off of the wall, "Then she's too much for you. Come on, we'll escort you back to the square." He began to lead the way out, the pair on that side of the alley parting for them. Zerek followed, with Endel timidly following behind him.

"Oh, and do yourselves a favor," the man looked over his shoulder, glancing first at Endel, and then at Zerek. "Don't come into an alley again unless invited. Wouldn't want her latest crush getting killed."

Zerek's cheeks flushed, and he looked at Endel excitedly. Did the blue-eyed man just admit that the girl had a crush on him?

That put Zerek in a love-induced daze for the rest of the day.

***

The civilian that Amaya had addressed was also the reluctant 'volunteer' to take her to the forge that Trebor used as his 'command post.' Those were the exact words the civilians had used, and she almost laughed outright at hearing him say it.

They were highly inexperienced, and if the Warriors decided to intervene by force, it would be a slaughter. Doing so would have one of two effects on the kingdom: it would either legitimize their cause, turning who knows how many innocents into martyrs, or it would strike terror into the hearts of any who would dare stand up against the war effort.

She wanted neither for her kingdom.

The forge was one of several large warehouse-sized structures in the Forge District, and seemed no more special than any of the others. That didn't exactly sit well with her, the uniformity that had begun to crop up in large structures. Where was their unique character? The first one had been special, but the fifth? Tenth? Anything that made them special was lost.

They also didn't serve as stores, she quickly realized. Or at least, the one she went into didn't have a store front, not like what could be found at a traditional blacksmith's shop. It was all about production.

Amaya and the volunteer entered through a wide set of double doors akin to a barn's. *Why in the world would they need such a large entrance?*

It didn't take her long to figure it out. There were several horse-drawn carts stored just inside, some with what appeared to be raw ore in them, others with boxes marked as containing weapons – swords, maces, axes. It was the shipping and receiving center of the forge. She also suspected this particular forge was meant to craft only weapons, as she saw no other labels on the outgoing boxes.

Her own sky-blue sword was unique, every Warrior's was. There was no other longsword exactly the shape and size of hers, with the unique channeling lines etched into it to help her focus currents of magic through the blade. The weapons they crafted here? They weren't unique or special. They were just common, ordinary swords, bound for common soldiers. In wartime, Warriors might be forced to use such common weapons, but it was always to the detriment of their combat prowess.

Just past the shipping center, she saw a group of four people talking together. Their conversation quickly ended as Amaya and her unlucky guide approached. The others spread out around one man, whom she assumed was Trebor.

He was actually quite an unremarkable man, at least at first glance. He wasn't much taller than her, and kept his walnut-colored hair short and tidy, along with his goatee. His eyes were the most unremarkable shade of brown she could imagine. Visually, he inspired very little, and she wondered how he could have rallied so many townspeople to his cause.

Then he spoke, and she understood why. "Well hello there," he smiled easily, a charm previously absent suddenly altering her opinion of him. He stepped up to meet her and extended a cordial hand. "I am Trebor Tem."

It wasn't what she expected. She was prepared for an aggressive man, ready to sacrifice lives to make his point. Instead, he was friendly and kind, and his voice was disarmingly buoyant. She took his proffered hand and replied in kind, "Amaya Kenla."

"I think she's a Guardian," her guide said, looking her up and down. Amaya was a little surprised that the guide had figured that out, but did her best to hide it.

"Oh my," Trebor tilted his head to one side in genuine shock. "It appears I've finally caught the attention of the King."

She narrowed her eyes at him and, after he refused to let go of her hand, forcefully yanked it back. "Yes," she shook her head. "Shutting down the Forge District has that effect."

"Well good," he laughed easily and looked around at his companions, who all nodded in agreement. They all appeared much more concerned about her presence than he did. "Excellent, I'm glad to hear that."

Something didn't feel right about the cook. He was just too jubilant, too friendly, smiled too easily. How could someone like him rally regular citizens to take up arms against their own people? She immediately went on guard, and tried to prepare herself for the unexpected.

Looking at his companions for a moment, she then leveled her eyes at Trebor and squared her shoulders. "By order of the-"

"Can I see the brand?" Trebor interrupted.

She paused, her line of thought broken. "Uh, yeah. Sure."

It was a tiny mark, branded by hot iron onto the inside of her left wrist, twin longswords crossing each other, like the logo of the kingdom itself, but instead of guarding a mountain, they guarded a crown.

As quickly as she could, she loosened her left wrist guard and pulled back the cloth beneath to show off the mark. Trebor examined the mark as if he were examining a small sample of ore or food, with skeptical eyes. "Uh huh, I see. Looks fresh," he looked at her. "A new recruit?"

It was a clever ploy on his part, to try to make her seem less legitimate, inexperienced. She knew better and continued with her original thought. While covering it back up and securing her guard, she continued her previous statement, "By order of the King, I demand that you lay down arms and go about your business immediately." She had said it with as much authority in her voice as she could muster, and in the past, that had always commanded the respect and attention of everyone. She also noticed that Trebor's companions immediately looked far more worried about her.

Trebor, on the other hand, laughed jovially and stepped back, crossing his arms. "Oh, I see. I thought you had come to actually listen to what we have to say."

"You mean what *you* have to say," her patience was running thin, and the tone of her voice reflected that.

"I speak for everyone on the side of the gods," he shrugged easily.

Some of the others nodded their agreement. "The kingdom has begun to lose its way. In fact it lost its way some time ago."

"I don't care," she lied. Initially she had come in to actually speak with him about his desires, to try to speak reason to him. However, his mannerisms made her realize that the moment she gave him any fuel to downplay her authority, he would have the upper hand. Perhaps he already did. "His Majesty, the King, has decreed an end to your activities. You will follow his command at once." She paused and narrowed her eyes, analyzing Trebor's nonchalant appearance. "Under my orders, everyone involved will be allowed to go home, resume their lives as if this never happened. No charges will be brought against you and your people."

"Oh how very kind of you," Trebor replied, his voice a little less jovial and a little more sarcastic.

"Yes, it is," she narrowed her eyes. "But the offer stands only so long as you accept now. If you refuse now, a dungeon is in your future, and in your," she glanced at his companions, "lieutenants'."

She expected Trebor to laugh. Instead, he simply furrowed his brow and looked thoughtfully at her feet. His companions looked genuinely worried.

"Tell me, Miss Kenla, do you believe in the gods?"

The question did not entirely catch her off guard, but she marveled at his ability to change the subject with no segue. "Of course I do."

"Then you should know that the gods are on our side," he unfolded his arms and planted his fists on his hips. She took note of the short sword strapped to his left hip. She also felt no power from him. Thankfully, he was not a Mage and would prove little challenge in combat, if it came down to that.

"Demons have been allowed to go free," Trebor continued, his voice slowly turning colder, less amused. "To influence our royalty. A weapon of the demons now rests in the hands of this 'Keeper of the Sword,' giving him unnatural powers. A member of the Covenant has been unfairly discharged from service, banished from the Order because he stood up to everyone to capture and interrogate a demon." His face was slowly turning to anger, venom in his voice. It was a frightening transition to behold. "Our kingdom has lost its way. And if we do not correct it, then the world will end in cataclysm."

She narrowed her eyes at him. "And letting the orcs slaughter us wholesale is your answer?"

A horrid grin crossed Trebor's face. "It is our reckoning. We must be made to pay for our sins, to turn the scales of judgment back in our favor. And only those who are righteous in the eyes of the gods will be spared the sword. By doing this," he waved to the cold forge, "we secure our futures."

With her fear increasing, she began to realize he truly was not in his right mind. There was no way she could reason with him, even if she used what knowledge she had of The Order to counter his assertions.

"And the wicked, the *dishonest,* the abhorrent will perish." He had emphasized dishonest. She cued on that. Something, she didn't know what, itched at the edge of her conscious mind, a clue in his words.

"Dishonest," she repeated quietly, narrowing her eyes. "Abhorrent. Who among your peers would you say that describes?"

"Any who do not follow the teachings of the Cronal, of the Covenant, our leaders in faith and righteousness." He looked at her with confidence in his eyes, spoke with anger in his voice, all of his calm demeanor gone. Something was angering him. Anger, not fear.

He wasn't afraid. That was key. Why wasn't he afraid? She could understand people fearing the new reality they all lived in, that the Covenant was wrong and there *were* other intelligent beings in the universe. The most devout of the Order feared it more than any others, everything they believed put into question in one nearly cataclysmic week.

So why wasn't Trebor afraid? Anger could be fueled by fear, but she neither saw nor heard fear in him. Just cold anger.

Anger and hatred.

"And any," he finished, "who disobey their oaths."

Those were the words that connected it in her mind. That made her realize where she had seen that kind of anger before. Where that anger came from.

Her face slackened, and she asked him softly, "Where is she?"

Trebor's lieutenants all looked at her and each other in confusion or shock. Trebor's face only hardened. He said nothing, but she could almost feel the anger rolling off of him. Or perhaps felt it within herself.

"A girlfriend? Wife?" She glanced at the lieutenants as their eyes widened when she said wife. "Ex-wife?"

She noticed Trebor's hands began to shake, his fists still on his hips, but clenched so tight now that his knuckles turned white. Still Trebor did not respond.

Folding her arms, she nodded. "So that's it, then? That's what this is all about? Your wife left you?" Anger began to boil up in her, and she felt her face harden. "You would risk thousands of lives, the defeat of our entire army at the hands of the orcs, because you can't stand the fact that she left you."

Trebor's hands began to lower, still in fists, but no longer on his hips. She paid as close attention as she could to his hands without taking her eyes off of his. The anger she saw in him was a reflection of her own. "Shut your mouth, you filthy witch."

A surge of adrenaline coursed through her, but she managed not to act, not yet. She likewise slowly lowered her arms, ready to draw at any moment. "That's it, isn't it? She left you for another man. And you can't stand that." She noticed his right hand slowly reach across his waist towards his sword. It was still shaking.

"She broke her oath," he growled. "She vowed before the gods to be with me always." His voice grew louder, his anger becoming almost uncontrollable. "A traitor like you could never understand. You don't know," he shook his head, looking her up and down. "I had you pegged the moment you walked in that door. You've never earned the loyalty of a good man." Now she felt her own hands shaking, and it was all she could do to keep from drawing. "You don't deserve a good man."

It almost happened. In her mind's eye, she saw herself drawing, charging her sword instantly with an ethereal charge, and throwing it out in a wave of destruction that killed Trebor on impact, threw him into the forges, breaking his skull upon the lead basins...

No, she thought to herself. *Don't let him beat you.*

"I see," she said, trying desperately to keep her own emotions out of her voice. There was just a slight tremor in her words. "She was unfaithful to you." She tilted her head to one side. "What did you do to lose her loyalty?"

Even she couldn't have expected his reaction. In an instant, his sword was unsheathed and swinging at her in a fast, angry arc. It was only instinct that allowed her to push out a magical shield just enough to deflect the tip from cutting her throat.

Backing away, she resisted the urge to draw her own weapon, and simply maintained her shield. He came at her again, swinging with an enraged shout, the blade missing her cleanly this time as she dodged and stepped to the side. When he came at her again, she used her open palm to try to push him away with magic. Mages used weapons, and sometimes even armor pieces, to focus their powers, weapons allowing the most deadly concentration of magic. But without using such focusing techniques, her power was weak, and that was what she wanted.

He stumbled backwards as the wall of magic pushed against him. She glanced at the lieutenants, all of whom appeared ready to defend their leader, but none actually drew. The man who had escorted her in had drawn his weapon, but he did not attack. In fact, he backed away against the wall, horror on his face.

"I'll kill you!" Trebor lunged at her. She finally drew her weapon, but only used it to deflect him and carry his weight past her. For good measure, she gave him a little boot to the butt to help him along. He almost crashed into a crate, but managed to steady himself.

"You don't care about righteousness," she scowled at him as he reeled on her. She continued talking as she easily deflected his untrained, undisciplined, angry attacks. "You just think that the orcs will take her life, and spare yours." She parried. "You want them to do what you don't have the courage to." He lunged again, and she just stepped aside, nudging him away with another unfocused push of magic. "To take her life, to satisfy your vengeance."

He stopped his attacks, his breathing heavy and ragged, his eyes full of fire. "You don't understand," he spat at her. "She ran away with *him*." Coming at her again, he swung is sword from overhead in a wide arc.

Deflecting the blow easily and stepping aside, she laughed, "So you want them to take her life *and* her lovers. What a coward…"

"That's not what I mean, you blind idiot," he pivoted on one foot and swung for her legs, but her blade met his, and she slid his up and over to plant his weapon's tip firmly into the ground. "She ran away with my son!"

That stopped her from doing anything else. With his weapon safely immobile for the moment, she looked at him in shock. "After

I caught her and that bastard together, she took my son and ran away." He tried to pull his weapon back, so she disconnected their blades and stepped back to a safe distance.

Trebor held his weapon ready, but he did not strike again, his breathing hard and his face red. She could keep him at bay indefinitely, his skills and fitness far inferior to her own. "She took my boy. Said I wasn't worthy of him, of either of them. I couldn't stop them," he lowered his weapon, staring at her with pain in his eyes. "He's just a baby. He can't choose for himself. He's innocent. He's…he's not like her. Not evil. Not treacherous. Not yet…"

She did not lower her guard, but she did look upon him with a better understanding. Her own anger finally subsided, and she was thankful for that. It wouldn't have taken much for her to destroy him, and the longer they fought, the more she was tempted to take his life.

That would only turn him into a martyr. Instead, this is what she needed. This is what his lieutenants needed to see.

Furthermore, she realized she was wrong. The Order wasn't just a weapon for his anger. "You think the gods will protect the innocent. So you think the orcs will slaughter her, spare your son, and somehow reunite the two of you."

He looked down at the ground, finally looking defeated. For a long time, he didn't reply. Amaya watched as multiple emotions contorted his face. Anger, despair, deep sadness.

"Only if I am worthy," he finally said.

He was defeated. Not so much that she had defeated him in combat, but in that he felt unworthy. Trebor Tem had failed himself, failed his son, failed his family.

Slowly she lowered her weapon, eyes fixed on the sky-blue blade, her own pain coming to the surface. Her own failures. And the man before her was no longer one to be feared, nor respected. She simply pitied him.

A deep void formed in her stomach when she realized that. A darkness that began to consume her soul. *What does that mean for me?*

"Trebor…" she began, but found that words failed her. What could she possibly say to him?

And then the bells rang. Only one at first. Then another. And another, until it was a cacophony of rings echoing through the walls. They were soon followed by the horns of the Warriors.

The sounds didn't quite register at first, and she looked around in confusion, as did everyone else.

Then her heart hardened when she realized what those bells were for. Why the Warriors called out with their horns.

The orcs had come.

Episode 5

THE SIEGE OF VALARAS

When Arkad cleared the tree line, the sun had not yet fallen behind the Ilari Mountains. They found a vast clearing marked only by thousands of tree stumps, echoes of the great woods that once reached all the way to Valaras.

Their timing was perfect, even if they had arrived far sooner than he had planned for. The sun helped conceal their approach, and even once they reached the range of enemy archers and Mages, their adversaries would still be blinded by the light.

If they reached the city walls fast enough. "Faster!" he shouted, the city still miles away. Then he let out a battle roar that surged his troops ahead.

They had a clear line of sight to the farms ahead, the tree stumps closer to the city having long been cleared out for fresh new farmland.

He knew of no two-legged species that could run as fast as orcs, so he felt confident. Confident that they could tear through the farmlands, killing any who stood in their way, and reach the city walls before the sun completely fell behind the peaks.

This was their time. This was their victory.

His group reached the first farm in a matter of minutes, and fell upon it like a great wave. It was surrounded by fields of grain, but just off to his right he saw a small stable. Several humans streamed out from the house to his left, running desperately for the safety of the city walls, still so far away.

Someone in the stable must have seen them coming - a moment later two humans broke out and raced upon the backs of their horses towards the city. That was fine. Even if they didn't catch the horses, the cowards would perish soon enough.

He reached the house, and reveled in the power he wielded in his enchanted axe. He pointed the head of his weapon at the house and willed the tantalizingly powerful energy within to stream forth in a concentrated burst. The house instantly exploded in a fiery death, and he found himself roaring in cheer.

To his right, Kilack used his own enchanted weapon to pelt the stables with shards of ice, tearing it to pieces and slaughtering the animals that remained inside.

Arkad wanted to lead the charge forward again, but they had to investigate any potential secret tunnel in the farm he had just destroyed. While the house was badly damaged, its frame remained intact and the fire was far too hot to enter. He looked to another of his orcs wielding a dark-steel mace, the silent command clear. The orc swung his mace, releasing an explosive wave of arcane energy that obliterated the failing structure and scattered its burning carcass out into the fields.

He and his group entered the remaining hulk of the house, pieces of the frame and chimney still intact, all burning. He felt the heat all around him, and many of the flames licked at his armor, raising even his enchanted armor's temperature. He was used to heat, in fact he missed it, and he was sorely tempted to remain a moment.

It was for naught, as they found no signs of a hidden passage in the building's remains, nor did Kilack find one in the stable. That would leave it up to one of the other groups. So with another battle roar, he led the charge to Valaras.

It was a calculated risk, breaking the line to investigate the farmhouses, barns, and stables. But he smiled in satisfaction when he noticed one group, off to his left, disappear into the ground. They had found it, and as he expected, it was one of the most outlying farms.

His heartbeat thundered in his ears as they drew closer and closer to the city. The bells rang and horns wailed, probably since long before he could hear them above his own pounding pulse. The humans knew they were coming, and would be prepared.

Not prepared enough, he thought. This would be the shortest siege in history, he was sure of it.

With renewed excitement and bloodlust, he surged forward, leading the charge for his people, for his entire species. This was their chance. This was his destiny.

Everything became a blur, moments in time that passed in a blink. He covered the miles faster than even he thought possible. Those who did not stop to investigate or destroy farms made it first, and waves of energy bolted from atop the city wall. Mages attacked, and many of his kin were killed before they could reach the wall. Those few who wore the dark-steel armor were fortunate enough not to be killed outright, but it hampered their advance.

However, the humans were far outnumbered, and their wall offered little protection. Arcane and elemental energy streamed forth to converge on the humans, burning, freezing, obliterating, *destroying* the enemy, decimating their numbers before he arrived.

With the bloodlust ever increasing, he willed the power of his weapon to leap from the darkened blade and burst forth upon the wall. Elation filled his veins when two of the humans were engulfed by his attack, screaming in their demise and falling back into the city.

Orc archers added their own assault to the mix. Human Mages threw up shields to try to protect themselves from the onslaught, to protect the city from errant attacks. They gave up their attack against the orcs, and focused only on protection.

When he could finally touch the wall, his madness began to wane, the bloodlust fading under strained control. Control he had lost in those minutes on the fields.

Taking in deep breaths, his nostrils burning with the smell of charred flesh, he calmed himself as best as he could. His anger made him useless to his people. Flashes of his own past failures echoed in his mind, and threatened to anger him further, but he pushed the images of burning homes and his kin on their knees out of his mind.

This was their moment. He could not lose it.

Kilack immediately joined his side. The guardians above were too busy defending to pay attention to what went on below their field of view and did not attempt to attack them. Together they looked back out into the fields and saw the qrishag lumbering towards the city, still miles away. Did the humans even notice them yet, or were they too focused on the closer, more immediate threat?

"The assault proceeds well, General," Kilack smiled, his fangs and the red of his gums making him look amazingly terrifying. "The humans were completely unprepared for us."

Arkad wanted to celebrate with his companion, but something was amiss. Something horrible. "Where are the Wizards," he asked. "Have you seen any Wizards amongst those upon the wall?"

His smile fading, Kilack glanced around and then shook his head. "No. Not one."

A dark pit began to form in his stomach. "We cannot wait for the qrishag," he growled. He finally took in his surroundings well enough to get his bearings, and realized he was only a short distance north of the southern gate.

"Gather as many darksteel brothers as you can," he placed a hand on Kilack's shoulder. "Quickly. We must use our powers to try to breach the doors now."

Kilack obeyed without question, and drew himself out from under Arkad's heavy hand to issue orders to their soldiers. Tightening his grip on the axe, Arkad lumbered south along the wall. Most of the orcs stayed far enough back that they could help keep up the assault. Every common soldier, whether they had archery skills or not, had come with at least rudimentary bows and arrows for the initial phase of the attack.

He ordered the few dark-steel-clad soldiers he could find to follow him, knowing the risk he took. Arrows could not last forever, but the enchantments could. If so many of his brothers hadn't been killed in that attack upon Archanon...

Suddenly a blast of magic smashed into a cluster of three orcs before him, and he looked up to see that a Mage had wisely decided to peak over the battlements and unleash an attack upon them. Arkad, along with the two other darksteel orcs behind him, lashed out with their enchanted weapons. The Mage ducked behind the battlements, and if their return fire did not slaughter him, he was too frightened to look over again.

After several minutes and a handful of similar engagements, Arkad made his way to the southern gate. This section was much more heavily guarded. The wall was intentionally recessed to give those upon it more room to focus on defending it, and they used this to great effect. None of his orcs had made it into that deadly zone, not alive.

His anger flared greater with every orc loss, and he struggled in desperation to control his rage. To keep the memories at bay. To not let fury overcome his intellect.

The humans were smart. Mages kept shields up, and the few wielding crossbows ducked between them to fire a bolt, then duck back to reload. There were enough of both that little could be done.

Before long, Kilack joined him, bringing nearly a dozen dark-steel orcs with him. With the couple Arkad had found, he thought it would be enough. "Bring weapons to bear upon the defenders," he shouted, raising his double axe and pointing it towards a Mage. "Do not stop until none remain upon the battlements."

With a battle roar, he unleashed the fiery power contained within the core of his weapon. Again, and again, and again, he let loose the power, as did his soldiers. The Mages' shields held, at first, and only because of their combined strength.

But the orcs had numbers, and greater power imbued within their weapons. Arkad did not know if it had been Klaralin or some other powerful being that had enchanted their weapons and armor, but he silently thanked them as he watched the shields fail, and the Mages either duck out of the way, or suffer the terrible consequences.

When there were few left upon the battlements, he looked over the sea of orc heads as they began to surge forward.

"No," he bellowed, his soldiers stopping their advance at once. Flanked on either side by several of their elite, dark-steel brethren, he could only imagine how terrifying he looked to the common, unrefined, uncivilized orcs that they had brought from the Wastelands. "Move," he shouted, waving his hand for them to part.

In seconds, the way was clear, the heavy ironwood doors directly in front of them.

Without giving the order, Arkad led the attack, marching forward and launching the most powerful fire attacks he could at the door. His kin joined him, and the space between the battlements became a torrent of magic. Fire blew against the door, ice shattered against it, arcane energy blasted it.

Ironwood was a special kind of wood, and its special properties was why they had sent a contingent of orcs into those woods to try to

procure some. When first cut from their roots, the wood of those trees were completely normal, bendable, burnable, breakable. But when tempered in the right kind of heat and infused with the kind of arcane energy that all Mages wielded, the wood became as hard as iron.

But even iron could not withstand the intensity of their unstoppable attack. It took well over a minute, but by the time they marched into the cul-de-sac between the battlements, the doors clearly bent inward, and moments later, they burst, their attacks spilling into the city and tearing apart the buildings beyond.

None of the defenders had been stupid enough to stand behind the doors, but he knew they stood to the sides, ready to attack the orcs the moment they entered.

He cried out their success in a terrifying roar, calling all of his soldiers who could hear to the entrance. Those not clad in dark-steel near them began to stream past, their bloodlust blinding them to strategy. He sneered at them, and almost ordered them to stop, but knew their numbers were too great, and the enemy would fall before the wave of his kin.

The enemy walls had been breached. The siege was over.

The invasion had begun.

***

It happened fast, faster than Amaya could have imagined. She swore the bells and horns had sounded only minutes ago, but by the time she had left the Forge District and made her way to the western side of the city, the orcs had reached the wall.

With her team right behind her, minus Nia who had left to report the orc attack, they had run to the wall near the southern entrance. This brought them closest to the Warriors' Guild complex, and she knew they would need to protect it at all costs.

As they approached one of the many staircases that led up to the battlements on the wall, they all came to a sliding stop as there was a sudden explosion of magical energy that assaulted the defending Warriors and soldiers protecting the southern gate. Parts of the battlements crumbled against the onslaught, the walls never having received the enchantments that Archanon had to protect them.

A city soldier flew off of the wall and landed a dozen feet away from Amaya and her team.

She immediately knew what was happening, and what they needed to do.

"Elic, Idalia, Nerina, get on the other side of the doors." They immediately moved without question, and she added, "Stay clear of the doors."

The southwestern entrance was like any other entrance to a city, and led into an open square, giving room to defend against any attackers. Usually defenders had time to setup additional defenses, but for the orcs to already be here, she realized they had been given little warning, and there were no other battlements in the square.

Looking at the nearest stairs up to the wall, she saw that there would be plenty of room for an extra body at the top of those stairs without impeding troop movements. "Peren, get up there," she pointed. "Do not expose yourself to the other side, wait for them to breach into the square. The rest of you, stay with me."

More Warriors arrived, led by Commander Argus. He took one look at Amaya's troop formations, looked up at the battlements where streams of magic flew overhead, and grimaced. Without saying a word to acknowledge her quick thinking, he issued orders for his troops to bracket the entrance.

"Commander," she nodded to him as he came up beside her to await the inevitable.

"Lieutenant," he responded without looking at her.

The assault finally began against the ironwood doors with a reverberating thunder. The constant pounding, the doors vibrating, pushing further and further inward like a steady war drum, it almost terrified her. But she had no time for terror. None of them did.

"I never expected to defend this city against orcs," Argus stated with an almost casual voice. She barely caught the hint of anger in his voice.

Thinking back to her encounter with Trebor, she realized that it hadn't been his anger or his agenda that had allowed him to inspire others to take the Forge District by force. It was their fear. Fear of everything that had changed in the past few months.

Maybe change has become the new normal, she thought to herself. *Maybe we either adapt to the change, or we get run over by it.*

Realizing what they were about to face, even though she hadn't looked over the wall to see how large of a force was pitted against them, she shuddered and looked at the Commander. "I need you to know, should something happen to me." She paused and waited until he looked at her. "Trebor won't be a problem anymore. Or at least, his group won't." It wasn't entirely a lie. Those who followed Trebor hadn't outwardly renounced him, but she had seen the look upon their faces when he admitted his motives.

Argus made little effort to hide his surprise, and in that moment, his demeanor towards her changed forever. "Perhaps I was wrong about you."

She did not take any comfort in his words, did not revel in his admission. She couldn't. There was too much pain behind her, and too much work ahead of her.

The doors bent inward around the central brace, the iron bar itself groaning and bending and creaking, threatening to give way.

"We only need to hold them off long enough," Argus stared at the doors as he spoke.

"I know," she nodded. "Reinforcements will be coming soon."

And then the doors breached, a torrent of magic following, shooting between the two flanks to smash against the buildings at the far end of the square, destroying their walls and laying waste to anything inside.

The stream of magic continued only for a short time, and then ceased. It was soon followed by a terrifying roar that made the hairs on the back of her neck stand up on end. What monster had made such a terrible roar?

Only a few moments later, the orcs streamed in. The moment the first had stepped through, clad in scaly leather armor and wielding a haphazardly crafted sword, Peren's first loosed arrow struck it right in its neck, catching it off guard.

With trained ease, Amaya charged her blade with ethereal magic, her skin tingling as she extended her will into the cold, sky-blue steel. More orcs streamed in, tall, muscular creatures that she had become too familiar with in the past month.

Drawing her sword up beside her, making the blade parallel to the ground, she thrust it forward and willed the arcane power out. It flowed easily and instantly along the etched markings in the flat of her blade, gathered in the point, and shot out like an impossibly fast arrow. It caught one orc square in the chest and threw him back into his following companions like a sledge hammer. Every Mage present did the same thing, destroying the front ranks of the orcs in an instant.

But more kept coming, streaming through the entrance like a horde of angry ants issuing forth from their mound. She charged again, fired again, managed to do so a total of four times before the first orc was upon her and the Commander.

In that moment, chaos reigned. The orcs were strong, powerful, but not well protected or trained. Amaya used a combination of magic shields, sword play, and charging her blade to give it strength against their weapons and armor, and cut through three in a matter of seconds.

But the stream of enemies did not end, and very shortly into the battle, orcs clad in the darkened steel armor joined the battle. As she had noticed in previous battles, they fought smarter, were stronger, and their armor and weapons were reinforced with enchantments.

She tried to make her way to the nearest one, cutting through the lesser orcs as she went. Her target was focused on others, not her. He was focused on Peren.

Wielding a blackened sword, he pointed it up at Peren, and she felt the surge of magic. "Peren, down!"

Somehow he heard her above the roar of battle and jumped away from the stairs, towards the other side of the wall, just when a blast of lightning shot out of the sword's tip. It missed Peren, barely, and lanced into the sky.

Amaya's distraction was enough to allow another orc to get in past her sword, and its mace connected with her arcane shield, softening the blow enough that she wasn't wounded, but it still hurt when it clanged off of her shoulder armor.

The pain and anger fueled her, and she jabbed her sword straight into the orc, using the magic she had pre-charged in it to force her blade completely through her opponent. The blade had a clear shot at the darkened steel orc, and she let loose what power was left in it.

But another orc got in the way, and the blast caught it in its shoulder instead, spinning it around until it crashed to the ground.

Now she had the darksteel orc's attention. It looked straight at her, and pointed it's sword at her.

Pulling her weapon free of the slain enemy, she ducked behind her dead opponent, who slammed into her when the blast of lightning magic immolated one side of it. She could smell the biting stink of burnt flesh. Falling back to one knee, she pushed the corpse aside, and gathered her powers into the strongest shield she could between her and her newest enemy.

Another blast of lightning struck her shield, and her shield held, but only barely, and she felt herself instantly grow weary and disoriented. She had no choice but to rush him, or his next blast would tear through her shield and cook her in her armor.

Springing forward, she shouted her challenge at the orc. He smiled and pulled back into a defensive stance, keeping his sword between them. Raising her weapon above her head, she brought it down hard, the orc pivoting to deflect her blow. But training had taught her long ago not to put all of her strength into such an attack, and instead of deflecting her and throwing her off balance, she pulled her weapon back at the moment of impact, and jumped back so that the orc's counterstrike missed her.

Before she could even think about attacking again, Vin leapt up onto the orc's back, daggers in hand, and used both to slice open the orc's throat. The monster dropped his weapon and clutched at his throat. He fell to his knees, Vin still riding his back.

The orc glared at Amaya, shock at his defeat evident in his eyes, and then he fell face-first.

A lesser orc tried to attack her as she watched, but she saw it coming, deflected it's stone axe, and cut its back open from upper left to lower right, severing its spine.

"Thanks, Vin," she huffed, the battle already wearing heavily upon her. They had not been involved in a pitched fight like this yet. All of their previous assignments had been attacks upon smaller groups of orcs. Attacks they had planned ahead for, and executed nearly flawlessly. This was the first time they defended against an overwhelming enemy.

But in that moment, everything changed. From over the wall, she heard the distant wale of horns. One of those horns she recognized instantly as the deep, throaty horn of Tal. Another she recognized as the higher-pitched horn of their ally, Erien. The others she had never heard before, but she knew what it meant.

The horns of the Allied Forces. The Wizards had come through on their promise. Out there, in the fields, the combined armies of all four kingdoms had arrived and surrounded the attacking enemy.

Orcs everywhere suddenly stopped their assault, and time seemed to stand still. Even the defenders ceased battle and looked around in excited hope. Then came several roars from the other side of the wall, different from the triumphant roar that had initiated the invasion of Valaras. These roars were filled with fear.

It must have been an order to regroup, since every single orc turned tail and streamed back out of the city.

The defenders cheered, Amaya with them. Commander Argus gave the next order, "Make safe the city!"

As the last of the orcs streamed through the destroyed doors, a line of his Warriors formed up at the entrance, and used their powers to erect a line of shields that protected them all. More Warriors and city soldiers climbed the stairs to the wall to help incur more casualties in the retreating orcs.

Victory was theirs!

***

The city would be theirs, Arkad knew it now. His army was an endless, unstoppable stream of terror that flowed through the gates, and it would only be a matter of time before they pushed past the defenders. Even if they didn't, the unit that had found the hidden tunnel would stream forth from within the city to attack the enemy from behind.

He smiled when he realized that they would not need the qrishag. At most, they might need them to help hold the city against counterattacks, but that was it.

With a fanged smile, Arkad brandished his axe and decided it was time to join the troops. He lumbered forward into the stream of his kin, standing far above them all, able to see into the square beyond, at the chaos of the defenders falling back, further and further.

And then the first horn sounded. A deep, throaty howl that he almost mistook for a qrishag bellow. That thought was soon dispelled when three other distinct horns called out.

All of them from the west.

He and the stream of orcs came to a sudden stop, and all turned towards the mountains. The sun was just falling behind the cliffs, but it did nothing to hide the new arrivals.

An army of humans stretched from north to south, completely cutting them off from the mountains. Their army was just far enough out that they contained the still-advancing qrishags. Countless shafts of blue-white light dotted the enemy line, from which more troops emerged, some mounted on horses, others on foot, all led by Wizards.

There were more Warriors and soldiers in their ranks than he thought existed on all of Halarite. All clad in gleaming, brand new armor, and wielding steel swords.

The last spark of the sun died behind the mountains, casting the city in shadow, and his spirits sank with it. "Impossible," he whispered. How could they have gathered such a force against them so quickly, even with Wizards?

As lessons long ago taught passed through his mind, he felt his face grow warm and his hands numb. *Never underestimate your enemy,* a master once taught him. *Always assume the worst, and you will never be surprised.*

He had committed the worst sin any general could. And it was about to cost him everything.

"No," he growled. "NO!" With his stomach turning in disgust and hatred, he roared out the call to retreat. "To the desert," he shouted at those closest to him. "Retreat to the other side of the city, make for the desert and make for the Wastelands!"

Then he looked around for his second in command. They could not all escape if the enemy over-ran them, and there were still orcs running with the qrishags. "Kilack!"

His most trusted friend was at his side in moments, "General!"

Grasping his friend's shoulder tightly, he looked intently at him. "We have to give them time to escape. We have to turn the qrishags around, and I need your help. Where is the rest of our unit?"

As he looked around, Kilack scowled, "All of the Wasteland orcs are fleeing."

That was what Arkad had ordered, so he did not share his friend's disdain. However, to his relief, many dark-steel orcs began to gather around him. They were fearless, and always loyal to their general.

He began shoving his way through the lesser rabble towards the now-advancing enemy. "Spread out, tell those lieutenants to turn around and fight!" With a roar, he cleared the way in front of him, and he and the remaining dark-steel commanders took off at a run, as fast as their charge to the city had been.

Arkad bellowed out another roar, a command to the qrishag unit directly ahead of him to turn around, but they were still a mile out, and his roar could not be heard above the noise of battle.

It was then that the Wizards let loose their first attacks against the qrishags. Bolts of lightning, streams of fire, shards of ice, all loosed at once upon the lumbering beasts that still had not turned around.

Many orcs were struck down in that first salvo, but there were dark-steel among them, and they used their enchanted armor to absorb as much of the initial attack as they could. They countered with everything they had, sending out salvos of their own elemental and arcane attacks, all of which vanished harmlessly against the Wizards' shields.

As Arkad and the others broke completely free of the Wastelands orcs, his companions spread out and began to run down the line, roaring their commands. Whether or not they were heard, the unit commanders must have seen them charging, and must have realized what they intended. The qrishags began to turn around, and within moments, lumbered into a run.

The giant beasts could run faster than even the orcs, when necessary, but only for very short distances. This must have surprised the attackers, for there was a sudden lull in their stream of elemental attacks.

Off to Arkad's left, he saw the enemy cavalry break off and begin to run south, no doubt to circumnavigate the battle and attack the escaping orcs. He grit his teeth and clenched his fists, frustrated that there was nothing further he could do for his troops. Their only chance would be in the sands of the desert, where he hoped the enemy horses were ill prepared for the shifting sands on the dunes.

Turning back to the battle at hand, his grimace turned into a face of elation. The qrishags had reached the Wizards' shields, and even with all of their power, their shields failed against the salvo of enchanted attacks and the physical power of the beasts.

His heart pounded harder, and for the first time that day, sweat began to bead his forehead. He was beginning to tire, and he imagined that the rest of his dark-steel troops felt the same. It was worth it, however, as they were now moments away from catching up to the intense battle.

The world before him exploded in magic, in clashes of steel, in roars, cries, shouts. The human Mages and Wizards focused their powers on the attacking qrishags, and the first one fell before it ever reached the first human. The others, however, plowed right through the enemy ranks, impaling with their horns, trampling, knocking over. The orcs behind them fell upon the enemy ranks with a brutality that rivaled anything he had previously seen.

Bloodlust began to take over Arkad's senses again. He smelled the rage in the air, felt the frustration in his veins. They had taken his victory. The closer he drew to the new front line, the worse his vision hazed, and the greater his murderous intent became.

Never again. He had sworn never again to watch his people fall, but the humans had taken his one and only chance at victory away from him. Tightening his grip on his axe, he surged forward. It didn't matter if they won or lost now, he just wanted them to pay.

As the battle unfolded before him, he roared, a terrifying, enraged cry of pain, anger, and intent. Even his own kin were startled by it.

And then he was upon them. Leaping into the air as high as his adrenaline-fueled muscles would send him, he split his first opponent down his left shoulder, the heat of Arkad's enchanted weapon cutting through the steel chain and plate armor.

From there he went to the next human, a Mage, and let loose upon her a wave of fire that her pitiful shield could not defend against.

It was stupid of him. Enchanted weapons had power of their own, but they still drew upon their wielder for their energy, and he was wasting his in acts of fury. The beads of sweat on his brow turned into streams, but he didn't care. He didn't care how tired he was, how foggy his mind was. He turned to another Mage and cleaved his head off.

Another victim, another Mage, another Warrior, he tore them apart. His soldiers gave him a wide berth, fearful of errant axe swings and bursts of fire.

Then he came upon a pair of Wizards. A young one had defeated him last time, but this time would be different. They were focused on taking down the last qrishag, driving shards of ice into its head as it charged at them. More atrocities. More horror.

So he charged at them with a renewed burst of speed, and roared his challenge. The qrishag crashed to the ground, letting loose a whimper of a roar, and slid to a stop. Just as Arkad was upon them, the Wizards turned. The first didn't stand a chance, never saw the axe blade coming, and she fell in a heartbeat.

But the other, a much older looking woman, blasted him with an arcane attack, the impact of which knocked the air from his lungs and threw him back two dozen feet. He slid to a stop, and cursed. Had it not been for his enchanted armor, he would not have survived.

Grunting and groaning, Arkad slowly stood up and faced his opponent. She wore emerald robes with considerable gold embroidery. Her dark wooden staff was a prim and pristine dark brown rod with a forest-green emerald at the top, an emerald that she now pointed straight at his face.

Without thinking, he swung his axe at her and let loose the most powerful blast of fire he could manage, but she threw up a shield to absorb it entirely. She was temporarily blinded by the wall of fire, so he pushed off of his knees and charged at her, swinging his axe with all of his strength.

She was fast, and powerful, and with a flick of her staff, he was flung to the side, crashing into the corpses of two of his kinsmen.

As strong as his rage was, as badly as he wanted to tear her limb from limb, he realized that he could never defeat a Wizard as powerful as she was. His campaign would end at the hands of a frilly little human in simple cloth robes.

Once again, she pointed her staff at him, but did not slaughter him. Not yet. "I know you are their general," she spoke in a gruff, tired-sounding voice. The sounds of battle rang all around them, and she had to shout to be heard. "I know you command them all. You can end this!"

He snarled at her and picked himself up. She kept her staff trained on him, brandishing it warningly like it could ever hold him back. "You have defeated us here," he growled, "but there are more of us than you know."

She raised an eyebrow, "I assume you refer to your forces deployed to the west? Bound for Saran?"

Stopping short of charging at her, he felt his face slacken. Valaras had been their key target, but it wasn't their only target. It wasn't their only goal in the war.

Looking around at the battlefield, she asked, "Do you really believe this represents the combined forces of the four kingdoms? Even now, half of the Allied troops are engaged in battle with your other army, and they are winning." The Wizard stared at him intently, her eyes pleading. "No more death. No more carnage. You are their general. You can stop this." Her words were passionate and moving, beginning to calm his blood lust just enough for his rational mind to assert itself.

They were defeated, and for a moment he almost wanted to surrender to her. Almost.

But then what? He had seen what the humans had reduced his kin in the Wastelands to. He had seen how a once proud, strong race had been reduced to shambles, to living like animals. Treat a person like an animal long enough, and that's what they become.

If they surrendered, he had no doubt it would continue. Never trust a human. Never trust *these* humans. Never surrender.

"Never," he growled.

She looked sullenly at him, but he prepared himself to charge, crouching low so that he could spring forward. The Wizard gripped her staff with both hands, ready to strike him down. He knew he couldn't get past her powers, could never defeat her.

Not alone, anyway.

With the chaos of the battle around them, she never saw them coming. Orcs from further afield, charging into the fray from behind the enemy ranks. The one who led the reinforcements was smart, he did not roar a challenge, nor did the two dozen orcs behind him.

At the last possible second, the Wizard turned to face the incoming attack, and she managed to begin erecting a shield, but the leading orc barreled right through it and slammed into her, sending her sprawling to the ground, smacking her head against a fallen Warrior's steel breastplate. It didn't knock her out, not immediately, but she was out of the battle.

Arkad stood up straight and nodded to the young dark-steel orc. "General," the leader replied. He recognized the voice as belonging to a young orc named Tezarik.

He also recognized the troops from earlier. They were the ones that had found the hidden tunnel in the farm. "Why didn't you attack the city from within," he demanded. As grateful as he was for the help, victory still might have been possible had Tezarik succeeded.

"The tunnel was sealed off," he shook his head, brandishing his dark-steel claymore. "Almost a mile in. We had to turn back."

Arkad cursed, at the humans and at himself. He had assumed that he knew how humans thought, but clearly things had changed.

These humans had changed.

Arkad took a moment to assess the battlefield. The orcs were falling back towards the city wall, where archers and Mages were prepared to finish them off. There were no enemies in the immediate area, but that wouldn't last long.

Then he felt a small smile creep onto his face as another dark-steel orc appeared from behind the fallen qrishag, clutching a squirming, struggling Warrior by the neck. "Kilack," he breathed. His best friend, his trusted lieutenant. At least he had survived.

Snapping the Warrior's neck, Kilack dropped the body into a crumpled heap, and ran towards them. "General, we should leave, now!"

Grimacing, Arkad looked again upon the battlefield. A unit of Warriors not far away saw them and charged towards them.

They could stay and fight. Die side by side with the rest of their companions. Or worse, be wounded and captured. His troops fleeing through the desert would be hunted down or intercepted. If none of the troops near Saran survived, then there would be no one left to fight for his people.

Unless…

A wicked, toothy smile stretched across his face. "I know how we can strike back at them." He stared with loathsome anger at the approaching enemies. "I know how we can strike at their heart, remind them of the terror they now face."

It would not bring ultimate victory, but perhaps it would make the humans stop long enough to reconsider them, and lick their wounds. He looked back at the mountains to the west, and then at Kilack and Tezarik. "Come. We must retreat back into the mountains."

It was not the first time he had ordered a retreat. But it was the most painful. With only the two dozen orcs surrounding them, they did not have to roar their orders. Silently, Arkad led them into a westward run.

He was exhausted, defeated, his spirits in the darkest depths. It was only the thought of the revenge he would bring down upon them that kept him going.

They would retrace their run through the mountains, and return to the south. It would take weeks to backtrack, especially as exhausted as they were, but they would not stop. Once they reached the south end of the mountains, instead of running back into the Wastelands with their tails tucked, they would turn west.

Towards Archanon.

***

Zerek shivered and wrapped his cloak tighter around himself as he snuck outside of the servant's quarters. The nights were getting colder, with fall just around the corner. He hated the cold.

It was a fool's errand, he knew it. How in the name of the Six was he going to get past the guards at the gate to the Castle District? How was he going to get into the Guild complex, and climb the tower? It wasn't like he could just go explain it to someone.

The conversation played out in his head, *Hey guys, so I'm supposed to meet this beautiful girl on top of the tower, who just happens to be a thief. You don't mind, do you?*

He'd be tossed out on his butt in an instant.

But he had to see her. Had to find her. Had to prove to her that he was worthy.

With that thought, he drew the hood up on the cloak and stalked off as quietly as he could towards the edge of the wall. There were regular guard patrols through the Castle District, so he knew that his best bet would be to cut through the gardens and yards of the rich houses that surrounded the castle grounds.

He had meant to leave his room much earlier, and grimaced when he realized that it was close to midnight. Endel had wanted to go with, but Zerek knew that was a bad idea, so he didn't wake the young boy at the appointed time. Some of the other men in the quarters, however, had stayed up later than usual.

The cloak he wore was black and he hoped it would hide him well enough in the night. Neither of the moons were full, but they still cast enough light that he would have to be careful. Creeping outside of the castle grounds, he was surprised that there were still lights on in some of the houses. Why would anyone still be awake at this hour?

Then he realized that *he* was still awake. And he also realized that some servants did most of their work at night in the castle, and he could imagine the same being said for the wealthy's servants. Would any of their servants work outside at night?

His heart beat faster and faster, and his hands began to shake.

This was stupid, he shouldn't be out doing this. What if he was caught? Or worse, what if he ran into muggers again, out there in the dark? He had his dagger, but the encounter in the alley frightened him.

Standing at the foot of a stone path leading into a small garden, he stopped and stared down at his hands. They were rough hands, miner's hands, calloused and dry. Even only a few weeks since his last shift underground, they still reminded him of what he'd lost.

Suddenly that was all he could think about. His father. Elina. Everyone and everything he'd ever known.

The darkness began to close in around him, and he felt terrified. Every noise, every cricket, the rustling of leaves in the breeze, everything startled him. He moved off of the path and fell to his knees beside a bush, struggling to breathe. He tried desperately to gasp for breath, tears welling in his eyes.

What was happening to him? What was wrong? Why couldn't he breathe or stand or think?

He wanted to go back, but to what? Where? To the quarters? Where he would live a life without his father, without his friend, without...

A leaf crunched under a footstep, and he whirled around, dagger drawn on pure instinct. A small figure stood in the shadows, stared right at him, unmoving. Was it a demon? A ghost?

His hand shook, the dagger threatening to fall out of his sweaty palms. "W-who are you?"

The shadow stepped into the light, revealing a worried, pale face. "It's me," Endel spoke, raising his hands disarmingly.

The weight in his chest lifted, and he heaved a sigh of relief, falling back the last few inches onto his butt. "Endel..."

"What's wrong," the young boy asked, taking another tentative step closer.

Zerek's face grew warm, and he shook his head. "I don't know. No, it's...it's nothing. Don't worry about it."

"You're white as ash, Zerek," his friend shook his head. "What's wrong?"

Glancing at the dagger, Zerek slowly drew in a deep breath, forcing, *willing* his heartbeat to slow down.

Slowly, Endel crouched down in front of him, and looked him in the eyes. Zerek shook his head, gulped down his tears, and pushed himself up. "It's nothing. Just forget about it, please." His friend stood up with him, and the concerned look never left his face, but he nodded his assent.

After Zerek sheathed his dagger, he frowned and asked, "What are you doing here?"

"I woke up and saw you'd left without me." His young friend pouted. "Why'd you do that?"

Heaving a sigh, Zerek shook his head. "Because if I get caught, I don't want you getting in trouble, too."

"Yeah but I know this city better than you do," Endel narrowed his eyes and folded his arms. "Lots better. Do you even know how you were going to get out of the Castle District?"

Zerek looked west, towards the only entrance he knew of. "Sneak past the guards."

Endel rolled his eyes. "Yeah, thought so. Come on, there's more than one way out."

Without hesitating, Endel took off at a run, his boots clomping in the grass. Zerek looked around for any guards, but none came running to the sounds of Endel's steps, so he took off after his friend.

They ran through yards and gardens, hopped over stools and leapt over low hedges, until they came to a section of the inner city wall on the north end. They stooped next to a stone statue of...someone. He didn't recognize who it was and he couldn't read the plaque in the dark.

From there, they had a perfect view of the stone wall, and of steps that led up to the top of it. Steps for guards, Zerek realized, as there was no doubt a walkway along the top of the wall for the guards to patrol.

Except this was an inner-city wall, and there wasn't a guard in sight.

"Where are the soldiers?" Zerek whispered.

"They usually don't patrol the wall at night," Endel shook his head. "What's the point? If any bad guys make it into the city, the outer wall will be the first to deal with them and sound the alarm."

Zerek nodded, realizing it made sense. He'd learned that the Castle District sat within the original city boundaries, but Archanon had expanded outward thousands of years ago, long before Klaralin. The inner wall was a relic, kept up only out of tradition and most likely to separate the richest from the rest of the city.

They waited for a few minutes longer, just to be sure, until Endel led the way to the stone stairwell. They ascended quickly, ducking low so as not to be seen from a distance. They came to the top landing, glanced down both sides of the walkway, and then Endel led the way to the right, bending low below the level of the turrets.

After only a few hundred yards, they came to a stop, and Endel quickly glanced over the ledge into the rest of the city. "Okay, this is it."

Zerek frowned, and then looked over the ledge as well. There was a narrow road on the other side of the wall, and a series of three-story buildings. "This is what," he asked.

"We're gonna jump to that building."

His heart skipped a beat, and he looked at his friend in bewilderment. "What?!" Again he stood up, this time high enough to look over the edge of the wall. Where they stood was level with the roof across the street, but that also meant it was a three-story fall to the street below. "No way!"

Endel looked at him skeptically. "So you're supposed to climb up the watch tower at the Guild, but you can't make this one little jump?"

Zerek's face burned red, and he smirked. "Funny."

Rolling his eyes, Endel stood up and climbed onto the ledge. "Come on, it's easy. The street is really narrow right here."

Without any fear or hesitation, Endel crouched, and then leapt the distance effortlessly. Zerek bolted up to watch, and saw his friend land on the pitched roof easily, dropping to his hands and knees to steady himself. The roof didn't have a very steep pitch, but enough that Zerek feared slipping off and falling to his death.

Once again he looked down at the street below and muttered, "Oh gods…" Someone walked by beneath, completely oblivious to the death-defying acts going on above. Zerek looked up at Endel, who also noticed the passerby, and waved his hand impatiently for Zerek to join him.

He didn't want to. The drop was too far, the risk too great. But then…then he remembered facing off against an orc in the forest, only minutes after his father was murdered. He didn't care about the danger then, he only cared about helping Elina.

And then he remembered the thief's amazing, beautiful face. Her depthless brown eyes. That smile she gave him when she called him 'lover-boy.' He wanted to see her again. He *had* to see her again.

Without another thought, he climbed up onto the ledge. It was only a few inches thick, so it was hard to stay balanced, and he suddenly felt his stomach flutter when he almost fell forward.

Not today, he thought. *I'm not giving in to fear today.* For a moment, he closed his eyes, and pictured everything that made him feel courageous. The thief, Elina, his father, the Wizard from the Allied Council. He grasped the handle of Elina's dagger and drew strength from it, as if her soul inhabited it and flowed into him.

He could do this.

With every ounce of strength he had, he pushed off of the ledge, his eyes flying open as he sailed across the distance. The random passerby was already several houses away. The roof before him seemed to stretch further and further away, as he began to fall downward...

Until his feet made it, right on the very edge of the roof. He fell forward and caught himself with his hands, and in that instant, his spirits soared. He'd done it!

Endel gave a silent cheer, and then helped hold on to him when his left foot slipped off of the edge of the roof.

His stomach sank, but his other foot stayed firm, and he pulled himself up. He collapsed onto his hands and knees, and then turned and sat down, staring back at the wall he had just leapt from. "I can't believe we just did that," he smiled at his friend.

Rolling his eyes, Endel just crouched next to him and clasped a hand on his shoulder. "I used to do it all the time. You'll get used to it."

Raising an eyebrow, Zerek again looked back at the wall. Would he get used to it? Was this going to become the new normal for him? If he met the thief, found out her name, and she fell hopelessly in love with him, would he be sneaking out to meet up with her and have adventures with her over and over again for the rest of his life? *Gods, I hope so.*

Then he realized he'd completely lost touch with reality for a moment. His eyes focused, and he looked back at Endel.

"You okay?" his young friend asked.

Zerek smiled, and replied, "Never better. Come on, it's almost midnight!"

Much to his surprise, they didn't actually climb back down to the street. Endel took them across the rooftops at a dead run, and the ease in which the young boy made every jump, the fact that he knew exactly where to go so that they never ran out of rooftops to run atop, he suddenly suspected that the young boy had lived more in his short life than Zerek thought possible. How many times had he snuck out to scramble across the rooftops? Climbing up to higher roofs, leaping down to lower, leaping across alleys without giving it a second thought.

It suddenly occurred to Zerek that for all Endel's talk, the young boy rarely talked about himself. He always cared more about Zerek's history, or telling Zerek the history of Archanon. So Zerek decided to make it a point to find out more in the morning.

Though their route was rarely direct, they eventually made it to the Red District, where Endel stopped them and they crouched behind a parapet. The watch tower was in sight, but that meant that *they* were in sight of it.

"Why would she tell me to meet her up there," Zerek whispered. "Aren't there guards up there?"

Endel frowned and glanced over the parapet. Then he took an even longer look, smiled, and shook his head. "Apparently not. But someone else is."

Feeling his face flush, Zerek looked up at the tower, and there she was. They were still a block away, but even from there, there was no mistaking her in the moonlight, her slender figure, her tattered cloak billowing in the breeze. Her pale face glowed in the moonlight.

She was looking right at him, and he realized that she had probably watched their entire approach.

Nudging him, Endel said, "Go on. Go get her."

Keeping low, Zerek began to move along the parapet until he was close enough to the next roof, and he leapt across. He still felt uneasy about each jump, but slowly, unsure without the guidance of Endel, he drew closer, until there were no more buildings between him and the Warriors' Guild complex.

It wasn't exactly a fortress, not like the ones he had seen in the smaller towns in the wilderness. The building itself was made of wood, not stone, and where there should have been turrets were instead pitched, pointed rooftops. In fact, if it weren't for the watch tower that dwarfed all surrounding buildings, he would have thought it nothing more than a mansion.

A mansion patrolled by Warriors. The Warriors were all about appearance everywhere he went, and here was no different. Two pairs of Warriors crossed paths near the complex, all of them wearing full chainmail and plate armor. One was a Mage, the other three carried the shields of non-magic Warriors. The two pair conversed for a moment, and then passed by each other, continuing their circuits around the building.

The mansion would be easy to climb, thanks to the latticed wood framing, but getting up it without being seen by Warriors would not be easy.

Zerek looked back up to the top of the tower, and saw the girl staring down at him, her arms folded as if to say 'well, I'm waiting.' He was so close! So close that he couldn't give up now, no matter what.

With an inexperienced eye, he began to search for a good place to climb. Part of the reason the complex stood out was that a large courtyard surrounded it, encircled by a low mortared rock wall with only a handful of arched entrances, and that meant that there was no chance that he could find a place to leap from rooftop to rooftop to get on top of the mansion. Besides, even if he didn't count the tower, the Guild complex was far taller than any surrounding building at five stories. Surely there would be a tale Endel could tell him as to why it had more floors than any other building in the city.

There were a few places that could be promising, but he felt too frightened to even consider climbing down to try them. There were hedges in the courtyard he could hide behind, but if just one Warrior spotted him...

The red torches didn't light up the area as well as the yellow-white torches of the merchant district, so he had that advantage, even with the moonlight. But where on the building could he actually climb up?

Zerek looked up at the thief and saw her shaking her head. She then pointed down and to her right. Following her finger, he saw where she pointed, at a giant tree near that corner of the building. Did she want him to climb up the tree and leap across to the building? That would be a huge mistake, the rustling leaves would make it impossible for him to remain hidden.

Then he realized what she meant. If that corner of the building was like the others, the flat-faced wall would bow out into the rounded turret-like corner, creating a partial natural cover. And the tree would hide him from being seen from a distance once he got above the ground floor. If the latticework framework was the same there as it was on the rest of the building, it would be an easy place for him to climb up.

So she wants me to succeed, he thought with a smile. He waved his thanks to her, but then felt like an idiot for doing it, and ducked down, realizing a guard might have seen his flailing hand. He felt so embarrassed that he almost didn't want to move, but he glanced over the parapet and saw her still waiting for him, and knew that he had to try.

Glancing around to make sure no one else looked his way, he moved along the roof to find a place to climb down. He found a 2nd floor balcony that he was able to jump down to, and then stopped, his feet clomping down harder on the stone balcony than he expected. With his heart pounding, he slowly turned and looked into the house, but the windows and door were closed, and the light was out. No one stirred inside.

His hands shook and his breath was starting to turn a little ragged in fear, but he pushed on and moved to the side of the balcony. He could easily hop down from the balcony to the ground, but now he was afraid a Warrior might hear him.

Zerek looked again at the rock wall, wondering about the lack of defensive structures. Shouldn't there have been a tall steel fence or something to protect the Guild? Or were they so confident that nothing could get that far into the city that they didn't need a big wall? What of common criminals?

With his chest thumping, he hefted over the wall and held on to lower himself as far as he could, until he finally could go no further and had to let go. He fell the few feet left to the ground, and cringed. But no one shouted, no one appeared to have heard him. He was safe.

For now.

He crouched as low as he could and crossed the narrow street to the rock wall. It was only three feet tall, he could have easily hopped over it. Anyone could have. It just made no sense!

Then again, he realized, *there probably aren't a whole lot of people dumb enough to try to break into the Warriors' Guild.*

Unless a girl was involved, apparently. He looked up at the top of the tower, but then his heart froze. She wasn't there! His mind raced, and he wondered why. Had someone seen her? No, no one had raised the alarm, and no one was shouting. Maybe someone looked up and she had ducked down to avoid detection.

Yes, that had to be it. She was an expert thief, so of course she knew when she needed to hide.

Realizing that, he slowly edged his head above the rock wall to look at the grounds, but there was no one around. The patrols must have moved around to the other side of the mansion.

Looking up and down the street to make sure no one approached, he steeled himself with a great big breath, and then vaulted over the wall.

Or tried to.

His face smacked right into a solid wall of nothing, and he bounced back into the street, landing with a thud and an aching nose.

"Owe!" he said, then clamped his hand over his mouth. A bright light had flared when he hit the wall of nothingness, and that flare stretched high up above the wall. That was when he realized the Guild complex was surrounded by a magic wall.

"Oh gods," he whispered through his hands. Someone had to have seen it. "No, no, no," he clambered onto his feet and peaked over the wall. Shouts came from within the complex, and he saw rapid movement. Someone was coming.

He turned to run, only to have hands suddenly grab him by the shoulders and whip him around. Panicking, he tried to squirm free, but then she spoke, "Easy there, lover-boy."

It was the thief! He frowned, feeling his face flush while his mind raced with questions. "Hey! Wait...how did you get down here so fast?"

"Never mind that, you fool." She sighed and glanced behind her, where he saw one of the archways that led into the grounds. "Just run!"

Grabbing his hand, she pulled him along at a run. He chased after her in a daze, his mind focused intently on her handhold. And once again, he found himself chasing after the most beautiful girl in the city.

Scarcely aware of what was going on, he followed her willingly, running as fast as his legs would take him, trying desperately to keep up with her as she constantly tugged on his arm. He was afraid she would outrun him and he'd lose his grip on her, but she wasn't trying to get away from him, not this time, and she let him keep up with her.

"Over there," someone shouted from behind. Moments later, they turned down an alley and ran as fast as they could towards a dozen boxes stacked conspicuously.

"We're going up," she glanced back at him. He wanted those eyes to never look away, but she only gave him a moment, and then looked back at the boxes. Without breaking her stride, she let go of his hand, much to his dismay, and clambered up one box after another. Not paying attention, he ran right into those boxes and almost toppled them over.

She hissed down at him, "Pay attention, I said we're going up."

Feeling his face burn bright red, he put his hands on the first box and pushed up, following her as fast as he could. She clearly had done this before, and was on the building's roof in moments. His own ascent took much longer, precious moments that they didn't have.

"On the roof," he heard that same voice shout from behind.

The thief cursed and grabbed his hand to help him the rest of the way up. "Great, now we have to outrun them."

Once he was secure on the roof, she took off ahead of him, and he tried desperately to keep up. She leapt from one roof to the next, and then climbed up a late addition to that building to a third story effortlessly. He tried to follow, but he had difficulty climbing the latticework frame, and she had to reach back over and help him again.

Once on top, he looked back to see a Warrior climbing up from the alley. He had a harder time, thanks to his armor.

"Move it," she yanked on his sleeve.

Once again, they took off running, and he followed her lead as best as he could. She knew exactly where to go, where they could easily leap from one roof to another, and never break stride. Twisting and turning, hopping over streets, alleys, using pillars, never slowing, never breaking stride.

He struggled to keep up, but his short sprint with Endel had helped him understand how to navigate the roofs well enough. If it hadn't been for Endel...

Something clicked in his head. Endel? Had he once run with these same people, scrambling across rooftops, evading guards? Excitable little Endel? No, surely he wasn't a thief, he worked in the castle for crying out loud.

Banishing the thought, Zerek focused on following the girl. On her billowing cloak, her short hair flowing in the wind, and her beautiful pale face in the moonlight. He'd finally done it, he'd finally found her!

Now he just head to make sure he didn't lose her again. They ran, as fast as the wind, faster even, certainly faster than the guards. His cloak billowed out much like the girl's, and he wondered if his looked as adventurous as hers did, flowing behind her like a hero's cloak. He only paid close enough attention to their path to ensure he leapt from rooftop to rooftop, climbed up or hopped down from one level to the next, and never tripped or fell.

So when the girl suddenly came to a stop, he nearly crashed into her. Realizing they had run out of rooftops, they looked out at the green district across the river. She'd brought him to the river again, and she hopped down onto another stack of boxes, and finally onto the street. Zerek followed, finding that going down was a lot easier than going up.

They had long ago lost the guards somewhere in the center of the city. Once they were at street level, he bent over and rested his hands on his knees, heaving breaths. For as much running as he'd been doing in the past few weeks, he clearly hadn't caught up to her level.

She folded her arms and tapped her feet impatiently, but she still waited for him. He looked up at her, felt his breath stolen from him when he gazed into her eyes, so dark in the night, so deep, so beautiful.

"Come on," she tugged on his sleeve and drew him along. "We should get out of the street, they'll be looking for us tonight." She led him along towards the southeast wall where the river wound back out into the world. It was well past midnight, and there was no one around.

He wanted to talk to her, to hear her sing-song voice again, but what should he say or ask?

"So, do you always run on the rooftops like that?" It was the first thing he could think of, and he felt stupid just asking it.

Looking back at him, she smirked, "No, only at night. It's easier to lose them in the crowds at street level during the day."

That he believed, after having chased her once before. In fact, he realized that both times he'd seen her, she had led him on a grand chase.

She picked up the pace some, and before long they were running again. He'd just caught his breath, but this time they ran a little slower and he had no trouble keeping up. She smiled and commented, "You've gotten faster."

Feeling his face burn, he smiled. "I wanted to be able to keep up with you."

Her smiled broadened, and he felt a fluttering in his chest from it. She reached out and took his hand in hers. Her hands were rough, not as bad as Elina's had been, but clearly the thief had spent most of her life in the elements and doing hard work.

They came to the end of the street, right up against the city wall, and she stopped them at the edge of the low walkway wall. She looked down at the river, and then at him. "We're going down again."

Not waiting for him to ask what she meant, she let go of his hand and leapt over the wall. He looked over and saw that unlike up river by the bridge, this part had a constructed stone landing. In fact the entire area was built up as a completely artificial canal, with easy access to the heavy metal grating that covered the arched mouth in the wall for the river to run out. The grating was interlaced close enough that not even a child could climb through, ensuring no one could ever sneak into or out of the city by river.

Glancing around to make sure no one saw, he hopped over the railing and clomped down with a thud. By that time, the girl had moved to the edge of the landing and had sat down. She was in the process of taking her makeshift shoes off, which he found to be curious, until she swung her bare feet over the edge and stuck them in the water.

"Isn't it cold," he asked.

"Not yet," she shook her head, splashing the water. "Not until the first snowfall in the mountains. Which will be any day now."

Smiling, he sat beside her and took his own boots off before he plunked his feet into the water. It splashed up his leg, and it was actually quite cold, but not so bad that he couldn't keep his feet in. She playfully splashed water on his legs, and he splashed back, eliciting a giggle from her.

Their eyes met, and he found that he couldn't look away. She stole his breath, stole his heart. In every sense, she was a thief. His thief.

"Hi there," she smiled, her cheeks flushing visibly even in the night.

He didn't know what else to say, his head was completely numb. All he managed was a quiet, "Hi."

"You're a persistent one," her fingers brushed against his. He looked down and stared at her hand, wanting desperately to take hers, but not knowing if he should. When he looked up again, she'd raised an eyebrow at him. "Have you been searching for me this whole time?"

"Uh," he stuttered, "Yeah. I have. I had to find you." He tilted his head, "I don't even know your name."

With her smile still broad, she giggled again. "All this time and you haven't even found that out?"

Suddenly he realized they'd drawn closer to each other, and his heart, which had only just begun to slow down, suddenly raced again. "No one knew who you were."

"Well," she whispered. Then, before he knew what he was doing, he leaned in closer to her, and their lips touched. Tingles exploded across his face, and his chest felt ready to burst with his pounding heart. She didn't pull away, and a moment later, she pushed her lips a little harder against his.

It was both the longest and shortest moment of his entire life. Their hands had connected at some point, he didn't know when. And when she pulled away from him, his mind was completely blank.

Until she told him something he swore he would commit to memory for the rest of eternity. "My name is Laira." She stared into his eyes, her face as bright as his felt. "And I am very pleased to meet you."

***

The dungeon in Valaras was among the largest that Amaya had seen, and was also one of the worst smelling. It didn't help that the few surviving orcs from yesterday's battle now occupied half of the dungeon cells.

She found herself having to cover her nose, and forced a gag back down. This was no time to show weakness. The orc cages were not her destination, but any fear she showed would be incentive for them to try to attack. As they had found out often since the war had begun, captured orcs were far more dangerous than caged animals.

Passing by one of the orc cages, she didn't dare look inside, but she could feel several eyes from within following her. Hungry for her.

For her blood.

Several more paces ahead, she came upon her destination. The jailor that accompanied her, a tall, broad-shouldered man with deep green eyes, stepped in front of her and unhooked the keys from his belt, fumbling with them. He was nervous, but not about the prisoner she was visiting.

Amaya stared through the bars of the door at the only occupant of the cell. And he stared right back at her, his eyes calm, discerning, even disarming. Trebor Tem's composure had returned, and he sat calmly and unshackled within his cell.

The jailor finally found the correct key, and the iron door swung up with a screech. That set off some of the nearest orcs, and they roared and pounded at their prisons. Trebor flinched, but otherwise showed no sign that he was perturbed.

"Thank you," she smiled at the jailor. He tried to smile back, but glanced around nervously at the surrounding cells. Several Warriors assigned to keep watch over the orcs began shouting at them to shut up, but that did not help.

Stepping inside, Amaya waited patiently. The jailor closed the door behind her, but did not lock it, and did not leave. She didn't need him there – Trebor was an unarmed man with no magic. He could not hurt her no matter how much he wanted to.

A charming smile crossed Trebor's face, but she knew to look through it now. She knew the anger and desperation that existed beneath the surface of his face. The same anger that coursed through her veins.

She never diverted her eyes from Trebor's, and they remained locked in a stare of wills, waiting for the orcs to quiet down, waiting to break each other down. The chance came after several minutes, when the orcs finally settled down.

"I was wondering if I would see you again, Guardian," Trebor spoke, his voice cheerful. "I hoped you would come."

Raising a curious eyebrow, she folded her arms. "Oh? I'm surprised, after the humiliation you experienced at my hands."

His face darkened, but only a little. "Hardly a fair fight."

With a sigh, she shook her head. "I wouldn't say that. You were rather crafty in your attempts to deface my authority. At first."

Very slowly, Trebor's smile faded. He looked tired. Exhausted.

"Yes," he spoke quietly, the false bravado gone and the pain in his voice clear. "At first."

She let that sink in for a moment, and slowly paced around the cell. She passed very near him, a signal that she was not afraid of him by any means. He did not look up, but she saw his eyes follow her feet.

"Your riot has been disbanded," she stated. "You've been discredited with all of your followers. And the attempted siege has left the people frightened and determined enough to resume work in the Forge District with a renewed fervor."

She approached the door again, and stood facing away from him, looking up at the ceiling. "You should see it, Tem. Countless chimneys all pouring smoke out." She grimaced, but did not let him see it. She thought it was actually a disgusting sight, but she also knew it meant that the soldiers of Tal would not go without desperately needed arms. They would win the war.

Looking over her shoulder, she smirked at Trebor. "We're not pressing charges against the others in your rabble."

He raised his eyebrows and looked at her in genuine surprise. "I admit I am shocked. The anger I saw in your face. The hate in your voice. I thought you would have arrested them all."

Her cheeks warmed and she looked away from him. Her hands clenched into fists, and she felt her earlier rage return.

"Don't deny it or hide it," Trebor continued. She could hear the victory in his voice, knowing that he had successfully pressed her wound again. "I don't know your story, but I know your pain. I know that only betrayed love can create such horrible darkness within one's soul."

She spun around to rebuke him, but was surprised to find that he had stood up and had closed half of the distance. His hands were at his side disarmingly, but it still startled her, and she prepared to draw her sword. Trebor raised his hands to show that he meant no physical harm to her.

"There is no darkness in my soul," she said at length. "Do not try to compare me to yourself."

With a smirk, he shook his head. "It's already begun," he lowered his arms. Somehow he looked menacing to her now. Dangerous. "Just give it time. I think by the time they let me out, you'll be consumed by it."

For a moment, she looked down at his feet, feeling fear, anger, regret. Was he right? Was this pain twisting her soul?

Those months in the Archanon dungeon had given her plenty of time to mull over everything that had happened. Everything that she now refused to face. And after yesterday, she realized that it had continued to build up within her. Pressure building, growing stronger and stronger. How much longer could she push it down? How much longer could she keep the darkness at bay?

The worst part was that she felt completely alone. She had her team with her at almost all times, but they were her subordinates and she their leader. There was no one she could talk to. No one to help her sort out her feelings. No one she could trust with the terrible secrets of her past.

What was she doing? Why was she doubting herself? Doubting her ability to control?

It wasn't long before it dawned on her. It was Trebor. His words. His demeanor. She was the one armed and armored, the one with power in the room, and yet he had just torn her down. Just like Din.

He was dangerous. His voice, his reasoning, his charisma was dangerous. She looked up at him, her brow creased in a deep frown. The anger seethed within her. His smirk faded, and she reveled in the fear that suddenly entered his eyes.

With slow, deliberate steps, she closed the distance between them, until she could whisper to him.

"You are mistaken about one very specific assumption," she spoke, her voice shaking. "You will never be granted leave from this place."

"You can't keep me here forever," he growled.

She looked at him, their faces inches apart. "Oh no? I am a Guardian. My orders are backed by the King. And I shall leave orders that you are never to leave this dungeon again. Not alive."

The fear in his eyes deepened, and suddenly he seemed so much smaller.

For a moment, she wanted to justify her decision. She almost told him why. That he was too dangerous, that she knew he could rally another uprising, or worse. And as the world continued to change around them, more might be drawn to his cause next time.

However, she had no reason to explain herself. No responsibility to. Her order would be final.

With that thought, the anger subsided, and she pulled away from him. "Goodbye, Mr. Tem." Turning, she approached the exit and called over her shoulder, "You will never see me again, I promise you."

The jailor opened the door for her, the screech setting off the orcs again. They howled and roared and banged, and she felt as if they echoed her own heart. The door screeched close behind her, and she paused there, not sure if she should look back at him.

There was a part of her that wanted to gloat, to let him know that she felt satisfaction at winning.

Until that thought scared her. No, not scared, *terrified* her.

What was she becoming? What was her heart becoming?

The jailor locked the door, and began to lead the way back towards the stairs. She hesitated only a moment, but finally steeled herself and walked away.

Had she really won this battle? Or had Trebor?

Worse still, one question echoed in her thoughts as she passed by the enraged monsters. Was Trebor right? Was the pain and rage within her heart changing her? Was she losing herself?

Who were the real monsters?

Episode 6

CROSSROADS

Try as he might, there was no chance Zerek's smile would fade, even when faced with a disgruntled Warrior lieutenant. He stood in the courtyard of the Warrior's Guild complex in Archanon, the very complex that Zerek had tried and failed miserably to break into a few weeks ago. Only this time, he was there on official business in the middle of the day.

The Lieutenant before him, Daisha Melin, scowled down at the letter that Zerek had just delivered. He never knew the contents of the sealed letters, he just knew that he had once again been trusted with a letter bearing the seal of the King of Tal.

As Daisha continued to read, another Warrior walked by on patrol, his full set of armor no doubt keeping him warm against the cool weather. Fall was in full swing, and unlike his previous visit, he was able to enjoy the beauty of the Guild compound. Every tree, including the one he'd considered climbing to meet Laira, was a myriad of reds, oranges, and yellows, their leaves just starting to fall.

In fact the courtyard was littered with dead or dying leaves, and he was glad that he didn't need to try to sneak in now. He stole a look at that tower, the sun glaring down at him from just above it. Closing his eyes, he let the warmth of the sun wash over his face, and his smile grew wider.

"You're in good cheer today, kid," the Lieutenant said, bemusement in her voice. Opening his eyes, he looked at her to see a small grin. Zerek's face suddenly felt warmer, even against a cool breeze.

That only made Daisha's grin turn into a full blown smile. "Oh my. Look at you, little one." This wasn't his first time meeting the Lieutenant, and every time she used one of her nicknames for him, he felt embarrassed. That coupled with his thoughts of Laira, the girl who stole his heart, made his face burn ever brighter. "You're in love," she exclaimed.

"Umm, I..." He shook his head, but she just started laughing, the letter hanging from her hand. He looked down and away, not sure how to react, not sure what to say. He wanted to deny it, but he didn't even know why. Was it love? Could it be? After only knowing her for a few weeks?

Daisha stepped closer and clasped a hand on his shoulder. "Hey, it's okay kid. It happens to us all, and that's not a bad thing." She looked to the side and frowned for a brief moment. "Well, not always." Then the smile returned. "What's her name?"

Zerek looked dead center at the Warrior, but his mind suddenly went blank. He knew her name, he'd committed it to memory, that wasn't what made him feel a sinking sensation in his stomach. No, he was actually afraid to say. What if Daisha recognized the name? What if she realized that Zerek was spending time with a thief? Worse still...what if it somehow led to Laira getting arrested?

His hesitation registered on Daisha, and she shook her head. "It's okay, if you're too embarrassed to tell me about your girlfriend, you don't have to." She beamed at him and added, "But I'm happy for you. Really. After everything you've been through..."

The sinking sensation he'd felt earlier turned into a giant lump, and his voice caught in his throat. It still hurt every time he thought about the Relkin Mining Camp. When he remembered his father, Elina, and everyone else.

He could only imagine what his face looked like now, and Daisha's smile quickly darkened. "Hey, I'm sorry. I didn't meant to bring up the memories."

"It's okay," he lied. "Really. I just need to be going. Is there anything you need me to return to the castle?"

She shook her head. "No, not at the moment. But thank you." She squeezed his shoulder, and then released her grasp on him. "Now go on. I get the feeling there's somewhere you want to go before you go home."

His grin returned, even if it was a weak one, and he nodded. "Thanks."

When he turned to walk off, she added, "And hey. Take care, okay? You're a tough kid, but..."

Zerek stopped long enough to look over his shoulder and give her his best fake smile. "I will."

He left Daisha and the Warriors' Guild behind him. The memories still hung in his chest like a great weight, one that never quite left him. How long had it been? A month? Month and a half? He wasn't quite sure. So many of the days following the attack were a haze in his memory.

A haze that seemed to be lifted by only one thing. One person. He needed to see Laira. He needed to see the light of her smile, her deep brown eyes, hear her laugh. Even if only for a second.

There was no telling where she was, of course. But she always seemed to find him. Anytime he asked her how, she side-stepped the question with a light-hearted joke, but he had his suspicions. They always started with the beggars in the alleys, and the thieves that no doubt roamed the city. He'd begun to see the signs of a vast network, and he wondered if they kept track of the habits of every single person in the city.

It certainly would make stealing from them easier.

All Zerek could do was wander aimlessly through the streets, although he did move in the general direction of the river. They always ended up there, at that landing by the wall. Where he'd had the first kiss of his life.

The warmth on his face returned, and so did a genuine smile. He'd never known something could excite and terrify him so much in a single moment. Never in his life could he have imagined such elation.

He let that memory fill every fiber of his being, his steps no longer his own. He simply walked wherever the tide of people took him. The city was massive, and he still hadn't journeyed down every street or alley. In fact he was sure he could spend a lifetime wandering the streets and never find every single nook and cranny.

Then he heard the clearing of a throat off to his right. "Hey, lover-boy."

A full smile blossomed across his face, and he turned to see Laira standing in the middle of an open door into a shop. His thoughts faltered for only a moment when he wondered why she was openly standing in a shop's door, but he banished any dark thoughts he had about her, and he rushed forward to embrace her in a hug.

But she didn't let him. The moment he moved towards her, she suddenly ran down the street. "Catch me if you can!"

And just as it always did when they met, a chase ensued. Laira loved to run! Everywhere they went, they ran, and it had done wonders for his stamina. He could keep up with her now, even when she was at a full run. In fact, he was sure this time he would actually catch her.

Through the streets, around people, under outstretched arms, over crates, they moved with a fluidity that she had begun to teach him. Every now and then, Zerek still stumbled, but he never fell anymore, and he never gave up.

Closer and closer he drew to her. She turned down one avenue that was very busy, and as he stumbled between a couple of larger men, he wished she would have taken them up onto the rooftops again. Unfortunately, it was a little more dangerous to do so during the day, since city guards would often spot them and shout after them. The last thing he needed was to be recognized and reported back to the castle, back to the steward.

Laira moved faster than he did through the crowds, but once they broke through and she ran down another smaller street, he started to catch up again. However, it was too late. When he was only a few feet behind her, she burst out onto River Street. It was their unsaid finish line, and as always, she won the race.

He was out of breath, but he felt some comfort in the fact that she was too. Despite how long she'd been doing this, she had to run faster now just to stay ahead of him, and as they leaned against the stone railing overlooking the river, she laughed. "I'm going to have to start cheating if I'm going to keep winning."

Huffing, he laughed. "How do you cheat in a race like that?"

"Like this," she pushed him away, giggling.

"Hey!"

And suddenly she was running again, down-river towards their spot. Shaking his head, Zerek chased after her again. They almost ran into a pair of city soldiers along the way, the soldiers telling them to watch it.

She managed to stay ahead of him, and right when they reached the wall, she came to a quick halt and turned to face him, reaching a hand out to the stone rail and leaning against it. A second later, he skidded to a halt right by her, and she shook her head. "Took you long enough."

His face burning, he laughed and said, "Well if you hadn't cheated…"

Smiling, she reached out her other hand, grabbed him by his tunic, and pulled him in for a sudden, deep kiss. Light exploded across his soul! His lips, and for that matter his entire face tingled. Then as quickly as she had pulled him in, she pushed him away and hopped over the edge to the landing below.

He looked over the edge, his heart ready to beat out of his chest, and saw her casually walking away, as if their run had actually been an easy walk for her. Glancing around to make sure no one would yell at him for hopping down to the river, where it was 'dangerous,' he planted his hands on the stone and leapt over.

His landings were getting lighter. Thanks to Laira, he knew now to land on the front of his feet, turning them into springs that helped prevent his feet from clomping down. He walked along to join her at the edge of the landing.

The river was lower than it had been on the night that they first kissed, so when they both sat down and dangled their feet, they no longer touched the river. That was fine, the first snows had already blanketed the tops of the mountain, and the river was freezing cold.

After only a moment, she leaned in closer to him so that they could wrap their arms around each other.

He reveled in the warmth they shared. Even if the weather wasn't freezing yet, just being with her made him feel like the world was a warmer, brighter place. He listened to the river waltz on by like a flow of dancers, glistening with sunlight. Across the river, farmers tended to their fields or livestock. The couple looked up and watched a flock of birds flying in a giant V formation southward.

It was a perfect day.

It was also the perfect moment to ask the question he knew he needed to ask her today. A question he had wanted to ask her for days, but he hadn't worked up the courage. He wasn't even sure why he was afraid to ask her.

What if she said no? What if she freaked out about it? What if...

"What's wrong?" She pulled away just enough to look into his eyes. "You're shaking, Zerek."

Feeling like a child caught stealing sweets, Zerek's face blushed for probably the hundredth time that day. But instead of trying to deny anything, as he had with Daisha earlier, he just blurted it out.

"You should come live and work in the castle."

Her face grew pale, and she slowly drew away from him, eyes widening with shock. "Live in the...Zerek, are you serious?"

Her reaction wasn't at all what he expected, and he felt as if his soul had just dropped out from his stomach. "Yeah," he said, hesitant. "I mean, you wouldn't have to live on the streets anymore, or steal or eat scraps. You'd have a roof over your head. And, well, we could be together in the open. Not have to hide."

The more he talked, the more she withdrew. He couldn't tell if it was because she was appalled by the idea or surprised, but he already feared the worst. Should he recant? Tell her not to think about it again? But if he did that, nothing would change, and all they could ever do was chase each other around the city, hiding from anyone who might recognize him and report to Kai that he was with a thief. That he was falling in love with the very thief that had stolen his first charge.

"Zerek, I can't live in the castle," she shook her head. "They would never take me."

"They would if I told them you were a good person," he quickly countered, feeling an uncomfortable sensation rising in his chest. "That you would be a hard and honest worker."

She outright laughed. "Are you kidding me? I'm a thief, Zerek, I'm hardly an honest worker."

He felt a wave of an unfamiliar sensation roll across his face, but it wasn't the heat of embarrassment. This was something different. It moved down into his chest, his stomach, made him feel like someone had just stamped on his heart.

"But you don't have to be a thief anymore. You can stop stealing, stop lying." He twisted his body, brought up one leg to sit on it, so that he could face her. "And then we can be together, and…"

"Stop," she stood up, backing away from him. "Zerek, I don't want to live in the castle. I can't. You…you wouldn't understand." Laira looked ready to turn and run, but all she did was stop, fold her arms, and look down at the landing, her face a contortion of emotions.

Slowly standing up, Zerek felt like the world had grown much darker, much colder in just a few seconds. She wouldn't look at him, wouldn't say anything to him, and she looked positively outraged. What had he done wrong? What was so wrong with what he was asking?

"There's so much you don't know about me," she said, looking at him through angry eyes. "About who I am. About my past."

"Then tell me," he begged, stepping closer to her. She backed away in response, lowering her arms.

"I can't," her voice trembled. "You…you've been incredibly kind to me, and I know you're head over heels for me. But I just can't, Zerek. I'll never live in the castle. I'll never be an upstanding citizen of the kingdom. Not while it…" She trailed off and looked away.

Zerek didn't know what to say, or how to react. He wanted to shout that it wasn't fair. He'd found something to make him happy in life, and now…now he felt like he was losing it. Losing her. All because she wouldn't tell him what was going on. It wasn't fair.

When he was finally ready to say as much, she looked up at him again, the anger having faded to regret and uncertainty. "You've been kind to me up to this point, Zerek, even knowing I'm a criminal. I've loved that about you. And I know you just don't know any better. I've taken advantage of that fact." She looked down, her face turning bright red. "I've taken advantage of you. I can't do that anymore."

Before he could ask her what she meant, she turned on her heels and ran up the stairs along the wall, back to the street level. He was too stunned at first to follow, but when he finally realized what was happening, he ran up to chase after her.

Only this time, when he made it to street level, she was nowhere to be seen.

Leaving him alone again.

***

By all rights, Amaya should have been in high spirits. The weather was beautiful for fall, just a hint of cold in the breeze. The sun shone down upon her body, stretched out upon a stone bench in the courtyard of Archanon Castle, keeping her warm. It was one of those rare moments when she was out of uniform, and instead wore a simple blue tunic, brown trousers, and a brown cloak, which lay open around her.

Yet she couldn't keep her mind quiet. She couldn't relax. As she stared at a small cloud passing by, all she could do was seethe.

Rage.

Anger.

She caught herself grinding her teeth, and forced her jaw to relax. What was she doing? Why was she out here, away from her team, alone?

Alone.

Always alone, now. It wasn't quite what she expected her life to be like. Or at least, not what she expected it to feel like.

The conversation with Trebor Tem in the Valaras dungeon played in her mind again. How she felt. What she thought. Everything. Over and over and over again.

She clenched her jaw and fists again. "Dammit," she grumbled, sitting up and staring down at her feet. "What is wrong with me?"

It was a question she had asked herself so many times in the past few weeks. And every time, she came up with more questions than answers. Her thoughts dwelled on Trebor, and on his failed marriage. On Din, and how her relationship with him had ended.

This wasn't who she was. She was once a Warrior, and now a Guardian of Tal. She was strong. The past shouldn't hold power over her!

And her nightmares. Gods, the nightmares. Where she took her anger out on Trebor. Of all people, on Trebor Tem, a weak, defeated barkeep sentenced to a life in the dungeons, surrounded by enraged orcs. He could do no harm to her. No one could. Yet in her dreams…

Shaking her head furiously, she stood up and started walking towards the gates to leave the Castle District. This wouldn't do, sitting around seething. She needed to walk it off.

Her head was bowed low as she walked, so she only saw in her peripheral a group of people exiting the castle, marching out onto the same road she was heading for. If she had noticed them earlier and looked up, she would have turned around before they saw her.

A dreadful voice spoke up and turned her veins to ice. "Amaya," Din called out.

She stopped short, her fists automatically balling up. When she looked at him, he also came to a stop, his blue eyes piercing hers. She wanted to tear his head off. Instead, she bowed, as little as necessary for etiquette. "Commander Din." What in the name of the Six was he doing in Archanon?

Leaving behind his entourage of Warriors, all of whom she recognized from her hometown of Everlin, he approached her, a grin on his face. "Well, isn't this a coincidence. I had hoped to see you today."

Could she say to him what she wanted? Was it permissible? He was no longer her Commander, after all, she reported to Draegus Kataar. But she also knew the importance of maintaining good relations between the throne and the Warriors' Guild. It was, after all, the Warriors' Guild on the front lines right now, not soldiers.

So as much as she wanted to tell him where to stick it, she couldn't. Nor could she tell him that the feelings were not mutual. She had to remain diplomatic, if at all possible.

"What may I do for you, Commander," she asked in her best stoic tone.

He frowned and closed the distance between them to a dozen feet, making her very uneasy and inducing a panicked need to run. "Still angry at me, I see."

Dammit, she thought to herself. There was no hiding her emotions from him. She never could, he knew her too well.

"My apologies," she gave another small bow. She should have called him sir, but she couldn't bring herself to. Never again.

Raising a curious eyebrow, Din shook his head. "You're going to have to get over our past, my dear." Her fists twitched when he called her 'dear.' "After all, we're going to have to get used to working together again."

All feeling drained from her arms and legs, her face going cold. "…What?"

"Yeah," he jabbed a thumb back at the castle. "Why do you think I was here? We're outnumbered by the orcs a hundred to one, we need more Warriors. So I came to barter for you and your team to return to the Warriors." Something snapped inside of her head, like a leather belt breaking from too much tension. "Under my command, of course."

"You..." she started moving towards him, "Son of a..."

Before she could lay a hand on him, another pair of hands grabbed her by the shoulders and held her back. "Amaya, no," Elic's voice was strong, and brought the light back to the darkest recesses of her soul.

Din had taken a step back, fear in his eyes. She'd never seen that in him before, genuine fear. Fear of her. Fear of the look in her eyes. The rage no doubt pouring from her soul, that any Mage or Wizard nearby could feel.

His reaction coupled with Elic's strength smothered the anger, and turned it to something worse. Something insipid, and dark.

"Commander, please leave," Elic commanded. When Din did not reply or look away from Amaya, her friend took a step closer to the Warrior Commander. "Please don't make me order it."

Din scoffed at that and looked at Elic for the first time, but then he noticed the uniform and tabard Elic wore: a castle guard's uniform, but with the kingdom's symbol on the tabard embroidered in silver, not white, distinguishing him from the common Tal soldier. He also held his left hand out so that Din could see the brand of the Guardians on it.

Scowling, Din spun around, his cloak flowing around behind him, and stalked off. His entourage was quick to follow.

All of this Amaya barely noticed. Her thoughts were turned inward, her eyes downturned. *The look on his face,* she thought, numb but for the horror she began to feel in her heart. *My gods, his face...*

Feeling a light pressure on her shoulder, Amaya turned to see Elic, his brow furrowed and his dark eyes searching hers. She wanted nothing more than to allow her friend to wrap his arms around her, embrace her and let her cry into his chest.

But she couldn't. She was his Lieutenant. It was already bad enough, him seeing her nearly assault a Warrior Commander. He was her friend, yes, but she still had to maintain some distance, some semblance of leadership.

Steeling herself, she pushed the anger away, the darkness, the hatred, all of it. She pushed it deep down into herself, into the very lowest reaches until it was nothing but a trickle of annoyance. *I am a Guardian. I must act like it.*

"Thank you," she managed to say without any emotion. Looking back to the castle, she decided she needed to find her bunk, and fast, before she lost control again. "Please excuse me..."

Elic didn't let her go. His hand was firm on her shoulder, and the look he gave her was one of annoyance and determination. "Come with me," he stated, not leaving room for debate.

She was about to object, to remind him who commanded whom, but he simply turned on the spot and walked away. Curious at his newfound disobedience, and even fearful of everything he had seen in Everlin and just now, she decided to follow after him.

To her surprise, he led her right back to the bench she had lain on only minutes ago. When he sat down, he motioned to the spot next to him and said, "I think it's time we had a talk."

"My, aren't we brash today," she chided, folding her arms and refusing to sit.

He remained motionless for a while longer, but when it became clear that she wasn't going to join him, he sighed and leaned forward, resting his elbows on his knees. After some thought, he looked up at her, genuine concern on his face.

"Alright. I know you've never had a second in command, not officially, but the others look up to me as such."

She felt something stir inside of her, apprehension at where he was going to take the conversation, and anger at herself for allowing it to come to this.

"You managed to keep it under wraps, but ever since Ironwood, and especially ever since Valaras..." Elic trailed off, his face betraying his uncertainty at how far he should go. "I know you and Din had a relationship. I know that it must have hurt you far more than it ever did us when he betrayed our team. Amaya..."

Feeling like she had lost control of the situation, of herself, of her subordinate, Amaya very nearly lashed out at him verbally to remind him who she was and that it was not his place to lecture her. Until she realized that she had no one else to talk to. No one else who cared about her. No one else she could truly call 'friend.'

"Something set you off this time," he continued, sitting up straight. "I didn't hear what, but something did. If you won't tell me what happened in the past, then at least tell me what he said just now."

Turning her head down and away from him, she discovered that she had clenched her fists again. Unfolding her arms and forcing her hands to relax, she decided to sit on the bench, and then with considerable effort, managed to look Elic straight in the face.

"He is here to convince the King to release us back into the service of the Warriors."

Elic couldn't have looked more stunned. "What?!"

She shook her head and massaged her nose bridge forcefully. "The son of a whore thinks we're still his to command!"

Even Elic was at a loss of words at hearing this news. Some of the color in his face drained, and he covered his mouth with his hand.

"The Warriors are spread too thin," she continued. "They need reinforcements."

Pulling his hand away from his mouth, Elic asked, "Do you think he actually has a chance?"

"If he pulls the 'we need every sword to win this war' card, then yes." She shook her head. "We're winning the war now, we've just about driven the orcs back to the Wastelands. But scouts have already confirmed the orcs are retreating into another army. They'll have fresh troops to hold the line just south of the border."

Elic closed his eyes in silent resignation. "And if we want to end the war quickly, we need the numbers to overwhelm them."

"Precisely," she folded her arms. "He said he came to barter, and you know the kingdom's gold reserves are dangerously low. Any concessions the Warriors give on how much they charge the King for fighting this war will be welcome."

Elic shook his head and stared at her, his eyes betraying the emptiness he felt even when his words spoke of hope. "We're Guardians." He pulled back his sleeve to show the brand. "There's no coming back from that, Draegus warned us of that fact."

She shrugged, feeling the anger seethe and writhe in her stomach, threatening to burst forth again. "Desperate times, remember?" It was true that their numbers were constantly being bolstered by the Wizard Sal'fe using his staff to resurrect fallen Warriors, but every time he did, he rightfully charged the kingdoms a fee, to help his kingdom pay for their recovery from Kailar's occupation, and the ongoing war effort. That only hurt Tal's dwindling gold reserves more.

The kingdom needed relief. It needed every edge it could get.

"What are we going to do," Elic asked, his voice strong, but with an edge that made her hairs stand up on end.

Searching inside of herself for answers, Amaya wished, even prayed for something. Some hope. Some way to make her feel like the world wasn't about to end.

But nothing presented itself. Her mind was blank.

"I don't know," she whispered.

***

"In what realm did anyone think this would be a good idea," Tezarik grumbled, his darksteel armor rattling from his shivering. Arkad growled a warning against the young orc's statement, but found that he couldn't help but agree. Then again, nothing could compare to the warmth of their home. Not even the Wastelands.

He and the surviving darksteel orcs from Valaras were huddled together, their energy spent, their spirits broken. Even orcs had a limit to how long they could run at full steam. Now they huddled in a small clearing surrounded by a dense cluster of trees in the Ilari mountains, their destination finally within reach.

"It does not matter," Arkad replied while awkwardly trying to kneel in his armor. The armor pinched and poked in very awkward places at the joints, and was definitely never designed for stealth. "We will return to the Wastelands soon, where it is warm even in this land's winter."

"We won't survive long enough," he heard someone whisper.

Arkad jerked his head to the right to see who spoke, but whomever had spoken was not brave enough to do so again.

His troops' bold statements was enough to worry him. These were not the downtrodden orcs that had been born and raised in the Wastelands. They, like him, were once residents of the great city of Akaida, and their spirits had not been broken by thousands of years of mistreatment at the hands of the humans.

If they were losing their spirit, he realized the situation was far worse than he realized.

"We will survive," he looked around, making eye contact with every orc that he could. More than two dozen had survived the battle and retreated with him, each wearing enchanted armor and wielding powerful weapons. "We are strong, and cunning. We are not the common rabble, and we are far more than foot soldiers."

"Which is why we should not have diverted," another orc, Telark, piped in. When Arkad glared at him, a sight that usually made even the toughest orc cower, Telark continued, "Forgive me for saying so, General, but the Wastelands rabble need our help to survive."

Something in Arkad began to rise up, and he was ready to beat his subordinate down for questioning his orders. In fact, in days past that was exactly what he would have done. That was how he had always commanded his troops, it was what he had been taught by his former master.

Then he realized what he was asking his troops to do. Archanon was one of the most well-defended cities he had ever heard of, and he wanted them to attack it. Two dozen orcs, even in darksteel, would not likely breach the wall. Was he, in fact, asking them to do something hopeless?

Was it worth it? Worth the sacrifice? If that question was on his mind, then it must be on theirs. He realized that they needed convincing. And so did he.

"You're right," he nodded to Telark. "They do need our help. Two armies of our kin are running for their lives right now, and they need our help. Did you see how organized the humans were? How quickly they rallied, how efficiently they formed up against us through portals?"

Arkad's second in command, Kilack, nodded. "Only once before have I seen such effective use of portals for battle."

The memory Kilack had just conjured made Arkad shiver, his heart feeling empty. The day he had been forced from his home.

No, he inwardly yelled at himself. *Do not dwell!*

Banishing the thoughts, he focused on what was before him. His kin. His people. The future of the orcs.

"Even now," he continued on, "the humans are harassing our armies as they retreat. They need at least another week, maybe two, to make it back to our lines in the Wastelands. But the longer they run, the more will be lost to the harassment of our enemy."

Pointing northwest, and almost taking Telark's head off in the process, he raised his voice, "We can do something about that here and now. The humans believe that they can walk all over us without fear of reprisal. They think they have us outmaneuvered. So now we will make them pay for their arrogance." He stood up, towering above his orcs. "If we attack their capitol now, they will fear how many more of us are out there, ready to strike at their heart. They will pull back. And our armies will be able to make it back to the Wastelands in far greater numbers."

"He's right," Kilack also raised his voice. "We can make a difference, right here, today."

Another thought occurred to Arkad, and while he did not wish to lose the momentum he had just begun to build, he knew that they couldn't just flat-out attack the capitol. They needed a plan.

So he looked at Tezarik. The young orc had impressed him at Valaras, and he had survived the first Battle of Archanon when Klaralin had ordered them to attack. "You know this land better than any of us," he narrowed his eyes. "Is there a weakness we can exploit?"

Tezarik turned his dark green eyes down and searched his memory. Over a thousand orcs had died that night, so Arkad did not envy the young orc having to return to those memories. Like he always did, Arkad wondered if the battle would have turned out differently if he had been present to lead the troops.

If only he had come to Halarite sooner.

"Yes," Tezarik's eyes opened wide. "Yes, there is! I fought along the far right flank, the northern flank. North of the gate, there is a great river, and that river flows into and out of the city. I remember seeing a grate there, it looked to be nothing more than iron or steel." A wicked smile crossed Tezarik's face. "If we could sneak up to that point, past the river docks, we could use our weapons to breach into the city."

Arkad felt his own face twist into a smile. "Then that is our target." He nodded to Tezarik. "When night falls, you will lead the way."

Standing tall, Arkad looked north, feeling his chest swell and his spirits rise for the first time in weeks. "Tonight, we will strike at the heart of the humans.

"Tonight, we will make the humans fear us again."

***

With barely contained rage and absolute determination, Amaya stormed through the castle towards the Allied Council chambers. She would not falter, not this time.

Twice already she had sought out King Beredis, ready to do and say whatever was necessary to convince him to not transfer her back to the Warriors' Guild. Back under Din's command. Each time, her courage faltered, and she stopped short of entering his wardroom. She had missed her opportunity then, the two hour long lunch break in the ongoing sessions between the four kingdoms, the Wizards' Guild, and the Covenant.

Now it was just past the usual dinner time, and she knew that the Allies would break session for the evening. For as much work as they needed to do, royalty did not like to miss their meals.

When she came around the final corner and saw one of the doors that led into the council chambers, her courage began to falter again, and so did her pace. Two of the King's personal guards bracketed the door, resplendent in their black and silver Tal tabards, and they looked at her curiously, even cautiously.

She was well known by all of the King's guards by now, but she could only imagine what she looked like, barreling around the corner in her civilian clothes, a dagger strapped to her left boot in plain sight.

It suddenly occurred to her that she should have changed into her guard uniform. She might otherwise stick out when the Allied leadership emerged. Unsure just how long she had before the doors would open, she looked around, and found a bench in a recess just down the hall.

Glancing again at the guards, she nodded and waved awkwardly, and then sat down on the bench, resting her elbows on her knees. Hopefully she would look like nothing more than a castle servant waiting to serve her master.

The minutes ticked by, and she grew impatient and anxious. She almost stood up to start pacing, but managed to control herself. She had to do this, she had to make her case and convince the King that she served him better as a Guardian.

This was where she belonged. Not with the Warriors. Even if she could be assigned to another city, under another Commander, she realized she didn't want to return to the Guild.

That realization surprised her. There was a time when she never could have imagined being anything other than a Warrior. It had been her dream for as long as she could remember, it was the only life she knew.

The Guild was too restrictive, she realized. As a Guardian, she could wear whatever armor she wanted, wield any weapon, and she was given a great amount of latitude in how she accomplished her missions. She reported to no one but the King and Draegus Kataar.

No, she could not go back to the Guild. Never.

She jumped when the doors suddenly clunked open. The two guards stood aside, and from within, a stream of servants, royalty, and dignitaries streamed forth.

The Allied Council Chambers was once the strategic command center from which the King would plan strategy and command the Tal armies in wartime. What was once a seat of war was now where peace was brokered. No, not brokered, fought and struggled for on a daily basis.

Queen Leian and her entourage walked by, and while she looked gorgeous in her navy-blue court dress and with her white crown, she appeared exhausted. Amaya couldn't begin to imagine the stresses of creating an alliance between the four kingdoms when there was so much bloody history between them.

Amaya looked anxiously for the King, knowing that he often came through this exit, but neither he nor Draegus marched through. When the stream of people, paying little or no attention to her, were past, she stood up excitedly. The guards looked in, and then remained at attention, still glancing at her nervously.

Realizing she had once again clenched her hands into fists, she forced them to relax, and then did her best to walk casually towards the doors. Since the guards hadn't closed the door or left their post, it meant that King Beredis was still inside.

The guards did not attempt to intercede as she passed through into the chamber, and she was relieved to find the King and Draegus alone. She very nearly turned around and left, but the moment she entered, Draegus saw her.

"Lieutenant," he looked at her wide-eyed. He and the King were hunched over their table, reading a piece of parchment.

The King also looked up, frowning. She felt her face turn bright red, and suddenly she didn't know what to say. The three of them stood still for what felt like ages, her eyes darting back and forth between them.

Finally, King Beredis stood up straight and folded his arms. "Is there something you need, Lieutenant?"

Before she could stop herself, she suddenly blurted out, "I am one of your most loyal and effective servants, Your Majesty!" Without realizing what she was doing, she began pacing back and forth on the other side of the table, her hands thrusting about in emphasis as she spoke. "Surely I have proven that to you, and proven my worth to you. My team has defeated more orcs than any single unit of Warriors or soldiers. We've followed your orders, we're loyal to you, I am loyal to you, absolutely and without question. You'll never find a more loyal Guardian, that I can tell you. Uh..." She looked at Draegus sheepishly. "Present company excepted."

Draegus raised an eyebrow at that, but did not interrupt her. She stopped her pacing and slapped her palms onto the tabletop. "I belong here, Sire! I belong under your command, I belong with the Guardians, we all do. And I swear to you, we will make you proud, and I will never, ever fail you!"

Her pulse was racing, and she started to feel lightheaded. She had just shouted at her King! Hadn't she?

Suddenly she wasn't sure just how loud her voice was. No doubt her slapping her palms on the table would draw the attention of the guards. The King frowned at her, exchanged confused glances with Draegus, and then nodded to her. "Good," he spoke in his court voice, louder than casual conversation and with authority. "Why do you think I chose you to be a Guardian? Now would you mind telling me what has you so riled up?"

"Din!" She had almost shouted at him. Catching herself, she stood up straight, doing everything she could to keep her hands open. "Commander Din, I mean. He came here to convince you to return us to the Guild to bolster our forces on the front."

The King's mouth hung open for a second, and he frowned deeply. "Commander Din came to report on another orc incursion into Ironwood. Your name never came up during the briefing."

Amaya's heart skipped a beat, and the edges of her vision blurred, tunnel vision setting in as she stared, horrified, at her leaders. "O...oh. I see." Slowly she backed away. "I am so sorry, my Lord. I didn't...I shouldn't have barged in here like this."

A small grin suddenly tugged at Draegus's face, and he brought a hand up to cover it. The King, on the other hand, raised his eyebrows. "Indeed. And if you were anyone else, I would have you sent to the dungeon for your outburst."

Color had drained from her face, but now it returned in full force. "I, um, should go."

She started to turn to leave, but King Beredis raised a hand to stop her. Feeling like a child being lectured by her parents, she clasped her hands behind her back and remained, feeling utter shame at what she had done. More than that, however, she had to fight back a building rage inside of her. *Din*, she thought, the name seething inside of her head. *This was another one of his games.*

"Lieutenant, do not for one moment underestimate your value to me," the King spoke carefully, each word enunciated clearly. "You do not know who all of the other members of the Guardians are, but every single one of them works alone." Her thoughts of disdain for her former Commander suddenly ceased, the surprise at her King's statement taking her off guard. "Yours is the first *team* of Guardians I have brought into the fold, and I have done so because of your decision not to followed Commander Din's orders."

She frowned at that statement, recalling that the King had openly disapproved of Din's orders and actions, but had taken no further action on the matter. She also didn't think it had any bearing on their induction into the Guardians. Not knowing what to say, all she could do was hesitantly ask, "Sire?"

Beredis smiled at her, his eyes gleaming like a proud parent's. "Amaya, I saw a spark in you the very moment you stood before my throne. And I saw it in your team too. Every day since then, you have shown me that I was not wrong." He shook his head slowly and began to walk around the table to stand in front of her. "I promise you, here and now, that I will never make you leave. I will never let the Guild take you back. You are a Guardian now, and that is a life-long commitment."

Once he was in front of her, he reached out and clasped a hand on her shoulder reassuringly. "And by that, I mean a commitment on both sides. You serve me, and I take care of you. For the rest of our lives."

Something inside of her broke, but not in a bad way. Something she hadn't realized she had been holding on to, and for that moment in time, the rage was calmed by a wave of soothing warmth.

Knowing that she was breaking every rule in the book, she reached her hand up to clasp his. Something welled in her chest, and her vision blurred with barely contained tears. "Thank...thank you." As an embarrassed afterthought, she added, "My King."

His smile grew only larger, but then his own sense of propriety took over. He stepped back, slipping his hand out of her grip, and nodded. "Now go and rest, while you still can," he smirked. "It will not be long before I call upon your team for another mission."

The moment was gone, but the calming effect of the encounter was not. With the deepest bow that she could manage, she said her farewell to the King and to Draegus, and then made her exit. The guards watched her go cautiously, no doubt still uncertain about her after her outbursts. She didn't care.

As she aimlessly walked the corridors of the castle, she began to realize why King Beredis was the most loved ruler of Tal in generations. She also realized that he was beginning to treat her like he might have treated a daughter, if one had been born before the Queen had passed away.

Suddenly she realized why she wanted to stay so badly. For all of the danger she was faced with on every mission, this was the first time in her life that she did not feel afraid.

This was the first time she felt safe.

***

The sewers of Archanon always stank, and given what flowed through its canals, Laira knew why. It was a smell she had grown accustomed to in her brief life, but it was also one that kept many other people away. Thankfully she did not have to travel far through the smell to get to her destination, where the smell was kept at bay naturally by air flow and a flow of clean water. After all, it would be hard to be a thief if people could smell her a mile away.

Passing through a tunnel with high winds, which made her cloak billow out around her, she paused, letting the wind wash over her. The water that passed through the tunnel was clean water diverted from the river, not sewage, and it made all the difference in the world.

She paused there, on top of a stone bridge that crossed the underground canal. Everlasting torches, stolen over time from various districts on the surface, provided ample, if varying light. Her stomach twisted as she considered what she was thinking.

That Zerek was actually so infatuated with her that he would want her to leave the dregs and live in the castle…

She never could, of course. That would be akin to slavery, and she would rather live poor and free than under the thumb of a failing monarchy. But still, he really had started to fall desperately for her.

Something inside of her twisted her stomach into a knot. A feeling she hadn't felt in such a long time. A feeling that made her want to never talk to Zerek again. Not out of spite, but out of caring. Out of regret. Out of guilt.

Could she do it anymore?

Steeling herself for the conversation to come, she crossed the bridge, which came directly to a sealed, steel door. She banged twice, slapped three times, and waited a moment before giving one final knock. Slowly the door groaned open, revealing a man dressed in rags as tattered as hers on the other side.

"Laira," he spoke in a deep, grumbling voice. "So good to see you again." He grinned, a sloppy smirk with half of his teeth missing.

As she always did, she tousled the man's hair as she walked past. "You too, Mekan."

He beamed at her action, and closed the door, leaving her to enter the Thieves' Sanctuary. Within was a wide-open, massive chamber that was crisscrossed with aqueducts going deeper and deeper under the city. It was quite literally on the opposite side of the city from the fabled Tomb of the Ascended, and seemed utterly redundant and useless, stretching deep into the ground but providing no actual water to the city above.

The chamber seemed to have been long forgotten by the rest of the city, and with only a couple of sealed off entrances within the sewers, it made for an excellent hiding place for the thieves, and a sanctuary for the city's homeless during the worst of the winters. Or at least, those whom Sorin deemed friends of the thieves.

That was whom she needed to find. He'd been the de-facto leader of their little faction for years, and no one seemed anxious to step up to challenge him. Which was fine, he actually had helped them organize well. They were no longer a disjointed scattering of thieves. Rules of conduct had been established, most of which she rather liked, such as never to steal from someone who clearly had to struggle to make ends meet.

Laira checked all of Sorin's usual spots. The first place she looked was in a little walled-off section he had built, to act as his own quarters and an office, but he wasn't there. Nor was he eating at the community kitchen. He also wasn't in the map room, which wasn't exactly a room as it was just a little alcove where city maps had been nailed into the ancient stone walls marking homes and businesses that were off-limits to the thieves or those that were considered prime targets.

Beginning to suspect that Sorin was still out in the city, Laira felt relieved. Already she was feeling apprehensive about what she had come to tell him, to ask of him. For as young as she was, she'd earned his respect long ago, and she didn't want to lose that by appearing weak.

Then she heard him call to her, "Hey, Laira!"

She had just left the map room and was ready to find her bed, but now she cringed at hearing his voice, and slowly turned to face him. With two of his friends, Dak and Emira, in tow, Sorin appeared in good cheer as he made his way from the entrance to the map room.

Trying to smile and look pleased to see him, Laira nodded. "Sorin."

When she tried to keep going, to not have to speak with him, he suddenly jumped in front of her, "Hey, wait a moment." He pushed a lock of his black hair behind an ear and frowned at her. "What's wrong?"

Feeling herself blush, she tried to push past him, but knew that was a futile effort. "It's nothing," she shook her head. Now she *knew* she couldn't tell him. But she also knew he had a way of getting her to tell him everything. He had that affect on everyone.

For a moment, he stared into her eyes, searching them for a clue. Then the edges of his lips pulled down into a grimace. "Give us a minute," he spoke to his friends. They looked at each other, then at Laira, before they turned and headed for the kitchen.

There wasn't much in the way of privacy in the Thieves' Sanctuary, but the little alcove of the map room helped them watch for prying eyes. Resigned to her fate, Laira walked back in with Sorin. Two blue-white everlasting torches illuminated the alcove with a ghostly glow, and did little to hide the concern on Sorin's face.

Gently placing a hand on her shoulder, he said, "It's something to do with Zerek, isn't it?"

Once again she felt her face burn, and knew that he could see it even in the blue light. She couldn't look into his eyes, knowing the guilt she would feel. "Yes…"

Sighing, he released her shoulder and leaned against a wall, folding his arms and nodding. "What happened?"

Looking everywhere but at him, she shook her head, trying to fight the urge to tell him everything. But before she knew what she was doing, she just blurted it out. "Zerek wants me to move into the castle." Out of the corner of her eye, she saw Sorin's eyebrows rise in surprise. "Wants me to leave this life behind and become a castle servant. Says he could help get me in."

When she did finally look at Sorin's face, his face went from surprise to concern. "Do you think he's told anyone on the inside about you, or who you are?"

"I doubt it," she shook her head. "He's talked about the castle's attempts to counter the increase in thievery, especially of castle personnel. I think he's afraid that if he tells anyone that he's involved with someone like me, they'll punish him or tell him he can't see me again."

Sorin drew his lips into a thin line and nodded. "At least there's that, then. What did you say to him?"

Again, she blurted it all out. "We got into a fight over it, and I told him that I've taken advantage of his kindness, and that I can't do that to him anymore."

Drawing her eyes down, she shook her head. Her stomach twisted, and her thoughts ran back and forth between her guilt over leading Zerek on, and failing Sorin. Failing the thieves. Failing the city. All over a damned boy.

For a long while, Sorin was quiet. He stared at her at first, but then he looked down, his brow furrowed deeply. Finally, he pushed off of the wall, approached her, and gently touched her shoulder. When she looked into his eyes, she could see a mixture of disappointment and kindness in his eyes. "You're in love with him."

Butterflies exploded in her chest, and she felt her cheeks flush. "He's just a boy," she turned around and walked to the other side of the alcove.

She heard Sorin chuckle. "He's only two years younger than you, Laira."

"You know what I mean," she scowled over her shoulder. "I can't relate to him, he's lived a normal life."

"Has he, now," Sorin asked. "Then it's normal to have your entire family slaughtered before your eyes?"

A renewed pang worked its way into her inner being, and pain long-forgotten returned to her chest. Laira wrapped her arms around herself, willing the pain to go away, and doing everything she could to keep the memories at bay.

She turned to look at him, her eyes opening as she took in the image of him. The only father figure she knew now.

His face relaxed into realization, and he smirked. "You haven't told him, have you?"

Laira shook her head. "No."

Sorin brought his hand up to slowly stroke his stubble of a beard. "I see. So it isn't just that you've fallen in love with him. He has fallen in love with you, even without you using your past to grow closer to him."

"I thought it would make me feel less guilty." She threw her arms up in exasperation, "You don't know what he's like, Sorin. He's..." She closed her eyes and clenched her jaw, frustration mixing with affection for Zerek. "He's so kind to me. He doesn't see a thief. And he is so damn naïve about the way the world works here."

"Laira, he lost his innocence the day the orcs attacked," Sorin said, shaking his head. "He's not the innocent boy you think he is, not anymore."

Scoffing, she walked to the back wall and stared at the city's map. She looked at the Merchant's District, where she first met him, quite by accident. She looked at the river, where he had chased her to. To the Warriors' Guild. To the landing on the river.

Sorin was right. She had fallen in love with Zerek, and that was going to make everything complicated from here on out.

"I don't know what to do." She closed her eyes, tears of frustration threatening to come out. She pushed it back, like she would push on a door to keep it closed against a horrible monster. She couldn't show anymore weakness. Not today.

Sorin was quiet for a long time, and she felt like punching the wall, even though she knew it would hurt. She wanted to punch Sorin. To slap Zerek. She didn't want to feel this way anymore.

"He loves you," Sorin stated flatly. "So he'll come find you again.

Make sure he finds you."

Laira turned to object, but the look on Sorin's face told her it wasn't a request. "You know how important our mission is, and he's our best bet. Keep working him, Laira. Put your feelings aside. He's a mark, remember?"

Could she ever do that? Ignore her feelings and use him further? She doubted it.

The doubt must have shown on her face, because Sorin stepped forward and clasped his hands on both of her shoulders, this time firmly. "Our kingdom is lying to us, Laira. Our own people on the inside don't have the access that he has or will have to sensitive documents. We need him. Which means," he crouched to force her to look into his eyes, "we need you. You're the one he's fallen in love with. You're the only one who can do this."

She clenched her jaw, and used that same image of a door in her mind to push her feelings back, to keep them away. He was right. Something was very wrong in Tal, and a lot of people were counting on her.

"Alright," she nodded. Looking into Sorin's eyes, pushing the guilt she felt away, she sighed, resigned to her job. "You're right."

Slapping her shoulder encouragingly, Sorin smiled, "There she is."

Frowning, she asked, "There who is?"

"The tough woman I always knew you were," he pulled away. "Now go on. You know what to do."

With a single nod, she turned away from him and walked out, her head held high. Not because she felt confident, but because she had to make a show of it. Dak and Emira watched from across the open hole that delved deeper into Halarite than she thought possible. It mirrored the hole that kept threatening to form in her stomach. If they saw hesitation on her face, they would report it to Sorin, and he might pull her off of the task. Who knew what they might do to Zerek then.

Sorin had, in fact, inspired her. But not in the way he thought. He was right. She could do this. She could do what needed to be done.

What was right.

***

Night had fallen, and Zerek's tasks for the day had all been finished with time to spare. He wanted more to do, *anything* to keep his mind off of what had happened earlier. He didn't want to think about it.

Yet that's all he did now, sitting on his bunk, legs pulled up to his chest. What had been so wrong with what he'd said? With what he'd asked? Why had Laira reacted the way she did?

Had he lost her forever? He had, hadn't he? Somehow he had messed up so badly that she ran off, and he'd never see her again.

Why was asking her to live in the castle so bad? She lived on the streets, and even faintly smelled of the sewers, though he never told her. He was offering to help her get off of the streets. Why would anyone choose that life?

He sighed, resigned to his loss, resigned to all of his losses. Everything he ever cared about, everyone, they just kept getting taken away from him. He should have known better than to grow close to her.

As lonely as he felt, as isolated as he suddenly felt, he was annoyed when Endel entered the room and immediately came over. They shared a bunk bed, with Zerek on the top bunk, so it was expected, but he wished his friend didn't talk to him. He hoped Endel would only get into his bottom bunk and go to bed.

Of course, Endel never did that, he was always too full of energy. Zerek also wasn't exactly hiding his foul mood, so before he knew it, Endel had climbed up on the bed and sat across from Zerek, his brow furrowed in concern.

"Okay, what's going on," Endel asked after several moments of silence passed.

Zerek's cheeks burned a little. He averted his eyes at first, but then sighed heavily, scratching his head.

"Something happened today," he spoke quietly so that no one else could hear him. Several other male servants were in the room too, either in their bunks or enjoying a late dinner at the common table.

Endel's eyes turned upwards. "With Laira?"

Zerek nodded. "Yeah. I, umm…asked her to become a castle servant. Told her I could help her get in to become one, put in a good word, you know?"

Endel's face turned downward, and Zerek could almost see the sinking sensation that his friend felt. "You…wow." He shook his head, looking downward. "I...why did you do that?"

Zerek frowned. "Because I want to help her get off of the street. And I don't want to have to hide us from Kai or anyone else anymore. I want us to be together in the open. I want..." The darkness he had felt in his stomach returned, and he rested his head on his knees. "I wanted something I was stupid to think I could ever have."

Endel frowned, his head jerking up and to one side. "What do you mean something you could never have?"

He was about to say companionship, but then he felt guilty for not considering Endel a companion. No one else had stepped forward to become his friend in the servants' quarters. Most others were friendly, sure, but Endel had been a *true* friend.

"It doesn't matter," he sighed, leaning back against the wall. "It's over now."

"Oh?" Endel looked at him with a smirk. "Giving up so easily, are we? After how desperately you pursued her before?"

Zerek shook his head. "You should have seen the look on her face. She was so mad that I wanted..." Just as he was about to say it, he realized his mistake. "That I wanted her to change her ways. To change her life, for me. Oh gods, Endel, I'm such a fool."

Stretching out a leg to fake-kick Zerek, he nodded vigorously, "Yeah, you are. But not for the reason you think."

He frowned and looked at his younger friend. "What do you mean?"

Shrugging, Endel replied, "Hey I may just be a kid, but I know a thing or two about love. And trust me, she's in love with you. So this isn't the end. In fact," he looked around, and then grimaced. "Well, when the night shift is gone and everyone else has gone to bed, you should get out there and find her."

Shaking his head, Zerek said, "I couldn't find her if I wanted to. I never know where she goes, she always finds me."

"I know," Endel nodded. "And I guarantee you, she'll be out there looking for you right now." His confidence that he was right was surprising, and seemed a little out of place. Turning to the side, he prepared to jump off of Zerek's bed, but then paused. "Seriously. Don't leave her waiting tonight."

The earnestness in Endel's voice was curious, but it was enough to make Zerek think that his friend was on to something. It would be at least another couple of hours before he would have a chance to sneak out, and that annoyed him.

Endel jumped down, and then started getting ready for bed. All Zerek could do was wonder. Wonder if his friend was right, and if it wasn't over. Could he hope? Should he hope? Or had he really lost her?

Slowly, Zerek lay down under the covers, and then reached for the dagger under his pillow, where he always put it before he went to bed at night. He felt the cold steel handle wrapped by leather. And every time he did, he swore he could feel Elina's soul. Like she was still with him.

It was a lie, he knew it. She was gone. So was his father. But it still comforted him, in the worst nights when he cried silently into his pillow.

He didn't want to lose anyone else. Not again.

Not this time.

***

Despising how cold it was at night, Arkad scowled as he kneeled down in the shadows of the forest by Archanon. The river was only a hundred feet away, and several hundred feet further up river was the great wall of Archanon.

He felt bile rise in the back of his throat at the thought that this was all they had to look forward to. Part of him even considered whether or not the Wastelands were so bad. If drinkable water wasn't so scarce, and so many deadly creatures didn't prowl the night, he would have been content to simply setup defenses along the Wastelands' borders and call it home.

Realizing that possibility was yet before them, he inwardly sighed, trying not to let the troops that knelt beside and behind him see his disheartened state. They looked to him for leadership, and he could not afford to show despair.

Between them and the wall was an open field that would make them easier to spot, but their darksteel armor would help conceal them. Furthermore, they would approach from the lowest ground possible, from the river itself.

From their vantage, they could see the torches lit upon the river dock. While the river was wide and deep, only small boats and rafts

194

could navigate it, especially as low as it was now, so the dock did not look busy, and what he supposed were normal operations had been shut down for the evening. There were only two small river boats docked, one on either bank.

Several guards were visible, city guards, not the more elite Warriors he had fought previously. They would be easy enough to sneak up on and subdue. From there, he could see where the river emerged from within, and through the iron grating, he could see pale green light from within.

Was this really necessary? Would they truly accomplish what he wanted with this raid upon the humans' First City?

Was it worth the lives of his men?

He looked to his right, at his friend and trusted lieutenant, Kilack. Was this worth sacrificing his life? Or the life of young Tezarik to his left?

They had failed so miserably. The war had gone horribly wrong, and he was about to send them on a mission that could easily end in death. He didn't want to watch more orcs die. So many had been slain back home. So many had died on Halarite.

He sighed, realizing they needed to make the humans think twice about harassing their retreating troops. Now more than ever, he had to believe in his own words. He had to lead his people to victory, or at the very least, survival.

But he could not just order his men to die. "Remember," he whispered. "We do not need to sacrifice ourselves here. The goal is to get in, raise the alarm, and show them that we are strong and they should fear us. Make them think twice about leaving their cities unprotected." He looked specifically at Kilack. "Do not throw away your lives needlessly. Inflict casualties, destroy their buildings, and then retreat back into the wilderness."

Kilack nodded, "Yes, General."

"And if we are separated," he continued, "make for the Wastelands after the battle." He turned back to the towering wall before them. With a bitter taste in his mouth, he finished with, "Return home. And defend it at all costs."

Without another word, he motioned for his men to follow, and he made his way to the river, keeping low so as not to be detected by any sentries on the wall.

They made it across the open hundred feet to the water's edge, and as carefully and quietly as he could, he crawled into the waters. The cold bit at his skin, flooding into his armor and instantly chilling him to his core.

As he carefully waded deeper and deeper into the river, fighting against its current, he pulled his double-edged axe from his back and held it below the surface. Glancing behind him, he saw his men follow suit.

With only his head and neck above the water line, he began to slowly walk against the surprisingly strong current, trying to ignore the awful bite of the cold. His muscles quickly began to ache, and he felt fatigued as his heart beat faster and faster in his chest. He tried to keep a steady, slow pace so as not to alert the guards, but it was not easy.

None of them watched the river, or at least they didn't look down at its dark, glassy surface. They looked for boats coming up river, as unlikely as that was, or for travelers who walked along its shores. They never saw the shadows beneath their feet.

Already having divided his troops into two units before they arrived, the orcs split up, one group crossing to the other side, and spread out along the stone docks, made of the same stone as the wall, he realized.

Two of the city guards conversed not ten feet from the edge where Arkad waded. He could not use magic, nor could any of the others in his troupe. Not if they wanted to have enough time to burn through the grating. So they would have to climb up and use their weapons.

There was only one thing he could think to do. Slowly he reached a hand out of the water and grasped onto the edge of the dock, his companions nearest him doing the same. Then he whistled, not so loud as to completely startle the guards, but enough to alert them that something was amiss.

The two guards that conversed nearest his edge stopped talking, and he heard their heavy boots clomping towards him. His heart raced even faster, his fatigued muscles forgotten for a moment as the blood rage grew. He let that feeling give him strength, hoping it would not consume him as it had at Valaras.

He heard the thump of a weapon striking a body. An alarmed shout, and another thump. A moment later, the two guards nearest him were at the edge, looking across the river to where the shout had come from.

With all of his strength, Arkad pulled up and swung his axe, cutting straight through one guard's armor into his chest, obliterating his heart. Another of Arkad's troops hauled up and stabbed his sword through the other guard's armor.

Arkad yanked on his axe, and the guard tumbled over and fell into the water.

And it was over, as fast as that. There weren't many guards, and no workers were on duty. He heard the sound of more guards being slaughtered moments after his kill, but that was it.

The way was clear. They could sneak up to the grate, and use their enchanted weapons to break through.

They would finally strike back.

***

Gathering her cloak about her to stave off the cold night, Amaya wandered down one of Archanon's countless narrow streets. Her mind wandered, her thoughts dwelling on Din, on the anger she felt, the frustration.

How many months since his betrayal? Since she had been imprisoned? Yet he still knew exactly what to say to throw her off, to anger her, to unhinge her. By all rights, how she had barged in and practically shouted at her King, she should have been thrown back into the dungeon. If he hadn't been so patient and understanding...

What was wrong with her? She was strong, wasn't she? She had fought in countless battles, witnessed horrible atrocities, taken the lives of monsters and humans alike. She had felt the guilt, overcome it, found ways to deal with it so that she could sleep most nights. Yet this one man, a man who wasn't even a part of her life anymore, continued to tear her apart.

Amaya felt the rage and frustration boil up within her, her hands clenching and unclenching in fists. Her pace increased rapidly, but she paid no attention to where she walked. She could see Din's face, imagined smashing it to a pulp. Imagined throwing her most powerful spell at him, wanting to feel satisfaction for it, but it wasn't enough. In her mind's eye, she imagined smashing him again and again, with fists, with magic, with the flat of her sword, until she imagined thrusting her blade straight through him, lifting him up, her anger giving her unreal strength, and throwing him across the street to slam into a wall...

In that moment, she realized where her thoughts had gone, and her stomach sank to the lowest depths of her being. She stopped, blinking, feeling guilt and a terrible void open up in her chest. An emptiness. No...fear. Intense fear. Not of Din. She no longer feared him.

She feared herself.

Whether from the cold or from her frozen soul, she suddenly shivered. Looking around, she realized she had somehow wandered all the way down by the river.

Looking by the stone wall bordering the river, she sighed, the sound of flowing water working to calm her just a little. It was late, very late. Almost no one else wandered the streets.

Except for a young man who emerged from another cross street by the river. No, not a young man, just a boy. He glanced at her and froze, the look of fear clear on his face in the pale moonlight. There was no curfew, why should he fear her?

Her own introspection forgotten, she was ready to approach him and ask what he was doing, why he seemed so afraid to be noticed. Until another figure approached him, a young, slender woman, also donning a cloak, but much more ragged than his, full of holes. He looked at her, cautious at first, but she said something to him. A moment later, she planted a kiss squarely on his lips.

Feeling her own face warm, Amaya smiled, and placed her hands on her hips. She could not hear what they said, but the young boy seemed to forget Amaya for a moment, the kiss clearly having stunned him. She suspected a forbidden love had just revealed itself before her, though she did not recognize who the boy was.

When he returned to reality, he looked back at Amaya, who smiled, shook her head, and then waved him on. The girl looked her way, her pale face flashing in the night. She looked terrified too, but Amaya did not know who she was either. The boy smiled, said something, and then together the two walked away from Amaya.

Something warmed in her heart at seeing them. A warmth she had not felt in a long time. One she never expected to feel again.

Love still existed. Even after the atrocities of the Battle for Archanon, amidst a horrific war against the orcs, love could still blossom. Even class borders, if their differing attire was any indication, could not separate or thwart love.

She shook her head, and then realized just how tired she was. Sighing, she got her bearings, and then turned back towards the Castle District. Tonight she would sleep. And perhaps tomorrow, a new assignment would await them. Then she could vent her anger on her kingdom's enemies.

With that thought helping lift the darkness in her heart, for now anyway, she made her way back home.

Until she felt a flare of power that stopped her dead in her tracks. She had felt that flare before, many times.

Turning slowly back to where the two lovers had gone, she felt it again, and saw from the river a flash of bright, orange light.

Enchanted weapons.

Orcs.

***

Zerek's heart soared, pounding in his chest in excitement, relief flooding every inch of his body and making his fingers and toes tingle. He had gone to the river to look for Laira, afraid she would not be there, that he'd never see her again. Instead, not only was she there waiting for him, but the first thing she had done was grab on and kiss him.

The cloaked woman that had seen them had worried them both, but she seemed amused by their late-night rendezvous and had waved them away. Now they rushed towards their landing on the river.

He couldn't wait that long, he had to say what he had been thinking ever since he'd talked to Endel. "I'm sorry," he said to her.

Laira squeezed his hand, still pulling him along. "I know," she said quietly, looking at him with those deep, dark eyes. "So am I."

They weren't far from the landing, but he was bursting with what he wanted to say, so he tugged on her hand and pulled them to a stop. She turned to face him with a smile and a look that wondered at what couldn't possibly wait. She moved to kiss him, but he put up a hand to stop.

"Wait, Laira," he smiled. "I...want say something. To make up for what I'd said earlier. For what I'd asked of you."

She started to say something, but then stopped, and nodded, squeezing his hand encouragingly. "Go on."

"I, uh…" He stumbled with his words, looking down at his feet, shuffling them. His heart raced ever harder. Not because he had just run across the rooftops of Archanon to reach the river, but because of what he was about to offer.

Finally, nodding his head, he looked into her eyes, trying not to lose himself in them. "It was wrong of me to ask you to change your life for me. I shouldn't have. I just thought…" He paused, realizing what he was about to say was no better. "Look. I want to be with you, okay? No matter what. So here it is. I'll leave the castle, leave my job, and come be with you on the streets."

As what he said registered on her, her jaw slowly fell open, her eyes growing wider. "Zerek, no," she breathed.

Grasping both of her hands in his, he smiled in excitement. "It's okay! I'll do this for you, Laira."

"Your dreams," she shook her head, "you want to become a soldier some day, don't you? Or a Warrior?"

A small void opened up in the pit of his stomach, and he shook his head. "I'm a fool to think that could ever happen. I'm no solider. Torick, the guard that's been teaching me, says I'm learning quickly, but I'm just a miner." He caught himself, felt a rush of despair as the memories flashed through his mind. "No. I'm not even that anymore."

He looked away, loosening his grip on her hands, trying to pull away from her. "I'm no one," he said, a void bigger than the greatest mining pit opening up in his stomach.

She wouldn't let go, and she suddenly pulled him close to her, until they were nose to nose. Looking intently into his eyes, she said, "No. Damn you, Zerek, don't you dare give up on your dreams!"

"Laira, I…" He paused, the thought of what he was about to say creating a lump in his throat that caught his voice. He had to force himself to say it. To tell her what she already knew, but what he had avoided talking about. "I have nothing left. No family. No life. I'm just a messenger in the castle, a pity case for the King. The first victim of a new war."

Before he could prattle on more about how horrible his life was, she suddenly pulled him in and kissed him fiercely. When the moment passed, and she pulled away, she smiled. "Thought that might shut you up."

His mind was blank, but when she said that, he shook his head and tried to clear his mind. "I, um..."

"No," she shook her head. "You aren't nothing. You're everything to me. And that's why I have to tell you something." She closed her eyes and took in a deep breath. Her hands shook a little, and he glanced down at them.

"What's wrong," he asked, almost afraid of what she was about to say.

An ironic smile crossed her face. "I never thought I would tell you this." Opening her eyes, she looked intently into his. "But I have to. I can't do this anymore, Zerek. You need to know that..."

There was a bright flash from downriver, near their landing, bright enough that even Laira noticed it and turned around to look. A metallic clang reverberated up the canal.

"What in the name of the Six," he mumbled, moving to the edge of the road and peering over the railing with Laira.

A deep dread filled his heart when he saw what had happened. The iron grating that covered the mouth of the river was red hot and melting, and several pieces of metal had exploded into the canal. Through the freshly-made hole in the grating streamed his nightmares. His nemeses. The one thing he hoped never to see again in all of his life.

"Orcs," he said quietly.

And one of them immediately spotted Zerek and Laira. Its darksteel armor made its body hard to see in the night, but he could see its pale, mottled face clear as day, and it sneered at him.

"Orcs," he called, looking back into the city, only to realize the city was asleep. "ORCS!"

Now all of the monsters saw him, and he realized he had just sealed their fate.

Laira grabbed his hand, shouted, "Run!" and pulled him along.

Even before they left the edge of the river, he saw one of the terrible beasts climb up over the edge of the canal wall. Without another thought, they ran for their lives.

***

Amaya's heart raced, until she heard the metallic clang. The couple she'd seen earlier were close to the wall and had stopped, but now they peaked over the edge. Even before the young boy shouted

"Orcs," she knew what it was. Reaching for her sword-

Her heart skipped a beat. She didn't have her sword!

The young couple ran towards her, as fast as they could, but one of the orcs was already over the edge and racing towards them, faster than they could possibly outrun. With no sword, she could only fall back on the steel dagger she had bought after her release from prison, which she pulled from the sheath on the outside of her left boot.

She quickly charged the blade with magic, though with so small of a blade, it could not hold much. Willing as much power as she could into it, she pointed it straight up, and loosed a bright red flare high into the sky. A warning flare. An alarm for all of the guards.

With at least that accomplished, she ran towards the couple. But she was too late, the orc had caught up and grabbed the girl's flowing cloak, bring her to a sudden stop with a gag as the cloak wrapped around her neck.

"Laira!" the boy shouted, pulling a dagger of his own. Her heart leapt into her throat, and she wished she could run faster. The boy stabbed at the orc, but it used its sword-arm to deflect the blade with ease. The boy was undaunted, ducking beneath a swing of the orc's weapon, and then taking that moment to step in, his rudimentary training apparent in how he moved his feet. Before the orc could react, the boy jabbed the long blade deep into its armpit, the weakest point in most plate armor.

The orc roared in surprise, and then elbowed the boy in the head so hard that he sprawled to the ground in a daze.

Amaya was almost to them now. The orc turned his attention to the girl, but she was back on her feet and spun around, the cloak literally tearing free. She had a dagger of her own, and like a dancer, she dodged several attempts by the orc to take her head off, until she was so far inside of his defenses that she leapt up and buried the dagger deep into its throat.

Coming to a stop only a few feet away, she watched as the dagger slid out, and the orc dropped his sword so that he could clutch at his throat, blood oozing through his fingers as he fell backwards.

Stunned that the two were not so helpless or defenseless, Amaya smirked. "Nicely done!"

The girl spun around, looked Amaya up and down, and then turned to the boy, helping him stand up.

But they had no time to celebrate their victory. More orcs were already over the edge of the canal wall, including a very large one. Thankfully neither the large one nor most of the other two dozen that had climbed up focused on them. Explosions rocked the city as they fired the full force of their magic into the storefronts and homes that lined the riverfront.

"Go, get out of here," she shouted, pushing past the two to stand between them and the three orcs charging their way. She noticed more flashes to her left, and saw a few orcs had gone into the farmland on the other side of the river, and were blasting away at crops and farm houses.

Cursing the gods, Amaya charged her dagger again, and then fired as powerful a blast as she could at the lead charging orc. The blast of magic bounced off of its enchanted armor, and did little more than slow it down.

Without her armor to help her focus her shield magic, she was vulnerable, and facing three darksteel orcs, who were notoriously more intelligent and skilled than their normal Wastelands ilk, she was dead.

But she wasn't about to go down without a fight.

Turning to the anger she had felt only moments ago, she shouted, "Come on, then!" and leapt right into the oncoming storm.

***

Flashes of horrors past. Elina facing off against three orcs. Zerek helpless as he watched. He managed to take one out, but the other two... Elina's look of surprise and shock as she and the last orc killed each other. The light in her eyes fading as she pleaded with him to find someone, to warn that the orcs were back. Her empty body, the fire of her soul gone.

As the mysterious woman charged the oncoming orcs with an enraged battle cry, he knew he couldn't stand by and watch it happen all over again. He looked at Laira, who looked back at him in fear and with a clear desire to run. "Go," he simply said. And without another word, he charged in behind the woman.

"Zerek, no!"

The woman was a Mage, and she used her magical shield to help her deflect the first blows of the orcs. They focused only on her, an obvious threat with her magic, and within moments she was surrounded. Presenting an orc's back to him.

The orc was at least twice his size in bulk, and the armor gave it an intimidating profile, but that just meant that he was able to leap onto his back, climb up, and try to jab Elina's dagger into the back of its neck. It didn't penetrate enough to kill the monster, but it was enough to make it arch back and roar in pain and surprise.

The orc spun around, throwing Zerek down so hard that he skidded up against a shop, whose storefront suddenly exploded from a magical blast. Wood splinters and glass rained down on him, some of the glass cutting at his face and hands and tearing his cloak.

When the debris stopped raining down, he pushed up, pain searing his left hand from a fresh cut.

Looking back to the battle, he saw that the woman was somehow holding off the other two orcs. But the one he'd attacked was facing him, its axe glowing with a magical charge. Time stopped for a moment, and he wondered if this was when he would finally see his father, see Elina…see his mother again.

The orc lowered his weapon at Zerek, but in that moment, Laira suddenly was there, holding the first fallen orc's sword in her hand. "Hey!" she shouted.

The orc turned to look at her, instinctively bringing its axe up to block her blow. But her blow did not connect with its weapon. It took its hand off!

Roaring in pain, the orc used its other hand to swipe her aside. "NO!" Zerek charged forward, not caring that the orc was going berserk. He ducked under its flailing arm, and tried to swipe at its throat, but missed. It noticed him, and tried to bash him, but he had learned how to dodge attacks well, thanks to his recent training.

The orc tried to swat down on him like a fly, palm-open, so Zerek jabbed his dagger up, straight through its gloved hand, the point splintering through the darksteel from inside. The force still brought him down to his knees. Roaring in pain, the orc yanked back, tearing the dagger out of Zerek's grip, now stuck in its hand.

Laira was back on her feet. She was stronger than she looked, but he still didn't think she had the muscle to penetrate the orc's armor. She must have realized this, and decided to use its size against it. Swinging low, she caught the back of the orc's knees, another weak spot in its armor, and cut the tendons and muscles through the bit of leather protection.

The orc roared again and began to fall backwards. Laira planted the pommel of the sword into the ground and ducked as low as she could, holding the sword with both hands. The orc impaled itself upon the blade, its weight carrying the point through its armor.

The scene seemed surreal at first, Laira nearly crushed under its weight, the tip of a blackened steel blade pointing through the monster's chest. It writhed a little, but soon fell silent and still.

Rushing forward, Zerek helped push the orc off to the side, the blade now stuck. Laira stood up and huffed, glaring down at their opponent. "Gods they stink," she waved her hand in front of her nose.

Laughing despite himself, Zerek wrapped his arms around her in a quick hug. Until he remembered the mysterious woman. He pulled away and looked down the street, to see the woman just finishing off the second of the two orcs. The rest of the attacking horde had moved further into the city, until an ear-splitting roar broke into the carnage of the night. As one, the orcs stopped, glanced at one another, and then immediately turned back towards the river.

Blasts of magic followed them. Zerek smiled when he realized what it meant.

They were no longer fighting alone.

Then his heart skipped a bit when the giant orc that led the others barreled out of one alley, and came face to face with Amaya.

***

The invasion had gone better than Arkad had hoped, despite the initial setback of two children spotting them and raising the alarm. They had damaged or destroyed several buildings and, while the children and another woman were handled by some of his men, he led his troops deeper into the city.

They weren't going to go too far, they couldn't. They needed to stay close to their only escape route. But the damage was exhilarating, and as he blasted fire into a two story building, he reveled in the screams of horror and pain that followed.

Several of the humans streamed into the street to investigate the noise, many armed, but none were soldiers or Warriors as far as he could tell. One literally ran right into him while fleeing a burning building. Arkad shoved the human away and swung his heavy two-sided axe, taking the man's head off with ease.

Suddenly a blast of magic slammed into his armor, catching him by surprise. Looking down the smaller side-street he was thrashing his way through, he saw half a dozen armored humans charging towards him and his soldiers.

That was it, then. The human reinforcements were coming. They had arrived faster than he had hoped, but the damage his troops had inflicted was good enough. Taking in a deep breath, he roared out the call to retreat. Then, with barely a thought, he swung his axe and unleashed a wave of fire at the charging Warriors.

Their leader was the Mage that had attacked him, and that human put up a shield to deflect the worst of the fire, but it still gave them pause. Pause enough for him to close the distance between them in moments, and to tear through them like they were nothing. His sheer size and strength gave him a great advantage over them, and as his axe burst through the Mage's magic shield and embedded into his shoulder, his opponent fell.

The others were not Mages, and took even less effort for him to dispatch.

More were coming down the street, and he knew he could not fight them all off. He turned and ran after his retreating brethren, right back out to the riverside street. And into the unarmed woman.

She had picked up one of his fallen kin's darksteel axes and held it in her hand. That was when he also felt the spark of magic in her. She wasn't so defenseless after all.

For a moment, they stared at each other, his heart pounding, the blood lust almost making him tear right through her. Until they heard the sound of footsteps running towards them. They both looked up-river, and saw the two kids from earlier running towards them.

"No!" the Mage shouted, suddenly moving to place herself between the kids and Arkad.

He was almost incensed to attack, especially when he felt the Mage's powers flare. But then he realized it had flared because she had put up a defensive shield. She wasn't preparing to attack, she just wanted to keep the children safe.

They stopped behind her, both of them armed with daggers and looking ready to fight. Children, fighting orcs.

Suddenly he felt his face grow cold. An image of his home flashed through his mind. A terrifying army slaughtering orcs wholesale. Slaughtering children.

"No," he grumbled. "No more."

Slowly he lowered his axe, and the Mage frowned at him. For a long moment, they simply stared at each other, neither speaking, neither moving. She, like him, was just trying to protect her people.

"General!" he heard Kilack shout for him from the river. He looked over towards his friend, and then down the road at the incoming enemy soldiers.

And he saw the carnage they had wrought on the city. At the buildings they had destroyed. At the homes they had destroyed.

Homes with children.

Looking again at the Mage, he bowed his head at her, and then ran for the river, leaping over the edge and splashing knee-deep into the waters. His boots sank into the mud, but he was undaunted, and he quickly made his way down river to the melted grate, now cooled by the water and the cold night air.

All of the other survivors were out, so only Kilack waited for him. They made their way through the opening and climbed up the docks on the other side, no longer caring about stealth. As quickly as they could, they ran for the cover of the forest.

His blood lust was dead. And he wondered if it would ever come back. His rage at losing almost everyone he cared about, and not being able to do anything about it… It was gone now. Finally gone. Replaced by a deep sadness that threatened to consume him.

In that moment, he knew he could never see it happen again. Never watch children be slaughtered again. Never take part in their deaths.

Not even human children.

Episode 7

REVELATIONS

In the blink of an eye, everything around you could change. Your status, the very course of your future could change from one act. Zerek never imagined that facing off against a bunch of orcs invading Archanon would do anything more than save himself and Laira.

Now, as he entered the men's quarters in the servants' house, he was greeted jovially by everyone.

"Hey, it's Zerek!"

"Buddy, you're back!"

"If it isn't the Defender of Archanon himself."

In a way, he was already used to the attention. But when he stopped to think about it, it seemed surreal.

Him, a simple miner from the Ilari Mountains, now lauded as a hero by everyone he knew. Never in his wildest dreams could he have imagined this.

With the battle already two weeks behind him, he had expected the commotion surrounding his presence to subside, and in actuality it had a little. But only a little. Speaking with everyone in turn, all of these like-aged or older men that he had spent the past few months bunking with, he'd found that they all weren't such bad people.

In those early days in the castle, he had avoided talking to them, and they avoided talking to him. Little Endel had been his only companion, his only friend.

In fact, he was saddened to see that Endel wasn't there. It was not yet midday, so he was probably out in the stalls performing his duties. Zerek was usually out running errands, and it was an especially busy time since the Allies were reinforcing every city in the wake of the orc attack on Archanon. But not today. For whatever reason, today Kai had no more orders for him, and had granted him leave to do as he pleased.

He hadn't had much time to speak with Endel in the past few weeks, so Zerek excused himself from the crowd and quickly left, making his way through the hallway and out into the courtyard as fast possible. The stables were on the other side of the castle, so he took off into a run, anxious to find his friend.

Until he heard Kai's voice call out, "Zerek!"

Screeching to a halt, Zerek turned to find the Steward of Archanon Castle coming out of one of the castle's back entrances. She wore another pencil-thin dress, this time a burgundy colored one. She wasn't rushing towards him, which disappointed him – she always looked comical trying to rush in those outfits.

The Steward waved him over, and his heart sank. The lull in assignments was already over, and he wouldn't get to see Endel after all. He jogged over to the entrance to meet Kai, where she looked him up and down appraisingly.

"You've been summoned before the King," she spoke sternly. His heart skipped a beat, and a feeling of shock slammed into his chest, so much so that his hands went numb. "We both have."

"The...the King?" he stumbled over his words.

Ignoring his blabbering, she nodded in approval, "You look well enough for a court appearance. Come along at once." Spinning on the spot, she made her way through the entrance, the castle guards opening the doors for her once again.

Zerek was too shocked at first to immediately follow, but within moments, he was chasing after her. "Why are we being summoned?"

He'd only appeared before the King twice before, three times if you counted the Allied Council meeting. The first time had been to bring the news of the orc attack on his mining camp. The second had been to tell the King about the orcs' incursion by the river.

"I imagine it has something to do with your heroics," she scoffed.

Zerek couldn't figure out why, but she had treated him with increasing coldness ever since the battle. Was she jealous of the attention he was getting? She didn't seem the jealous type, but then again, Zerek really didn't know her.

In fact, the Steward never talked about herself with him, or it seemed with anyone. How lonely must she be?

Their trip through the castle was quick, as it always was following the bustling storm that was Kai. They did not enter the throne room through a side entrance, as servants usually did. No, as they skipped all of them and moved to the front, Zerek realized that this was an official audience with the King, and they were going to enter through the main doors.

Twice as tall as the servants' entrances, and twice as wide, the double doors were already wide open, bracketed by two castle guards in their finest leather armor and black and silver tabards. Suddenly Zerek was very conscientious of his own clothing, a simple blue tunic and brown trousers, well-worn leather boots, and his dagger, still strapped to his belt in one of the scabbards given to him from the castle armory.

He was a commoner. Worse than that, he was just a servant.

As they came to stand in the center of the door, he could see King Beredis standing before his throne atop the stairs at the back of the throne room. The giant statues that lined both sides of the red carpet intimidated him, as they always did, and he felt as if the kings and queens of old judged him while he and Kai walked towards the King.

At the foot of the stairs stood the king's most trusted guard, Draegus Kataar, father of the now-famous Cardin Kataar. Like the other castle guards, he wore leather and the kingdom's tabard. However, unlike those other guards, he was a former member of the Warriors' Guild, and the hilt of his longsword, strapped to his left hip, set him apart from the other guards.

Beside him stood yet another unexpected figure. Another castle guard, also wearing the standard armor, and also bearing a unique looking sword that indicated she was once a member of the Warriors' Guild. It was the woman he had fought side by side with two weeks ago against the orcs.

"Steward," the King spoke jovially, descending from the throne to greet them.

Zerek and Kai stopped a dozen feet away from the foot of the steps, and together they bowed. "My King," Kai spoke with absolute respect.

"Please stand tall," King Beredis said, coming to a stop at the foot of the steps. "I believe you both know Commander Draegus Kataar."

Kai nodded respectfully to the Commander, "Of course."

Moving to stand next to the woman, the King added, "And this is Lieutenant Amaya Kenla. I believe you, young Zerek, have already met her."

Unsure what to say, he glanced first at Kai, and then at Amaya. He did not know her name before now, the chaos during and following the battle had not allowed for pleasantries to be exchanged. "Yes," he said. Thinking he should say more, he added, "I think I owe her my life."

"As I owe you mine," Amaya nodded. "You aided me when you could have escaped. I'm not sure I could have faced all of those orcs alone."

Zerek felt his face grow warm, and he averted his eyes from her appraising smile. A part of him found her to be very attractive, and he loved the attention from her. But upon thinking of that, he immediately felt guilty, and he thought of Laira. He'd seen her maybe twice since the battle, his own duties keeping him from seeing her more than that.

"In fact," King Beredis continued, smiling, "the Lieutenant has spoken very highly of your skills, and that of your companion, the young woman you were with that night."

Naturally, Zerek also considered that the Kai was still furious with him for being out so late at night. And the existence of the 'young lady' he had been with was no longer a secret, though she had slipped away and never had appeared before the King.

She had explained later that she was afraid she might be recognized as a thief by a castle guard. He wondered if there was more to it than that. Something about what she wanted to tell him that night, moments before the orcs invaded.

"And I have spoken with your defense trainer, Torick Alixton," Draegus added. "He tells me that you have advanced quickly for what little training he's given you. Your physical fitness, your reflexes, all are higher than he expected."

"In short," the King stepped closer to him, "you have impressed a great many people in recent days. And you have proven yourself a willing defender of your kingdom."

His cheeks burning even hotter, all Zerek could think to do was bow his head, "Thank you, my Lord. It…" Pausing, he considered his next words. Was it appropriate to confess to the King his greatest desires? "I have always dreamt of being a Warrior. Of protecting others. Fighting for others."

A giant smile blossomed upon the King's face. "So I have heard. That is precisely why I have called you before me today." He then turned to Kai and nodded to her. "I know that he is your newest servant and our newest messenger. However, could you bear to lose his services at this time?"

The look of shock on Kai's face didn't quite mirror his own, but it came close. She looked completely taken aback, and even shifted backwards, as if she wanted to step back in shock. "My Lord? I, well, of course. I mean, he is not *my* ward. He is a servant of the castle, and therefore he is your servant to do with as you please."

It was the first time he had ever heard Kai stumble with her words. Her response was one of complete shock.

"Excellent," the King smiled. "Then we have quite the offer for you," he turned to Zerek. "If you feel up to the challenge."

Draegus stepped forward and nodded to Zerek. "There's a spot open for training to be a city guard, and it's yours if you want it." This time it was Zerek's turn to stagger backwards. They were offering to make him a soldier!

"I know it's not the Warriors' Guild like you wanted," Amaya stated, "But trust me. This is better."

Zerek wanted to rush forward and hug her, hug Draegus, shake hands with the King, do anything to express the joy that rushed into every corner of his body. "I…it…it's beyond my wildest dreams! I accept! Of course I accept. Yes. Absolutely!"

Almost everyone laughed at his emphatic response, and he felt himself blushing again. Except for Kai, she did not laugh. She did not smile. In fact if anything, her face grew longer, but Zerek seemed to be the only one who noticed.

"Excellent," the King replied. "Then, unless you have any duties for him to perform at this very moment, Steward?"

She slowly shook her head. "No, Sire."

"Then go pack your belongings," Draegus nodded. "Torick will meet you and escort you back to the Red District. You'll join the latest trainees in the training barracks for the next few weeks."

Brimming with excitement, Zerek very nearly ran out of the throne room at that very moment, but then stopped when hard-learned etiquette kicked in. He paused, and looked to the King.

No doubt seeing Zerek's excitement, the King nodded his head. "You may leave. Steward, if you would remain behind for a moment..."

Without another thought, Zerek ran out as fast as his legs could take him. It felt as if his legs had an unlimited supply of energy, and he would never stop running so long as he was fueled by the fact that dreams he never thought possible were finally coming true.

However, it wasn't the servants' quarters that he ran to. He had to tell someone else.

He had to find Laira!

***

Blessed warmth.

It was the first thought Arkad had as he and his surviving darksteel orcs crossed onto the brown, crunchy grasses of the Wastelands. They had finally left behind the wretched cold in the north, with only warmth ahead.

The Wastelands were aptly named. Very little of sustenance grew there, unless you knew where to look. The orcs that had lived in the Wastelands for millennia had survived there because orcs were very good at finding food in the unlikeliest of places, and they could drink almost any water without fear of poison or disease.

More than that, they thrived in heat. While he wished it were a bit more humid, it was the closest thing to home they would find.

Home... Should he resign himself to this fate? Would the Wastelands forever be their home? If so, then they could never rise to the empire they needed to become to protect themselves against the coming storm.

If he knew his troops well, the ones that had retreated from Valaras and the borders of Saran Kingdom, then any survivors would have made it back to the Wastelands by now. He felt his stomach twist and turn. Had their gamble paid off? Did their assault on Archanon force the humans to pull their troops back and allow his kin to make it home?

He hoped so, but mostly he just wanted to stop running. He was tired, so very tired. Even as strong as he was, he was reaching his limits to how far and how fast he could run. If he felt this tired, he could only imagine how the rest of his party felt.

More than that, however, he was tired of…everything. Of failing. Of being an outcast.

Of killing.

Shaking his head, he tried to banish the feelings from his heart. He was an orc general, he should never tire of the battle! That was what he was born to do. That was what he was meant to do. From birth until death, until the gods came down to relieve him of his duty.

He was a soldier. Arkad had to remember that.

As the sun drew high in the sky, he caught his first glimpse of the most welcoming sight he had seen in months. Through dry, gnarled forests, he saw orcs. Hundreds, no *thousands* of orcs spread out in a wide frontline in a deep valley, with trenches dug, pikes laid out, and catapults and archers ready to defend.

The defenses were still under construction, so he knew the line had only recently been formed, but orcs were efficient, and very soon, they would be dug in so deep that the humans couldn't hope to penetrate them.

A dark hole formed in the pit of his stomach when he realized how false that thought was. When he had first come to the Wastelands, he had been told just how difficult the Wastelands were to traverse for humans. The landscape changed so quickly from swampland to dead plains to impassable brambles. Orcs were tougher, more robust, and could make it through the worst that Halarite could throw at them. It was why they survived in the Wastelands, and why the humans had never wiped them out.

Now, however, the humans had Wizards, and portals. The front line could be bypassed and their enemies could attack from behind. Whoever had ordered the creation of this new frontline had not taken that into consideration.

Never-the-less, to see so many of his kin in one place warmed his heart. They weren't all dead yet.

There was still hope.

Even though they were still well within the cover of the trees, someone must have spotted them coming, and a deep, throaty horn sounded to alert all troops to their arrival. He felt that tone vibrate his very core, and he felt, for a moment, at home.

At first the orcs on the front formed up to defend against an assault, but the moment that Arkad broke through the tree line, he could see their formation slacken. When they finally approached the front line and slowed to an exhausted march, they were greeted with great fanfare. The orcs roared in hearty cheer, shouting in triumph at the return of their General.

Their troupe was surrounded, jostled about as their kin brusquely slapped them on the back or tried to shake their hands. Arkad's heart swelled, and no matter how he felt or what he thought about their situation, in that moment in time, he felt welcome, wanted, *needed*. He was their General, and despite his failures, they still loved him.

As he looked around, he saw very few darksteel orcs aside from his party. Almost all had been deployed in the two armies that had marched upon the human lands. Had any others survived, or were these all the ones who had been left behind to defend against counter attack?

When the initial celebration had ended, he and his team were taken to a large camp in the rear, where a fire roared, and he could smell fresh meat cooking. His stomach growled angrily at him and his mouth watered. How long had it been since they had eaten fresh meat?

They all sat around the fire, Kilack sitting next to him, looking completely spent. However, when food was in-hand, served by their lowest ranking soldiers who looked simultaneously terrified and in awe, they had the energy to devour their food in minutes. The taste of the sweet, juicy meet exploded in his mouth, and he was ever so grateful to be back.

That is, until he heard that horrible voice call out, "General!" The voice was clear, confident, and for a female, very low. The voice always annoyed him to no end.

Looking to his left, Arkad snorted at the approaching figure. When both stood, she was half of his height. Now, however, with him seated, she was able to look at him face to face as she stepped up next to him. She still wore her simple leather armor, blackened to try to make her look like she belonged amongst the other darksteel warriors.

"Orinda," he looked away. "Couldn't I have gone one more day without seeing your abysmal face?"

Orinda grumbled at him, but ignored the jibe. "I always knew some day you would fail so horribly that even She wouldn't be so forgiving of you."

A sudden lump formed in his throat, and feeling drained from his arms and legs. It was the inevitable conclusion to his epic failure. Punishment was due, and he would get no stay of execution.

The entire camp grew deathly quiet at her words, and all eyes fell upon him. Normally he would have glared at them for their stares, but all he could do was stare into the blazing fire. Somewhere in there, he saw his life behind him, and wondered if only his fate with the gods remained in his future.

Knowing that there was nothing else to do, he stood up from the ground, pulling his axe along with him. He couldn't help but grin when Orinda watched his axe nervously. But he would not take her life. That would only make his position worse.

Securing the axe on his back, he narrowed his eyes at her with a confidence that did not mirror what he felt inside.

Somewhere inside, he found the courage he needed to tell Orinda, "Do not worry, whelp. I will survive long after you have perished. I promise you that."

For a long moment, she stared up at him, her eyes searching his for the terror he felt but would never show. Scrunching up her nose, she shook her head and pulled out a lilac-colored vial. "We shall see about that, General."

Turning on the spot, she threw the vial against a rock, where it shattered and spilled out its contents. Within moments, a lilac-colored wall of light appeared before them, stirring the dust and broken, dry grass around them in a flurry of wind.

Without hesitation, Orinda walked through the shaft. Arkad scowled after her. He'd give anything to twist her head right off of her shoulders. If only...

He looked at Kilack, and nodded. "Take command, and reform the line to protect from all directions."

With a grimace on his face, Kilack nodded. "Yes, General."

Without another word, Arkad faced his fate, and walked forward with as much pride and confidence as he could muster. If he was to die for his failure, then at least the last memory his men would have of him would be that of a proud General.

Even if he didn't feel like it anymore.

***

It was as if every single person in Archanon was out in the streets today and wanted to get in Zerek's way. Somewhere in this gigantic city was the one person on Halarite that he wanted to talk to, and he couldn't get to her!

Of course, he didn't even know where to find her, so he was running through the streets as fast as his legs could take him, dodging every person meandering about, running into a few, eliciting more than a few grunts and complaints from random people.

Where could she be? In the past couple months, when he'd wanted to find her, he found that she often stayed near their spot, the landing on the river. But now, even after hasty repairs to the grating where the river passed through the city wall, the landing was under heavy guard. No way she would ever go near a city guard, not if there was even a slight chance that someone would recognize her as a thief.

So where, then? He thought maybe where he had finally found her, near the Warriors' Guild complex, but she wasn't there. Nor was she near the alley where she had snuck that note into his belt. And the bread lady also hadn't seen her that day. The bread lady wanted to reminisce with him about her own love-filled youth, but he was too excited to listen and excused himself.

When he found Laira, it turned out that she was near where they had first met, what felt like a lifetime ago. The Market District, where she had stolen his dagger and his first charge from the King.

She was perusing a stall, and he noticed her pouch looked a little full, so he assumed she had or was in the process of stealing food. He didn't even give her a chance to react or notice him, he simply grabbed her by the hand and pulled her along.

"Zerek!" she objected, trying to resist, but only just enough to let him know that she was annoyed.

"Come on, I have to tell you something," he said excitedly, his heart racing and his mind spinning with the reality of what had just happened.

Within moments, he pulled her into an easement between two

shops. Laira yanked her hand free and glared at him. "You almost got me caught! What's gotten into you?" Then she stopped, an eyebrow raised as he practically jumped up and down in excitement. "What's going on?"

"You're never going to believe what happened," he started. "You see I was out walking when Kai called me into the castle and said the King wanted to see me about something she wouldn't say what but I thought I was in trouble and then-"

"Woh," she clamped down hard on his shoulders, "Slow down there, lover-boy. You're talking too fast. Just breathe."

Zerek's face grew warm in embarrassment, not just at what she had called him, but at his own outburst. So he took a moment to close his eyes and take in deep breaths, an exercise that Torick had taught him.

When he finally forced himself to calm down, he opened his eyes, and felt a smile blossom across his face when he saw her own gorgeous smile aimed right back at him.

Zerek launched into another explanation of what had just happened, only this time he managed to keep his excitement under some semblance of control. When he finished, Laira's smile had grown ever bigger, and she clutched her arms around him in the biggest hug she had ever given him.

"Oh my gods, that's amazing, Zerek," she pulled away, giving him a kiss that made his lips explode in tingles. "I'm so excited for you!"

His own excitement and happiness was palpable. Finally, after so long, everything was going right! His dream was coming true, and he was falling in love with a wonderful, exciting woman. He was making a name for himself, and had the respect of the King of Tal and his guards. His life was finally coming together.

Remembering that he had left one final piece out, he added, "Oh I almost forgot, I'll be moving out of the castle today. I'll be in the training barracks for the city guard, over in the Red District."

It was as if a dark cloud had overcome Laira's face. Her hands stopped squeezing his in excitement, and in fact quickly seemed to grow cold, colder than the fall air around them. Her smile didn't just fade, it vanished in an instant, replaced by a look of dread.

She started to pull away from him, but he held on to her hands. "Laira?" He heard his own voice tremble when he said her name. Fear struck deep into his heart, his mind racing with how what he had just told her could elicit such a reaction. "What's wrong?"

Closing her eyes, she stopped pulling away and stood still for a moment. Something terrible was coming, he felt it. He didn't know what, he just knew that he had only ever seen her react this way once before, and suddenly he suspected what was coming.

"I have to tell you something," she finally said, opening her eyes. Her voice was quiet, barely audible over the din of the Market District. There was a world still moving all around him, but he was scarcely aware of it, of the dozens of people streaming by on the street behind her. The entire world didn't matter to him, only she mattered.

Her hands trembled, so he tried to step a little closer to her, but she backed away to maintain their distance. Afraid that if he let go of her hands, he'd never get to hold them again, he held on tight, and wouldn't let her move further away. Somewhere deep in the pit of his stomach, he thought he was about to lose her.

"I should have told you this a long time ago," she started, shaking her head, unable to look at him. "Maybe…maybe I never should have let you find me in the first place." She took in a giant breath, and then let it out in a long sigh. "Zerek, I've deceived you. I mean, not entirely. Well I did at first. But I've been lying to you. Or holding something back."

He felt his heart twist. What could she have lied to him about that was so horrible? Dread filled him, and ridiculous situations began to play through his head. Was she really an orc in disguise? No, that was stupid. Was she a murderer? He'd never seen any evidence of that. The only thing she had ever killed, as far as he knew, was an orc. So what? What was making her act this way?

Finally, she explained. "When I stole from you the first time, you were just a random target, a mark carrying the very documents we needed from the castle. But then, you started looking for me, telling everyone you could find in the city that you were looking for me." She shook her head. "It was apparent that you were infatuated with me."

He frowned and tilted his head. "Infatuated?"

She stared at him for a moment, then shook her head, "Sorry. It means you are, well, head over heels for me."

He nodded, that dread in his stomach mixing with the warmth he felt towards her. "Yeah, I am. So just…tell me already. What's wrong?"

"I'm part of a...I don't know what to call it. Like a guild, of thieves." She shrugged. "Nothing official, just a bunch of us working together for mutual benefit. We do, however, have a leader. And he decided your interest in me was worth..." She trailed off and stared at him, sorrow and regret in her eyes. When she took in a shuddering breath, she finished, "Worth exploiting."

At first, what she said didn't sink in. When it did, his heart sank to the deepest, darkest pit of his stomach. All warmth faded, and the edges of his vision grew dark. "You...what?"

He didn't know how to interpret the look on her face. He didn't know how to interpret anything going on around him. All he could focus on was the horrible darkness that had just clutched onto his heart and squeezed.

"Our leader ordered me to let you find me," she continued, her voice almost a whisper now. Or was that just his perception? "Told me to win your heart, so that I could someday convince you to join our cause. Not to become a thief, Zerek, just to help us prove that the monarchy was hiding something, and was doing everything it could to prevent its own downfall, at the expense of innocents."

Zerek couldn't think. It was as if his mind had stopped working completely, and there was just that moment in time. That moment of shock, that the world he had built up around himself was frozen. Nothing moved forward. Nothing went backwards. Only that moment existed.

Until the anger grew. First as a light simmer, then a boil, until it was ready to explode.

"You lied," he spoke. He was barely aware of how his voice sounded. Was it angry? Was it hateful?

Her eyes turned downward, and she nodded. "I did. But something I didn't expect happened, Zerek." She looked up at him again, her eyes pleading and hopeful. "I really did fall for you. I really...I really do love you, Zerek."

He'd let her hands go, but he didn't know how long ago that was. A pain he had never felt before welled up in his chest, as if something or someone had taken a hold of his heart and was squeezing it, harder and harder until it felt ready to crumble.

"Shut up," he said. "I don't...you lied." He backed away from her. "YOU LIED!"

There must have been more rage than he realized in his voice, or he must have shouted louder than he intended. She backed away, as if he had physically hit her, and what color there was in her face drained completely. A couple of people in the street behind her stopped and gawked at them.

"Zerek, I…"

He didn't let her finish. He didn't want to hear anything she said. He didn't want to be there anymore. Tears blurred his vision, and he didn't want to cry in front of others, in front of her. He had to get away, to find some place to hide. He had to escape. From her. From the world. From everything!

Zerek ran. He didn't know where he was going, he wasn't aware of any of the people he ran past, he just knew he had to run.

He had to find somewhere safe.

***

For the second time that day, Amaya was called before the King. Only this time, the King was in an unplanned meeting with the Allied Council, so she was stuck waiting in the corridor outside of the Council chambers.

The last time she had sat on the bench that she currently warmed, she had been enraged by Din's false claims, and had been ready to storm into the room to demand that the King retain her services.

Sighing, she leaned back against the stone wall, the cold seeping through her leather tunic. Annoyed, she sat up straight again, adjusting her posture to try to relieve the pain in her butt from sitting on stone for so long.

A voice from her right startled her, "Used to be you could sit anywhere for hours and never get uncomfortable." Elic strolled up and folded his arms. He too wore the castle guard armor that helped them blend in when they were not on a mission. His black hair was pulled back into a very short pony tail, and he grinned at her. "Getting old, are we?"

She rolled her eyes, and then slid over a bit to give him room. He sat to her left and leaned back against the stone, never unfolding his arms.

"We've barely started our lives, Elic," she sighed. "Yet right now I feel like I've lived a hundred years."

221

He shrugged and looked at her. "Gods know you've been through a lot lately." For a moment, his eyes took on a distant stare, and he added, "We all have."

With a nod of her head, she asked, "Have you heard from Denora?"

One edge of his face turned up in his attempt at a fake smile. "Yes I have."

When he didn't elaborate, she figured it was a subject he was not ready to discuss, so she didn't press further. None of them had been given leave to visit family since the war started, so all correspondence had been through letters. The quiet smile that Elic usually wore had faded over the past month, and she wondered if that had to do with his wife, Denora.

As always, however, Elic turned the topic of conversation to Amaya. "How are you holding up?"

Letting out her own giant sigh, Amaya leaned back, no longer caring about the cold. "I'm not."

That admission startled even her. Amaya had always tried to keep her emotions covered up around her subordinates. She had to look strong, look infallible, so that they could trust her command. Trust her.

Then again, she realized that they were no longer Warriors. There was no official chain of command amongst them, they simply looked up to her for leadership because that's what they were used to.

"You must be doing alright if you can hold off darksteel orcs with nothing but a dagger," he said, genuine enthusiasm in his voice. She felt something stir inside of her, a memory of her anger from that night. "You clearly didn't lose control."

Shaking her head, she looked into his eyes, their darkness mirroring the darkness in her stomach. "Yes, I did. I left it out of my report, but when those three charged, and I thought I was dead…" She paused, looking down at her hands, palms facing her. They were gloved, but she could feel blood on them. If she scrubbed for the rest of her life, there would still be blood on them.

"I felt so much anger, Elic," her voice trembled a little. "I just launched myself at those orcs without a care in the world. I wanted to hurt them. Hurt *someone*. Anyone I could, and they were just there, conveniently."

For a long moment, Elic was quiet, and she continued to stare at her hands. She wouldn't allow herself to cry, but the feelings inside of her were enough to make her shake. Even the memory of the anger she felt was terribly strong.

"What you did to them, you wished you could do to Commander Din," Elic spoke softly.

She nodded, looking at him with a small smile on her face, glad that he understood without her having to say it. He just looked back, sorrow on his face.

"What you're feeling is normal, Amaya," he nodded. "He betrayed you. He betrayed all of us, and if I feel the way I do about him, then I can only imagine…"

"It was stupid of me," she scoffed, leaning forward and planting her elbows on her knees, her head turned down and her black hair falling around her face. "I should have never gotten involved with my commander. Even if he wasn't a gutless, backstabbing rat, it was still a stupid thing to do. We were taught early in training never to get romantically involved with your commanding officer."

"Hey," he rested a hand on her back, a physical connection that she wanted to shy away from at first. "The blame doesn't lie solely on you, you know. He was the commander, it was his responsibility to follow and enforce the rules. He failed. He failed you, and he failed all of us."

She shook her head, glancing at him through her hair. "That only makes it worse. My failure hurt more than just me, it hurt all of you."

"Really?" he asked, something strange in his voice. She looked at him and saw a skeptical look staring back at her. "You're going to take the blame for all of our misery? We supported you when you decided to disobey him. We've always supported your decisions. So don't try to take the blame for everything."

She felt herself give a half-hearted, silent laugh. "You're all fools for following me."

"And damn proud of it," Elic patted her back, and then retracted his hand.

Sitting up straight again, she stared across the corridor at the opposing bench. "One thing is for sure. I don't think I can ever be in another relationship again." She felt her throat clamp up for a second, the realization of what she'd just said sinking in. "I don't care what that means for my future. I don't care if it means I never have a family. I can't…" She trailed off, gulped, and then finished,

"I can't risk going through that kind of heartache again. Not when you all are depending on me to have a clear head."

Elic said nothing to that, and for the next several minutes, they remained silent. Finally, when the air felt so heavy that she could slice through it with her sword, the doors to the council chambers opened, and a crowd streamed forth. She and Elic stood up and remained where they were, watching as the Allied leadership passed them by.

A moment later, Draegus was next to them, beckoning her to follow him in. She looked at Elic and was about to bid him farewell, but then another thought occurred to her. "Come with," she nudged his arm towards the chambers. "You're my second in command, it's about time you saw how these meetings went."

Elic glanced at the chamber doors, and then back at her. Shrugging, he motioned his hand, "After you."

Passing by him, she followed Draegus into the council chambers. After Elic passed through, the doors were closed by guards behind them. The chamber was void of people except for King Beredis, Draegus Kataar, and Amaya and Elic. The doors on the opposite side were also closed by the guards outside.

King Beredis wore his usual black and silver robes and stood in front of the Tal table. He glanced at Elic curiously.

"With your permission," Amaya looked at her friend, and then back at the king, "I thought Elic could join us this time."

The King raised an eyebrow, but nodded. "I have no objections. He would have learned about your next mission soon anyway." Turning his eyes to her, he asked, "What do you know of the orc General?"

Once more, the night of the Archanon attack flashed through her mind. Taking a moment, she nodded, "I know that he is called Arkad, and that he is one of the most formidable orcs anyone has ever faced. Even the Keeper of the Sword could not defeat him."

Stepping up beside the King, Draegus nodded, "He has killed more of our soldiers and Warriors than any other orc. We also know that all orcs look up to him as their greatest leader."

"Yeah, every time he's been in a battle, the orcs have fought with a noticeably greater ferocity." She frowned, and added, "but he also has eluded us quite readily. We had no idea where he was until he attacked Archanon."

"Indeed," the King nodded. "We need to eliminate him."

Glancing at Elic with a raised eyebrow, she asked, "We've found him again?"

Draegus folded his arms and nodded. "He was just spotted by our scouts entering the orc frontline in the Wastelands. All of the orcs that survived their invasion attempt have gathered there, and have recently been reinforced from further into the Wastelands. They formed up a line facing north to defend against us, so with the help of the Wizards, our forces are forming up behind enemy lines.

"It was a perfect plan, until General Arkad showed up. Our scouts couldn't keep him in sight for long, but shortly after his arrival, the orc line reformed to defend from all directions, effectively canceling our advantage."

The King sighed deeply, his brow furrowed tightly. She noticed that, as the war raged on, his face looked harder and more wrinkled. "We need to eliminate him, and we need to do it fast while we know where he is at. I am afraid that this mission will be a longer, less directed one, but I feel that your team is the only one truly up to the challenge."

"You're orders are simple in principle," Draegus stated, though she felt her stomach twist a little. Nothing was simple where Arkad was concerned. "Find General Arkad, and eliminate him."

Amaya looked to Elic, who frowned. "Obviously a frontal assault won't do the trick," Elic stated, planting his hands on his hips. "If their entire army is gathered around him…"

"We'll have to find a way to separate him from the rest," she finished, nodding to the King and the Commander. "Or wait until he does it himself."

"Which could happen very soon," Draegus nodded. "Arkad is smart, and has a propensity to go off with his darksteel orcs on their own. So you're going to keep an eye on him, and follow him if he leaves."

Elic frowned and asked, "What if he uses a portal? We can't track him then, and we know he has those strange vials that make portals."

Draegus and King Beredis exchanged hesitant glances. "Wizards can determine where a portal leads to when it is created," the King stated, surprising her with that news. "However, they must be in close proximity. You must get Nia close to the camp to watch until he leaves."

Amaya sighed deeply, looking down at the chamber floors. She wanted to say it was a ridiculously impossible mission that would require a lot of things to go right for them to succeed. Nothing felt right about the mission.

"This will be a long one," Draegus stepped closer to her, resting a hand on her shoulder. She looked up into his blazing blue eyes, and he smiled. The confidence behind that smile, even if it was false, was enough to make her own courage stir a little. "And it is a vital mission. We need to eliminate Arkad to demoralize their troops." Draegus hesitated and looked at the King for a moment, before looking at her and Elic again. "We're fortunate that Sal'fe can resurrect all of our fallen troops, but it costs us a lot every time he does it. The sooner we can end this war, the better for everyone."

With a deep sigh, Amaya nodded. She did not feel confident at all, but she had to show confidence. She had to make sure that the King did not lose faith in her. So she said, "We will not fail you."

***

Only two months had passed since Arkad had last seen the black Fortress of Nasara, but when he emerged from the portal and the great monolithic structure stood before him, he was shocked at how much his perception of it had changed.

It had once filled him with hope, and even pride as his kin worked on finishing the repairs that Klaralin had ordered. Fewer worked on it now, and he noticed that some of the repair work looked completely abandoned. Many must have been pulled away to bolster the front line.

As he and Orinda strode towards it, he felt a chill crawl down his spine. This was no longer the seat of growing strength and power that he thought it was. It was not the beacon of hope for the rebirth of his culture and heritage. It was nothing more than an ancient, damaged building that held within it the last leader of a dying race.

Arkad could feel her power even now. Her magic flowed from the Fortress as a mist flowed from a lake down a river. It coated everything he saw, gave a sickly smell to an otherwise pleasantly pungent Wasteland. Of course, it was all perception, and none of that was real. But it twisted his stomach none the less.

And yet, it was his reaction to it that gave him pause. Was his perception of the feeling different, or was the magic itself somehow different? Tainted, somehow, like poisoned water. It also felt like it affected him far less than it should have, and that made him wonder even more.

They passed through the main gates and into the foyer, the black stone absorbing the light of the blue-white everlasting torches. Two guards, clad in darksteel, remained on guard, but there were no others around.

As the general of the army, he should have been aware of how great their losses were. Yet the fact that there were not enough of his darksteel kin to guard every corridor meant that their losses must be staggering. Nothing was more precious than the one who resided within these dead walls.

Orinda looked back at Arkad and smirked. Grunting, he furrowed his brow and asked, "You have something to say?"

"I can smell your contempt," she narrowed her eyes before looking forward again. "I hope it is towards me and not towards her. You will be fortunate if she does not take your head off on sight."

Though he dared not show it, he genuinely felt fear for a brief moment. Their leader was powerful and respected, and honor demanded that he bear the brunt of any punishment.

Never-the-less, a spark of doubt entered his mind. He was the most powerful orc alive, more skilled and cunning, and by far stronger than any other. Coupled with his enchanted armor and weapon, he could likely destroy their leader.

The thought was scandalous and he felt his stomach twist in greater fear. Orinda brought them to a halt before a single iron door and sniffed the air.

Looking back at him with a leer, she nodded, "That, General, is more like it."

He wanted to take her head off at that remark, but knew that such an action would surely result in his execution. His hands clenched into fists, but he did nothing more. Orinda opened the doors and preceded him into the library.

The carpet was old and dry, the dark finish on the furniture worn almost completely off, leaving only hints of the grandeur of the library. Stacks of book shelves lined the square room, and within them were books of all shapes and sizes. In fact the only thing they held in common was that they all looked ready to fall apart with the lightest touch.

In the center was a circular table with a gap in the center, surrounded by opulent chairs. Even the orcs did not know who had once held council in that chamber, nor did they know who built the ancient fortress. All he did know was that their leader, the last orc shaman that any knew of, now used the library as her personal study.

Even compared to Orinda, the Shaman was quite scrawny. The skins she wore hung loosely around her body. She could have easily had clothes tailored to her size, but she seemed not to care about her appearance. She stared at him, emotionless, her eyes piercing into his very soul.

Did she see the spark of doubt he had felt only moments before? Were shamans truly as powerful as legends spoke of?

More importantly, would she give him a chance to defend his failures? Could he even defend them?

Realizing he had momentarily forgotten his manners, Arkad bent to one knee, his body aching in protest after months of running and fighting. "My Shaman."

For a long time, the shaman did not speak. Arkad bowed his head and studied his boot carefully. His heart thundered in his ears, and he began to suspect that this truly would be where the gods would forever relieve him of his duties.

Finally, the shaman let out a long sigh and walked from the stacks to stand near Arkad. He flinched, fearing the worst.

"Our hopes and dreams have been dashed, General," she stated coldly. Her words were very proper and held a confidence that could only come from a shaman. "You have failed not only me, but every single one of your brothers and sisters."

He didn't know what to say, he didn't know if he should say anything at all. Should he defend himself? Could he? Had the battles before him been unwinnable, or had he simply failed to account for all possibilities?

As he debated those questions, a sudden, staggering thought occurred to him. He should have focused on figuring out the answers to those questions for the past several weeks. Instead, he had mulled over whether he wanted to continue to fight or not, whether or not he was doing the right thing.

Were the human lands making him weak? No...no, he could not blame external factors for his own internal battles, his own failings.

He had to take responsibility for his actions, his thoughts and feelings. No one else could possibly be to blame.

"Our entire future is at stake, General," the shaman spoke again, her voice making him flinch out of his reverie. "Do you not take this effort seriously?"

Without looking up, his reply came automatically, "Of course I do, my Shaman." Even as he spoke those words, he suspected that it was no longer true. Considering his next words carefully, wondering what really was important to him, he added, "The future of our species is of utmost importance to me."

She reached a hand down, and he prepared for the inevitable death to come. He knew the Shaman kept a long, impossibly sharp dagger on her at all times, and all it would take was a quick swipe across his throat to end his life. It would be a shameful death, but perhaps it was no less than he deserved.

Instead, her fingers touched his chin, and beckoned him to look at her. Despite his shame and failure, he brought himself to look her in the eyes...and felt nothing.

Those eyes had always instilled the greatest fear, commanded only the greatest respect, and her voice alone was usually enough to make any and all orcs follow her every command without question.

Her eyes had no affect on him.

"As you have always said," she narrowed her eyes at him. "And so I have believed from the moment you arrived." Her voice was soothing, even understanding, until she spoke again. With contempt, she spat at him, "Yet your failure is almost complete." She pushed his chin back down. "We now stand on the brink of complete extinction. You know what the future holds, what dark forces grow in the Universe."

She turned away and began to pace, her hands clasped behind her back. With imperfect posture, it almost made her look comical, but of course Arkad could not say that or laugh.

What was wrong with him? Why had he lost respect for her? Why did he no longer revere her? Was he losing his mind? The moment she realized his inner betrayal, she would strike him down without a second thought. He had to hide it from her, from everyone.

"Worse still, more orcs have dissented," her voice grew louder, anger spilling into her tone and her arms, waving about in frustration.

She turned and looked at him, though he only glanced at her eyes, unwilling to look deep into them again. "An entire tribe has defected, refusing my orders to join the front line and defend the only home we have left."

This news startled Arkad more than any other. An entire tribe? Even at great range, the Shaman was able to directly influence orcs if she chose to. She had the gift of sight, able to conjure visions of her children from hundreds of miles away.

Which was also why he was unprepared for her next order. "If you wish to redeem yourself, you will track them down." It was as if all thoughts evacuated his mind, and he was left stunned. "Those are your new orders. Find the rogue tribe, and any who joined them. Execute half of them as an example, and offer the others a chance to return. Any who still refuse should be executed in front of all others."

Execute his own people?! Such had not been done in centuries! Not since the great revolt that tore their people apart in civil war. How could she possibly ask him to destroy their own people?

Yet as startling as that order was, the fact that she didn't know where the rogue tribe could be found was a far more distressing revelation.

Realizing she awaited his response, he quickly came up with the only reply that was appropriate. "It will be done, my Shaman. They will regret ever crossing you."

Once more, she closed the distance between them and extended a hand, holding a single lilac-colored vial. As he reached up to take it from her hand, she said, "This will take you back to the front. Gather your darksteel brothers, the ones who share in your dishonor, and find the To'kar tribe."

Placing the vial in a pouch on his belt, he lowered his head further in one final act of reverence. Without another word, he stood up...and looked one more time into her eyes. He should have felt her power, should have felt her control. Instead, he still felt nothing.

Turning away immediately, he left the library, barely noticing as he passed by a disappointed Orinda.

The Shaman's powers were waning. Such had not happened in a long, long time, not since the days of the civil war. Legends say that the only reason a Shaman loses her power is because she has failed the gods in such a manner as to anger them beyond reckoning.

He still felt magic all around him, but she could no longer control him, and she could no longer see from afar. So what should he do? What could he do?

Barely paying attention, he walked through the Fortress of Nasara until he stood at the portcullis, staring out into the empty fields. The fields that were once filled to the brim with his kin, preparing for a war that was, perhaps, unwinnable.

So much death. Thousands of his brothers on Halarite, millions at home. Were his people in danger of vanishing from the Universe completely?

Staring out into those fields, and further still into the dead forest beyond, he realized how lost he suddenly felt. Everything had fallen apart in the past year, and it was only getting worse. What was the point of it all? Why did he continue to fight if there was no hope?

Suddenly he realized that this was neither the place nor the time to show his uncertainty. The Shaman could still kill him if she suspected his internal battle. *Then again, she might already suspect it,* he realized.

Without another thought, he pulled the vial from his pouch and threw it against the nearest wall. The two orcs guarding the entrance were startled by the sudden action, but relaxed when the portal appeared. By now, they were no doubt accustomed to such events.

He took one more moment to consider his options, and decided on at least his next step. So he passed through the portal to return to the front. To return to his friends.

Arkad needed time to decide what to do with everything he had just learned. The only way he could do that was to pretend to look for the To'kar Tribe, as he had been ordered to do. Out there, in the field, away from the army and any possible spies the Shaman might have amongst his people, he could think freely.

***

When Zerek had run away from that alley, he had no idea where he was going. He didn't even really care, he just ran. Unexpectedly, he found himself back in the Castle District, at the royal horse stables. When his mind cleared a little, he found himself standing in the middle of the long walkway between the stalls. The horses were accustomed to his presence by now, he had spent enough time there with Endel, so none of them reacted.

Through tear-blurred eyes, he looked around frantically, needing to talk to the one and only real friend he had. But Endel was nowhere to be found, and Zerek realized he was likely out training or exercising one of the horses.

The hole in his heart threatened to consume him entirely, and he didn't want to talk to or see anyone else. So he found one of the only empty stalls and went to the darkest corner he could find. Sliding down into the hay, ignoring the pungent smell of a stall in need of mucking, he buried his face in his arms, and he let himself go.

Everything came crashing back all at once, all in a torrent of visions that he couldn't hope to control.

His father, cut down by one of hundreds of orcs. The sudden emptiness he felt at the sight, how his limbs had begun to grow numb. He even remembered hearing someone scream out "no!" and, after a moment, realized it had been his own voice. Somehow, Zerek was remembering more now. Remembering what he didn't want to. The three closest orcs that heard his scream. Elina grabbing his arm and pulling him along.

Elina... He saw the light fade from her eyes, as if her very soul had expanded out from her body, leaving only an empty shell behind for him to cry over.

An empty shell...like the nothingness he felt inside of himself now. Crawling from his chest out to the rest of his body, consuming every fiber of his being. Until he thought of Laira. And then the emptiness was suddenly replaced with a rage beyond reckoning. He jumped up from his corner and began pacing back and forth, not caring if he stepped in the muck. His hands were clenched in fists, and he tried to hold back the pressure that was building inside of him, threatening to tear him apart in one great explosion.

Visions of their time together came to him, visions of chasing her, of their first kiss, holding each other at the riverside, her smile, her kind words to him, her encouragement, he remembered it all. With each memory, the pressure inside of him grew ever greater, until he couldn't hold it in anymore.

Zerek let forth an enraged roar, and he pounded his fist into one of the support beams. But it wasn't enough. He punched again. And again. And again. Until his entire hand screamed in pain, and he collapsed to his knees.

Cradling his throbbing hand, the tears came back again, in a flood that he could not stop, no matter how hard he tried. And he gave up trying. He gave up holding it all in.

He gave up...

Until a quiet, worried voice called his name. Startled, and feeling embarrassed, he tried to sniff back the tears and looked behind him. At the entrance to the stall stood the small, skinny figure of Endel, a giant of a horse waiting nervously behind him.

"Endel," he managed to say through his tears.

"My gods, what's happened?" Endel hesitantly led the horse into the stall. The horse stomped a bit, and Zerek realized his anger spooked it. Fully aware of what could happen if the horse decided its life was in danger, Zerek retreated back to his corner, giving the graceful beast all the room he could under the circumstances.

"I...I don't know where to begin," Zerek slid back down to the ground. His fist throbbed even more, and he feared he had broken it in his rage. How would he explain that to whomever his new trainer was to be?

He could imagine the conversation. 'I'm sorry, I can't hold a sword for the next couple months, I broke my hand in a stupid act of rage.' Yeah, he'd be rejected from the guards before his training had even started.

Taking off the lead rope, Endel left the horse on the other side of the stall, dropped the rope over the stall door, and then came over to Zerek, where he knelt and looked at him through worried eyes. "Zerek, tell me. What happened?"

Barely able to keep the tears from coming forth again, he looked down and stared at his swelling fist. "It's...it's Laira. She..."

"She broke up with you?" Endel asked.

That almost would have been better, Zerek thought. He shook his head, "No. No, she betrayed me. She lied." He looked at Endel, the anger within flaring again. "She lied, Endel. The entire time I've known her." Which he suddenly realized wasn't a long time. But when there were so few people left in his life that he loved, every moment with every person counted. Didn't it?

Endel hung his head low, the look of regret and sorrow in his eyes almost driving Zerek to cry again. At length, Endel sighed and rocked back on his feet, somehow balancing in a way Zerek found uncanny.

"I'm so sorry, Zerek," he shook his head. "So very sorry."

Zerek clenched his eyes shut, forcing the tears to stay back. Forcing the emotions that wanted to burst out back into the depths of his soul. He had to control himself, before he did something worse than punch a pillar.

Looking at Zerek's swollen hand, Endel grimaced. "That looks bad. Come on," he stood up. "I know just what to do."

Reluctant at first, unwilling to go out in public with how red and swollen he knew his eyes must be, Zerek finally assented and stood up. He followed Endel out, closing the stall door behind them, and into the fenced off area where they sometimes let the horses roam when they couldn't take them out into the fields.

The air was getting colder, and clouds had begun to build up overhead, partly covering the sun. Zerek shivered and tried to rub his arms, but that made his swollen hand hurt even more.

"I know it's cold," Endel said as he led Zerek to a water trough, "but trust me, this will help with the swelling. Stick your hand in the water."

Gawking at Endel, Zerek replied, "Are you kidding me?"

His young friend looked at him with exasperation. "Would you just trust me? It'll hurt at first, but give it a few minutes, and it'll start to feel loads better."

Grimacing, Zerek sighed and began to lower his hand towards the water. The moment his fingertips touched the cold, he retracted it, and shivered.

Rolling his eyes, Endel grabbed Zerek's wrist and plunged his hand into the water. With how cold the air had become, the water bit at every inch of his skin, and the ache in his hand increased.

"Hey!" Zerek objected.

"Just do it already, will you?" Endel shook his head.

Zerek wanted to pull his hand out, but he did not try too hard, and just resigned himself to the pain, gritting his teeth.

"This had better work," he glared at his friend.

Endel rolled his eyes again. "Big baby," he whispered.

"I heard that."

After another few moments, the biting sensation faded, though the ache did not. Not at first anyway. More and more, he wanted to pull his hand out, but Endel kept stopping him.

"Tell me what happened," Endel said idly. "What do you mean, she betrayed you?"

Sighing, Zerek shook his head and stared down at the water, watching the rippling surface reflecting the sky. "Where do I begin?"

"Usually at the beginning," Endel replied evenly. Zerek looked at him, and his friend stuck his tongue out at him. Before he could think to stop it, a small chuckle escaped, and then quickly turned into an outright laugh.

"Yeah, I suppose," he shook his head, trying to stop the laugh. He wanted to stay angry, he wanted to stay sad, but apparently Endel wasn't going to let him.

Finally, with another heave of a sigh, he launched into the description of the conversation he'd had with Laira. At first he was afraid it would bring back the pain in full force, but as he spoke, it felt like he was describing something that happened to someone else. In doing so, it helped him feel better about it, or at least feel numb about it, and not react.

When he was done, Endel's face had soured, his attempts to humor Zerek defeated. Or so he thought. Suddenly a great big smile drew across his face, "Wait, you're going to train to be a soldier?"

Feeling his own glee from earlier in the day threaten to return, Zerek nodded. "Yeah. I start tomorrow. In fact," he suddenly felt his stomach drop, "I'm supposed to be packing right now."

That's when he realized he had forgotten about his hand. He pulled it out of the water, which no longer felt cold to him, and examined it. His knuckles were still swollen, but the swelling had noticeably gone down. A slight breeze cooled his hand further, but the ache was so much better now.

"Hey, that actually worked," he smiled. Then he looked at Endel. "How'd you know how to do that?"

His friend's smile faded, but just a little bit. "I wasn't always a stable boy, you know. I learned a thing or two before they brought me into the castle as a servant."

Feeling shocked, Zerek tilted his head to the side. "Wait, you never told me that before!"

"Yeah," he nodded. "I've only been here a year."

Then it clicked in Zerek's head, and he felt his stomach suddenly fall into another endless pit of darkness. Thinking of how Endel knew how to get in and out of the Castle District unseen. How he leapt from rooftop to rooftop effortlessly. Just like Laira could.

The look on his face must have changed to reflect the horror he felt inside. Endel's smile faded completely, and he looked at his feet. "You just figured it out."

It didn't make sense. "But, you can't be. You're younger than I am!"

"I'm thirteen, remember?" Endel shook his head, resting his hand on the water trough. He looked Zerek in the eye, "And I'm not a part of them anymore. Not exactly."

The rage threatened to come back, Zerek could feel it boiling up inside of him. First Laira, now Endel? Had everyone lied to him from day one?

"You're a thief," he whispered, afraid someone else might hear him.

"I was," Endel shook his head. "I'm not anymore. I mean, I still agree with what they sent me in here to do, but I won't go back. Doesn't matter that I didn't do what I was supposed to do. I messed up and didn't get the job I was supposed to." He gulped. "You're job."

He wanted to shout, to scream at the kid, to hurl something at him, to run. Gods, he wanted to be anywhere but there. Anywhere but near Endel.

"Zerek, I-"

"No," Zerek backed up further. "Just, no, Endel. Shut up."

When he turned to walk away, Endel put a hand on his shoulder to try to stop him, but he jerked his shoulder free and stomped away. He completely ignored Endel's calls for him to wait, to let him explain. Endel stopped following him after he left the small pasture, leaving him to his emptiness.

Leaving him to his loneliness.

***

After Arkad's return to the front, he quickly found his team again. He hadn't been gone that long, but his team was dedicated, and they had wasted little time on their meal. The orc troops were already in the process of a massive reorientation to protect from all directions.

Kilack was at the center of the camp now, directing the restructure with only some amount of frustration. Only a handful of the rest of his team was actually present, but Arkad soon learned that the rest were out helping the less intelligent Wastelands orcs figure out how best to redeploy.

He was fine with that for the moment, but they would need to depart soon. The camp's Commander, Zinrel, was also at hand. Also a darksteel orc, Zinrel was one of the best strategic minds Arkad had come across. But he lacked actual combat experience against the humans of Halarite, and like Arkad, underestimated the Wizards.

"General," Zinrel nodded, his unusually dark face giving him a more ominous appearance, even to the taller, stronger Arkad. "I have trusted that your Lieutenant has conveyed your orders, but I must protest at this rearrangement of our troops. It weakens our northern line too much."

Arkad was tempted to quite literally take the Commander's head off with a swipe of his axe, but managed to restrain himself. "It is not your place to question my orders, Commander. Especially when we have fought our enemy and you have not. I guarantee you, if they have not already formed up on our flanks or rear, they soon will."

Zinrel raised an eyebrow, and then nodded. "By your command, General. I place my trust in the hero of Akaida."

It was good someone still trusted Arkad, even if he no longer trusted himself. Maybe that was where he was going wrong. He had started to doubt himself after his failure at Valaras. But now…now he doubted their Shaman.

After allowing Zinrel and Kilack to finalize the redeployment, Arkad asked of the Commander, "Tell me, what do you know of the To'kar Tribe?"

The fact that Zinrel did not look surprised told Arkad that his mission was not unexpected. "Their village is not far from here, so they were expected to bolster our numbers when the decision was made to hold the line here. They refused, and even managed to persuade several of our Wastelands soldiers to join them in their dishonor. By the time additional troops were sent, they had cleared out of their village completely."

Arkad frowned at that revelation. Honor was important even to the Wastelands ilk. To disobey their shaman… Did they know about her powers waning? Hoping for a clue, he asked, "Why would they disobey so blatantly?"

"I don't know," Zinrel scowled and spat on the ground. "Cowards, all of them."

Smirking, Arkad refrained from pointing out that every single orc now considered the To'kar Tribe traitors and targets of opportunity. It was likely courage that spurred them into rebelling. Or stupidity. He wasn't actually sure yet.

Then Zinrel said something even more curious. "Rumors abounded that their tribe was led by a female that had begun to lose her mind. Tana, I think. You know the influence a female can have over males."

All too well, Arkad grimaced. No matter what, he had to talk to them, to find out what they knew. Maybe Tana was crazy. Or maybe she knew why the Shaman had begun to lose her control. Either way, the only real recourse he had was to take his troops and move out. At least give the appearance he was following the Shaman's orders, until he knew what his next move would be.

Turning to Kilack, he ordered, "Recall every darksteel that fought with us at Archanon." When Kilack raised a questioning eyebrow, Arkad added, "We've been ordered to hunt down the To'kar, as punishment for our failure at Valaras."

Grimacing, Kilack nodded, and turned to a messenger to pass out the order.

"Until you receive other orders, remain in this formation," Arkad spoke to Zinrel. "Be prepared to retreat in any direction if the enemy brings an overwhelming number."

The Commander did not object to his orders, but for Arkad it felt strange leaving someone else in charge this time. Troop strength was dangerously low. Arkad should be with his men, ready to fight off the humans, to the last orc if necessary. Instead, he was leaving them behind with an inexperienced Commander.

He knew he had no choice. But that didn't mean he had to like it.

***

When Amaya passed through Nia's portal, the stark change in temperature was like walking into a furnace. Fall was in full swing in Archanon, with winter not far behind, so the oppressive heat of even the northern Wastelands shocked her.

She preceded her team through the portal and into the designated arrival area near the Allied army that had begun to form up for what many had hoped would be a final assault against the orcs. It was an area deep inside of a forested area, several miles behind the orc front.

Of course, calling it a forest was a bit of a stretch. Sure, there were plenty of trees and she could not see further than a few hundred feet beyond their small clearing, but the trees all appeared lifeless and twisted, with not a single leaf in sight.

And the stench, oh gods the stench! She gagged a little, never having breathed such a wretched, foul smell before in her life. It was as if someone had thrown month-old corpses, rotting fruit, and rotten eggs into a room and let the smell permeate every corner.

Coughing and bringing her hand up to her nose, she stepped aside to allow the rest of her team to follow unhindered. A squire was there to greet them, though unlike the squires of Archanon, he was clad in leather armor and armed with a simple sword and shield. This was a war zone, where everyone was prepared to fight, regardless of title, rank or purpose.

The squire bowed deeply before her and said, "Lieutenant Kenla. We've been expecting you, milady."

Elic stepped through the portal after her, and likewise began to gag. Amaya pulled him away from the portal, and then looked at the squire to ask, "Is it always this bad?"

Pointing to the west, where the sun marched steadily towards the horizon, the squire replied, "It gets worse as the day wears on, especially in the evening. You get used to it after a while."

"Not likely," Elic gagged, his eyes watering.

As more of her team came through, she asked, "How long have you been here?"

The squire considered her question for a moment, and nodded, "I believe three days. It's already starting to blur together."

When Peren, Idalia, Nerina, Vin, and Gell had followed, Nia finally passed through, and the portal closed behind her. Everyone stared at Nia, waiting for her to react to the stench. Even after nearly three months of working together, the Wizard still seemed deadpan to them all, and never spoke of her life in the Grand Wizard Hall.

Her head perked up a bit, and she took in a few tentative sniffs of the air, but did not gag or cough. Instead, she simply replied, "Intriguing."

"No doubt," Gell replied. "I'll bet you don't smell anything like that in your Guild Hall."

Raising a curious eyebrow, she planted her staff in the barren dirt and shook her head. "No, we do not."

Gell exchanged a smirk with Peren and Idalia, then caught Amaya's stern look. His smirk faded, and he nodded.

Then to everyone's surprise, Nia added, "That has been my favorite part of our journeys together. New experiences, new smells, new feelings." The slightest hint of a smile crossed her face and she looked at Amaya. "New friends."

In the dead heat of the day, silence fell upon them all. No one replied or made a single sound. Amaya didn't know how to react. It was the most personal thing Nia had ever said. And the friendliest.

Hoping to spare their Wizard friend embarrassment, Amaya stepped closer to her and clasped a hand on her shoulder. "Well said, my friend."

The slight smile on Nia's lips stretched up just a bit more, and she swore some color reached the Wizard's cheeks.

Letting go, Amaya then turned back to the squire. "Well, then. Take us to the General."

Bowing again, the squire led the way out of the clearing and into the forest. Within minutes, Amaya began to sweat profusely, and she was glad that they had brought extra water in their travel packs. She was also glad that they had been warned not to wear full plate armor. Leather would be hot enough, and their goal wasn't an all-out attack, but an ambush. Steel armor would only hinder such an attack, especially in this climate.

The Allied army was spread throughout the forest, the trees bunched together too closely for them to form any real ranks. The Warriors and Wizards were gathered in between the trees and dried brush, conversing quietly and suffering together. No one dared start a fire, for fear not only of creating smoke, but of also starting the dry trees and dead leaves on fire.

Before long, they reached another small clearing, where a tarp had been strung up between the trees to give some cover from the sun. Beneath it, a small table was setup with a makeshift map drawn out, surrounded by the highest ranking leaders of the Allied forces.

Stopping at the edge of the clearing, the squire bowed, "General Artula. May I present Lieutenant Amaya Kenla of the Tal Guard."

Likewise bowing to show her respect, Amaya waited to be invited under the tarp. General Artula looked up from the map and met Amaya's look with a stoic face. "Lieutenant," he nodded. "I was told to expect your arrival. Please, come in."

She nodded, and then motioned for her team to wait for her outside of the clearing. The squire stepped away, but did not go far, no doubt awaiting further orders. Three other commanders from other Guilds were also in the clearing, and all turned to face her. She did not recognize any of them, but that was not surprising, since their tabards showed them as Warriors from the other kingdoms.

Stepping up to the table as the others moved to make room for her, Amaya took a moment to glance at the map. It was a simple drawing of where the Allies waited, and the orc forces. If it was relatively to scale, they were at least five miles away, not the three that she originally thought.

Looking up, she met the General's gaze. He was a man of legend, not just in Tal, but in all of the kingdoms. A veteran of the last Lesser War, and of the Battle for Archanon, all respected him, and none questioned his orders.

Yet even the legend had his limits, and he was not clad in his full steel-plate armor, as he was always rumored to be in. Rather he wore leather armor not unlike Amaya's, his gold-dyed longsword the only hint of steel on him. It was unusual, and yet he still had a presence about him that awed her.

It startled her when she suddenly realized she had now met every person of the highest command in Tal. Her King, Commander Kataar, and now General Artula. Had her life really changed so much that meeting legends was common place?

The General glanced down at her wrists, and then back up at her eyes, an unsaid question in his eyes. The Guardians were not entirely secret, but she knew that the King preferred that their existence not be overtly acknowledged. Thankfully, the General did not ask her to show her brand. He would simply have to trust that she was, indeed, a member of the King's elite.

"I understand that you have specific orders from the crown," the General nodded. "Concerning the enemy General."

"Indeed," she nodded. "General Arkad of the orcs, probably the most infamous of our enemies. The Allied Council fears that his return to the enemy ranks will bolster their spirits." She took in a hesitant breath, looking at each of the Commanders before settling her gaze back on the General. "My team and I are to find a way to isolate the General and either capture or kill him."

"The latter being the most likely," the Saran Commander, a stocky, strong-looking woman scoffed.

"Even the Keeper of the Sword could not defeat him," the Erien Commander looked at Amaya skeptically. "How do you propose you and your team can succeed where he has failed?"

Amaya knew of Cardin Kataar's encounter with the giant orc. It was said that Arkad had managed to actually disarm Cardin, before a Wizard stepped in and forced the orc to flee.

Wondering how much she was required to justify and defend her position and her orders, she simply looked at the General and said, "A frontal assault obviously won't work. Thankfully my team has experience in other methods of attack."

"Is that so," the General raised a curious eyebrow. "Well in any case, the mission is yours, not ours. However, several minutes before your arrival, we received word from our scouts." Looking to the map, General Artula pointed to the eastern side of the orc encampment. "Arkad was spotted leaving the camp with several of his darksteel soldiers. We do not know where he was going, but a team is tracking him as we speak. They will be returning via a Wizard's portal to report their position within a few hours."

"That's a good thing," she smiled, thankful for the turn of events. "He'll be much easier to isolate if he isn't in the main camp."

The General nodded, and then narrowed his eyes. "We were due to attack their main camp tomorrow morning, but they have repositioned their forces, apparently at Arkad's command, and no longer have a vulnerable flank. We must re-assess our situation. However, what I can tell you is that I will not be able to spare my Warriors to help you."

She nodded, having expected that. "So the moment we take over tracking Arkad's position, we'll be on our own."

"As was specified in the orders I received," Artula patted a folded-up note in his belt. "We're to leave you to your mission."

Looking at each of the Commanders present, she nodded. "Very well. Where can we expect your scouts to report back?"

He pointed to the squire and said, "Gorman will take you to the designated location."

Backing away and bowing, she smiled. "Thank you, General. It has been a great honor to meet you."

Smiling warmly, he actually returned the bow, though he did not bow nearly as deeply. "Good luck, Lieutenant. I do not envy the task before you."

The sudden change from business to warmth was a bit startling, but she was glad for his honesty, and his personal touch. Her cheeks grew warm, or rather warmer than the heat had already made them.

Turning around, she retreated back out into the forest, where her team and the squire awaited. She quickly filled them in on what she had learned, and then looked to the squire to lead them.

As they walked, Elic was the first to speak of the impossibility of their task. "How can we keep up with them? They travel faster than any human, and even if we had horses, they would not do well in this heat."

She looked at her second in command, knowing he only spoke out about their missions if he felt it was of the utmost importance. Amaya also knew that he was right. But she had given it a lot of thought, and an idea finally struck her.

Feeling her stomach flutter in excitement, she looked at Nia, and then back at Elic. "Well, you know how the scouts tracking Arkad are going to use a Wizard to report back to us?"

Elic also glanced at Nia, who seemed almost oblivious to this fact. "Yes," Elic nodded. Then it dawned on him as well.

"Nia," Amaya turned again to the Wizard, "How often can you create portals?"

Finally, the young Wizard reacted and looked at her. "I have never tested my limits," she spoke cautiously. "It does take considerable concentration and energy to create one."

Amaya then looked at Vin. "If we used portals to cover large distances, how hard would it be to pick up their trail again after each jump?"

Vin raised a curious eyebrow, then shrugged. "I guess it would depend, but I doubt they are taking special care to cover their tracks. Not to mention the terrain itself makes it kind of easy."

"It would certainly cut down on our pursuit time," Elic nodded. "We could actually catch up."

"But there is a risk," Nia pointed out, ducking under a low branch of one of the dead trees. "Portals are bright. They might notice us pursuing them."

"Well," Amaya shrugged, "We'll have to cross that bridge when we get there. Although I already have an idea about that."

The look of confusion that crossed Nia's face was almost comical. Her brow scrunched up along with her nose, and she tilted her head to one side. "Well," Amaya began to explain, "by the time we catch up, we'll have an idea what direction they are heading. If they catch us coming, create a portal several miles ahead of their destination, and then-"

"No, that is not what I am confused about," Nia interrupted.

Stopping short, Amaya asked, "Then what?"

Looking to Elic for a moment, Nia asked, "Have we found evidence that the orcs have built bridges within the Wastelands?"

At first Amaya's mind went blank. Why was Nia asking about bridges? But then she realized where the Wizard's question came from, and it took all of her self control to stop herself from laughing outright. Several chuckles passed through her team, including one that escaped the squire.

"I'm sorry, it's just an expression," she shook her head. "It means we will have to deal with the situation if and when it happens."

Nia did not visibly look embarrassed, but Amaya wondered just how much emotion the Wizard felt, and if she was simply adept at hiding her feelings. That moment of friendliness earlier made her suspect that there was much more to Nia than even Amaya suspected.

"I see," Nia looked ahead and nodded. "Thank you for clarifying."

Several more minutes passed by as Amaya and her team discussed possible strategies. Before too long, she noticed that she could see further, and realized that the forest was thinning out as they approached the edge. She also noticed that there were fewer Warriors and Wizards, too. This was definitely the eastern flank.

However, just when she thought they would have a moment's rest, a figure stepped out in front of their group, bringing them all to a halt, and causing Amaya's heart to skip.

Flanked by his two usual flunkies, Uric Din stood before them, his sword sheathed, but his intention to block their path was clear.

"Please excuse us, Commander," the squire bowed, and tried to walk around the trio.

But Din did not move. He stared directly at Amaya, and he didn't look the least bit happy. She imagined her own face looked as angry as his.

The squire stopped when he realized that Amaya no longer followed him, and he looked back at them. Amaya and Din's eyes never parted from each other, and she felt the anger boiling up within her, like a tea kettle getting ready to blow. He was the last person she needed to see right now.

When neither spoke, it was Elic who tried to come to the rescue. "May we help you with something, Commander?" Even he couldn't hide his rage from his voice.

"I understand you didn't take too well to my little joke," Din spoke, his jaw tense.

At first she frowned, confused that he would bother her about their last encounter, that he could be angry about it. He had thoroughly humiliated her, in front of Elic, in front of the King and her Commander. He had won.

Or had he?

The anger inside of her stomach turned to something else, something unexpected but not unwelcome. Satisfaction. "You didn't expect it to come back onto you, did you?"

Din narrowed his eyes and clenched his hands into tight fists. She watched for him to reach for his sword, almost wishing he would do it. It would give her an excuse to do to him what she had so far only imagined.

"Apparently, you have somehow become the King's new favorite pet," he scowled. "As if I needed more reason to lose faith in the throne."

That almost incensed her into attacking him right then, and she stepped towards him. Thankfully, Elic's hand stopped her from advancing. She glared at the offending hand, and then at Elic, but he didn't let go. He looked at her with an unsaid warning, even through the anger in his own eyes.

Realizing that Din's words were bait for her to attack, she looked again at their former Commander. He had his hand on his sword, but had not drawn it. His two guards likewise were prepared to draw.

On the eve of an all-out assault against the orc army, she knew they could not afford infighting in the camp. So she stopped pulling against Elic's hand and forced herself to calm down. The war against her inner anger was one she wasn't sure she could win. Anger that had built up with alarming force in the past few weeks. But she had to.

"You're in our way," she growled.

Smirking, Din shrugged. "Am I supposed to care?"

A small grin tugged at the corner of her mouth. "We are on an official mission from the crown. If you wish to incur further punishment from King Beredis, by all means, continue to impede us."

That wiped the smirk off of his face, and she felt her chest ready to burst in the joy she felt from her victory. For a moment, he continued to glare at her, and she was ready to order his arrest.

Finally, he stepped aside, motioning for his guards to do the same. When the path was cleared, she smiled and marched past him. A great look of relief overcame the squire's face, and she hadn't realized what that must have looked like to him.

She wanted to hurt Din, and she had genuinely hoped he would have stepped out of line further. As it was, his insult to the throne could have been enough to warrant arrest, if not for the war and their need for every sword available. Plus it would have forced her to abandon her mission while bringing charges against the wayward Commander.

It wasn't worth it. They had to stop Arkad, hopefully before he could rejoin his forces. Whatever had taken him away from the front, it likely wouldn't last long, so they had to act fast.

She would just have to take care of Din another time.

***

Zerek didn't cry, not again. When he left Endel in the training yard, he went straight to his bunk, not so much sad as angry.

No, not angry, furious! They had lied to him, both of them! Had Endel and Laira worked together? Arranged for him to meet her like he did, pushed him to fall for her?

When he reached the servants' quarters, he felt ready to explode.

Until he entered the room and saw Torick impatiently waiting for him by his bunk. That was when he realized he had actually disobeyed orders.

"You were supposed to come straight here from the throne room," Torick folded his arms and stared harshly down at Zerek. "I was about ready to send out a patrol to look for you. Where have you been?"

"I'm...I'm sorry." Zerek felt embarrassed, his face turning red. He had meant only to tell Laira the good news and then come back to the servants' quarters. How long had he actually been away? How long had he hidden in the stables? "I went to tell my friends the good news, and I was distracted."

He didn't quite meet Torick's gaze when he spoke, but if the castle guard noticed, he said nothing of it. Was Zerek successfully hiding his anger? Or did his face reveal all? He felt like Torick could see right through his wall.

After what felt like ages, Torick slowly stepped up to him and gently placed a hand on his shoulder. Zerek looked up at him in surprise. "Look, I know you're used to a certain amount of freedom. But at least for the next few weeks, that freedom will be lost. So whatever is bothering you now, you need to let it go. Understood?"

Could he? Was it possible for him to completely forget everything that had happened today, and just move on with his new life? Or would it haunt him for months or years to come? How could anyone ever get over the kind of pain that he felt right now?

Knowing that Torick would not let him go without an answer, he nodded and said, "I understand."

Patting his shoulder, Torick motioned his head back towards Zerek's bunk. "Good. Now gather your things, and do it quick. We need to get you to your new bunk. Your training starts in the morning."

Without another word, Zerek moved to his bunk and used a sack someone had left on his bed to pack up the few clothes he had been given since his arrival in the castle. Other than his dagger, he had no other belongings.

As they left the room, Zerek took one moment to look back in, at his bunk, and the bed beneath where Endel slept. His stomach twisted into a knot at the thought that he would probably never see the small boy again. Somehow, realizing that made his anger ease, if only a little.

Enough that he had to hold back a tear.

This was goodbye to one new life. And the start of another.

Drawing in a deep sigh, he nodded his head, and followed Torick out. They marched through the Castle District with purpose, Zerek taking every chance he could to look around again. Would he be assigned to the castle after he finished training? The city wall?

Somewhere in the streets? Out in the farms to the west?

Suddenly there were a million new possibilities ahead of him, and his excitement began to build. He had never been so close to realizing his dreams before, never thought he could get so close! This was what he had always wanted. This was the life he needed.

Their journey through the city was quick, a path to the Red District that he had become all too familiar with. His excitement only grew as he thought more and more about his future.

Until he saw the Warrior's Tower. They did not go to the Guild complex, they merely walked past it, but as they did so, memories flashed through his mind. He could see Laira standing atop the tower, looking down at him and pointing out where he needed to go. He saw where he had tried to leap the wall into the courtyard, only to slam into the invisible shield surrounding the entire complex. He saw where Laira had grabbed his sleeve and told him to run.

The excitement faded. The elation turned to a deep sense of loss. Everything that had happened to him since the orcs attacked the mining camp, was it all for nothing? The feelings he felt for Laira...

Not far past the Warriors' Guild complex, they came upon the training grounds, a walled complex in itself, but much colder and less elaborate than the mansion-style Guild complex. Simple stone brick and mortar walls, much like the outer city wall. Were they protected by a shield as well? He doubted it.

They passed through an open pair of wooden doors into the training courtyard, and that was when he caught a glimpse of the kind of training he would endure. Ten men and women, clad in simple training tunics and trousers and wielding wooden swords, were lined up in formation. They all looked to be about his age, maybe a little older.

At the command of a Lieutenant, they stepped forward, jabbing their fake weapons forward, and then pulling them up, shouting as they did. Another command, and they stepped to the side, swiping their swords in the same direction, and another shout. With each command, there came another move and another shout in response.

Basic sword combat, the kind Torick had already taught him. As he watched and they walked around the edge of the field, Torick explained to him, "There are set start and end dates for training for each set of new trainees, and normally you would be required to wait for the next class. However, since I have been training you already,

Lieutenant Oban has agreed to take you in with this class. She'll assess your skills tomorrow, so be prepared. And for the sake of the gods, don't embarrass me."

Zerek smirked. "I wouldn't dream of it."

The Lieutenant commanding the soldiers, whom Zerek assumed was Oban, paid them no attention, and focused only on her charges. A moment later, they passed through another open set of doors and into a dank, stone and brick corridor. Zerek noted that, even though the castle was made mostly of stone, it was decorated such that it felt far warmer. Here at the training complex, the walls were sparsely decorated, and the lighting much lower. It felt cold and dark.

They passed one room that appeared to be an armory, and on the opposite side was a lecture room. At the end of the corridor, they passed into what was clearly the barracks, with bunk beds stacked three high. There were two small windows, one to the left and one to the right, at the end of the rows of beds, but they let in very little light.

"This is where you'll be staying," Torick explained. "Find a bunk without blankets, that's a sign of an empty bunk." He pointed over to one side where there were several large chests against the wall, "Grab a blanket or two from one of the chests when you find your bed."

Stopping them in the center, he looked at Zerek and smiled. "For what it's worth, you've impressed me in training."

Feeling his face grow slightly warm, Zerek frowned and replied, "I thought I did pretty badly."

"For a kid with absolutely no prior training?" Torick shook his head. "There's a reason you're here. Don't expect a lot of positive feedback, though. Training isn't about making you feel good, it's about getting you into shape and giving you the most basic combat skills. Your mornings and evenings will involve physical training, like what you just saw. Mid morning and after lunch will be classroom lecture for things like tactics."

Zerek nodded and commented, "Sounds fun."

He'd meant it seriously, but Torick laughed as if he'd joked. "Yeah, loads of fun. Someone will come get you for evening meal. Stay here until then. And whatever you do, get a good night's rest."

In reality, Zerek knew that wasn't going to happen. Not with how he felt. Not after what had happened today. His heart felt heavy, like his chest now weighed an extra fifty pounds.

But he couldn't tell Torick that.

Much to his surprise, the soldier extended his hand to Zerek. Taking the offered hand gingerly, Torick gripped it and gave it two good pumps. "Welcome to the city guard, Zerek." A grin stretched across his face, and he added, "You belong here."

That compliment momentarily spurred his spirits higher, and he smiled. "Thank you. Uh, sir."

Nodding his approval, Torick left Zerek to his own devices. His elation was already fading, so he quickly chose a bunk, found a set of blankets, and made his bed. It was the bottom bed of a set that looked completely empty, exactly what he needed. As much space and alone time as could be afforded in the barracks. The chest next to the bed was even smaller than his old one, but it was just large enough to fit his few clothes in.

With that, he laid down on the bed, unable to sit up due to the lower height of the middle bed. Staring up into the darkness, he let out a great sigh.

Almost immediately, he felt like the darkness surrounded him, pressing in all around, clinging to his skin like he was buried alive. Him, a miner by birth, suddenly feeling closed in. That was certainly not normal.

Something was eating at him, terribly. And it took him several minutes to realize that it wasn't the darkness closing in around him, nor was it the strange sensation that he almost couldn't breathe.

It was something about Laira. About the first woman his heart had throbbed for.

The first woman he had loved.

The first to love him.

Suddenly his heart stopped and he felt numb, when her last words passed through his mind. *"I really did fall for you,"* she had said. *"I really...I really do love you."*

Right before he'd run away from her, away from the disbelief, the pain, the heartache.

"Oh gods," he whispered. "She loves me!" Zerek sprung up, only to smack his head on the bunk above. He bounced back onto his bed and rubbed at his forehead in annoyance.

It startled him to realize that she loved him, to realize she had admitted to him what he had been afraid to say for so long. In doing so, she had risked her mission. Risked everything, for him.

Had he made a mistake? Was he wrong to be so angry with her? No, no he wasn't wrong to be mad. He wasn't wrong to have felt betrayed. But every time her words played through his head, every time he saw her pleading face when she told him that she loved him, it softened his heart, and somehow, even if only a little, it eased the pain.

Was her declaration of love another lie? Another attempt to lure him back into her games? Or was it genuine?

Zerek closed his eyes and tried to remember the exact look on her face, but it was blurry, incomplete. Like trying to remember a dream.

Try as he might, he just couldn't remember, and frustration grated at his heart. His hands clenched into fists, and he wanted desperately to know. He *had* to know.

Voices from out in the corridor caught his attention, and he realized that it was probably close to dinner time. His stomach growled viciously at him, and he realized he had missed lunch.

When the first of the soldiers ambled into the barracks, he sat up, keeping his head low this time.

In that moment, he vowed that he would find out if she was sincere. He would seek out Laira, look her in the face, and ask her for the truth. He would look into her eyes, and he would see either honest love, or the empty eyes of deceit.

One way or another, he was going to find out.

***

Arkad huffed in relief when their destination finally came into view. Night had fallen hours ago, and he and his troops were still exhausted from months of running. Even orcs had limits.

The second moon was gloriously full, casting a dim light upon the Wastelands. For all of the features of this new world that he hated, Arkad loved the moons, especially the slight orange tint to the larger one.

Small insects called lightning bugs were out in force, and they cast an eerie yellow-green glow upon everything. Never before had he seen such a sight, thousands of the glowing insects inhabited the swamps! They were harmless to most living creatures, but once the sun set and they came out, anything dead or dying was consumed by them.

It was also a double-edged sword. While their ambient glow made it easier to run across the uneven, sometimes dangerous terrain, someone inevitably swallowed a lightning bug every few minutes, and their coughing fits would slow the troupe down. Between the bugs and the orcs' fatigue, what should have taken only a couple of hours of running took them until nearly midnight to reach their destination.

The To'kar tribe's abandoned camp. He hadn't realized just how big their tribe was, until he saw the ruins. Dozens upon dozens of huts, each large enough to hold a small family, were shredded or burned to the ground. Charred remains of bones and gnarled wood along with scorch marks upon the ground silhouetted where tribe members' homes once stood.

But no bodies. Not a single To'kar corpse. Clearly the original orcs sent to investigate had taken out their frustrations on everything else, but he was surprised that no To'kars had remained behind to defend the camp. No orc tribe would leave behind perfectly good materials for building their tents. They would have to hunt and scavenge for new building materials when they finally settled down. It made no sense...

He and his forces came to a stop just inside of the borders of the ruins, and stared absently at the carnage. Above the heavy breathing and the hacking of one orc still trying to clear his throat, Arkad could hear murmurs of surprise and confusion.

Kilack was beside him, his breathing a little lighter than the others. "What should we do now, General," he asked quietly.

Shaking his head to clear away his own awe, Arkad waved his arm out ahead and replied, "Spread out. Look for tracks leading away from the camp. Look within the ruins for clues."

His orcs rumbled in response. In their darksteel armor, they looked like ghosts or shadows moving through a dead village. It actually sent chills down his spine, especially when he thought about how similar the armor was to the same enemy that had driven them from their home world.

Latching onto Kilack's shoulder with one hand, Arkad said, "You stay by me."

His lieutenant gave him a quizzical look, but did not object. Arkad saw how nervous his friend was, his fist clenched over the base of his mace, ready to pull it and defend his General in a heartbeat.

When the rest of his unit was out of earshot, Arkad began to walk through the dead fields, Kilack at his side. It was then that Arkad finally, and quite reluctantly, told Kilack about his experiences with their Shaman.

It was shocking enough news to make Kilack stop jumping at every noise, no longer disturbed by the carnage around them.

"I believe it would be our duty to remove the Shaman from her position if she is unfit to lead us," Kilack said quietly, as if afraid the Shaman could still overhear him.

"She still has power," Arkad shook his head. He reached his hand back for his axe, wondering if Kilack was right to be afraid. "I do not know how or why, but she has either become weaker, or something is blocking her power."

"I have never heard of such an occurrence," Kilack shook his head, looking around nervously. "Shamans are so rare, their power remains absolute until the day they die." He looked at Arkad, his golden eyes intense. "General, you know our laws. Weakness is unforgivable."

Arkad wanted to point out that they were the laws of a dead world, but he refrained. His lieutenant did not need to be reminded. Arkad also knew that if they had any hope of rebuilding their civilization someday, they needed to hold onto the values that had made the orcs strong for generations.

They needed to remain true to themselves.

Arkad and Kilack reached another edge of the camp, and remained there, staring out into the darkness of the night, watching the lightning bug clusters float about in lazy circles. The stench of a nearby swamp caressed his nostrils, and he breathed deep, thinking of home. He remembered a little tent outside of the city, where his father had taught him to wield an axe. Arkad could have chosen any life, any orc was free to. But for as long as he could remember, he had chosen to be a soldier.

It was a memory of a home that he would probably never see again, no matter how much he wanted to.

"This isn't so bad, is it," Arkad asked, trying to mask his sorrow. "This land. It's no wonder our brothers and sisters here have been content to remain in the Wastelands."

"It could be better," Kilack snorted. A moment later, he nodded once and added, "but truly, for an alien world, it is agreeable."

Arkad considered the fact that the number of remaining orcs, even Wastelands orcs, was frighteningly low. Maybe there was enough land left in the Wastelands that they no longer needed to invade the human lands.

If only that had been the case before they had attacked the humans.

Suddenly Arkad caught a strange scent that made his skin crawl, and his other senses perked up. He heard a twig snap in the distance. Sudden movement in the moonlight. Kilack caught it to, and in an instant, they drew their weapons. They looked around for the rest of their unit, but the soldiers were spread out and nowhere nearby. Whatever moved, it wasn't one of Arkad's men.

Focusing on his enchanted axe, Arkad prepared to for battle.

But he never saw the first strike. All he remembered was a bright flash, a great blow to his chest that sent him sprawling into the village, and then a sharp blow to the head. He was on the ground, his body ached, and he had a sense of rapid movement all around him.

Then he saw her. A small, petite orc female emerged from the shadows as if passing through a curtain. She did not wear the normal skins that their Wastelands kin wore, nor did she wear anything resembling their darksteel armor. Rather she wore leather reminiscent of what the humans wore, and a set of un-dyed steel pauldrons.

She looked at him, tilting her head to one side, before she pointed a finger at him. There was another bright flash, but this time, when the flash subsided, there was only a cold darkness.

***

When Zerek awoke that night, he cursed himself for having fallen asleep. He had intended to sneak out as soon as he was sure everyone was asleep. But thankfully, many of the exhausted trainees snored very loudly, and sneaking out would not be difficult.

It had to be around or even past midnight now. The doors into the courtyard were sealed, and guards patrolled along the top of the wall, so it took him a while to find a way out. Thankfully the brick and mortal walls of the complex were old, and climbing up and down them was not difficult. He only needed to ensure that he was not caught by the patrols, a task made difficult by the bright moons.

Once he was out, he snuck away as quickly as he could, until he was far enough away that he felt comfortable climbing onto the roofs and running at full speed. With the wind whipping past him, whistling in his ears as he raced along through the cold night air, he felt a renewed sense of freedom. And despite all of the darkness he had felt that day, his heart felt light again.

Zerek had thought all evening about where he would go. He had no idea where Laira slept, if she slept at all, and the landing by the grate was probably still well-guarded. That left only one common place they shared that she might go to.

When he arrived at the edge of the canal, he second-guessed himself. While he remembered the guards stationed at the river grate, he had forgotten that they had added patrols all along the river.

The river was the one common thing with Laira. It was where she had led him when they first met, and where she had somehow disappeared. The key was the river. No, not just the river, but the bridge just upstream from the grate.

So that was where he headed. A stone bridge that crossed over into the Green District, simple in design. They had never gone there together again, the landing had always been their spot. But somehow, that bridge was important, he knew it.

Zerek tried to take a direct route, but when he was close, he came across a wide avenue. He could have backtracked further into the city to find a place to cross the avenue under cover, but he didn't want to delay seeing her anymore. He was too close.

Climbing down from the roof, Zerek felt more exposed than ever. He wasn't just an errant castle servant anymore, he was officially a trainee of the city soldiers, and he realized that he would be scrutinized heavily for being out of his barracks. In all reality, he had abandoned his post.

So he moved carefully and quietly, sticking to the shadows where he could, and he avoided the patrols at all costs. He was almost caught once, when he came around a corner and found a Warrior leaning against a wall, her arms folded and her head tilted down. He froze, his heart skipped a beat, but then he realized that her breathing was slow and deep. She had somehow fallen asleep on her feet!

Careful to be as quiet as he could, he passed by the Warrior until he was in the middle of the street, and then he walked faster to get to the other side of the avenue and into the shadows again.

After another few close encounters, he finally made it to the riverside, where he hopped over the wall without hesitation and landed on the dry river bank. The river was a little higher than when the orcs had invaded, the first snowfalls in the mountains melting just enough.

The sound of the rolling river helped conceal his movements, so he no longer feared being caught. As long as he stayed in the shadow of the retaining wall, he was safe. He was up river from the bridge, not far from where Laira had first hopped down. He looked into the shadows under the bridge, only a couple hundred feet ahead, and felt a chill run down his spine.

This was where it had begun.

He looked down to see if there were other footprints in the river bank, but it was completely in shadow and he could not see. Taking in a deep breath, and reminding himself that he had faced orcs twice and survived, he walked under the bridge.

Each step made his heart beat faster. Would he find Laira under the bridge, or danger? Or something else entirely?

Step after step, heartbeat after heartbeat, he drew closer to the center, until he couldn't see anything.

It took a long time for his eyes to adjust, so he remained as still as he could, waiting, listening. Then he noticed it, an almost imperceptible flicker of light just a little further ahead. With a frown, he walked closer, his eyes fixed on the low, flickering blue light. Until he came to the center underneath the bridge, and found himself staring down a long tunnel that ran beneath the city.

"By the gods," he whispered. What appeared to be an everlasting torch was a couple hundred feet inside of the tunnel, not enough to cast illumination out onto the river, but enough that he could begin to navigate the tunnel.

That was how Laira had disappeared that first day! In the shadow of the bridge, he couldn't seen the tunnel, and she must have ducked in there after she gave him his dagger back. It also explained where the smell had come from. This was an old sewer tunnel!

So what was down there? Thieves? Beggars? Murderers? Who was she involved with, exactly? And what would they think of him sneaking his way in? Would they simply kill him for knowing too much, or would they…

A sudden shadow appeared, and he yelped and fell back onto his butt, splashing his behind into the icy river. The shadow rushed forward, eclipsing the torchlight. Fearing the worst, he moved his muddy hand towards his dagger.

"Zerek!" a sharp whisper called to him.

His heart leapt into his throat and his insides tingled in excitement. "Laira," he whispered back.

Laira stepped closer to him, though all he could see was her silhouette. She reached down, grabbed him by the arm, and helped him up.

Pulling him into the tunnel, she shoved him against the wall, and then stuck her head back out under the bridge.

"Hey, I…"

"Quiet," she whispered angrily.

He clamped up, feeling his face grow warm. Then he realized that the increased patrols could have meant someone heard him splashing around on the edge of the river. After several tense, silent moments, Laira sighed in relief and ducked back into the tunnel.

He couldn't see her eyes, but she looked at him, and he heard the annoyance in her voice. "What are you doing down here?"

His heart continued to race, and he stammered around his words. "I, uh, I mean, I came looking for you. I, umm, had to find you."

When she didn't reply, he tried to stammer out additional details, but only embarrassed himself further. So he shut up, and he waited for her to say something.

The moments passed in silence, until she sighed and shook her head. "You weren't supposed to find this tunnel. But I guess I'm not surprised that you did."

"Laira," he finally said, feeling butterflies in his stomach. "I…I'm sorry. I screwed up."

"No," she quickly replied. "No, don't you dare blame yourself for this. I lied to you. I manipulated you." Her voice shook a little bit as she added, "You're right to hate me."

He reached out, blindly searching for her hands. Instead he found her waist, and he kept his hands there. Until he remembered that his hands were muddy. He apologized and tried to pull away, but she stopped him and held his hands against her.

"Laira, you came forward and told me the truth." His eyes had adjusted more to the darkness, and he could just barely see her eyes, so he stared into them intensely. "And more than that...you said you love me."

He couldn't see the color of her face, but he still knew she blushed because of how she turned her head down and away. So he had remembered right!

"I was wondering if you caught that or not," she spoke just loud enough to be heard.

The butterflies in his stomach fluttered even more, and he felt his face grow warm. His palms were sweaty, and his heart was ready to burst from his chest. There was only one thing he could say now. The only thing that mattered in his heart.

Taking in a deep breath, he reached his hands up and gently nudged her chin up, looking into her eyes and willing her to feel what he felt for her. Finally, he said it. "I love you too."

He wished he could see her face, see how she responded to what he'd just said. The moment lasted forever, his heart suddenly going from beating insanely fast to stopping altogether, and he waited. And waited. Until he couldn't stand it anymore, and he almost said something.

Before he knew what was happening, she threw her arms around him, and she kissed him fiercely, holding him tighter than ever before. The world exploded in giddy happiness, and he wrapped his arms around her and pulled her in tighter.

When they finally came up for breath, he suddenly started giggling, and couldn't stop himself.

"But...wait," she pulled back enough to look into his eyes again. "What about everything I told you? You aren't just going to forgive me, are you?"

His spirits dampened a bit when she asked that, and there was just a hint of the rage he had felt earlier stirring in his stomach. She was right of course, and he knew he had to be completely honest with her. So he replied, "We need to talk more about it. But I can't ignore the fact that you love me, and...Laira, so much of my life has been lost this year. I can't lose you, too."

She remained quiet for a long time, but she didn't let go of him, nor did he let go of her. He gazed into her eyes, wishing he could see their color, wishing they had met somewhere with more light.

When she did talk again, her voice was barely above a whisper.

"So what do we do now? Where do we go from here?"

He drew her closer and touched his forehead to hers, sighing deeply. "We talk," he replied simply. Then he added, "You tell me more about what's going on, why you and the thieves are trying to infiltrate the castle." He had closed his eyes, but now he opened them and looked at her intently. "And then...I help you get what you need."

She pulled away just enough to look at him with skepticism he could see even in the low light. "But we already failed. You're no longer in the castle."

Grinning a little, Zerek shrugged. "That's okay. Sneaking in and out of the Castle District was one of the things I learned how to do just so I could find you." He hesitated, thinking back to his last conversation with Endel. "And...I think I know someone on the inside who will help us."

He realized what he was committing himself to, and the trouble it would lead to, but he didn't care anymore. He had to see this through. Either to show Laira that there was nothing wrong in the castle, or to find out if she was right.

No matter what, he couldn't lose her.

He didn't want to lose anyone ever again. No matter the cost.

Episode 8

THE LOST TRIBE

So cold.

Would Arkad ever grow accustomed to the cold of Halarite? Or would he forever long for the warm, humid days of home? Was he doomed to be miserable for eternity?

So very cold.

He felt his entire body shiver, right down to his very core. Nausea overcame him for a moment, and it took every ounce of strength he had not to turn onto his side and empty his stomach onto...onto what? Where was he?

A dull ache overcame every muscle in his body, so he was definitely alive. Considering the last thing he remembered, that was a good thing. Wasn't it?

The ache turned into a sharp pain in his head. Drums reverberated in his ears, but it was several long moments before he realized that the drumming was his own heart beat. What was happening? What had happened to him?

Tana, he thought. The To'kar tribe leader, and if his blurry memories were right, she was a shaman. One whose power rivaled his own shaman's.

He opened his eyes, but they felt dry and itchy, and the world was a blurry mess at first. He felt his chest vibrate when he groaned. He felt every muscle when he brought his hand up to rub his throbbing temple. He felt *everything.*

Blinking to try to get moisture into his eyes, his vision began to clear. The world coalesced enough that he realized he was in a tent or hut made from animal skins. A Wastelands orc tent.

Arkad gingerly turned his head to the right and saw the entrance, along with four orcs. So, no, not a tent, much larger than any tent. His mind was so foggy that he couldn't think of the word. He couldn't think of much of anything.

Until everything came into sharp clarity with one thought – he was a prisoner.

The guards were Wastelands orcs, but their clothes were of much nicer quality than the usual rabble. There was actual craftsmanship and tailoring in their design, and they fit the four orcs such that he could see that their muscles were well defined, even for orcs.

The pain began to diminish, and the banging drums in his ears faded to a dull thump, but he knew he could not defeat the guards, not unarmed. He was a prisoner, and there was nothing he could do about it.

His groans must have alerted them, for all four now stared at him. When he met each of their eyes, they snuffed at him, and then finally turned back to look at each other. The one closest to the entrance ducked out.

Though every muscle in his body protested, Arkad eased himself into a sitting position. That was when he realized that not only had he been stripped of all of his armor, but someone had put something on his lower body…what did the humans call them? Trousers? That was what they looked like, leather trousers. Why had his captors begun to emulate their human oppressors?

His head spun, and nausea overcame him again, but he wouldn't let himself fall back down. Then the worst thing yet happened to him – the scent of cooking meat wafted inside, and despite the nausea, his stomach growled fiercely.

After several moments of allowing his stomach and his head to settle, the entrance flap opened up, and a petite female orc walked in. Despite her small size, the three remaining guards stood at attention and gave her plenty of space. She covered half the distance of the structure, about twenty feet, and stopped. Plenty of room that her guards could defend her.

Then again, if she was as powerful as he suspected, she really didn't need guards.

"General Arkad," she spoke to him. He was surprised at how clearly she spoke. She was supposed to be a Wastelands orc, and they were not known for their intelligence or clarity of speech. "Welcome to the To'kar."

Arkad absently reached up to touch his enchanted necklace, only to realize that it was gone! It was the only thing that allowed him to understand the human speech that the Wastelands orcs spoke. He looked at her neckline, ignoring her perfectly-formed cleavage, and saw no necklaces around her throat either.

"You speak az'ork," he frowned at her.

Tana studied him carefully before she nodded. "Yes. I am quite fluent in our native tongue."

He rubbed his temples some more, his head still feeling foggy. Had she said 'our native tongue?' No Wastelands orc had ever heard az'ork. So he asked the obvious question, "Where did you learn our language?"

She raised one eyebrow, her mottled gray skin flushing a little darker. "From my mother, who else?"

His mind raced with possibilities. Had a single line of Wastelands orcs passed down the traditional language over the millennia? Kept the spirit alive, while the rest of the orcs assimilated into their new world? That seemed highly unlikely, based on the history of the orc presence on Halarite. The humans had hunted them down, treated them like animals. Culture was lost, education was lost, until there was nothing left but the animals he was forced to call their last hope.

Yet, the To'kar were obviously different. The posture of the guards, their backs erect, their chests puffed out, their heads held high. Their tailored leather clothing.

Still studying his face closely, Tana took two steps closer. Arkad tensed, ready to take an opportunity to grab her and hold her hostage. He quickly abandoned that thought, her powers giving her an advantage he could never overcome without his enchanted weapons and armor. Even then, he probably wouldn't stand a chance.

She looked at him intently, and nodded. "I was born in Akaida."

Color drained from Arkad's face, and he stared at her dumbly. "But...how is that possible?" He shook his head, "No, I helped evacuate the city, I fought to the last portal. You weren't there, you couldn't have been! You've been here, a part of the To'kar tribe since long before I arrived."

Tana nodded. "That is true. However, I did not evacuate the city when it was invaded. I have lived on Halarite for over a year."

"What?!" He shook his head, and then regretted it when the world threatened to spin. "How is that possible? Why?"

Tana studied his face for a moment, before she raised her right hand, palm up, and said, "Because of this." In a sudden flash, there was a ball of blue fire hovering above her palm. "I am a shaman. More than that, my power comes to me with little effort."

Arkad stared at the flame, mesmerized as a moth would be. The tiny blue flames flickered and danced before him, and a sense of wonder filled his chest. She had conjured the flame with no effort what so ever, as if it had always existed, and she merely opened his eyes to its existence.

"My powers grew faster than anyone could have imagined," she explained. "And our Queen, sensing my powers," she snapped her hand closed, snuffing the flames out, "ordered my execution."

His head snapped up in shock. "Why would she have done that? You were obviously meant to be our next Queen."

Tana stepped closer, close enough that she could have reached out to touch him if she wanted. "Exactly."

Shock quickly gave way to understanding. Even through his fog, everything made sense. The Queen had barricaded herself in her bunker the moment the invasion had begun, and had committed half of their military to guarding that bunker, despite Arkad advising that they needed to engage the enemy on the outer defenses.

He knew now that no matter what, their city would have fallen. But it would have given everyone more time to evacuate. More of their kin might have survived. His Queen had cared more for her own well being than that of her people.

In the end, her fear and selfishness had been her undoing. She refused to leave her seat of power, even when Klaralin had arrived and offered to take them under his wing. One shaman, the same woman who now led their remaining kind, had taken him up on the offer. Even when they had all fallen back to the Queen's bunker, and all hope was lost, the Queen refused to follow Klaralin to Halarite. Instead, she created a portal to who knew where else on their own world, and left Arkad and his remaining men to die.

The only reason they had survived was because the shaman had given a portal potion to Arkad before she had left with Klaralin, and when the Queen had abandoned them, they used it to evacuate to the Wastelands.

Now that very same shaman he had sworn allegiance to was failing her people, just as their Queen had. Her powers were weakened, no doubt by Tana's influence, and she had ordered him to kill his own brothers and sisters. In another time, he would have followed orders without question. Now, however…there were too few orcs left to waste their lives on killing as punishment.

A wave of fatigue suddenly washed over Arkad as the monumental reality set in. Here stood what should have become the new Queen, having been forced to abandon her people long before the invasion because of a selfish old woman. Perhaps under her leadership, they would have stood a chance, even against the hopelessly powerful enemy.

Perhaps Tana was their chance to save the future of the orcs.

Another orc suddenly entered the tent, drawing everyone's attention. He did not approach Tana, but instead dropped to one knee and bowed his head. "My Shaman."

"What is it, Vertek?" She turned just enough so that Arkad could see her profile. She wouldn't turn her back on Arkad.

"If I may approach?" Vertek asked.

Tana nodded, so the orc drew closer to her and whispered in her ear. Arkad strained to hear, but there was no way that he could hear the other orc's words. When Vertek finished, he pulled away, and Tana remained silent for a long time. Finally, she turned to Arkad and nodded.

"I must attend to other matters." She reached out a hand and rested it lightly on his shoulder. There was a momentary green glow, and suddenly the lingering pain in his muscles vanished, as if taken away by her touch. "Please rest here. You and your men are safe, and will be our guests for the time being."

The healing effect of her touch surprised him, so when she did finally turn and show him her back, he did not even think to attack.

He simply remained seated on the bed, only now realizing that it *was* an actual bed and not just skins piled up on the floor. That was also when he realized that all of the fog in his mind had lifted.

What did she just do to me?

In moments, Tana was gone, along with Vertek. The other three remained inside to continue to watch over Arkad, joined by their former fourth companion moments after Tana was gone.

Arkad slowly swung his legs over the side of the bed and sat up straight, grateful that all of his pain was gone.

Looking at the entrance, willing himself to see through the flap, he sighed deeply.

It seemed that he had much to think about.

***

Another curse escaped Amaya's lips when another sharp piece of needlegrass managed to poke in-between her bracers and her gloves. That was what they called it now, needlegrass. Long, dry, sharp-edged grass that somehow found every weakness in her leather armor better than any orc blade ever could.

She was down on her belly, creeping forward up a hill with Vin and Elic on either side of her. Vin had spotted smoke while tracking ahead of them and had told them all to stay down. Amaya ordered the rest of the team to stay behind, and then led the other two as they crawled up the hill to get a better look.

They slowly crested the hill, keeping their head low while trying not to let the needlegrass tear their faces apart. Her view was too obstructed, so she risked raising her head just a little more above the grass, and felt her jaw drop.

It was the remnants of a large village, now nothing more than burned husks. Some of the fires still smoldered enough to puff smoke into the air, but otherwise there were no signs of life, and all structures were mere shambles of whatever they had once been.

"What in the name of the Six happened here," Elic whispered. "Our troops aren't this far into the Wastelands, are they?"

Amaya shook her head, "Not that I know of."

"Well it isn't a human settlement, that's for sure," Elic whispered. "Look over there, they used bones for the framing of that building."

He was right, it was clearly an orc village. She looked over to Vin, who had so far been his usual silent self. "What do you think?"

At first, he didn't respond or even acknowledge her. When he did, it was by pushing up onto his knees, letting everyone know where they were. Her heart suddenly skipped a beat, but when nothing happened, she sighed in relief, and the three of them climbed onto their feet.

"I don't see anything moving down there," Vin finally spoke. "But over there, on the western side, are the only bodies in this mess." Amaya followed his pointed finger, and saw the corpses. They were too far away to see any details, but close enough that she could identify that they belonged to Wastelands orcs, not the ones armored in blackened steel.

Looking back down at the rest of the team, she waved them up. Then she looked to Vin and asked, "What about our quarry?"

Pointing to their right, he nodded, "Their tracks go right into the village."

Looking out beyond the village and around them, she noted that they stood on a rather lonely hill. The terrain was relatively flat elsewhere, but the village was nestled in a cove of a rather thick and gnarly-looking forest. If Arkad and his troops went into that forest, traversing through there at any great speed would be difficult at best. She also didn't know how well Nia could create portals when she had no idea if there was a tree at their destination or not.

When the rest of the team was with them, Amaya quickly explained their observations while leading them down into the village. She drew her sword, a signal that the others should draw their weapons as well.

Once they reached the bottom of the hill, she ordered her team to spread out, and to cover Vin as he tracked their prey's footsteps. The well-worn paths through the village made it harder to follow their quarry's tracks, but that didn't appear to slow Vin down.

After a moment, he paused and looked ahead. Right at where all of the bodies were. "Looks like they went towards them," he frowned. "Or else..."

Amaya's eyebrows peaked upwards. "Or else what?"

Once again, Vin didn't reply, and he simply continued forward. Amaya kept up with him, staying only ten feet away, but started to take a closer look at the village around them. It was once a large community, easily home to over a hundred orcs. No, probably closer to a hundred families, if the orcs even lived together as families. She realized she didn't know anything about their culture.

She stepped on something hard and paused, lifting her boot up to look. It appeared to be a child's toy, made out of dry twigs and lashed together by a type of grass that was more bendable than the dreaded needlegrass. Its eyes were drawn onto the twigs with coal from a fire, as was its mouth. Either a very poor craftsman, or a very determined child had created the little humanoid doll.

Amaya bent over to pick up the toy, almost afraid to touch it. Something in her stomach twisted, wondering if the child whom this had belonged to was still alive.

Her boot had crushed the arm, but otherwise it was intact. It had to have been a child's creation. She didn't know how she knew that, she just knew. She held the doll around the torso, wishing, hoping that the creator was still alive.

Their mission since the war had started was to hunt down every last orc and end their threat once and for all. But they weren't the mindless, monstrous creatures she thought they were. And she only now realized that hunting down every one of them would mean slaughtering innocent children.

The image of Arkad refusing to attack her and the two kids in Archanon flashed through her mind again, and she clutched the doll tightly.

They weren't mindless beasts.

Not sure why she did it, Amaya stuffed the doll into a nearly-empty pouch on her belt. It barely fit, but she didn't care. She needed to keep it. If only to remind herself of whom their enemy actually was.

Suddenly realizing Vin and the others were very far ahead of her, she gripped her sword tighter and rushed to catch up. She reached Vin just as they made it to the corpses. The rest of the team had fanned out quite a distance from them, and Idalia even approached the forest, looking into it for signs of activity. Peren, their archer, had stayed far behind to cover them, his bow at the ready, an arrow already nocked.

Vin went from corpse to corpse, staring at the ground around them, occasionally crouching to get a closer look. The frown on his face grew deeper and deeper, but he still said nothing.

Finally, Amaya's patience wore thin, and she grabbed him by the arm. "What do you see?"

He looked shocked to have been stopped, but she gave him a stern look and gripped his arm tight. Finally, he shook his head, as if bringing himself back to the real world. "Uh, well the orcs we're after were a part of this battle," he waved his free hand around at the bodies. "But they weren't part of the burning of the village. That happened before they arrived."

She frowned. "So, what...they came to investigate what happened to the village?"

Vin shrugged, and then tugged his arm free from her grip. "I don't know, but I do know that our targets engaged these orcs," he waved at the bodies around them. "But that's not the strangest thing. Some of the tracks of our targets don't show any sign of actually fighting. As if they were defeated from a distance."

Amaya shrugged easily and commented, "Well we know they have enchanted weapons." Then she caught herself. "Well, no. The ones in darkened steel do. The Wastelands orcs do not." She placed her free hand on her hip and looked around at the bodies. "Huh, that *is* weird."

"Best I can tell," Vin continued, "All of the darkened steel orcs were dragged away, except for one," he pointed to Amaya's right. She followed his finger and saw one of the corpses was not like the others.

They slowly approached the body, its armor obviously darkened steel and not the leather skins that the other orcs wore.

"Wait," she paused, looking again at the other orc bodies. "Wait a second, look at their clothes, their weapons."

"Yeah, I caught that too," Vin nodded. Elic approached them, his family longsword gripped in one hand, ready for anything. He looked at the bodies as well. Vin continued, "Better craftsmanship than any other Wastelands orc we've encountered."

Elic stopped by the darkened steel orc's body, Vin and Amaya joining him a moment later. "Why is he the only one left?" Elic asked. "Where are the bodies of the other dark steel orcs? Or signs of a greater battle? I count a dozen Wastelands orcs."

Vin nodded, "But tracks indicate there were many more."

He looked around some more, and then started following something on the ground towards the tree line. "All of the tracks converge in that direction. Including signs of dragging bodies, or deeper footprints indicating they carried heavier loads, likely armored bodies."

Amaya's head spun a little at all the details he was able to get from just tracks, but she knew to trust his judgment. They drew closer to the forest, until Vin stopped only a dozen feet from the tree line. She looked into the shadows of the forest, almost expecting to see a dozen orcs suddenly appear and attack them.

But Vin wasn't looking into the forest. He stared at his feet. She approached him and looked down, and even she couldn't mistake what she saw. All of the footprints and drag marks seemed to just end. As if the orcs ceased to exist. Or...

Amaya looked around, saw their Wizard companion, and called, "Nia, over here."

"It was a portal," Elic frowned. "They created a portal?"

"And most likely came through one, too," Vin nodded.

"How is that possible," Amaya asked. "I mean, the reports from the first battle said Arkad had a vial he used to create a portal, but..."

"There are no glass shards around here," Vin shook his head. "Nothing to indicate it was a shattered vial containing a potion."

When Nia approached, Amaya pointed to the ground where the footprints disappeared. "We think they created a portal to escape. What do you think?"

The Wizard's usually emotionless face crinkled into a deep frown. She lifted her staff up, and then slowly lowered the focusing gem to the ground, until it touched right where the footprints ended. Amaya felt a wave of energy pass over her, giving her goose bumps, and the jade-colored gem in Nia's staff flashed.

A moment later, she brought her staff back up and nodded. "Yes, there was an outgoing portal in this location. From the energy left in the ground, it was sometime last night. We barely missed them. I..."

Suddenly Nia's head snapped towards the forest, and a moment later Amaya felt the surge of energy too. From behind a tree came a shard of ice, headed right for Elic. Nia reacted fast, and a shield surrounded Elic, shattering the ice shard into harmless slivers and pellets.

From behind that same tree emerged a darkened steel orc.

"Orcs!" Elic shouted.

But something was wrong. The orc didn't charge. He didn't try to send another shard of ice. Instead, he slowly emerged from the tree line, a giant mace clutched in both of his hands. The orc breathed heavily. Then she saw a black substance dripping from his elbows onto the forest floor.

Orc blood.

Vin started to charge at the orc, but Amaya shouted, "No!"

The orc roared, and swung his mace at Vin. He ducked under the swing, and then tried to use one of his daggers to cut the orc's throat, but the beast actually managed to hit him, sending him sprawling to the ground.

Knowing that Peren was an expert shot, Amaya looked back at him and waved her free hand, "Don't attack him!"

Everyone looked at her in shock, but they followed her orders. She looked at Vin, worried he was hurt badly, but he was already on his feet, and looked ready to disobey her order.

"Vin," she shouted. He looked at her, the anger and murderous intent clear in his eyes. "Stand down, that's an order!"

At first she wasn't sure he heard her, but then he sighed and lowered his daggers ever so slightly. Amaya turned back to the orc, only to find that it stared at her in confusion. Then his eyes rolled into the back of his head, and he fell forward, the thump vibrating the ground.

For a long time, everyone simply stood still, too stunned at what had just happened for it to really register. When it did, it was Elic who asked, "What just happened?"

"He's wounded," Amaya lowered her sword. "I saw the blood dripping from his armor."

"You noticed black orc blood against black armor?" Nia asked, raising her eyebrows. "Impressive."

"I'll check to make sure he's out," Vin stated, moving towards the orc.

Fearing he would kill it, if it wasn't already dead, she shouted, "No! I'll take a look. Nia, Elic, on me."

Vin clearly looked disappointed, but did not disobey. Elic walked beside her, while Nia remained a step behind as they approached. It was conceivable that the orc was faking his wounds to draw them in, but she very much doubted that. She had never seen an orc employ deceptive tactics like that. Of course, there was a first time for everything, but she didn't think he was faking it.

She hoped.

There was no denying the fear she felt as she drew closer to the massive body. Though not nearly as large as Arkad, the orc was still much larger than she was, and much stronger. He could easily tear her limbs off.

When she drew closer, she could see that he was still breathing, but his breaths were very slow and appeared labored. His mace was at his side, but his hand had released it when he fell. Cautiously, she approached the mace, and motioned for Elic to be ready to strike.

With all due caution, she reached her free hand down to the mace just below the spiked ball, and lifted. It weighed far less than a weapon of its size should have, but that no longer surprised her. She also felt a surge of energy from the enchanted weapon, a sensation she never got used to. The weapon sent a cold energy that chilled her to her very bones, but also made goose bumps rise up on her arms and the back of her neck with a crackle of energy.

Amaya backed away from the orc, and then tossed the mace behind her, as far from the orc as she could. The orc still didn't move, so she looked at Elic and motioned towards the orc, indicating that she wanted him to verify it was unconscious. She then focused her own energy, and felt her powers flow from her body, through her hands, and into the blade of her sword, ready to send an arcane blast at the orc if it made any sudden moves.

Elic drew closer, and then slowly reached his hand out. Amaya felt her heart racing, thundering in her ears, but she couldn't allow herself to make a false move. If the orc was alive but wounded…

Touching the orc's shoulder and shaking it a little, Elic jumped back and gripped his sword. The orc didn't move, didn't so much as make a sound. So he tried again, but did not jump back this time. When the orc didn't do anything in response, he tried to roll it over, but it was too heavy, its armor too bulky.

Sighing in frustration, Elic stood up straight and lowered his sword. "It's okay. I don't think it's getting up anytime soon."

Amaya sighed and lowered her sword, letting the arcane charge within the blade slowly flow back into her body, where she then let it dissipate into the Universe.

Then she smiled and looked first at Elic, and then at Nia. "Looks like we have our first prisoner of this hunt."

Nia raised a curious eyebrow, and said, "Indeed."

Amaya sheathed her sword, and then nodded at their prisoner.

"Let's strip him of his armor and bind his hands. Maybe he can help us find our quarry…"

***

Every single muscle in Zerek's body ached and felt ready to give out on him. Blisters were forming on his feet and hands, and he struggled to keep his eyes open.

He'd never felt so alive in his entire life!

Training to become a soldier was hard, but it was the closest he had ever come to realizing his greatest dream. Sure it wasn't the same as becoming a Warrior, but the training would be invaluable no matter what he did with his life.

It gave him a chance to make a difference.

In the training yard of the barracks, he was among the last of the soldiers to warily put away his training sword and shield. Both were made of simple wood, but they were certainly heavy enough. Especially after a morning of physical training, and several hours of evening weapons training.

The only real break they had been given was a couple of hours of lecture before and after lunch. And lunch felt extremely short.

The work load was very similar to working the mines, so he knew he could handle it. In fact, he almost relished in it, realizing that while his stamina for running had improved over the past few months, his upper body had grown weaker, his arm muscles decidedly smaller than when he had first fled the mines.

He rested at the weapon racks for a moment, holding onto the sword he had just placed in it, and closed his eyes. Yes, he was glad to be rebuilding his strength. But by the gods, it was hard, and this was just his first day!

Forcing his eyes open, he turned to follow the rest of the trainees inside. They would eat their evening meal, much later than he was used to, and then would spend the rest of their night in the bunks.

Just as he passed inside of the door, the last one in, Lieutenant Oban stepped out in front of him. She was a tall woman, very strong and very much a military officer. He had seen few soldiers, but never had he seen one who fit the role of a trainer or a leader as well as she did, not even Torick.

"Zerek," she looked down at him. He wasn't short by any means, but she really was tall. "Step into my office."

If his heart hadn't already been beating from their efforts in the courtyard, it would have started to race, and his stomach sank to his toes. Did she know about him sneaking out last night? Her expression gave very little away.

Knowing that he had no other choice, Zerek nodded and followed her down the hallway. While everyone else turned right into the mess, she took them into a door on the left, into a small office. He wasn't sure what he should have expected, but the office was surprisingly inviting. It was furnished very well, with what had to be a very old, though well-maintained desk in the center, and several small paintings of the former...what was Lieutenant Oban, anyway? Headmaster? Teacher? What did they call them?

Zerek felt embarrassed when he realized he had no idea. His life had been spent in the mines, not studying military protocol. Hopefully that would be one of the many things he'd learn about in future classroom studies.

The only thing that was uninviting in her office was that there was only one chair, a finely-upholstered, if ancient-looking, high-backed chair. There were none for her students or guests to sit in, and just from his crash-course in protocol and etiquette that morning, he knew it meant he was to stand at attention before the desk.

From behind him came another soldier, Morrison Tennit, one of Oban's trainers. Morrison had worked closely with Zerek throughout the day to help get him up to speed, but he hadn't been kind or easy about it. Zerek understood that was how the military was, but it didn't mean he liked being yelled at. He missed Torick.

Zerek still didn't know what to expect, and his pulse continued to race while his skin turned clammy. Or more so than it already was.

Oban stepped behind her desk and faced Zerek, but she did not sit down. She wore what he had learned was considered 'duty armor,' granted only to full-time soldiers and only those who had achieved a rank that meant they were not always on patrol or other duties. It was for those who spoke regularly to Commanders, Generals, and royalty. He also noted that she wore a tabard bearing the kingdom's symbol and colors, a black background with a mountain guarded by two crossed longswords in white.

Her face was still expressionless, and he had no idea if he was in trouble or what her reason was for calling him in. Should he start apologizing for last night now? No, what if she didn't know, and he revealed that he'd broken the rules?

No, he had to remain quiet, and find out what she actually wanted. So he simply stared at her chin, not knowing where else to look. It felt awkward to do so, but she was taller, and he definitely didn't want to look further down…

"Well, young man," Oban finally spoke, "I have to say that I am quite pleased with what I saw today."

Feeling surprised, he looked her in the eye, and asked, "Sir?"

"Your performance today," she nodded, clasping her hands behind her back, gathering her black and white-trimmed cape in the process. "Torick said you were a quick learner, and he was not exaggerating."

Feeling his cheeks flush, Zerek smiled and looked down at his feet before looking her in the eyes again. He tried desperately to force any fatigue from his eyes. "Thank you."

"Nothing to thank me for," she shook her head, "just an appraisal of your skills. As I believe was explained to you yesterday, today was your initial assessment, to see if you could remain with this class, or if you would be forced to wait for the next training session to begin." She looked to Morrison. "What are your thoughts?"

Zerek looked at him, worried that the blonde man would not endorse him. He had never hesitated to insult Zerek when he failed at something.

Yet when Morrison brought his hand up to stroke his goatee, all he did was smile and nod. "Indeed. Torick did well with you." Zerek resisted the urge to roll his eyes. Of course he gave someone other than Zerek the credit for his progress. "I would be willing to keep him on, so long as he doesn't stay up as late as he apparently did last night."

Zerek's face flushed again, but he did not say anything, fearful of revealing himself. He instead turned to Oban, who frowned at Zerek and nodded. "Yes. Some of your performance showed great fatigue faster than it should have for a boy in your physical condition."

"I apologize, Lieutenant," Zerek looked down, almost feeling like Madame Kai had just lectured him.

Oban brought her arms forward and folded them. "Well it matters little. Your performance was adequate when you were fatigued, I imagine you'll be even better once you've actually had a good night's sleep. Which you will, by the way." He looked up, curious as to what she meant. She clarified, "Whatever kept you up last night, it won't tonight. You'll fall asleep the moment your head hits that bunk, I guarantee it."

"I see," he nodded, fearing that she was right.

Zerek was supposed to meet with Laira tonight, so that she could introduce him to the leader of the thieves. He was to propose his infiltration method into the castle, and discuss what exactly they needed while he was in there. More than that, he needed more convincing that there really was something wrong, and that someone attached to the throne was deceiving the people.

He could scarcely believe it. The very people who had taken him in after he had lost everything he had known…could they really be lying to the people? It seemed unlikely, but he had to at least consider the possibility. If only because Laira believed it so passionately.

"Well, then," Oban nodded. "Go get yourself something to eat, and then rest up. Believe me," she leaned forward, a small smile cracking her cold exterior, "You're going to need it."

Nodding, he said, "Yes, sir. Thank you."

He turned to leave, but then Oban stopped him, "Oh, and Zerek." He paused, still fearful that she knew of his plans. He slowly turned to face her, but her smile only broadened. "Welcome to the Archanon guard."

Despite his fears, Zerek couldn't help but smile, feeling the pressure and fear within him lighten for a moment. "Thank you," he nodded.

Without looking back, he quickly crossed the hall to the mess, and gladly accepted every scrap of leftovers he found. Without looking at or talking to any of the others, he dug in and ate up every bit of food that he could, not caring that it really didn't taste all that good. It was food. It was *meat,* for that matter. Fowl of some sort, he wasn't actually sure what.

However, when he came to the end of his meal, guilt began to creep into his soul. He looked around the room as most of the other trainees had finished and were getting up to turn in for the night.

He was learning how to stand side by side with these men and women, and defend the city from threats. Yet tonight, he would be discussing how to betray the oath he had given just that morning, just so that he could break into the castle and find some evidence of wrongdoing on the throne's part.

Something didn't sit well with him when he thought of that. Something dark and uncomfortable began to grow in his stomach, and he had to work at keeping the meal he had just finished down.

After he turned his plate and utensils in for cleaning, he walked back to the bunks in a daze, suddenly not sure what he should do. He knew he wanted to be with Laira, despite everything. He really did love her.

Yet the more he thought about betraying these people, his city, his King, the more it made his stomach twist and turn.

He needed more time, more convincing.

And without even realizing it, he gave himself another day. He found his lonely bunk and lay down on it, intent on giving the situation as much thought as he could before the others all fell asleep and he snuck out again.

Except that within moments of lying down, his eyes closed, and his nightmares found him.

***

When dawn came the next morning, Arkad's mind had become a flurry of conflicting thoughts. He mentally flogged himself for even considering betraying his shaman, no matter what evidence was presented before him.

Honor and loyalty. These were the tenets central to an orc soldier's life. He could have chosen a different life for himself in his youth, but he had chosen to become a soldier to defend his people, knowing what it would cost him.

Orc soldiers had no personal lives, pure and simple. He would never be allowed to find a permanent mate, never allowed to have children of his own, nothing that could jeopardize his service, his loyalty. That was the price all soldiers paid.

Honor and loyalty, above all else.

Yet why did he feel like he was the one betrayed? First by the Queen, for putting her life above all others, and then by their shaman, who directed the orcs into a hopeless, unwinnable war.

It had seemed so clear before. The shaman had saved him and his people where the Queen had failed. Brought them to a world they could take as their own and rebuild the orc civilization. All they had to do was clear the humans out of the way.

All they had to do…was kill.

He literally reeled on his bed in anger, the thought of what that entailed enraging him, startling the guards in the hut.

His Shaman, a woman whose name he didn't even know, had sent him and his people out to kill not just soldiers and Warriors, but innocent men and women. Children.

Their mission had been to exterminate the humans to make way for a new order for the orcs. What angered him the most, what made him growl and glare at the guards in a near-blind blood rage, was the realization that he had allowed himself to be manipulated, allowed himself to view humans as lesser beings, as unworthy of life.

As the guards drew their weapons, his anger redirected back to the humans. Weren't they the ones who had mistreated his people? Had they never bothered to try to live peacefully with the orcs?

Arkad didn't know when he had risen to his feet, but his four guards looked absolutely terrified. His hairless head pushed up into the ceiling, and no doubt made him look foreboding.

Who should he be angry at? The Shaman? The Queen? The humans? Klaralin, for bringing them all here to fight his war?

It was as if everyone had used and manipulated the orcs, and he hated them all!

Letting loose a terrifying roar, Arkad took one step towards the guards, ready to shove them aside and rescue his men. Until the flap opened, and Tana stepped inside. She held her hand out before her, a blue flash emanating from it, but not making contact with him.

"Arkad," she shouted, her voice surprisingly powerful. "Do not!"

The blood rage abated just enough to stop himself from charging. He knew that she could simply use magic to incapacitate him again, and he did not relish the idea of waking up with that cold feeling, or those aching muscles, again.

"Do not let the blood rage control you again," Tana's voice had softened ever so slightly. "That is how she controls you."

That was enough to completely push back the rage. Instead, his anger was replaced by a sudden emptiness, a sensation of his stomach sinking into the depths of the world, right to the very center.

Silence engulfed the tent, and Arkad felt his shoulders slouch. His eyes fell to the ground as emptiness consumed him.

"It's how she controls everyone," Tana spoke softly, taking a tentative step towards him. The four guards looked nervously at her, but did not move. Their weapons were still pointed at Arkad, their stances uncertain, and still with a hint of fear.

In battle, the blood rage could be both a boon and a curse. While it gave one a single-minded strength and will, it also meant becoming blind to everything that happened around them, anything outside of their focus.

It was exactly what had happened to him, and to all of his people.

"I've been so blind, haven't I," he asked, his voice nearly a whisper.

Tana stepped closer, and gingerly reached a hand out to touch one of his forearms. He looked into her eyes, a striking green with just a hint of red. Whereas her words before had helped quell the blood rage, it was her touch that helped fill the emptiness, and drive away the darkness.

"We all have," she replied. "That is why I came here, to escape the lies. To escape the treachery. To escape the end of our civilization, and preserve what I could."

He frowned at her, and asked, "You knew the end was coming?"

She clenched her jaw and looked down at his feet. After a moment, she nodded and looked back up to him to say, "Not exactly what happened, but I knew it was inevitable. I felt the dread creeping into every corner of our world, anticipating the invasion. I saw the Queen's mind slowly losing control. And I felt the coming of darkness, like a wave overshadowing the shoreline."

Sighing slowly, Arkad eased back onto the bed, which creaked slowly under his weight. Tana allowed him to sit, her hand sliding down his forearm, then his hand, until the touch was broken. He feared the darkness would return, but it did not. Not yet.

"How can I trust you?" he asked.

Remaining silent for what felt like ages, Tana finally shook her head. "I do not know. But perhaps if I show you trust first, that would be a start. Come," she started to back away. "Let us go for a walk. Your men would be greatly reassured by your presence."

Seeing his men again would certainly raise his spirits, so he nodded and stood up again, careful not to push against the ceiling this time. The guards still had their weapons drawn, but one look from Tana and they quickly stowed them. She paused between the guards and looked at one carefully. "Remain here."

They did not question her order and simply stepped further away from the entrance, bowing their heads to her. Arkad was surprised at first, thinking it was yet another show of great trust. Perhaps that was what she meant it to be. However, he quickly remembered that she was more powerful than anyone he had ever encountered before. She would never need guards to protect herself. No, they had been stationed in his, for lack of a better term, prison to ensure only that he did not escape.

Watching the guards cautiously, he stepped forward and followed Tana through the tent flap, having to bend almost halfway down to fit through.

When he emerged, the sun blinded him, still low in the sky directly ahead. He stood up straight, feeling his muscles protest at finally stretching out, and brought his hand up to shield his eyes.

He couldn't even begin to guess where they were, or how far away the To'kar village was from the front. But one thing was for certain, the village's numbers had grown. He remembered being told that some of the orcs that had been sent to the To'kar to force them to fight had instead joined with the rogue tribe, but that couldn't possibly account for the sprawling collection of tents spread around the area.

There had to be thousands of orcs! Enough to stand against the Shaman. Enough, he realized, to start over again.

Arkad also noted that there were no permanent structures. Granted that was common in the Wastelands, but every hut, every structure looked easy to dismantle, pack up, and leave with. This wasn't where they were settling, it was just where they had stopped for the moment.

Tana gently touched Arkad's elbow and began to lead him further into the camp, so he followed while gawking at his surroundings, at the numerous orcs that he saw. It was families, pure and simple. More female orcs than he had seen in one place since his arrival on Halarite. More children.

Children...his orders had been to wipe out half of the To'kar. Did the shaman mean for his men to slaughter half of the children, too?

It wasn't long before they arrived at another tent, guarded on the outside by two orcs. Tana ordered them to bring forth their prisoner, and a moment later, Telark emerged. Like Arkad, he no longer wore his armor and had been clothed in a simple leather shirt and trousers. Once Arkad had spoken to Telark and was sure he was being well-treated, they moved on to the next tent, and the next.

When Tana brought him to the last tent, he felt his veins turn to ice. "If this is the last, then two of my men are missing."

She hesitated in her next response, but then nodded and looked him in the eye. "Yes. I thought you might notice, but I wasn't sure how to break the news to you. I'm still not sure how I can...how I can tell you."

Clenching his jaw and standing up straight, he nodded. "Two were killed in your attempts to capture us."

The energy he could see behind her eyes wavered, but she did not confirm what he suspected. Instead, she hesitantly said, "Two of your men would not be subdued easily, and they were wounded before I could incapacitate them."

Looking to the tent, Arkad felt his heart beat faster in fear. He had not seen Kilack yet, his best friend and trusted lieutenant. Was he in there? Or was he one of the ones left for dead?

"We are soldiers," he said quietly, his eyes never leaving the flap of the tent. Tana motioned to one of the guards, who entered the tent at her command. "To be captured is a grave dishonor. If you had not..." He felt his muscles tighten at the thought, and he shook his head. "I am glad to be alive, but I feel shameful for my dishonor."

At first, Tana did nothing more than stare at him. When the silence grew deafening, she approached him and lightly touched his elbow, sending pins and needles up and down his arm. Arkad looked into her eyes, and once again found warmth.

"I am sorry," she spoke to him softly. What surprised him most was the sincerity in her eyes. She truly was sorry, and it made his heart beat a little bit softer. "I hope you will one day feel like it was worth it."

It was then that something happened that had not happened in nearly a year. A smile crept across Arkad's face, and a small sense of hope kindled in his chest.

If only it could have lasted longer. The tent flap opened, and one of the guards preceded the occupant out. It was not Kilack.

While Arkad's spirits once again sank to a renewed low, he was pleasantly surprised by whom it was. "Tezarik," he approached the orc and clasped him on the shoulder.

"General," Tezarik nodded. "I am pleased to see you are alive and well."

"And you," Arkad replied.

"I overheard some of your conversation," Tezarik looked to Tana, then back at Arkad. "Who are we missing?"

Letting his hands drop uselessly to his sides, Arkad sighed deeply. "Kilack and Morkind."

Tezarik closed his eyes and clenched his jaw. "Not Kilack…"

For a moment, they remained silent by each other, each grieving for the loss of a great warrior. Arkad had lost so much in the past year that he was surprised by how deeply he felt the loss. Would he ever become accustomed to losing those closest to him? He had been taught from his youth that loss was inevitable…

"There is something else I must tell you," Tana spoke hesitantly, stepping closer to them.

Arkad turned to face her, but did not think there was anything she could say that could help lighten his spirits. If anything, he suspected that she had only more bad news for him.

Tana hesitated, but then nodded and said, "One of those two men still lives."

Feeling his heart leap into his throat, Arkad drew closer to her, "What? Who?"

"I do not know," she shook her head. "His wounds were grave, and he was unconscious when we left. We thought he was dead. But my scouts reported to me last night that a human party hunting your troops entered our abandoned encampment and were attacked by a survivor from your team. He was too weak to effectively fight, and he collapsed."

Arkad felt his hands clench into fists. "So he is dead after all." Why would she tell him only to dash his hopes again? Was she manipulating him, too?

"No," she frowned and stared up at him. "The humans did not kill him. They stripped him of his armor and have him tied up while they tend to his wounds. He has not woken up, but from what the scouts can see, he is still alive."

Exchanging a hopeful and determined look with Tezarik, Arkad said, "We must go rescue him, now!"

He began to look around, as if he could spot where she had placed his armor and axe, but she responded by gently touching his arm. "Not yet."

"It could be Kilack," he glared down at her. "We cannot leave his fate to the humans."

"I know, Arkad," she more firmly grasped at his arm, her hand that of a child's in comparison to his mass. "But think about it. Why did the humans not kill him? Why are they tending to his wounds? We have been led to believe that all humans treat all orcs as monsters, to be slaughtered without regard."

Feeling impatient, he shook his head and backed away from her, breaking their touch. "What's your point?"

"These humans may be worth speaking to," she replied. "If they know about you, and they learn about our tribe, the armies might never stop hunting for us in the Wastelands." She looked around, opening her arms up to encompass the camp around them. "I do not want us to live in fear of attack for the rest of our lives. I wish to find a peaceful corner of the Wastelands to try to rebuild. And if these humans do not view us as monsters, if they are willing to treat one of our wounded with respect, then perhaps they would be willing to negotiate a peace on our behalf."

Arkad almost told her that peace with these humans was impossible, but then he stopped himself short of that. His instinct still was to think of humans as horrible, evil beings. But that was what the Shaman had wanted him to believe, wasn't it?

Tana was right. They needed to think carefully about how to proceed, about how to rescue Kilack.

He also realized that she was already forming a plan, if she was thinking of negotiating with the humans. "What do you have in mind?" he asked, narrowing his eyes.

Tana drew in a deep breath, and then nodded. "I need your help."

***

When the orc awoke, it was already mid-morning, and the sun marched steadily upwards. Amaya sat in front of their campfire, a small fire with as little smoke as they could manage, and gazed into the flames.

Her thoughts had wandered all night, and sleep had been difficult to come by. She kept thinking about the Ironwood assault, and the choice she had almost made then. Looking up across the fire, she stared at the orc, slumbering in nothing but the simple undergarment that it had been wearing beneath its armor, and a blanket tossed over it to help keep it warm, and ensure its modesty.

Only a few months ago, she had nearly killed orcs in their sleep. Had ordered her team to do the same. So who were the real monsters?

The orc suddenly jerked, as if waking from a bad dream, and his yellow eyes shot open. He snorted, and tried to sit up, only to find it difficult with his wrists, ankles, and even his knees bound together. The blanket partially fell off of his chest, revealing the mass of muscles that powered him.

Amaya slowly stood up, and the rest of her team suddenly focused on the orc. Vin drew his daggers and began to approach the orc, but Amaya held up a hand. The orc continued to struggle, and she could hear the leather bindings strain, even though he was wounded.

She had pulled her sword and sheath off to sit on the ground, and she considered picking them up to lash back onto her belt, but then decided against it. Making the orc feel more threatened than it already did would only hinder her.

Then it began talking to her. But not in any language that she understood. With hard consonants and short vowels, it sounded like nothing but gibberish, and her spirits sank. The orc didn't speak their language.

"What in the name of the Six is it saying?" Nerina asked, her hands hovering over the mace strapped to her hip. Amaya lauded her for her restraint.

It was Nia who replied. "I believe it is their native tongue." Everyone stopped and looked to her, waiting for further explanation. No one on Halarite had ever heard orcs speaking anything other than, well, what she supposed she should call 'human language.'

In fact, no one had heard another language spoken on Halarite in thousands of years. Each of the kingdoms once had their own languages, or so history books stated, but those languages had been lost during Klaralin's reign. He had forced all kingdoms to speak one language. While the Lesser Wars had continued to rage long after Klaralin's first defeat, none of the kingdoms returned to their old languages.

At least, not overtly. Their written forms were often used to help keep letters secret during wartime.

"So they spoke another language before they learned ours," Gell asked. He was behind the orc and had to talk over its incessant rambling.

"It would seem so," Nia nodded.

It wasn't long before the orc heaved a giant sigh, blowing the dust beneath it into the air. It suddenly began to take sharp breaths in, and she wondered if its wounds were flaring up again...but then it sneezed, hard enough to blow out a renewed cloud of dust around it.

She almost laughed, especially when the orc shook its head rapidly to try to clear its sinuses. It growled then, and glared right at her. It clearly recognized her as the leader.

"Well that's useless," Elic walked up next to Amaya. "How can we interrogate it if we can't understand it?"

Idalia, off to Amaya's right, nodded in agreement. "Agreed. Even if it was willing to tell us where Arkad is-"

"Which I doubt it would," Elic nodded.

"-We couldn't understand it," Idalia finished. "We should send it back to Tal for imprisonment. Maybe someone there can figure out its language."

Suddenly Vin began walking closer towards it, and Amaya felt her pulse quicken. "Or we could just end its misery right here," he spoke quietly.

"Vin," she barked at him. Both he and the orc looked at her, startled. "We don't kill unarmed prisoners."

He frowned at her, his daggers still poised at the ready. "It's an orc. An animal. Who cares?"

A part of her wanted to agree with him. A strong part. Even with King Sal'fe using the Staff of Aliz to resurrect fallen soldiers and Warriors, the war had been devastating and costly. There was a time limit to the Staff's powers. If a person was dead for too long, they could not be revived.

Such as those at the Relkin Mining Camp. When that young man, Zerek, had lost his family. She had made it a point to find out more about him after he helped stop the orcs in Archanon.

Not to mention the fact that Sal'fe did not have time, nor did Tal have the funds to pay for the use of the staff to heal non-lethal wounds. Those Warriors would live with scars and, in some cases, great pain for the rest of their lives.

However, that thought gave way to Arkad refusing to attack her when Zerek and his lady friend had come to help her. He'd refused to kill children.

So she gave Vin her most venomous glare, and ordered, "Stow your blades and go walk it off." When he didn't move, she turned to face him fully. "Now!"

It was the first time any one of her team had questioned her orders, but if anyone would have, it would have been Vin. Not because he was defiant by nature, but because he held a greater hatred for the orcs than anyone else.

Grumbling, he put away his blades, and turned to stalk off. Amaya began to realize just how much trouble capturing the orc was going to cause her.

For several moments, she watched as Vin walked away, her thoughts wavering between being sympathetic to his desires and her unwillingness to kill unarmed…people. She was brought back to the situation at hand when Elic nudged her. "Amaya."

When she turned back to the orc, it was grunting and motioning its head, looking off to her right. She followed its eyes, and saw that it was motioning towards its weapons and armor, piled two dozen feet away from it.

"What is it doing," Idalia asked. "Does it really think we'll let it have access to its enchanted weapons or armor?"

When it looked again at Amaya, it stopped its motions and grunts and stared at her. Then it said something, a word she couldn't understand, and then looked at its armor. It did this three times, looking at her, repeating the word, and looking at the armor.

With a frown on her face, she walked over to the armor and knelt down. The orc nodded, and repeated the word again.

There was something in the pile that it wanted her to find. So she started sifting through it all, holding up various pieces of the armor. It used a different word for the first piece and shook its head. So she held up another piece, and he did the same thing. Over and over, she tried every individual piece of armor or clothing, and it said a different word for each one and shook its head.

Until she held up a necklace with a small black crystal. When she held it up, the orc repeated the first word, nodding its head emphatically.

"I believe the orc wishes you to give him the necklace," Nia tilted her head to one side.

Standing up straight, Amaya observed the necklace carefully. As with all of the orc's weapons and armor, she felt a power emanate from it that made her neck hairs stand up on end. It was enchanted, but with a power she had never encountered before the orc war. A powerful magic.

"I don't think that would be a good idea," Elic shook his head. "Who knows what that will do. It could give it greater strength, allow it to break through its bindings, protect it from a spell..."

Amaya shook her head, "We could guess all day at its purpose and never figure it out." Looking to Nia, she asked, "Can you determine its purpose?"

The Wizard was already walking towards her, and held her free hand out to accept the necklace from Amaya. She closed her fist around it, and then closed her eyes. There was a pulse of power that emanated from her, but it soon faded.

Opening her eyes and her hand, she shook her head, "I cannot say for certain. It does not appear to be offensive in nature, but beyond that..." She was about to hand it back over to Amaya, but then stopped. The look of suspicion on her face was palpable.

"What is it," Amaya asked, suddenly worried. "Is it dangerous?"

Nia looked at her in surprise. "No, but I think I have an idea of what purpose it may serve. How much do you know of the elf that visited Halarite?"

Tilting her head to one side, she shrugged and replied, "Not a whole lot. Just what rumors have been going around. The Order thought she was a demon, but the Prince determined she was not. And she ended up helping Cardin Kataar finish off Kailar."

"She was from another world," Nia looked at her, the first spark of excitement that Amaya had ever seen in the Wizard giving her eyes a glow. "And she does not speak our language. But she was able to communicate with everyone because of a pendant she wore. An enchanted pendant that allowed her to understand our words and us to understand her words."

Feeling her jaw drop, Amaya's eyes fell upon the unremarkable black gem on the necklace. It was magic beyond anything known on Halarite, but then again, so was the magic that enchanted the darksteel orcs' weapons and armor.

"We still can't give it to him," Elic insisted. "We can't get close to him, not while he's awake and, well, pissed off."

She looked at the orc, its eyes darting between her and the necklace. It grunted and nodded.

That's when it clicked. "No, that's not what it wants."

Everyone frowned at her, but instead of explaining, she picked up the necklace and began to pull it over her head.

"No!" several voices shouted at her.

But it was too late, and the necklace was already around her neck.

"You fool," Nia stepped away. "I said I suspected, I did not know for certain!"

"Can you understand me now?"

It was when that voice spoke that everyone stopped chastising her. Everyone looked between her and the orc expectantly, wondering if she had understood it. She looked into its sharp, yellow eyes, and nodded. "Yes," she nodded at it. "Can you understand me?"

Heaving a great sigh of relief, the orc nodded. "Yes, I can."

It spoke very well, very clearly, unlike the broken sentences that the Wastelands orcs formed. Then again, she realized it was likely far more comfortable speaking its native language, and the stone translated it into perfect human language.

Human language...that was a description that was going to take getting used to.

She slowly approached it, and then, ensuring that she kept her distance, she knelt down to be able to talk to it easier.

No, not it, she realized. Him. She had to stop thinking of it like a thing. Maybe, just maybe, if she treated him better...

"My name is Amaya," she said. "What's yours?"

The orc stared at her for a long moment, before it allowed its head to lie back on the ground, putting his neck at an awkward angle. He seemed to be considering whether or not to answer her question, as if giving her his name would somehow give her power over him.

Finally, he sighed, and said, "My name is Kilack. Lieutenant in the service of General Arkad."

She felt her jaw drop slightly, not having realized that they had one of their target's most trusted soldiers in their midst. This could work out better than she expected.

"Where is your General," she asked.

He narrowed his eyes at her, but did not speak.

"Is he still alive?" Again, no response. "At least one of your other darksteel soldiers was killed here, and your team appears to have been overwhelmed. You're on your own, and I have to assume that you wanted to be able to talk to me for some reason."

For another long moment, the orc did not respond. Finally, however, he lifted his head up, and looked intently at her. "We were ambushed. I believe by the very orcs we were sent to find."

She frowned at his statement. *Why were they sent to find other orcs?*

Instead of asking questions, she patiently waited for Kilack to continue. "Only they weren't supposed to have any sort of magic on their side. Our weapons and armor, our training, we should have had the upper hand. Yet they were able to defeat us quickly. They incapacitated the General at the very beginning. Smart, but cowardly. They have no honor…"

Amaya was surprised to hear that the orcs had a concept of honor. Everything she thought she knew about them pointed to them having no sense of honor, nor a sense of cowardice, just the basic animal instinct to survive.

He sighed and looked at the dirt. "I would have rather died in battle, but they left me for dead. Left me to die slowly of my wounds…"

She shook her head and said, "Hopefully that won't happen." She motioned towards his bandaged left rib cage. "Hopefully you'll heal."

Kilack was ready to say something, but then he clamped his mouth shut. "Yes. Hopefully."

She waited for Kilack to continue, but he said nothing more. Was that all there was? "Where is your General now?"

He continued to avert his eyes for several more moments, but then he looked at her and replied, "I do not know. I've failed him."

"Not necessarily," she shook her head. "If you were searching for these orcs, where were you going to go next?"

The orc once again took several moments to respond, no doubt wondering what he should or shouldn't tell her. "We never had time to figure that out. The ambush happened before we could begin to discern which direction the tribe fled."

"I see," she sighed and looked down. She began to lose her

balance for a moment from crouching down for so long, so she stood up and looked back at her team. They all waited impatiently for her to tell them what was going on.

For a moment, she thought the pendant had actually changed her words when she spoke. "What of all of that could you understand?"

Elic shook his head, "Only your words, not his."

"Ah," she nodded. "Well, apparently they were trying to find this tribe of orcs, only to be ambushed by them. Sounds to me like dissent in the ranks."

She looked back down at Kilack, but he did not confirm nor deny her assertion. "He also claims they never found out which direction the tribe had originally fled in."

"Then we're stuck," Idalia sighed. "We don't know where to go."

"For all we know," Gell spoke up, "They've already killed Arkad for us."

She looked for a response from Kilack, but then remembered that he could only understand her. "Maybe, but we have to be sure," she shook her head. "Or our mission is a failure."

"Perhaps I can help," Nia said. "I may be able to ascertain where their outgoing portal traveled to."

Amaya looked at the Wizard in shock. "I thought you could only discern the destination of active portals. You think you can figure out where a closed one went?"

"Perhaps," she shrugged. "I am quite skilled at portals for my age. However, it will require several hours uninterrupted."

Amaya nodded, and said, "Work as quickly as you can. We may not have much time before this other orc tribe moves on."

As Nia turned and began to walk to where they suspected the portal had been, Amaya turned back to Elic. He asked, "What are you going to do?"

For a moment, she hesitated, taking in a breath but holding it a moment. Finally, she let it out and looked at Kilack. "I'm going to see if I can't get to know our prisoner a little bit better."

***

"Ouch," Zerek whispered to himself, pinching the back of his hand as hard as he dared. It was all he could do to stay awake. After another exhausting day of training, he wanted to stay awake so that he could try to rendezvous with Laira.

He'd been distracted throughout most of the day, still performing his training, but his mind and his heart weren't fully into it. He kept wondering…was he doing the right thing? Should he sneak out that night? If he did, should he tell Laira that he'd made a mistake, that he couldn't betray the oath he had taken not two days ago to protect and serve the kingdom and the city?

The truth was, he probably wasn't going to be able to decide. Not unless he knew more about what the thieves were trying to prove.

Which meant that when he was certain everyone in the barracks was asleep, which given everyone's exhaustion wasn't all that late, he forced himself to ease up out of the bunk and sneak out.

It was certainly a different experience, sneaking out of what was essentially a small fortress. There were regular patrols, but his experience sneaking out of the Castle District proved invaluable. Especially since the main gate was left open this time, much to his surprise.

His originally rendezvous was somewhere that meant a great deal to both him and Laira – the rooftop across from the Warrior's Guild, that fateful night when he meant to climb the Warrior tower to earn her love.

Only even after his failure, she still ran with him across the rooftops, still spent the next couple of months holding his hand, making him feel like the world was a ray of sunshine. Had she stayed with him because of her mission?

It made his head spin, and he began to feel like he no longer knew which way was up.

Within minutes, he made it to that flat rooftop, climbing up with practiced ease, only giving a casual glance around for patrols. He knew that most of the patrols now focused on what were perceived to be the most vulnerable parts of the city, not in the center where there could be no surprises.

Laira was already on the roof waiting anxiously for him. She hadn't heard his ascent, but the moment she noticed him approaching, she didn't say a word, she simply flew at him and wrapped her arms around him, nearly knocking him over.

Her embrace was warm and firm, and he couldn't help but wrap his arms around her waist to hold her close. Wishing the moment could last forever, he closed his eyes and lost himself in that moment of happiness.

"I was starting to get worried," she whispered, pulling away just enough to press her lips to his. Further losing himself to her touch, to her breath, her taste, her lips, he wanted to run away with her right then and there. Leave the city, the thieves, everything behind. Everything that was making him doubt who he was and what he was doing.

When she finally pulled away, he slowly opened his eyes, searching for hers in the dark of the night. "I'm sorry," he said, touching his forehead to hers. "I fell asleep last night. The training is so exhausting…"

She smiled. "It's okay. You're here now, that's what matters."

They remained in each other's embrace for at least several minutes, his sleepiness long since gone. How long could they remain as they were, standing atop a roof across the street from the Warriors' Guild, unnoticed?

Not long, he wagered. So he pulled away a little, took her hand in his and nodded. "Lead the way."

With nothing more than a smile in response, she turned and pulled him along. Within seconds, they were in a full run, flying across rooftops, leaping over streets together with the grace of linked dragonflies, their movements synced as if they had known each other their whole lives.

Zerek had expected her to lead them to the canals, but instead she brought them to an old, abandoned building in the Blue District, where they walked in casually, as if they belonged there. Zerek was aware of the two guards just inside of the door, though hidden in the shadows. His experiences and his training were paying off. But the guards allowed them to pass without question.

Within the old stone building was a basement, where they found a small hole in the ground. It was obviously man-made, but the remnants of the original ladder were all but useless, and a makeshift wooden ladder took them down into the depths of the cold, smelly sewers.

It took him a long time to get used to the smell. No, actually, he never really did, but when they finally stood before the entrance to their destination, he had finally stopped gagging. It was all Laira could do to not laugh at him.

Once they did stand before the entrance, atop a bridge over an underground canal, a breeze helped abate the stench. The guard at the heavy steel door greeted Laira with a mischievous grin. Looking at Zerek, he laughed and remarked, "So this is the little heart thief."

Laira's blush was visible even in the flickering torch light. "Yeah. Is Sorin still in?"

Stepping aside, the large man grunted and motioned inward with his head. "Grumpy as he is over having to wait." He looked hard at Zerek. "Again."

He felt compelled to apologize to the big man, even though he had no idea why, but he managed to just keep his mouth shut. He was definitely in unfamiliar territory now.

"Thanks, Mekan," Laira said wearily, tugging Zerek into the sanctuary.

What Zerek saw then was completely unexpected. It looked to be ancient aqueducts, crisscrossing over and under one another. The everlasting torches could not illuminate the entire chamber, and it gave him the impression of being within a great cave, or a giant well.

No mine that he had ever stood in could compare. Mines were always dug out to their minimum heights, tall enough for a person to walk through, barely, but never anything so grand as this.

He didn't even think humans could build such things today, let alone however many thousands of years ago this was built.

Laira allowed him a moment to gawk, but then pulled him along the edge of the great pit, until they came to a small sectioned-off area. Against the back wall was a map of Archanon, and surrounding a large wooden table were what he assumed to be the ranking members of the thieves. Assuming they even had ranks of any kind.

The man in the center was the one who caught his attention. Long black hair pulled back in a pony tail, the shadow of a beard, and piercing blue eyes. The same man that had caught Zerek and Endel in the alley when he sought desperately to find Laira the first time.

"Zerek," she brought him up to the only unoccupied side of the square table, "May I introduce Sorin, our leader."

His stomach did back flips, and his mind immediately turned suspicious. Had Laira even left the note on his person as he originally thought, or had Sorin planted it on him? How much of him finding Laira had been manipulation?

Turning to look at Laira, searching her eyes for some sign that everything was okay, she instead seemed to avert her eyes, from both him and Sorin. She felt guilty, he realized. Could she know what he was thinking now? The pieces that had clicked together in his head?

After a moment of silence, he turned to Sorin, who regarded him with a frown. "Is everything okay, young man?"

Not knowing what else to say, Zerek simply shrugged and nodded. "Sure."

Clearly skeptical, but willing to let it pass, Sorin nodded. "I'm glad you agreed to meet with us. How much has Laira explained to you?"

Zerek shrugged again. "Not a whole lot. Just that you all believe the throne is lying to the people about something, and that you're willing to risk everything to figure out what, to find proof, and expose the lies."

He glanced at Laira, but she kept her eyes locked on the table. He looked at where she stared, and took notice of papers strewn across it. In fact, the one she stared at specifically was the set of orders from his first mission. The orders she had stolen from him.

In the span of a moment, he felt awe when he realized the chain of events that had led him to the sanctuary of thieves in Archanon. On one hand, he had gotten in serious trouble for losing those orders. Yet that failure had prompted his being given training to defend himself, giving him the skills to impress Amaya Kenla when the orcs invaded, and ultimately leading him to being enrolled to become a city soldier.

Was life really so interwoven and complicated?

"That's pretty accurate," Sorin leaned one hip against the table, showing Zerek his profile while he folded his arms. He wore dark clothes, pretty much what he'd expect for a thief to wear at night, and his clothes were in considerably better shape than Laira's.

Another one of the thieves at the table, a woman not much older than Sorin, chimed in, "We think the kingdom is, for all intensive purposes, broke."

Her word usage made him pause, but it was another person, a young blonde man opposite of her, that called her out on it. "Intents and purposes, you dolt."

The woman literally growled at his correction, and it was all Zerek could do not to chuckle at the exchange.

However, his grin faded when he realized what they had just said. "Wait, what?" His jaw dropped. "You can't be serious."

Sorin nodded. "We are. Look at what's in front of you," he

motioned to the papers on the table. "Every single one of these are orders we've intercepted from the throne. Orders. Nothing more. Did they provide you with gold to pay for the orders you placed or retrieved?"

Zerek thought for a moment, and realized that no, he had never been given gold. He had simply assumed it wasn't necessary, or that someone who *hadn't* failed his first mission would have been trusted to deliver payment.

He took a closer look at the papers, especially at the one he knew to be his first assignment.

The word "credit" stood out to him. A credit of three gold pieces to the blacksmith for horseshoes. A credit of two to Farmer Alexton for the vegetables and grains listed in the order.

He looked at another set of orders. More credit. Another set, and more credit. There were a handful that had statements like, "trade goods delivered with this letter," for payment, but mostly they all said credit.

No gold. Not one single piece of silver. No mention of precious metals or coins.

There were over two dozen orders strewn about the table, and he felt his stomach sink.

"How can the King be poor," he asked, looking up at Sorin in awe.

But it was Laira who answered. "Because the Prince was an idiot."

Looking at her in shock, he almost backed away. Such a statement could have easily landed someone in the stocks for a day, or worse. "Laira?"

Her jaw was clenched tight, as were her fists. She was leaning against the table, but now pushed off and turned to face him fully. "He overextended the kingdom with all of his new laws and enforcing them. He very nearly destroyed free trade in doing so, and then tried to tax non-existent trade. Started resorting to *other methods* to fund his stupidity." He immediately noticed how much emphasis she'd placed on the words 'other methods.'

Before he could ask about that, however, Sorin interjected, "The King is covering it up."

The woman that had spoken before chimed in, "But that's only making things more bad." After so much time learning how to speak properly from Kai Loric, Zerek cringed at her poor grammar. "And if they don't come forward soon, it'll only get worse."

Raising a curious eyebrow, and feeling like he might regret asking her to speak further, he inquired, "How so?"

Thankfully it was Sorin who answered. "The economy has surged in the repair efforts," he pushed off of the table and turned to face Zerek. "However, all of those credits, if gone unpaid, will soon result in everyone having no money with which to buy more supplies. Buy more seed. Pay people to work for them. Pay for repairs and equipment."

Zerek frowned, trying to wrap his head around it. He could see the point, no one worked for free. What good was credit from the throne if they could never use it to pay for the things they needed just to make their livelihood?

But could it really be all that bad? Plus, as he looked at the papers...was it really true anyway?

"I don't...I don't understand," he frowned. "The King protects us. We serve the King, and he provides us anything we need. Isn't that how it's always been?"

The incredulous look Sorin gave him made his face turn pink, his heart beating a little harder as if he'd just been frightened. "Kid...it hasn't worked that way in a very long time. Centuries at least, probably longer. The kingdoms have gotten too big for that old system to work. This world runs on gold and trade. The thrones merely govern us and, through money, pay the Warriors and soldiers to enforce their rule."

"How do you not know this," the grammatically-challenged woman asked. Hearing her say it almost made him break down, feeling like a total idiot.

It had never come up before. Not while working with his father, not while listening in on negotiations for their latest lodes. Not in Kai's teachings. Not even in the two days of training he'd received at the barracks.

He'd never thought beyond his own life.

Feeling completely lost, and wishing he wasn't the center of attention, he looked to Laira. She looked at him with sympathy, but didn't seem to know what to say. All she could do was draw closer to him and hold his hand, as if she knew that he needed her to confirm everything they had just said.

She nodded once.

Shaking his head, he again looked down at all of the documents. "So...if that's true, what do we do?" He looked up at Sorin's sharp blue eyes. "What are you planning to do?"

"We need evidence," Sorin leaned forward and planted his hands firmly on the table. "We need to show the people what the throne has done, force them to come clean. Let the *people* decide what to do."

He felt scared at the idea, all those people, hundreds, even thousands, finding out their city was rebuilt upon a fake foundation. Would they panic, like he was starting to do now?

Having no idea how to respond, what he should or shouldn't say about his fears, he looked again to all of the papers. "This isn't proof enough?"

Sorin shook his head. "It's all circumstantial. No one will believe this is proof of anything."

That's when he remembered that they wanted someone on the inside, in the castle, to help them accomplish their goals. He felt a horrible cinch in his throat, and had to gulp it down before he could meet Sorin's gaze again. Laira gave his hand a squeeze of encouragement, and it was the only thing keeping him from running away.

"I guess I should ask...what do you need me for?"

Standing up tall, now suddenly a very intimidating figure, Sorin folded his arms and looked down his nose at Zerek. "Well, we originally needed you to sneak into the coffers, or into the King's study, or into the Governor's offices, and find some document, some proof, that the throne has no gold to back itself. But since you don't work in the castle anymore, I'm not sure that you *can* help us. Laira said you might be able to get us in, though?"

Endel's innocent-looking face suddenly passed before his eyes. What sort of trouble might he be getting his friend into with this?

But at the same time, he felt like a complete idiot in front of these people. He didn't even know the basics of how society was built.

Once again having to gulp down a lump in his throat, he nodded. "Yeah. I know how to get in. And...and I know someone who might be able to help us sneak around the castle."

A wide grin crossed Sorin's face, one which twisted a knot into Zerek's stomach. "Good."

***

Amaya's dreams were always the same. Claps of thunder, flashes of lightening, and *him* standing before her. He was bigger in the dream, twice her size. And she was helpless before him. He would backhand her, hard enough to send her flying across the grassy field, until she tumbled to a stop.

She would fight back. Or try to, but he was too strong, too powerful. She couldn't touch him. But he could touch her, and he did so with such violence, asserting his will over her, until...

Until she awoke, a scream just ready to escape her lips. Amaya bolted upright, the world spinning around her, until she remembered where she was.

The orc village. She was in the abandoned orc village, surrounded by her team, and safe. Or at least, as safe as she could be in the wilderness of the Wastelands. Some creature, a small, hideous, furry one was only a few feet away, barely illuminated by the predawn glow. It hissed at her, baring fangs at least two inches long at her. With barely an effort, she flicked her fingers at it and released a highly uncontrolled and very weak blast of magic.

It did little more than nudge the creature, which she expected without using a weapon to focus her powers, but it frightened the...rat? No, rats were more attractive looking than it was. Never-the-less, it scampered away, terrified of the one that could touch it without touching it.

She noticed that Elic and Idalia, both asleep nearby, stirred at her use of magic, their Mage senses pulsing from her uncontrolled use of power. Further away, Nerina, who was awake and on watch, looked at her with bemusement, as well as an apologetic look for letting the creature get past her.

Amaya nodded to her, but did not move from atop her blanket. It was still warm enough, at least down in the Wastelands, that she didn't need to cover up at night, and she was thankful for the precious little cushioning that the blanket gave her.

She closed her eyes to rub them, but the images of her dream flashed before her, and she had to force her eyelids open to keep the images away.

Din had never actually forced himself on her like he did in her nightmares, but that didn't seem to stop her dreams from making her feel like he had. It didn't stop the images from haunting her. Why had they started now, six months later?

She realized that there was no sense trying to fall back to sleep. The sun would rise very shortly, and she wouldn't be able to close her eyes again for a while. With her body protesting every inch of the way, she stood up and stretched.

Then she felt it, a sudden surge in magic, like static electricity, raising the hairs on her arms. Someone nearby had just used powerful magic. Had it been Nia? Had she finally figured out where the orc portal went to, and tried opening one of her own?

No, she would have told Amaya first. She looked over to where the Wizard had stood most of the previous day, working to discern where the outgoing portal's destination had been. She saw Nia's form lying on the ground, but it had stirred at the same moment that the pulse of energy occurred.

Amaya's sensitivity to magic wasn't nearly strong enough for her to get an idea of what direction the sense had come from, but she knew it wasn't within the camp. Fearing the worst, she picked up her sheathed sword. Thankfully she still wore her light leather armor. Though uncomfortable to sleep in, the Guardians dared not take their armor off within enemy territory.

There was another pulse, and this time Nia shot up from the ground, the gem of her staff glowing a sharp green.

Feeling a surge of energy course through her body, Amaya started moving through their camp, shouting, "Up, everyone up, now!" As everyone was startled awake, trying to come to terms with what was going on, she added, "Arm yourselves!"

As she and Nerina ran towards the alarmed Wizard, Nia cast another spell from her staff, and a beam of bright light illuminated the tree line.

Amaya's heart nearly stopped at the sight she saw. Emerging from the trees, like a flood of ants from a disturbed ant hill, came orcs. Dozens of them, all clothed in leather armor, bearing well-crafted iron weapons.

Leading them was the very orc they were looking for.

Stopping beside Nia, they stared in awe. General Arkad likewise came to a stop, raising his free hand to halt his soldiers' advance. His other hand held his double-edged axe at the ready.

She frowned at his actions, having expected his troops to outright attack. When she could sense her own team coming up behind her, she raised her left hand with a closed fist, and everyone stopped in a line to either side of her.

It took her a moment to also realize that none of the orcs accompanying Arkad wore darkened steel armor. However, these also weren't the normal Wastelands rabble, their armor and weapons were far more refined. Suddenly she felt like she lacked very necessary intelligence on their adversary.

They were in a standoff, she realized, and she wondered who would be the first to flinch.

Then, much to everyone's surprise, a very small female orc stepped around from behind Arkad, and stood just in front and beside him. The orc woman wore surprisingly nice-looking leather clothes, dyed a color that she thought was pale blue, but was discolored by Nia's green-white staff light.

After several moments of tense silence, the petite orc waved her hand, and much to her surprise, all of the Wastelands orcs stowed their weapons. General Arkad did not, but he did lower his axe.

Suddenly Amaya felt the color drain from her face. She knew exactly what stood before them now. Before she could voice her revelation, Nia did so for her in a voice of shock and awe. "It is a shaman."

In the beginning of the war, many had suspected a shaman might have controlled the orcs. However, by the time they had routed the hordes back into the Wastelands, there was much doubt behind that assertion. The orcs had lost every battle since their initial victory at the Relkin mine. Surely a shaman would have stepped in personally to attempt to change the tides of war.

Now, however, she realized that wasn't true. Before her stood her greatest fear.

History books were vague about the powers of orc shamans. Their births were very rare, but it always marked a change in the behavior of the orcs. Any time orc attacks upon the Freemount Trade Passage had increased, they suspected shamans and sent in forces to find her and eliminate her. They were never far from where the attacks were, and the casualties the shamans inflicted were always high.

It had been three hundred years since the last one was found and killed. Yet Amaya couldn't help but think, *What are the odds that a shaman has appeared at the same time that Klaralin showed up?*

There was no refuting what was before her eyes, and the power that Nia no doubt felt. They were in trouble.

Yet the shaman had made her troops put their weapons away. Therefore Amaya was not entirely surprised when the shaman spoke.

"My name is Tana of the To'kar Tribe," her voice boomed across the void between them. She was surprisingly loud, and more to the point, very well spoken for an orc. "I believe you know General Arkad," she motioned to the giant towering behind her.

Flashing back to Archanon, Amaya stepped forward and said with a nod, "Yes, we've met. Briefly."

"We have not come here to attack," Tana continued. "We do not wish to engage you in battle."

"I find that unlikely," Vin grumbled from her right. She glanced at him in warning, and then looked back at Tana.

"Then why so many orcs," Amaya asked. "You outnumber us three to one. More, if you count your powers and the General's prowess." Arkad's face twisted for a moment into what looked very much like a smirk. She shuddered at that sight.

"To ensure we survived if you attacked us outright," Tana continued. "Human mistreatment of orcs is well known, and we...*I*," she corrected herself, "thought an overwhelming force might make you think twice."

"They're animals, we can take them," Vin grumbled. Amaya glared at him this time, making sure he knew to keep his mouth shut. He was starting to speak out of line more and more, and she was growing tired of it. This was definitely not a good time for it, either.

"Why do you wish to speak to us," Amaya called back. "No orc has attempted peaceful communications with us before. We have no reason to trust anything you have to say."

"And what of Kilack," Tana replied, motioning behind the Guardians.

Amaya glanced back to see that the bound orc was very much awake, and had shifted around to watch the proceedings. Was he afraid? Hopeful? What was he thinking? She'd spent several hours attempting to converse with him yesterday, but after their initial exchange, he had remained largely quiet.

"Our scouts say you spoke to him at length yesterday," Tana

continued. "You also refused to kill him when you first encountered him."

Amaya frowned back at the shaman. "What of it?"

"You are different," Tana said plainly. "You refused to murder a wounded, defenseless orc. This makes me think that there is hope for you." Tana stepped forward. "For all of us, perhaps."

It took only a moment for the meaning behind Tana's words to click into her mind, and just when she thought she could never be more surprised than she had just been, she was proven wrong. Unable to believe her own conclusions, she asked, "Hope for what?"

Folding her arms, Tana nodded once. "Hope for peace."

Peace…with the orcs? Did they even understand that concept?

All of her life, all she'd ever heard was that orcs were mindless killing beasts bent on wiping out humans. From the moment the war started, she felt as if all of those stories were true. The orcs invaded their lands by killing innocent miners. Not engaging against soldiers or Warriors, but killing people who were just trying to make their way through life.

They were animals…weren't they?

For the hundredth time since that night in Archanon, she imagined Arkad, refusing to attack her when Zerek and his friend came to her side. When their worst enemy had refused to kill children.

However, this time she saw something else when she remembered that night. A look on Arkad's face she hadn't noticed before. Shock and regret.

Maybe he wasn't so inhuman after all. Maybe none of them were.

Lowering her sword, Amaya nodded. "What do you have in mind?"

The smile that crossed Tana's face was somewhat frightening, but she realized that was only because of how different the orcs looked from them. Tana began to approach, Arkad staying behind and raising his hand to keep the other orcs in place.

Realizing that the shaman wished to meet Amaya in the center, alone, she sheathed her sword and lashed the sheath back to her belt. She started to walk towards Tana as well, until…

It happened so fast that she didn't have time to react. A blur whizzed past her from behind, heading straight towards the shaman. The shaman reacted quickly, raising her hand and deflecting the knife with a grey shield.

Amaya's eyes grew wide, and she spun around. "Torik!" she shouted Vin's last name. "Stop!" But he had already thrown another knife. She tried to intercept, but there was no way she could.

Only this time, the attack was answered with one from the shaman. A blast of lightning struck out at Vin, catching him in his right shoulder. He spun through the air like a dancer, until he crashed into a heap on the ground several feet back.

Before Amaya could shout any orders, Peren had drawn his bow and released an arrow.

"No!" Amaya shouted, looking back to the orcs. The arrow was deflected as easily as the two knives, but this time with disastrous consequences – the arrow deflected back into the ranks of the Wastelands orcs, piercing one in the leg. Though non-fatal, it was enough to incense them, and the orcs suddenly turned into a frenzy. They drew their weapons and charged, despite Tana's calls for them to stop.

Another arrow flew past Amaya, striking one orc square in his chest, penetrating his leather armor easily. And then Nia joined in, a bolt of lightning lashing out at Tana.

The rest of her team charged, weapons at the ready, no matter how much she shouted at them to stop.

The orcs had been their enemy for too long. There were too many battles where it was kill or be killed. It was the only reaction her team knew to the threat of orcs. She suddenly realized that it was no different for the orcs. Their shaman was under threat, and they had to save her, save themselves, at any cost.

Tana and Nia were locked in battle, leaving the orcs and humans to fight each other. Arkad joined in, no doubt intent on keeping safe those under his charge. And Amaya realized she had no choice but to do the same.

Perhaps there would never be an end to the war. Not unless one side was completely wiped out.

Drawing her sword, Amaya charged after her team, drawing energy into her blade. They were outnumbered, but that didn't mean they couldn't win.

That is, until Tana overpowered Nia. She hadn't even realized it had happened, until Tana was able to turn on her and her team.

And then the world went dark.

Episode 9

THE STORM, PART 1

At last, the time had come.

Only two months after the war had begun, Commander Uric Din reveled in the knowledge that the deciding battle of the war was upon them. In just a few hours, they would finally move forward with their plan to attack the orc encampment and destroy what ability the filth had to wage war.

It would become a day that history would forever remember, and for once he would not be left on the sidelines. During the last Lesser War, he had been a mere recruit, depriving him of any glory. Worse still, his Warriors were not called upon to defend Archanon when Klaralin attacked.

This time would be different. Finally he would make his mark on history.

He strode through camp, hidden in the dead forest of the Wastelands, nodding to his unit of Warriors as he did so. They in turn saluted him as he passed.

The orcs were stupid beasts, they should never have gathered their entire army in one place. Last night, the Allied armies had encircled the orc forces, cutting off supplies and hunting parties.

Now the time had come. He knew it would be any moment that

the horns would sound, and the first attack would commence. Their strategy was sound, and his units were among those that would attack from the north, drawing the orc defenses in that direction. Once the south was exposed, Warriors and Wizards to the south would charge their weakened line.

It was a sound strategy that he wished he had thought of first. It would have gone a long way towards ensuring his shot at making General some day. Never-the-less, his units would be part of the first strike, and that counted for something.

Stopping at the end of his line of Warriors, he looked further down the frontline, through the gnarled, twisted forest at the Warriors from Daruun. Their Warriors were legendary, having fought Falind on the Great Road only four months ago. The first battle of the Sword of Dragons.

Their leader, Commander Idann Kale would be his greatest competition for the General position.

The sound of rushing feet and breaking twigs caught his attention, and he turned to see a runner coming towards him. Instead of walking to meet the runner, he waited for the young girl to come to him. When she stopped, he folded his arms and looked down at her.

"Commander," she said, only slightly out of breath. "You must come quickly."

He frowned, shaking his head, "What could possibly be so important, girl? We're on the eve of battle."

Shaking her head, she said, "Lieutenant Kenla's team just came through a portal with a Wizard, just behind our forces, all of them wounded."

Feeling his heart skip a beat, he nodded for the girl to lead the way, and followed her at a run. He knew of Amaya's mission to locate and eliminate the Orc General, who was mysteriously absent from his assembled forces.

There was no straight line through the gnarled, twisted forest, so making the short distance took far greater time and effort than he would have liked. They passed behind his line of Warriors and went to what was previously the standard point of entry for Wizard portals, before they had redeployed their forces.

In that clearing was a disaster. Elic, Peren, Vin, every one of them had once been Warriors under his command, and every single one of them was wounded. Wounded, but none of those wounds appeared fatal, strangely enough.

A few of his own Warriors had been drawn back by the commotion, and quickly rushed to the aid of the wounded Guardians. The Wizard that accompanied Amaya's team, her name long forgotten, stepped closer to Din.

"Commander," she nodded, her face smug in typical Wizard arrogance. He noticed a rather nasty looking bruise near the Wizard's right temple. The orcs had managed to overpower her?

He knew that the King's mission for Amaya was a foolish one…

"What happened," Din asked, glaring at the Wizard. "Where is your Lieutenant?"

"It is complicated," Nia leaned heavily upon her staff, shaking her head. "We were confronted by the General and a unit of Wastelands orcs. He was accompanied by…"

"Nia," Elic suddenly called out. The young man was kneeling, but upon seeing Commander Din, he pushed himself up and made his way over, limping badly. Blood trickled down his left leg, staining his leather armor.

"Mister Morgin," Din narrowed his eyes. "Is there a problem?"

Elic thought for a moment, biting his lower lip, as if chewing on a problem in his head. His eyes darted between Din and Nia, clearly uncertain. Immediately Din's suspicions flared, and he knew that Elic wished to hide something from the Commander.

"If something has happened to Amaya, I would know of it," he stepped closer to Elic threateningly. The young man didn't flinch, which was quite a departure from when he had been under Din's command. Clearly his position as a Guardian had given him courage.

"I think I'd rather talk to another Commander," Elic shook his head. "Or General Artula."

"Are you kidding me?" Peren spoke up, holding the pieces of a shattered ironwood bow. "The longer we wait, the more likely something horrible will happen to the Lieutenant!"

"I agree," Nia nodded calmly, little emotion on her face or in her voice. Din found that lack of feeling to be unsettling. "I must return to the site and continue my divination of the orc portal. The longer we delay, the greater the risk to Lieutenant Kenla's life."

Adjusting his stance to take further weight off of his wounded leg, Elic shook his head, "I don't trust Din."

Reaching for his sword, Din glared at the Mage and shook his head warningly. "Watch your tongue, whelp. I am a Commander of the Warriors' Guild, and you will show me my due respect."

Raising up his left hand, Elic pointed to where a brand was hidden by his bracer. "And I am a Guardian. My word is the King's word."

Grinding his teeth, Din was so tempted to pull his weapon and strike down the insubordinate peasant. However, he did not need to.

The Wizard was the voice of reason, "I must return, with or without aid, and finish what I began yesterday." She slowly rested a hand on Elic's shoulder, eliciting a look of quiet surprise on his face. "However, no other Wizard knows the location of the abandoned camp. Therefore any reinforcements must come with me now." She stepped in front of him and stared into his eyes intently. "Time is our enemy today, Elic. Let me save her."

Finding the exchange almost amusing, if it weren't for his need to know what had happened, Din folded his arms impatiently. Elic looked down, clenching his jaw and searching the ground for answers. Finally, he nodded and looked at Din.

"I can't go with you, I'm in no shape to fight. Most of us aren't." He looked intently at Din. "Please go with Nia, and save her. Take any Warriors you can spare."

Looking over his shoulder towards the front line, Din sighed. The assault was about to begin, and his chance to make a name for himself was upon him. This was his battle to win. This was not the time to go off chasing after his former lover.

But then he realized that Arkad must have defeated them. Looking at Elic and the Wizard, he realized what it would mean if he was the one who defeated the great orc General where the Guardians had failed.

Plus Amaya would be forever indebted to him for saving her life. Not a bad secondary victory.

Finally, he nodded. Looking out at the Warriors that helped tend to the wounded Guardians, he pointed at each of them and said, "You will all accompany us on this mission."

"Sir," one of them asked. "What of the assault?"

"You are six out of sixty, I think they can spare us on the front line." He then turned to the runner that had retrieved him. "Find my Lieutenant, tell him to take command of our unit for the assault. Tell him we've gone to rescue a Guardian."

Without question, the runner nodded. "Yes, sir."

As she took off running for the front line again, Din turned, and saw Idalia approaching him. "Aside from some bruising, I'm good to go." She rested her hand on her sword, strapped to her hip. "I can still give those bastards some payback."

Knowing all too well how gifted Idalia was, he nodded. "Come if you like. Anyone else?"

None of the others volunteered. Elic shook his head, "Trust me, we would if we could. But we'd only get in the way with our wounds."

Din shrugged, and looked at Nia. "After you, Wizard."

With a smile, Din realized that today would actually turn out better than he expected. Perhaps the gods favored him after all.

***

In the deep, unending black, there was only one sensation that Amaya was painfully aware of, and that was how cold she felt. Not the kind of cold where you shivered and rubbed your arms to try to get warm. No, this was so much more. As if the very center of her being was frozen solid, as if her soul had become an ice cube.

There was no actual physical pain, not right away, just the torturous cold...

And then a voice. Deep, quiet, almost a whisper. "The cold will pass."

She tried to open her eyes, but the light stabbed at her and she clenched them shut. *That was a bad idea,* she thought.

"Do not try to move," the reassuring voice said. "Give yourself a moment. The magic is still wearing off."

Who's voice was that? Where was she? The last thing she remembered was trying to stop her team and the orcs from fighting. Rushing to the defense of her team when that failed. There was a flash of light, a force slammed into her, knocking the wind from her, and then darkness.

Which meant...what? Suddenly dread sank into her stomach, and she began to wonder just who spoke to her.

Pushing through the pain, Amaya opened her eyes. The world was blurry, but it began to clear before long. She saw that she was in a hut, or tent, something covered with animal skins. It was definitely not human-built.

Slowly, she turned her head and confirmed her fears. Sitting cross-legged on the floor across from where she lay was General Arkad of the orc armies.

She was a prisoner.

Except that her hands were not bound, and she still wore her leather armor. She searched for her sword, but sadly it was no longer strapped to her hip. With great effort, Amaya sat up and tried to get her bearings. She was atop a makeshift bed, one of three in the hut. A set of everlasting torches were stuck in the ground in the center of the tent, their blue-white light adding little to the ambient glow from the shaft of sunlight that beamed in through the entrance.

And then her eyes settled upon the orc General. Was that really his voice that had spoken to her? It couldn't be.

Then he spoke again, and it was all she could do to keep her jaw from dropping. "I experienced the same cold not long ago." His was a soft, deep, and even sympathetic voice, with so much intelligence behind his words.

Absently, she reached for the translation necklace she had put on after they had captured Kilack, but it was gone. No doubt Arkad had one as well, but...did he wear it? Or did he speak her language this well without it?

The longer she sat up, the more she began to feel a horrible throbbing pain in her temples. It grew worse and worse, until it was blinding, and she had to shut her eyes and push her fingers deep into her temples.

No longer caring who it was she spoke to, she asked, "Will this damned headache ever go away?"

"Of course," Arkad replied. "Just give a few more minutes."

The pain grew worse, as if someone had jabbed a pick through her head, and she slowly laid back down on her side, curling into a ball, wishing, willing the pain to go away. *Gods, make it stop!*

That was when she discovered that laying down helped, and the pain eased, slowly but at a steady rate. When she no longer had to clench her eyes shut and she could pull her hands away from her head, she looked at Arkad. He did not smile, nor did he did revel in her agony. He just watched, his mottled-gray face bearing a look of deepest sympathy.

A month ago, she would have been shocked, or would have doubted his sympathy. Now, however, she realized it was genuine.

He was genuine.

He was not a monster.

"I am sorry," he nodded at her. That was the first time that she realized he no longer donned his darksteel armor, but instead wore surprisingly well-tailored leather trousers and a leather shirt. The patchwork colors of the leather indicated that it was pieced together from smaller animals, but it was far better quality than anything she had seen an orc wear, aside from the darksteel armor.

Shaking her head, she asked, "What happened?"

Leaning forward and resting his elbows on his knees, he let out a deep sigh. "The situation quickly grew out of control. Tana, our shaman, could scarcely control our forces, they were so angry. Anger whose source was not linked to what was happening." Arkad paused, staring down at her with a look of pain and sadness. "It was anger fueled by centuries of mistreatment."

It took her several heartbeats to realize he meant at the hands of humans. Amaya opened her mouth to object, but the objection hung on the tip of her tongue, a wall of realization blocking her words.

The orc that sat near her was not a different species from the ones they had fought in the Wastelands for three thousand years. He was one and the same. Granted, Arkad was a giant even for an orc, but that didn't change the fact that he was the same species as the others.

There was a spark of anger in Arkad's voice when he added, "We are not the beasts you think we are. But if you treat someone like an animal long enough, perhaps they will never consider that they can be more."

He let those words hang in the air for a long time, and she felt a chill run down her spine. A thought that had once before come across her mind came back to the forefront – who were the monsters, really?

Then another thought occurred to her, filling her with dread. "What happened to my team?"

Arkad looked her straight in the eyes before he replied, "I do not know for certain, but I do believe they all live. It took every bit of control that Tana could exercise, but she held them back. We took you, released Kilack, and fled, hoping to avoid any further bloodshed. Your men killed six of us."

Resisting the urge to correct Arkad when he said 'your men,' she allowed herself a small feeling of relief. Maybe they were all okay.

Maybe the peace they had begun to speak of in the abandoned village could still be achieved.

Which brought her to her next question. "Why am I here?"

"You are here because I wish for my people to survive," a sing-song voice called from outside of the hut's entrance. It was then that the small, lithe orc she had seen moments before her blackout stepped inside. "You are here because I still wish for there to be peace between our two people."

Like Arkad, Tana wore finely–tailored leather clothes, including a pair of sandals that looked rather comfortable, even on the woman's mottled, four-toed foot. Her gaze felt like it penetrated Amaya's very soul, and she had to actually look away for a moment to catch her breath.

Tana stepped closer, and Amaya flinched, but she shushed her, and said, "Be still, young woman. I mean you no harm."

She still clenched her eyes, and waited for the shaman to do something horrible to her, but then immediately blushed at her reaction. This was the same woman who wanted peace, and whom associated with Arkad. Plus if she had meant to hurt Amaya, she could have done so when she was unconscious.

So she slowly opened her eyes and forced herself to look into the orc's green eyes, noticing for the first time a hint of red in them. Her eyes were sympathetic, caring, even nurturing, and her hand hovered over Amaya's torso. A moment later, a smile stretched across her face.

"You are fine, child," Tana said. "You should be okay to sit up now, however I advise you to do so slowly."

Raising a curious eyebrow as the shaman backed away, Amaya pushed back up to a sitting position. There was still pain, but it was a small fraction of its former intensity. Amaya gave herself a moment to feel steady sitting up.

"Peace," Amaya repeated slowly, looking to the shaman.

"Yes," Tana nodded once. "Peace between orcs and humans on Halarite. A peace which has never existed before, but which I believe is possible, and vital."

Creasing her brow, Amaya's first instinct was to shake her head. "I...I just don't see that happening." The look of disappointment on Tana's face made her quickly add, "I believe you, your intentions, I really do." She glanced at Arkad for a moment before looking back at the shaman. "And I really would love to see this war end in peace, but it just isn't going to happen. There are too many humans who view orcs as monsters. Too many who see you as the ones who killed their brothers and sisters, mothers and fathers, daughters and sons. That's all they see when they look at orcs."

After a moment of thick silence, Arkad grunted. "Monsters."

She didn't know if he meant humans were monsters, or humans saw orcs as monsters. Never-the-less, she nodded.

Tana let out a very deep sigh, but then a look of determination came across her face. "Let me tell you a story," she said, sitting down cross-legged next to Arkad. "A story of where my people come from. How we came to be on Halarite. And the future that both orcs and humans share."

***

Zerek took in a great big breath and held it for a moment, staring at the open gates to the Castle District. His stomach was doing back flips, and his palms were sweaty. This wasn't something he ever expected to do in his lifetime.

Letting out the breath slowly, he shook his head. What in the name of the gods was he doing? Granted, he wasn't breaking into the castle, not yet any way, but that was the point to today's visit. To prepare for when he would break in. When he would betray his oath.

The person he had mentioned to Sorin was Endel, and he had intentionally neglected to mention him by name. He knew Endel was once a part of their brigade of thieves, and had even been sent into the castle with the very same mission Zerek had inherited.

Now, after Endel had settled into a life in the castle and given up on his mission, Zerek was about to ask his friend to help finish it.

His friend...was he still his friend? They certainly hadn't parted on the best of terms. In fact, Zerek had felt betrayed, and hadn't been shy about letting Endel know that. Did this make Zerek a hypocrite?

It was only after someone said his name a third time that he suddenly came back to the present, and realized that one of the guards at the gate was calling his name.

Feeling a giant grin cross his face, Zerek stepped forward to greet his former trainer. "Torick!" he replied, genuinely happy to see him.

"Hey, there he is," Torick met him and clasped his hand in a vigorous shake. "Off in your own world there, eh kid?"

Zerek laughed and shrugged. "Yeah. I've only been gone, what, a few days?" He looked up at the wall and the gates into the inner city and sighed. "It already feels like a lifetime."

Raising an eyebrow and stepping back to get a good look at Zerek, Torick smirked, "And what's this? Wearing a military trainee's uniform?"

It was nothing, really, just a fine, black button-up tunic over a white shirt and black trousers, and a pair of very comfortable leather boots. He wore his dagger strapped to a wide leather belt, a silver buckle breaking up the dark colors. He'd been told it was what they were supposed to wear while out on their one and only day off of training every week.

"Hey, you ought to know," he shrugged. "I hear they asked you if I'd make a good candidate when the idea was first suggested."

"Well, yeah," Torick glanced at the other guard on duty. "I may have had something to do with it. You learn quickly, and you were already pretty strong."

Nodding, Zerek said with as much sincerity as he could, "Thank you. Really, thank you so much, sir." Feeling his head swim at what was in his future and what he was about to say, he sighed. "Your confidence in me...it means a lot."

Looking uncomfortable now, Torick just shrugged again and leaned against the gate frame. "Hey, kid, you earned it."

Feeling like he was a horrible liar, a cheat, a terrible soldier, Zerek shuffled his feet a bit and looked down at the ground. He wanted to say something, but he couldn't figure out what. The conversation had to move forward, but he felt too guilty, his mind was just racing with the what-if's of getting caught.

It was Torick who broke the silence. "Just came by to gawk at the gate, then?"

Looking up at the guard, he shook his head. "No. I, uh, actually have a favor to ask. You see," he felt his face turn red, and he hoped that his former trainer thought it was due to embarrassment, "I kind of left things with a friend in a bad place. I want the chance to make it up to him. To tell him I'm sorry."

Torick frowned and said, "Yeah? The only other person you ever hung around was that kid, Endel."

Sheepishly, Zerek nodded. "That's the one. I really need to talk to him. I..." He hesitated and ran his fingers through his hair, trying to think of what to say next. "I don't want to lose my only friend in this city."

For a long moment, Torick was silent, and Zerek couldn't bring himself to even look up at him. He waited for him to turn him away, which would mean he'd have to sneak back into the Castle District later that night.

Instead, Torick came close to him and rested a hand on his shoulders, prompting Zerek to look up into his face. To Zerek's surprise, Torick looked a little hurt. "He's not your only friend in the city, kid. But yeah, I'll make the arrangements. Come with me."

Together, the two walked through the gate and up the hill into the Castle District. Here the houses were three times the size of those in the wealthiest neighborhoods in the rest of the city, each belonging to the most influential families. Those who had the throne's favor, or had enough money to make themselves important.

Then again, Zerek thought, thinking back to his days going into towns with his father to sell ore and buy supplies, *if you're rich, it's probably because you have power. Can you have one without the other?*

He tried to awkwardly apologize to Torick for what he'd said, never having considered Torick as more than his defense trainer, but the guard brushed off the apology. "I'm in the military myself, and I know that you generally don't consider your trainer a friend." He grinned down at Zerek, "More like a slave driver, eh?"

Smirking a little, Zerek laughed despite himself. "Well, I wasn't going to say anything, but yeah."

"Hey, there's the jovial young man I started to shape into a soldier!" Torick nodded. "That's more like it."

Torick quickly led him to the castle's horse training grounds, on the backside of the castle and away from the other houses. Zerek looked towards the stalls with dread, knowing that Endel was likely in there mucking them out right now. Could he really do this?

Pointing to a bench at the edge of the training grounds, Torick asked him to wait there, and then went into the stalls to look for the stable boy.

Zerek sat impatiently, watching the main entrance with intense nervousness, his fists clenching and unclenching regularly. Would Zerek be mad at him for walking away? Or would he be understanding? Plus, what would he think of Zerek asking him for help? Would he laugh at him? Tell Zerek that he was a fool to think Endel would help after he left him behind?

He looked down at his hands, watching them work themselves nervously. Should he even be this apprehensive? It hadn't even been this bad when he finally found Laira... Then again, they'd not exactly had time to be nervous, what with the guards chasing them and all.

That memory suddenly sparked a realization in his head. This wasn't the first time he did something outside of the law. He'd snuck in and out of the Castle District before, ran along rooftops, ran away from guards, and spent time with Laira when he should have been attending to his duties.

Was this time so different?

Immediately he knew that the answer was yes, because this time he was betraying an oath he had taken a few days ago. And yet, he also realized that this time, it wasn't for personal gain. What if the thieves were right? What if someone in the throne, the Prince or someone else, was lying to and betraying the people, betraying the King? If he could find evidence, brought the betrayal to light, then those responsible could be brought to justice.

If the thieves were right, if Sorin was right, then doing so could potentially avoid an economic pitfall for the entire kingdom. What exactly that would mean, he wasn't sure, but he knew that if the most prosperous kingdom in the entire world suddenly had no money with which to pay its Warriors, its workers, its people, then they really were in trouble.

Zerek returned to reality when Torick emerged with Endel. Feeling a surge of energy, he stood up, ready to run to meet them, but then he stopped. What could he say?

However, before he could begin to work his mind into a greater frenzy, a giant smile suddenly stretched across Endel's face, and he ran the distance between them, wrapping his little arms around Zerek.

"Zerek!" he cried out. "I'm so glad to see you."

Feeling altogether shocked, Zerek returned the hug and felt himself smile more than he had in days. He didn't know what to say, so he ended up sounding dumb when he simply said, "Hey."

Torick smiled and shook his head. "Alright, Endel, I'm leaving him to you to keep an eye on while he's here. Remember, he's technically no longer assigned to the castle, so you cannot leave him alone until he leaves."

Finally unwrapping himself from Zerek, he turned and nodded. "Of course, sir. Thank you!"

With that, Torick gave them a mock salute, and then headed back to the gate.

After a moment of watching the guard walk away, a look of sheepish guilt crossed over Endel's face, and he backed away a little, looking down at his feet. "Are...are you still mad at me?"

For only a moment, Zerek toyed with the idea of teasing Endel and letting him think that he was uncertain, but he couldn't do something that mean. "No, my friend. No, I'm not." As he said it, he realized he wasn't, not anymore. Whether Endel had been complicit in Laira's deception or not, he wasn't mad at him.

A broad smile overcame the boy's face as he looked up at Zerek. "I'm glad. I was afraid I'd messed up our friendship."

Shrugging, Zerek said, "It was a really bad day. And I'm really sorry that I reacted like I did." He felt his stomach twist as he said it, the memories from that day flashing through his mind. His fist flinched a little, still a little stiff and sore from punching the pillar in the stalls. Yes, Endel had kept the truth from him, but did that excuse how Zerek had reacted?

Maybe, maybe not, but he swore to himself he wouldn't do it again. No one had been kinder or more understanding of him than Endel.

"Like I didn't earn it," Endel shrugged. "But I'm glad you came back to talk to me. So tell me, what's been going on? What have I missed in the past few days of your life?"

Feeling his face warm, Zerek nodded and began to walk towards the Castle District's wall. "Well, a lot. More than you'd believe."

Endel stopped them long enough to beam a smile up at him. "You and Laira made up?"

Laughing at his friend's excitement, Zerek nodded. "Yeah, yeah we did. She...well, I think I understand why you both did the things you did." He looked at Endel, hoping his sincerity showed through in his eyes. "Especially once I found out what's going on, and, umm," he felt his face grow warm again, "once it was explained to me, a few times, just how bad things could get if it wasn't fixed."

As they continued towards the wall, Endel nodded morbidly. "Yeah, I don't think I really understand it myself. But Sorin, he...he thought I'd have the best chance at getting in, being so young. That they would take me in as a pity case. Which they did."

"How long ago was that," Zerek asked, realizing he still didn't know a whole lot about Endel's past.

"Only eight months ago," she shrugged. "But I failed. I mentioned that, didn't I? I failed and I couldn't go back to face Sorin and everyone else, and the Steward and everyone here was so nice to me. So I stayed." He looked over towards the slave quarters, just coming into view around the castle. "I stayed thinking I'd be safe here."

He wondered something about how Endel had spoken of those events before, of how he spoke of them now. "Is Sorin dangerous? Are you afraid of him?"

Blushing, Endel shook his head vigorously. "No. He's intimidating, and he'll sometimes go too far with things, but he'd never actually hurt me or anyone else. He's a good guy. Well, as good as a thief can be, anyway."

Smiling up at Zerek, he continued, "He brought everyone together in the Sanctuary before I was found. Made them all work together. Created a sort of code that anyone who worked under him had to follow. Never steal from someone else who was poor. Never steal from each other. No killing. That sort of thing. It made things better."

Still hesitating, Zerek asked the one question that had been on his mind ever since he'd found out who Sorin was. "Is...can I trust that his intentions are honest? That he doesn't mean to hurt anyone?" He continued on nervously, looking around as if afraid someone else from the thieves would overhear him. "I mean, it sounds like he's not, but he really does frighten me."

"Don't let him," Endel shrugged. "And yes. You can trust him. If you're willing to take my word for it, anyway..."

Smiling, Zerek nodded and clasped his friend's shoulder warmly. "I am."

Endel smiled, and then stopped them when they came within arm's reach of the wall. They looked up towards the top, the midday sun having peaked over the wall.

Feeling his stomach twist a little more, Zerek looked at Endel, waiting a moment until he too looked at Zerek. "Endel, I don't have the right to ask this of you. And I feel horrible asking it, but..." He paused, clenching his fists at his sides. "We need your help. I know that I have no right to ask…"

"I'm in."

There hadn't been even the slightest hesitation in his voice, so Zerek frowned down at him. "You don't even know what we need."

"I have an idea," Endel shrugged. "Plus you need me."

Raising his eyebrows, he asked, "Do we, now?" Granted Endel was right, they needed him to help guide them through the castle, since he knew it better than any of the thieves.

"Yeah," Endel smirked with pride. "There's more than one reason I was originally chosen." Pointing both thumbs at his chest, he boasted, "I am the best lock-pick there is in the group. And I happen to know that what we need is behind a locked door."

Frowning, Zerek asked, "You know what we need? Where it is, and everything?"

Endel nodded, but the pride vanished and his face turned red again. "Yeah. But I couldn't get close to it. I'm a stable boy, I don't belong in the castle, and every time I tried to get close, I was found and told to get out. I can't do it alone. Neither can you."

Zerek nodded. "Alright. Then we'll do it together, along with Laira."

Endel smiled, and launched himself at Zerek to embrace him in another hug. "Good! I don't want to leave the castle, but I still want to help." He pulled away and beamed a smile up at Zerek. "If I can make up for my screw up, then maybe I won't feel so bad staying here."

Feeling amused, Zerek snickered and laughed. "I have no doubt you'll be invaluable, my little friend. Now come," he pried himself out of the kid's embrace and began walking along the wall. "Tell me what you found, and let's figure out how we're going to get it."

***

There was a change in the air, Arkad could feel it. As he, Tana and Kilack walked through the To'kar camp at a leisurely pace, he shifted his shoulders up and down anxiously. When he looked up at the sky, he could see only scattered clouds, nothing to indicate a storm was coming. However, when he took in a deep breath, he could smell it too, the smell of distant rain.

Tana, noticing his sudden diverted interest, paused for a moment, and then began to lead them towards the south. Arkad strayed at first, not noticing they had turned, but when he did realize it, he caught up quickly.

After a moment of silence, Tana looked at him with a raised eyebrow. "I think we may have begun to sway the human woman," she said idly.

It took a moment for her words to register on Arkad, but when they did, he looked at her skeptically. "Whether or not that is the case, she said it herself, she cannot control what the rest of her people do."

Kilack nodded from the other side of Tana and added, "The humans have always been content to keep the Wastelands orcs' population under control, but this time is different. We have declared all-out war on them. Twice. I do not think they will stop this time until there are none of us left."

Arkad recalled what he had been told of the first war, short-lived as it was. The orcs had invaded the ancient city of Archanon, only to be repelled when dragons arrived.

What if they *come back,* he thought to himself, shivering. *We cannot stand against dragons...*

Tana nodded thoughtfully, drawing in a large breath before speaking. "Perhaps, but I believe she can be convinced not to tell others of our existence."

They came to the southern edge of the camp and began climbing a steep hill, the dry, sharp grass crunching softly underfoot. He wondered where she was taking them, but gave it little thought as he continued to focus on the topic at hand.

Suspecting where Tana was going with the conversation, he wrestled with the idea in his head as well. "You would prefer that we not kill her," he said, keeping emotion out of his voice. He wanted to see what her intentions were.

Tana nodded. "Indeed. She is the first human we have seen on this world that is sympathetic to our people. She could have killed Kilack," Tana motioned to the other warrior, now wearing the same finely-tailored leather clothing as Arkad. "She didn't."

"In fact she prevented another from doing just that," Kilack nodded, looking over to Arkad. "I was surprised. I did not think a human would care whether we lived or died."

Raising an eyebrow, Arkad suggested, "Perhaps she wanted more information from you before killing you."

Looking towards the crest of the hill, which they were moments from seeing over, Kilack nodded. "That was my initial thought. However, she then took the time to try to speak to me, to..." The younger orc paused, a deep frown furrowing his brow. "To try to get to know me."

It took every bit of self control Arkad had not to let his jaw fall open. Up until now, he had been under the impression that all of the humans of Halarite treated the orcs like animals, and everything he had seen since his arrival confirmed that. To hear of one who treated them like actual people was astonishing.

It was then that he could see over the hill, and as they took the final steps to the top, Arkad's jaw really *did* drop, and a feeling he had not felt since he fled his home took hold of his stomach.

Fear.

A wall of black stretched across the horizon before him, reaching up into the heavens as if the stars themselves could not escape the encroaching monster. Flashes illuminated the interior, and even though it had to have been a hundred miles away, he swore he could see the clouds swirling in lighter and darker patterns. It was the most menacing sight he had ever seen.

At some point, they had stopped walking. The conversation died, leaving them in an eerie silence that belied the distant maelstrom.

"What...what is that," Kilack asked, fear giving his voice an edge that made Arkad shudder.

"A great storm," Tana sighed. "It came this time last year, and from what the Wastelands orcs have told me, it comes every year at this time. Always from the south. Always from the sea."

Kilack looked first at her, then at the camp, and finally back to Tana. "You're still here, as are many of our brothers and sisters..."

"The storm is survivable," she nodded. "The further inland, the weaker it will be." She smiled and looked at Arkad meaningfully. "In fact, by the time it reaches us here, it will be a mere torrential downpour. Oh there will be lightning, lots of it, and plenty of wind, but it is easily survivable. And it will wipe away all of our tracks."

Suddenly the pieces in Arkad's head clicked into place, and he gazed out at the storm, the fear subsiding. "I wondered why you had not fled the area sooner. You are waiting for the storm."

With a broad smile, Tana nodded. "We can travel further southeast, away from the orcs, away from the humans, and our tracks will be obliterated. No one will ever know how to find us." Crinkling her nose, she looked up at the sun, marching dutifully towards the west. "However, it will not reach us until an hour or two before nightfall, and we cannot travel in complete blackness."

She sighed heavily and turned towards the camp. "We will have to remain here for the night, and pack up in the rain tomorrow morning to move out."

Arkad grimaced, knowing all too well how annoying that would be. Still, it was the best plan available to them. Idly he wondered why Tana couldn't just move all of the orcs at once, but then he recalled that after their return through the portal with Amaya, Tana was completely exhausted. Obviously moving even a dozen orcs by portal was difficult, let alone an entire tribe.

Soon enough, they could be free. Free from the shaman, free from the humans.

Free to live as they saw fit.

Which made his thoughts stray to his brothers still in the field. Those ready to face an overwhelming human force. There were so few survivors from the exodus, so few who had come through to Halarite, and now the majority of those survivors were about to be slaughtered.

He realized that was perhaps another reason to give this human, Amaya, a chance. After hearing Tana's tale, Amaya had told them that the humans were preparing for one great assault against the shaman's army. The human could have just as easily not told them, so perhaps that meant she was worth trusting.

Tana looked at Arkad thoughtfully, and then slowly turned to fully face him. "Will you stay with us," she asked. "You don't have to, and I know you wish desperately to try to go back and save as many of our kin as you can from the humans."

Could she read his mind? Shamans were powerful, but he didn't imagine that there was anyone who could actually do that. Maybe it was just that she understood him.

However, he also realized that the future of his people did not lie with the shaman from Akaida. Nor did it lie in war with the humans.

That would only lead to the destruction of the orcs.

Tana's goal was not invasion or destruction, it was peace. Peace with the humans. Perhaps this was what made her such a powerful shaman, why orcs chose to serve her even when another shaman vied for control over their hearts and minds.

She valued their lives.

In Arkad's mind, this made her far more worthy to serve. Far more worthy of loyalty.

And then she did something he did not expect. She slowly reached out a hand and gently touched his. He looked into her eyes, and suddenly felt his face grow warm when he saw affection looking back at him.

"I would very much like it if you stayed with me," she spoke quietly.

Suddenly his head spun, and the world seemed to blank out around him. Was she implying what he thought she was? No, he was a soldier. He had given up the thought of finding a mate, of having children...

No, he could not think of that now. He slowly pulled away from her, but he did nod before she could react. "I will stay. For the future of our people, the only future where we might survive."

The heartbreak she felt was impossible to hide, and she withdrew her hand slowly, painfully. It hurt him to see her feel such pain, but he knew it was the best thing he could do, the *only* thing he could do. Their people needed both of them to be clear-headed.

"However," he said, anxious to move away from the uncomfortable topic, "I can't leave my people to be slaughtered. The other refugees who fight side by side with the Wastelands orcs deserve the same chance I am getting. A chance to make a new life for our people."

Tana looked up at him, shaking her head. "I know that you very much desire to help them, but if you go, the shaman would eventually learn of your betrayal, and would continue to hunt us down."

"Assuming she survives the war against the humans," Arkad shrugged. "If they do not know of her existence yet, they will eventually figure it out. They have to assume that is how I obtained portal portions in the past."

He folded his arms and stared down at her, unwilling to budge. "I must give them this chance. But I can't without your help. So I ask you," he paused, wanting to emphasize what he was about to call her. "Please, my Shaman, let me give my men a chance to come with us. I am still their General."

Tana clenched her jaw, her mind working over his request. Finally, she nodded and said, "Very well. But I cannot go with you, Arkad." When she looked into his eyes, he could see how much she feared losing him. How much she wanted him to stay. "You must go alone."

Arkad nodded slowly, already having anticipated that fact. He was about to reply, but then Kilack stepped closer to him and said, "No, he won't go alone."

With a great smile on his face, Arkad was about to tell him that he needed his trusted Lieutenant to stay behind and keep an eye on the To'kar camp, on Tana. But then he realized that he didn't want to go alone. He wanted his friend there to back him up, in case everything went wrong.

"Very well, my friend," he clasped Kilack's shoulder. Looking to Tana, he hastily said, "Don't worry. The rest of my soldiers will remain with you. I will command them to protect you and the tribe at all costs."

Tana nodded, "That is acceptable. I will begin preparing your return potion." She turned to leave.

As she walked down the hill back towards the camp, Arkad looked again to Kilack. There was much he could have said, thanking the one man who had stuck by his side through everything, even the very end of their world.

But words would be too little. So instead, they turned towards the camp, and descended.

***

Endel and Zerek had spent several hours together, and Zerek was grateful that he had been able to reconcile with his friend. After they had talked about Endel's discovery and had come up with a partial plan, he and Zerek spent time catching up. Even though very little time had passed since Zerek's training had begun, it felt like so much had happened.

Now Zerek and Laira strode through the sewers of the city.

Every now and then, he caught the scent of what sewage actually was, and it made him gag each time, but thankfully Laira knew the best path through the passages. Strong winds in the tunnels helped keep the smells tolerable.

He hadn't told Laira yet that Endel was his insider, and he could tell she was annoyed by his silence, but she said nothing. He knew that if anyone would be sympathetic to Endel, it would be her, but he still wanted to keep it quiet until he spoke to Sorin.

It was eerily silent in the thieves den when they entered. Most everyone was out in the city, trying to work as much as they could before winter set in. He knew what that meant, what work for the thieves meant, and it didn't sit well with him.

It felt like he was in too deep, now, that there was no turning back. How had he gotten caught up with these people?

When Laira took hold if his hand and led him towards the meeting place with Sorin, he remembered why, and felt his face flush.

The same group of people were already assembled and waiting, but that did not surprise him. He was right on time. Still, Sorin looked impatient.

"Alright, young man," he folded his arms and looked down at him. "Did you get everything you needed?"

Zerek started to say "Yes" but was interrupted by Sorin, "Because I don't very much like people under my watch keeping secrets from me."

Feeling his face flush, Zerek narrowed his eyes, and before he realized what he was saying, he replied, "I don't work for you."

Everyone remained dead silent after that, looking back and forth between them. Zerek glared up at the thief master, wishing he felt the confidence that he wanted Sorin to see. He wasn't even sure where his sudden courage came from, but he knew he was tired of everything. Tired of being misled, tired of being used, just tired.

A brief flash of a memory from his last argument with his father passed through his mind, but he knew he didn't have time to live in the past, so he just bit down and let what he'd said sink in.

After a very long moment of palpable tension, Sorin tilted his head to the side. "Very well, oh great master thief. Would you be so kind as to grace us with your expertise? Who is your contact in the castle, and how do you plan for us to get what we need?"

Ignoring Sorin's sarcasm, he looked around at the gathered

thieves. "When I first entered the service of the throne, there was one young boy who befriended me...Endel Marric." He waited patiently for there to be an outburst of some sort, for everyone to object to his plan before he could spell it out, but all he saw was a look of slight surprise in Laira. Sorin showed no outward reaction.

"I learned recently that he was once a thief like all of you," Zerek continued, "and that he failed in his mission. The very same mission you intended for me. Well, Endel got in. He even figured out where the ledgers are kept that record every bit of gold that enters or leaves the castle. The only problem is that it is too well guarded, and he was caught every time he tried to get to the ledgers."

"So you are making excuses for him, now," one of the other thieves scoffed.

Much to Zerek's surprise, it was Sorin who stepped up to defend the boy. "Be silent," he said. "Endel is just a child, and we asked much of him." Unfolding his arms and leaning forward over the table, Sorin nodded eagerly at Zerek. "Please continue."

Shocked at Sorin's sudden change in attitude, Zerek continued, "Apparently the castle treasurer or coin master or whatever he's called these days actually holds his office in the treasury," he continued. "And so the ledgers are in there too." He felt himself blush at the memory of having young Zerek explain to him what ledgers actually were. He should have known, because his mother had once kept ledgers for their mining camp, before she died. He just didn't know what they had actually been called.

"And those ledgers would be proof that the castle's coffers are empty," Sorin narrowed his eyes, nodding. "We never knew where they were kept. How did Endel...? Is he sure of this?"

Zerek nodded, folding his arms before he realized what he was doing. "He is positive."

"So," Laira looked down at the center of the table, her eyes unfocused as she thought, "the question is, how do we get in there to steal the ledgers?"

Sorin stared at her for a moment, but then looked again to Zerek. "You two already have something in mind, don't you?"

Zerek couldn't help but grin. "We do. But," he turned and reached a hand out to lightly touch Laira's back, "we need help." He turned again to Sorin to continue, but as he pulled his hand away from her back, she took his hand into hers, and drew closer to him.

That distracted him for a moment, but he was glad for her support, and her touch. "Endel told me that the entrance is down a short corridor," he continued, "and the entrance is always guarded by two soldiers without exception. There's no way to sneak by them, and no other way in or out."

"So you need someone to distract the guards, get them to leave the door unguarded," Sorin nodded approvingly.

"And since I'm one of the fastest runners here," Laira smiled, "you thought of me, didn't you?"

"I did," Zerek smiled sheepishly. Would she be mad at him for not consulting her first before making her a part of their plan?

A slight squeeze of her hand told him that he was okay, at least for now.

"I'm going too," Sorin nodded. That elicited a couple of gasps from the other thieves.

"Sorin, no," one shook her head. "You're too important, what if you're caught?"

"This task is too important," Sorin shook his head, standing up straight. "We've worked towards this goal for nearly a year, ever since the Prince took over stewardship of the throne. Now we're closer than we've ever been." He took a moment to look into the eyes of everyone present, including Zerek and Laira, before he finished, "I'm going to see this through personally. I started us on this path, and I'd be a coward not to finish it."

Yet again, Zerek found himself having to reevaluate what he thought he knew about Sorin. Sometimes he seemed like such an uncaring person, and yet, now he was taking a personal interest in the events that would affect the future of the entire kingdom.

Zerek began to suspect that Sorin had not always been a thief, but if not, then what was he before?

Ignoring his questions for a moment, Zerek said, "I don't think we should have anymore in our group than that. More people will make it harder to sneak around the castle." He tried to sound smart about it, but those were Endel's words, not his. The fact of the matter was that he was not an experienced thief, and he had no doubt the others could see through his façade.

"Agreed," Sorin smiled and nodded. "Good point, young man. So now the only question is, how do we get into the Castle District?"

"That's the easy part," Laira chimed in, smiling at Zerek.

"Because you've been sneaking in and out of there for months, haven't you?" She squeezed his hand.

Feeling his face turn bright red, Zerek nodded. "Indeed."

Suddenly Sorin laughed, not an amused or sinister laugh, but one of pleasant surprise. "I can't believe it. We actually have a plan. We actually can do this…" He looked incredulous, shaking his head and running his hand through his hair. "After all this time."

Zerek let the moment sink in, despite one question of his own he wanted to ask. All of the other thieves joined in Sorin's joviality, laughing and patting each other on their backs. It was amazing to see the sudden shift in everyone's moods.

When the congratulations and laughter died down, he finally asked his question. "So, when do we do this?"

Sorin paused in his breath, glancing around at the assembled thieves, before he shrugged simply, and said, "Tonight, of course."

***

Thunder rolled through the valley of the To'kar encampment, vibrating Arkad's chest. He felt a chill run through his body, one which even his fire-enchanted axe could not keep at bay.

Craning his neck to look up at the towering black clouds, he couldn't help but feel as if the clouds were a wave cresting overhead, ready to drown him and all of his people. It didn't help matters that the sun had drawn close to the horizon.

He recalled that there had been a storm just before the outsiders had invaded Akaida. A small storm compared to this, but the correlation still made his pulse race and his heart freeze.

Today will not be like that day, he thought to himself. *Whether I rescue one or dozens of my people, everyone else is still safe here.*

As if reading his thoughts, Kilack stepped up next to him, wearing his battered and worn darksteel armor. "We can weather this storm together, brother," Kilack looked up to him, nodding confidently. "As long as you're leading us."

Pride filled Arkad's chest, a sensation he had not felt in many months. It was a welcome warmth against the life-sucking cold that seemed to surround their very existence. He smiled down at his Lieutenant and nodded. "Then let us finish this."

Turning together, they both faced Tana as she stepped out from her hut and approached them. She seemed to pause for a moment, looking at both of them with her piercing eyes, and for a moment, Arkad felt an electrifying pulse pass through his body.

With a smile growing upon her face, she stepped up to Arkad and nodded. "I was prepared to give you an encouraging speech," she said, "but it seems your hearts are already steeled for what is to come."

"We are soldiers of Akaida," Arkad puffed out his chest proudly. "We are always ready to defend our people."

"Good," she nodded, and then extended her hand, a vial filled with a lilac-colored fluid in her palm. "Here is the potion." He accepted it from her and held the tiny, deceptively important potion up for inspection, the stopper seemingly jammed in almost too tight. "I apologize for taking so long to craft it, but it is not a normal one. I have tied it to your soul, General. Once you throw it down, the portal will open to just over the hill," she pointed off to the south, "and will not close until you step through. This will allow you to send back as many orcs as you can."

Nodding in satisfaction, Arkad stowed the potion in a pouch on his belt, and then hefted up his axe, ready to go.

But Tana was not yet ready to send them on their way. She raised up a cautionary finger, and added, "This is dangerous. Anyone can pass through the portal. Any orc, any *human,* anyone. You must not let our enemies through, at all costs."

Arkad stared down at her, the weight of what she'd just said pressing against his chest. This could be his greatest moment as a general, leading his people to safety. Or it could be what brings destruction down upon the last of his race.

He wouldn't let that happen. Not today. "I swear on my life, I will protect our people with every drop of my blood."

Expecting a satisfied smile from Tana, he was surprised when she grimaced, and reached out an affectionate hand to hold his. "Just come back safely, General. I...we need you."

Feeling his cheeks warm, he squeezed her hand and bowed slightly to her. "I will, my Shaman."

Releasing his hand, she turned to her right and raised her hands, open-palms facing away from her. The wind from the storm had already kicked up, but suddenly a new, stronger wind blasted from the opposite direction, and created a whirlwind of dust, twigs, and grass all around them. Tana's eyes began to glow a bright red, and as he had before, Arkad wondered if her magic was what gave her eyes their hint of red amongst the sea of green.

Within moments, a red-white wall of light flashed into existence a few feet away. He felt the air around him crackle with magic.

This was it. This was the moment. There would be no turning back once he stepped through that portal.

So he didn't step. He charged.

Right into chaos!

A blast of magic seared past his ear, a simple energy blast that was definitely not from a darksteel orc's enchanted weapon. He knew Kilack was right behind him, so he didn't stop moving, and let his momentum carry him into a shocked Mage bearing colors of gold and black. He barreled over the Mage, and allowed his momentum to carry him a dozen feet further before coming to a stop.

Turning around, he was glad to see Kilack had not faltered either, and had finished off the Mage that Arkad had shoved over.

Tana's portal had taken them right into the middle of the clearing where the orc army had formed their defense, and he grimaced to see that they were too late. From their vantage, they could see that the orc army was now completely surrounded, the humans and Wizards advancing on all sides...except one.

Looking east, he saw that his darksteel brethren had come together in one location and used their enchanted weapons to force a gap through the enemy lines, straight into the forest, where they had the best chance of escape. However, only some of the orc army was moving in that direction, most of them had not heard a signal to retreat.

For a long moment, Arkad considered sounding that retreat, but then he realized that Commander Zinrel had likely intentionally left the rabble behind, to cover the escape of the more valuable darksteel orcs.

It was a cold move, but from a tactical standpoint, it made the most sense. The enchanted weapons and armor could not be replaced, they did not know where Klaralin had obtained them from, and the loss of every single piece was a greater blow than losing 20 Wastelands orcs.

There was no time for him to debate the moral merits, who knew how long the battle had raged, or under what conditions Zinrel had given that order. Besides, Arkad was here for one reason alone, and he had come knowing that the Wastelands orcs' lives were forfeit anyway.

Waving for Kilack to follow him, they rushed towards the broken eastern line. Few humans made it through the orc line, and he admired that even against Wizards, the Wastelands orcs were still putting up a great fight. Their greater numbers alone gave them that staying power, but that advantage was quickly dwindling.

Still, after only having to fight off a half dozen Warriors and a single Mage, they made it to the breach point, just as the human army was close to closing it off.

Using his fire enchantment along with Kilack's ice-enchanted Mace, they broke through the closing line, and fled into the forest, seeking the last of his brothers.

***

The rumble of thunder vibrated the ground, sending shivers up and down Amaya's spine. The lightning strikes were getting more frequent, and fearing that a horrible storm was coming, she stepped outside of her hut. The pair of orcs standing guard looked at her in surprise, but she had been assured by Tana that she would not be hurt and that she was free to roam the camp.

"I just wanted to see the storm," she told them.

At first she thought the storm was coming from the west, since that was where she looked first and saw dark clouds closing in on the sun, which was less than an hour away from setting. Then she followed the storm south, and then looked straight up. The darkness was closing in all around them, and she felt her jaw drop as she stepped back away from the hut, fear gripping her heart. "My gods..."

"Do not worry," Tana's voice called from her right. The shaman was just coming around Amaya's hut, and at her presence, the guards visibly relaxed. "The storm comes every year."

Looking up again, she shook her head. "That is supposed to comfort me?"

Placing her hand on the shoulder of one of the guards, Tana eased that guard away, and nodded for the other to leave them. Once they were alone, Tana looked confidently at Amaya. "Yes. I was here to see it last year, and the rest of the tribe has told me tales. It marks the end of the warm season, and the temperatures in your lands will drop significantly in the next week."

Nodding slowly, Amaya said, "The official beginning of winter. Our first snow fall usually comes this time of year, though it melts within a day or two."

A sudden gust of cold wind kicked up, and Amaya clenched her arms around her chest, rubbing her ribs to keep back the cold. Was that gentle snowfall the remains of this massive storm?

With little warning, a shadow fell over them, and they looked west to see that the sun had fallen behind the edge of the storm. "The winds will likely take some of our huts," Tana shook her head. "There will be flooding, replenishing the marshes to the west. And lightning will strike everywhere, but the rains will stop any fires. We will survive this, Lieutenant."

Still not used to talking to an intelligent, well-spoken orc, Amaya looked at her in surprise. "Orcs never die from this storm?"

Motioning for her to walk, Tana led her away from the hut, probably in an attempt to distract her from the impending storm. "It happens, of course. And will become even more likely, given that tomorrow morning, we will pack up and begin our journey away from here."

Nodding her head slowly, Amaya said, "You wish for the storm to cover your tracks, in case anyone else finds this encampment." Then another thought occurred to her, and she felt color drain from her face. "What does that mean for me?"

Tana did not look at her, and she feared the worst. However, she was surprised when Tana said, "We will let you go in the morning. I do not know if that is a better fate or not, but we cannot allow you to accompany us. Even if you wished to."

Feeling her shoulders slouch in relief, Amaya said, "I understand. Believe me, if the storm can be survived, I'll survive it. I've had plenty of training. Although..." She looked around, shielding her eyes from the wind and dust. "I do not know where to go from here."

"Worry not," Tana smiled at her. "I will create a portal that will take you back to our original encampment. From there, I think you know the way home."

Once again, Amaya heaved a sigh of relief. "Thank you, Tana.

I...I don't believe I deserve such kindness."

She hadn't even meant to say it, it just came out before she could stop herself. The shaman looked at her curiously, her hairless eyebrows creased upwards. "Oh? Do you really think so little of yourself?"

Blushing, Amaya shrugged. "I'm a human. We've not exactly treated your kind that well, though in fairness, we had no idea..."

When she didn't continue, Tana added, "That we could be intelligent? That we were individuals with souls of our own?"

Amaya found herself wondering if they actually had souls, but then stopped herself. "You have to understand," she ran her fingers through her hair, "we've been taught since birth that humans were the only intelligent beings in the universe. Anything else that gave the appearance of intelligence were said to be demons. It was only a few months ago that we began to question those assertions."

Of course, what she didn't tell Tana was that she had been imprisoned during that time, when the elf Elaria had revealed herself, when the Prince, as wretched of a boy as he was, had declared that Elaria was not a demon. And when the dragons had appeared in the skies above Archanon.

The news had first reached her when she overheard guards talking about it. After, when she was released, she had sought out as much information as she could on the subject.

Everything that The Order had taught them was suddenly in question. And people were talking about it. Most often in complete fear of the future to come.

They had mistreated Elaria. They had mistreated the orcs.

"Maybe humans are the real monsters," she shook her head. "Maybe we're the real demons."

That little admission made her stomach sink, and she felt a great emptiness open up within her chest, threatening to swallow her whole. But then something unexpected happened. Tana lightly touched her shoulder, and stopped them so that she could fully face Amaya.

"Evil is not unique to humans, my dear," the shaman spoke, her green eyes piercing into Amaya's blue ones. "Orcs are capable of great evil. So are elves, and a host of other races in the Universe."

The idea of there being even more intelligent races out there made her head spin for a moment, but she should have realized that was the case. Elves, orcs, and dragons? Yes, there had to be more than just them out there. Perhaps thousands more. How big was the Universe, anyway?

She shook her head and asked, "Does that excuse how we have treated your kind? Does that excuse how we act even towards each other? Does it excuse the horrid, twisted ways we destroy each other, fight each other in wars, manipulate each other?" Her voice grew louder as she spoke, and she felt as if her chest were about to explode as rage and anger suddenly filled in the void she had felt moments ago.

When she became aware of that anger, she stopped herself and turned away from Tana. She had been so focused on her mission to find Arkad that she had not thought about her own troubles, but now they suddenly came back to her all at once.

Tana allowed her a moment of quiet, until a sudden bright flash of lightning lit up the sky, and was very quickly followed by a deafening boom. As if a signal to the gods, rain suddenly fell upon them. There was no gradual drip leading up to the downpour, it just hit all at once, soaking them instantly.

Without a word, Tana tugged on her sleeve and led them ahead. Amaya, fearing another lightning strike, followed without question, her heart pounding against her chest. They didn't even go for a specific hut, they simply ducked into the closest one, where an orc woman watched over three small children.

"Shaman," the woman exclaimed before bowing her head. She was actually a little taller than Tana, and it was just now that Amaya realized she had never before seen another female orc. Was Tana unusually small? Or was the other orc unusually tall?

"Be at ease," Tana smiled, and then looked at the children. All three were huddled as far away from the entrance as they could be, cowering in fear. Tana approached them, and held out a hand. A soft, golden glow extended from her hand towards the children, and she said, "Do not be afraid, young ones. The storm cannot harm us in here."

As the glow washed over the children, their fear visibly faded, and they even moved a little closer to the shaman. Even Amaya felt a little warmth radiating from the glow, and she stared in wonder at the shaman. She had never seen such a power before, and she began to suspect that there was more to this shaman than any previously encountered in history. What that was, however, she could not begin to guess.

Tana sat down cross-legged and beckoned to the children, and, tiny as they were, they crawled into her arms and lap and snuggled up. In that moment, she realized just how adorable they were!

She felt guilty for ever thinking of them as mindless monsters.

As if reading her mind, Tana looked at her and smiled. "Life is precious, Lieutenant. All life. And when you spared the life of Kilack, you proved to me that you were an honorable person. You are worthy, dear. Never doubt that. It is why I brought you here. Why I thought you were the only one who could help us."

Smiling and feeling her cheeks grow warm, Amaya stepped over to just a few feet beside Tana and sat down, drawing her knees up to her chest and wrapping her arms around them. The ground was cold, but it was better than being out in the rain. Her wet clothes didn't help matters, either, but there was nothing she could do about that now.

The glow from Tana's hands increased and filled the entire tent, so Amaya closed her eyes and basked in the soft warmth.

Tana was not evil. Everything she thought she knew about orcs was wrong. Everything she thought she knew about the world, about the Universe, it was all suddenly different.

She had to help. She hoped that, somehow, doing so would make up for the terrible things that had happened to her, and the terrible things she had done to other orcs.

Opening her eyes, she looked at Tana, watched as she rocked the young orcs back and forth, humming softly to them. It was a beautiful sight, and she realized how right Tana was. Life was precious.

All life.

"I have something to tell you," she suddenly said. Tana looked at her, but did not stop humming. Amaya hadn't told Tana who she really was before, fearing that the shaman might consider her a threat and execute her. Now, however, she no longer feared that. "I am not just a Lieutenant in the army, I am part of the King's Guardians." When Tana looked at her quizzically, she continued, "We are the King of Tal's most trusted guards and soldiers, and have the authority to speak with the weight of his voice. He trusts us."

Tana smiled and said, "Then perhaps it was destiny that you

would be the one to come to our camp."

Grinning a little, Amaya shook her head, "I don't know about that. But I do know this…I will tell the King of what I have learned. I know that the general population will not be ready to learn that not all orcs are the evil killing machines we believed them to be, but he is an honorable man. Perhaps he can help ensure the Allied Army never comes this way. Never finds you."

Looking thoughtfully at her, Tana added, "And perhaps in the future, he will be the one to help broker the alliance that must inevitably exist between us."

Earlier in the day, Tana had told Amaya about her prophecy, that humans and orcs would one day stand side by side against the very enemy that had driven the orcs from their homes. The idea of such a vast army invading Halarite terrified Amaya, but Tana had insisted that as long as the orcs and humans faced that enemy together, there would be hope.

This wasn't just about saving the orcs, she realized. It was about saving her own people, too.

If she could convince King Beredis, maybe everyone had a chance at surviving the coming days.

***

Pain seared through Arkad's arm when a blast of arcane magic slammed into him, shoving him into a nearby tree. Growling, he turned at the offending Mage, who looked determined…until she saw the look on Arkad's face.

With a violent swing of his axe, he blasted fire at her, as strong of a blast as he could conjure from the massive weapon. The flames engulfed a hastily-erected magical shield, but they danced around the edges and licked at her.

He could have continued to focus his enchanted weapon upon her, eventually destroying her, but they didn't have time to wait for that. Arkad was therefore grateful when Kilack came up behind her and swung his mace, shattering her spine and knocking her to the ground just as Arkad stopped the stream of fire.

They had tried to follow the orcs into their retreat, with relentless human forces pursuing them, diverting their attention frequently. Wastelands orcs also followed and tried to keep up, but all they managed to do was distract the enemy forces.

"Come on," Arkad shouted, waving his hand for Kilack and any nearby orcs to follow. He charged further into the forest, shoving aside branches, angry at the trees for blocking his path, and at the dying light of the setting sun.

They only made it another hundred feet before a group of enemy soldiers suddenly blocked their path, but only one Mage was amongst them. The rest were powerless.

Arkad didn't even have time to consider his next move, Kilack leapt past the General and swung his weapon, sending out a blast of instantly-freezing cold. The Mage managed to shield himself and those directly behind him, but the rest were on the peripheral and were rendered useless.

Tired of the delays, Arkad continued his charge, and swung his axe as he barreled into the Mage, shoving him over brutally and leaving him, and the other surviving Warriors, behind to tend to their wounded.

Kilack was right with him, as he always was. Ready to fight for his General, and his people, as they had done so together for so long.

And finally, when the General began to lose hope, after what felt like hours of pursuit, they stumbled into a clearing in the forest, onto the remaining darksteel orcs. All of their heads turned to him and Kilack as they burst through, a handful of Wastelands orcs following behind.

However, a moment later, he noticed that orcs were not the only ones in the clearing. His heart froze, almost as cold as Kilack's enchanted mace, when he saw on the other side of the clearing a group of enemy soldiers he had not seen in months.

The Keeper of the Sword, wielding the great red Sword of Dragons, and his three companions, the Wizard, a Mage, and a Warrior, along with three other Warriors that Arkad did not recognize. They had effectively cut off the retreating orcs, and as the sound of pursing enemy soldiers grew closer behind him, Arkad knew that their time was running out.

He looked up into the sky briefly, saw that they had minutes of daylight left, and darkness would only make things harder. Now was the time, but he knew he could not yet throw down the portal vial, not without risking enemy soldiers following through.

There was only one choice, and he felt his gut twist at the order he was about to give.

He thrust his axe high into the air, and shouted, "For Akaida!"

And with a roar, he charged through the group of darksteel orcs, right for the enemy, roaring a challenge that the other orcs echoed. The ground thundered when they all turned and charged at the enemy along with their General.

The Wizard and the Keeper had both grown in power, and their initial salvo of magic slammed into the front line of the darksteel orcs with devastating effect. Bodies slammed into each other, and bolts of lightning connected with a half dozen orcs, burning right through their enchantments and killing them instantly.

However, the darksteel orcs still had their enchanted weapons, and several used them to release salvoes of magic that forced the enemies to cease their attack and focus on shielding themselves, quite effectively thanks to their Wizard.

Until the orcs reached their line. Then it was all they could do to keep themselves alive. Several more orcs fell, but the humans surrounded the Wizard to protect him, and this allowed many of the orcs to run past. Arkad almost gave into his blood rage and charged into the center of the human defenses, wishing to destroy the Wizard that had defeated him at the mining camp, but he knew better. He circled around to chase after those who made it past the enemy.

However, the Keeper was not ready to let him go. Before Arkad knew what was happening, the Keeper suddenly landed in front of him, having used his powers to leap over the General.

Showing his youth and inexperience, the Keeper smirked and asked, "Going somewhere?"

But Arkad didn't stop. He charged right at the Keeper, and swung his axe with as much heat pouring out of it as possible, setting the surrounding grasses and trees ablaze, and slamming into the Keeper's magical shield...

To no effect. The shield held, and as Arkad tried to plow over the Keeper, he slammed into an immoveable wall, crunching his shoulder and bouncing back onto the ground.

As the flames quickly grew, igniting the dead and dry underbrush around them, Arkad scrambled to his feet. The Keeper looked shocked by the brutality of Arkad's attack, but held his ground, his blue-white shield fading.

"Not this time," he settled into an aggressive battle stance. "This time, you and I are going to finish what we started."

Arkad didn't have time for this. Neither did the Keeper. The forest would burn fast, and while that had the advantage of cutting off pursuers, it also meant he would soon be cut off from his troops. He wasn't going to let that happen.

The blood rage threatened to overcome him, but he held it back. Blind rage would not win this battle...in fact, he realized, he didn't need to win this battle at all. He just had to get away.

The Keeper seemed arrogant, far more so than when they had first fought, and that gave Arkad the edge he needed. Counting on the human to meet him blade-for-blade, he attacked with an overhead swing.

Handling the Sword of Dragons with a deftness and speed that belied its size, the Keeper deflected Arkad's attack and tried an upward swing to cleave open his belly, but Arkad had anticipated the attack and side-stepped it, though barely fast enough. The blade, impossibly sharp, cut up through his darksteel chest plate, sending sparks of conflicting magic to the ground and starting mini fires.

Spinning around, Arkad hefted his axe and swung with every ounce of his strength, imbuing his weapon with all of the power that he could manage.

Had it been any other Warrior, the attack would have destroyed his opponent, but the Keeper was fast and smart. A shield protected the Keeper, but it couldn't stop the force of the attack, and the human was sent sprawling to the ground.

Arkad sprinted several feet past the Keeper, and then turned.

Pausing for only a moment, he watched as the Keeper, stunned, tried to stand. And then he opened up his axe's enchantment, and sent forth a stream of impossibly hot fire into the forest surrounding the Keeper.

The flames did not engulf the Keeper, as he knew would be the case. The human threw up a shield and leapt backwards, impossibly high and far back, over the fires that had been set before, and to safety several hundred feet away.

For the moment, the enemy was cut off from pursuit. But at what cost? How many of his brothers were caught in that field behind the wall of fire?

Arkad's grip on his axe tightened, and he was tempted to find a way to rescue them. However, he also realized that many more of his brothers had made it past the Keeper and his companions, and were even now fleeing further into the forest.

Arkad had to rally them before they fled too far. Turning away from the flames, he ran into the forest, heedless of the danger behind him, or the danger still ahead.

Episode 10

THE STORM, PART 2

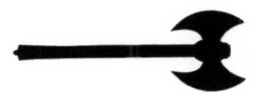

Amaya shivered, wrapping her arms tightly around her torso, wishing her armor would dry faster.

The mood in the orc hut was mostly somber, although at one point, Tana had begun to hum a tune to the children that Amaya did not know. The shaman's surprisingly melodic voice soothed her and the children. But nothing could stop them from jumping every time a lightning bolt struck nearby, the deafening boom rattling Amaya's teeth.

It was going to be a long night, one which she didn't think she could sleep through. Every time she felt like she could lie down and doze off, another bright flash and deafening crack jolted her awake.

Her backside was starting to hurt, and she tried to adjust her posture to alleviate the pain. She considered just lying down anyway, even if she knew sleep would not come.

Until Tana suddenly stopped humming and her head jerked to the right. Frowning, Amaya asked, "What is it?"

Tana's eyes searched the walls of the hut, as if looking for some clue to something, but nothing revealed itself. She looked at Amaya. "Did you not hear that?"

Turning her head to look in the same direction, Amaya listened carefully, but all she could hear was the endless pelting of the rain on the hut's walls, and the distant rumble of thunder. "I don't hear anything…"

Except she did, when it happened again. A far-off sounding wail that made her ears perk and her skin crawl. No, not a wail. It was something else.

Horns.

"That's the lookouts," Tana breathed.

Amaya's head snapped around and she looked at the shaman in shock. Tana was already extracting herself from the children, who must have sensed the sudden fear that both the shaman and Amaya felt, and began to fuss and cry. The caretaker helped Tana pull the children off.

Both Tana and Amaya stood when the horn sounded again, but it was still so difficult to hear over the roar of the storm. Amaya knew what the horns must have meant, but it made no sense. If the lookouts were sounding the alarm, the camp had to be under attack. But by whom? And during the storm? Who would be crazy enough to attack now?

"Come," Tana ordered, making her way through the flap of the hut. Amaya followed quickly, the storm instantly drenching her again while gusts of wind stole what warmth she had recovered.

The horn sounded yet again, and was much easier to hear out in the open. Only this time, the horn was cut off mid-blow.

Several soldiers emerged from their tents, brandishing their weapons and prepared to defend against whatever the threat was.

"Shaman," one approached them, "what is it?"

Tana motioned for silence and listened, but no more horns sounded, and they could hear nothing else above the wind and the rain. Amaya couldn't tell if the sun was still up or not, but she thought it must be, since there was still a little ambient light, despite the fact that they were now completely surrounded by black clouds.

A flash of lightning arched across the sky and struck the ground less than a mile away, the instant boom of thunder making her jump, and the hairs on the back of her neck stood up on end.

"I don't know which direction the horn came from," Tana shook her head, "but we must find out. You," she pointed to the orc that had just spoken to her, "Go to my hut and retrieve this woman's sword, immediately!"

Amaya looked at the shaman in shock, but Tana simply stared back at her confidently. "Whatever the threat, I trust you."

What if it's my people, coming to rescue me, Amaya thought to herself. Would she be forced to choose sides? Or would she be able to convince her people to leave the orcs alone? Would Tana be able to stop her orcs?

Her mind suddenly felt a little more at ease when Tana rested a hand on her shoulder and looked intently into her eyes, a flash of lightning giving them greater intensity. "I trust you," she repeated. "Whatever the situation, we will handle it together."

Amaya stared back for a moment, not sure what to make of the orc's soothing powers, but she was grateful. She nodded at Tana, and replied, "And I will trust you, as well."

Before long, the other orc returned with Amaya's sheathed weapon in hand. He gave it to the shaman, who then looked to Amaya and passed it to her. The other orcs surrounding them looked at each other with concern or confusion.

As Amaya strapped the sheath to her right hip, Tana looked to the other orcs and raised her voice above the storm to say, "This woman is under my protection, and you are not to harm her under any circumstances. Do I make myself clear?"

It was a giant leap of faith on Tana's part, and Amaya suddenly felt overwhelmed.

But before anyone else could react, several of Arkad's darksteel orcs came from the south. "My Shaman," one of them said. "We're under attack!"

They rushed to meet with the darksteel orcs, all of whom eyed Amaya suspiciously. She ignored their stares and stayed close to the shaman.

"Tezarik," Tana spoke to the one leading the darksteel orcs. "What's going on?"

"We did not see the actual attack," he replied, his eyes darting between Tana and Amaya. "But one survivor reported that a large group of humans appeared through a portal and attacked without warning or hesitation."

Amaya's face drained of color, though she doubted anyone noticed. So it *was* her people. Which put her in a rather precarious situation, and her mind raced. Was it just her team, or had they gone back for reinforcements? "How many," she asked.

Tezarik looked at her curiously, and then back at Tana. Tana simply nodded and said, "Answer her question. She is here to help us."

Still hesitant, the orc replied, "I do not know. Six or seven, plus a Wizard."

Then it could still be just her team, if the numbers were right and her entire team had survived the encounter.

"We don't know where they are now," Tezarik shook his head. "It's impossible to see or hear anything in this storm."

"And this camp is huge," Amaya sighed, looking around for any clue to follow.

"Let us start with where they were last seen," Tana nodded south. Without hesitation, the gathered soldiers followed her. Amaya stayed as close as she could to the shaman, fearful that the others might attack Amaya out of spite.

More orcs joined them en route, but the dying light made it difficult to keep track of them all. Before long, only the flashes of lightning could guide them. The sun had definitely set by now.

Amaya brushed her soaked hair back out of her eyes and looked at Tana, and said as quietly as she could, "I can talk to them, once we find them. They'll follow my orders."

"Assuming the chaos allows for them to listen," Tana nodded. "I would prefer to stop the bloodshed before it becomes any worse."

Grateful that the shaman agreed, she looked around and kept her eyes and ears open. If it was her team, they would follow her order without question, except perhaps for Vin, who's hatred of orcs seemed to have grown tenfold during the course of the war.

But if other Warriors or soldiers had reinforced her team, there was no telling who would be in charge of the attackers. If they were Warriors from another country, they might not care that she was a Guardian.

Their search took them to the south end of the camp, where they found a handful of slain orcs. Four of the huts on the outer edge were obliterated.

She was not a tracker, but even if she was, it would have been virtually impossible to see tracks in the muddy grounds, especially in the utter black of the stormy night.

Until there was a bright flash of light to the east. A flash that was definitely not a bolt of lightning.

She looked at the orcs around her, but they had all spread out and hadn't noticed the flash. Or they had and dismissed it as lightning, but she knew it was something else, especially when no thunder followed.

At first she was going to tell Tana what she had seen, but then she stopped herself. This was her chance to stop whomever it was without unnecessary casualties. After all, if she was accompanied by orcs, something similar to what happened in the other camp could occur, and one stray arrow or magic attack could start a conflict that could not be stopped.

No, she couldn't let that happen again. She had to keep everyone safe.

Knowing that time was short, she pretended to search around for clues, as impossible as it was to find anything. Slowly, she edged towards the east, until she came upon an orc hut. As quickly and quietly as she could, she moved around it, effectively hiding herself from the orcs.

She glanced one last time at Tana, before she disappeared into the darkness, moments after a flash of lightning.

Knowing that the sound of the rain and wind would cover her, she took off into a run towards the east, following the edge of the camp as her supposed rescuers had likely done. There was another flash of light ahead, one which she recognized as a Mage releasing a magic attack.

And then she felt her spirits sink when another orc horn sounded, alerting her, and everyone else, to the attackers' positions.

She was out of time, and tried to push herself to run harder, but the mud made that impossible. When she finally made it to the source of the horn and the flashes, she found death.

Her rescuers had just defeated several more orcs, and stood over their corpses triumphantly, weapons in hand. This she saw by the light of the staff of the only Wizard present, and her spirits soared when she saw that it was Nia. She even noticed a shadow of a woman hunched over a corpse and thought that it looked like Idalia.

However, as Amaya looked to the others present, she realized those were the only two from her team. The glow from Nia's staff did little to illuminate in the rain, but it was enough that she recognized the other men and women present as members of the Everlin Warriors' Guild.

Each turned to face her when they became aware of her presence. She looked to each of them, searching their faces, afraid of who was present, but was glad when she realized that Din was not among them.

"Amaya," one of them called out to her, a Warrior named Merrick. The rescuers gathered around her, but she knew time was short. She glanced over her shoulder, expecting orcs to come barreling after her at any moment.

"Stop what you're doing," she ordered, realizing she didn't have to talk as loud. The wind had died for the moment. "Do not attack any more orcs!"

Merrick and the others all exchanged confused glances. "What?" Merrick asked, taken aback. "Are you kidding me? We have the perfect opportunity to finish off this camp while the storm rages on!"

She glared at him and asked, "Is that why you came here? To kill orcs? Or to rescue me?"

He looked confused for a moment, and then shrugged. "Both."

Amaya clenched her jaw, wishing her team was all there. She looked at Nia and asked, "Where's Elic? And Peren? Where's everyone else?"

"They are fine," Nia replied, standing behind the others so that her staff light was not so blinding. "Wounded, but alive."

She heaved a sigh of relief, glad to hear that there were no casualties. However, she then felt surprise when another of the Everlin Warriors asked, "Where did the Commander go?"

Amaya's stomach sank, a great void opening up within her. Everyone looked around, but Din was nowhere to be found. "Maybe he went looking for you," Merrick nodded to Amaya.

Dealing with Commander Din was the last thing she needed. He wouldn't follow her orders, and would probably slaughter every orc that he could.

"Orcs!" Idalia shouted, pointing behind Amaya.

She turned to see several shadows moving towards them, obviously darksteel-armored orcs. Tana was right behind them.

"Wait!" she stepped out in front of her rescuers.

The orcs didn't seem inclined to stop, and Amaya very nearly drew her sword, but then Tana added her own order, "Do not attack them!"

Only a dozen feet away, the orcs slid to a stop. Their weapons were drawn, and they looked very menacing in the dark. The flashes of lightning only added to their frightening appearance.

Tana stepped forward to also stand between the orcs and Amaya's rescuers. "Amaya," she breathed heavily. "You made it here fast."

"I'm sorry for breaking off," she shook her head. "I wanted to stop them if I could."

"You wanted to stop us from killing orcs," Merrick asked, incredulous.

She glared back at him. "Yes! These orcs are not our enemy."

"All orcs are our enemies," a voice suddenly shouted from further inside the orc camp.

All eyes turned towards the voice. Standing atop a hill was a shadow, his sword held out to his side. A flash of lightning confirmed who she thought it was.

Pressure boiled up inside of her, the anger she had felt over the past several months surfacing. She turned to face him, and felt her hand reaching for her sword.

"It's no surprise that you don't know friend from foe," Amaya shouted at Din, her last word almost lost in another boom of thunder. "I'm ordering all of you to stand down, and to leave here immediately."

"Hold your ground," Din shouted. "We're not going anywhere."

She looked to her rescuers, but they didn't seem to know what to do. The Everlin Warriors looked at her, knowing all too well that she was a Guardian and therefore outranked Din. Yet he was their commander, and loyalty was instilled into Warriors from childhood.

Idalia was probably the only person present that looked ready to follow Amaya's orders. Nia seemed completely fascinated by the brewing conflict, curiosity more than any other emotion showing in her eyes.

When Nia's eyes met Amaya's, the fascination faded, turning to one of grave concern and sympathy. The look on Amaya's face must have made the Wizard realize just how much pain and anger Amaya felt.

When Amaya looked back to Din, he still stood atop the hill, unmoving. She had a very bad feeling about what he was about to do. About the fight that was about to happen. And yet, a part of her was looking forward to finally unleashing her wrath upon him.

"Don't do it, Din," she warned. "I'm a Guardian. You *will* follow my orders."

She then looked over towards Tana, who met her gaze. Din wasn't going to follow her command, she knew it. In fact, she knew exactly what he was about to do. She wished she could tell Tana what was going to happen next without giving away her hand. Thankfully, a flash of lightning illuminated the shaman's eyes and revealed a look of understanding. The shaman already knew.

Amaya then turned to her would-be rescuers. In a voice she knew was too quiet for Din to hear, she said to them, "If you hold any loyalty to the throne, you will not interfere or attack the orcs, no matter what happens next."

When she looked back at Din, he still hadn't moved or changed posture. She did, however, sense a draw of power into Din. He was trying to do it subtly, but like always, he had underestimated her. *Please let Tana be ready for him,* she thought.

And then it happened. He raised his sword and pointed it right at the orcs, firing off a blast of arcane magic. It slammed into a red-white shield several feet away from the orcs, and they roared in response, but Tana shouted for them to stay their ground.

Amaya, on the other hand, was free to do what she should have done a long time ago. With an enraged shout, she pulled her sword from its sheath, instantly charging it with anger-fueled magic, and fired a blast right at Din.

He raised his own shield to deflect, but the blast still knocked him off balance. In his moment of distraction, she charged up the hill towards him. It was a struggle against the mud, but those difficulties only fueled her rage.

Din recovered quickly and brought his sword down on top of her the moment she reached him. She deflected with both magic and her sword, but he literally had the high ground, and when her feet slipped out from beneath her, he pressed the advantage, trying to cleave off her dominant hand.

She spun down the hill, but the spin turned into a slide, the rain-soaked hill unable to hold their weight and the dead grass giving way. Realizing it was her chance, she pointed her sword towards Din, but instead of shooting magic right at him, she released it towards his feet. The hill exploded beneath him, and the ground gave way, forcing him to tumble down after her.

When she finally stopped sliding, she managed to stand up, and both the orcs and her rescuers backed off to give them room.

Din came sliding down faster than she had, and within moments was at the bottom of the hill. She swung down on him with all of her might, hoping to overpower him, but his sword met hers, and he thrust his open palm at her, blasting her with unfocused magic and making her stumble backwards.

Slipping and sliding as he went, he stood up and faced her. The mud was going to make this battle impossible for either to fight, she was already exhausted. But was there anywhere they could go to get away from it?

Looking behind her, she saw the trees of the forest, and wondered if it would be better or worse. Then she did a double-take on the forest, realizing in Nia's light that the once-dead trees were now alive with giant, green leaves. Could life really grow that fast?

Anything was possible, she realized. Amaya turned her attention back on her opponent and began to move towards the forest.

Din saw her movement, and seemed to think this meant he had the advantage, so he pressed in on her, covering the distance as quickly as the mud would allow, until their swords met in an arm-rattling clash.

She summoned forth energy and pressed it into her sword, charging it in the hopes that if she were lucky enough to get a swing in past his shield, it would cut through his steel armor and wound him.

Another swing from Din, and another, and another, until she nearly lost her footing. But then they made it to the cover of the trees, and while the ground was still wet, her footing felt far more secure, whether by the roots of the underbrush and trees or some other force.

Except that she had not accounted for the tree roots, and tripped backwards over one, crashing down onto her back. It was the second time he had her on her back, and her fury grew tenfold. He brought his sword overhead and was prepared to bring it down on her, but she had already channeled power into her sword, and with every bit of rage buried inside of her, she released it on him.

It struck him dead in the chest, crumpling his armor and throwing him back against one of the outermost trees of the forest. Crumpling to the ground with a grunt, he cursed at her.

She slowly rose up, letting the pain from falling back fuel her anger further. He looked up at her, and in a flash of lightning, she saw fear on his face. Good. Fear was what he should feel.

Din scrambled to his feet, and that was when she attacked. She started with a jab, which he deflected, but she was inside his defenses now, and she threw her shoulder into him, shoving him along the edge of the forest. She swung her sword at the hip, using all of her strength, and their swords met in a ringing clash.

Again, she swung, charging her sword with more power, forcing him back. She swung again, meeting sword for sword. And again. The world grew dim around her, and she realized that she had a very hard time seeing him, but her eyes had adjusted well enough, and she didn't care.

Each swing was more forceful than before, more brutal than before. Flashes of memories passed through her mind. Flashes of being with him, cuddled up in his arms, and she struck at him again. Flashes of patrols together, and she struck again. Their first night making love, and she struck again. The day he had sent her on the mission to kill the bandits, and she struck at him even harder.

The weeks in prison. She yelled out in rage, and struck for every single day in prison, again and again and again, never letting up, never giving him a moment of rest. He tried to change the tide of the battle by kicking low at her, but all she did was back-step away, and then press in on him again.

She shouted, "Not again!" Amaya struck again. "You think you can tear apart my life and not suffer consequences?" Another blow. "You think you can screw with me, with my team, with all of us and get away with it?"

He swung at her, but she batted his sword away easily, and then she swung in response, releasing magic she hadn't even realized she had channeled into her weapon. The blast slammed into him, ripping through his hastily-erected magic shield, and sent him sprawling to the forest floor.

She rushed over to where he had landed. He tried to attack her with an arcane blast, but she used magic and her sword to deflect the attack. She swung her sword against his, knocking his sword arm to the ground, and then she stomped on his hand, forcing him to release his grip.

Flipping the sky-blue blade around to point down, she raised it up, and prepared to plunge it straight into his chest.

She glared at him, right into his eyes. A soft green glow lit the surrounding area, allowing her to see the fear in his eyes. Amaya reveled in that fear, glad to have made him so afraid, to make him cower. He feared her.

...He feared her.

Her heart skipped a beat when she realized what that meant. He feared her, and she stood over him, holding his life in her hands. He could no longer hurt her.

Or could he?

What if she killed him now? She would never have to fear him again. He couldn't hurt her anymore if he was dead. He could never hurt anyone again. The world would be a better place without him.

But would she be better? Would killing him take away the pain she had felt in her heart for so long? Or would it only fester?

What would she become if she killed him now?

His life wouldn't be the first she had taken. It wouldn't be the last. But then she remembered the conversation she had once had with Trebor Tem, deep in the Valaras dungeon, surrounded by raging, roaring orcs.

Trebor recognized the hatred building inside of her. The same rage that he felt. So strong that it had changed him, turned him into something terrible, a monster of his former self.

She was breathing heavily, her sword still held high, ready to plunge through her former lover's chest. Looking to the source of the green glow, she saw that everyone had followed them into the forest, orcs and humans together. The glow came from Nia's staff, allowing everyone to stare at the scene solemnly.

Tana especially looked at her with concern, her jaw clenched tight, as if she wanted to say something, but the words unable to come forth.

Amaya remembered what she felt after that conversation with Trebor. She remembered asking herself, *who were the real monsters?* The orcs? Or her?

If she did this, she would have her answer.

She looked again into Din's terrified eyes. He was a coward.

That realization was so staggering that she almost lost her balance. He was a *coward*. And that was why he tormented her. And if she gave into her urge...

No.

Amaya lowered her sword and shook her head. "No," she said to him. She backed away, releasing his sword hand from her boot. Knowing he could not be trusted, she bent over and picked up his weapon, taking away his only means of actually hurting her. "No," she repeated, shaking her head and backing away further. "No…"

He looked at her in confusion, but there was an obvious look of relief in his eyes. "I will not kill you, Uric. As much as you deserve it, I will not kill you." She looked at Tana, and smiled. "I'm better than that."

After a moment of silence, he suddenly laughed. "Better than me? I think not." He wiped blood, sweat and water from his face. "I've caught you consorting with orcs, you pathetic wench." She looked at him stoically and allowed him to finish. "I will tell the King that you have betrayed your own kind. You traitor…"

His threat to ruin her life should have angered her, and it would have before. Instead, she just laughed. "Oh, Din. You don't get it yet, do you?" He looked at her quizzically. "You've lost. You have no power over me. You never will again."

She looked at his sword, a finely-crafted, grey-white blade, with a beautiful black and silver hilt. It was his pride and joy, and a symbol of his command. Smiling, she jabbed it into the ground and stepped back. Sudden exhaustion overcame her, so the effort of charging her sword with magic was greater than normal.

And just as she swung, Din yelled out, "No!" But too late. With the magic giving her sword an unnatural sharpness, she cleaved through his blade, snapping it in two.

"You are no longer a member of the Warriors' Guild," she looked at him. "By order of the King, I am hear-by stripping you of your rank, and banishing you from Tal." He was too stunned to react, he simply stared at his broken blade, unable to stand, unable to do anything but sit in the mud. She stepped closer to him, forcing him to look into her eyes. "Today I spare you, but if you ever show your face in Tal again…" She shook her head. "You will be executed."

Incredulously, he said, "You cannot simply banish me because you wish to. You must have just cause!"

She wanted to give him a satisfied smile, but even that was too great of an effort. "You disobeyed my orders, which is akin to disobeying the King's orders. You are no longer a citizen of Tal, Uric Din. Make sure I never find you again."

As the fatigue continued to drain her further, Amaya sheathed her sword and turned away. She wasn't ready to return to the orc village, or to talk to anyone else, so she walked past everyone, deeper into the forest. All she wanted was to be alone.

She wasn't sure how far she walked, but before long she could go no further, the darkness making it impossible to safely traverse the root-laden forest floor.

Amaya collapsed to her knees, letting the darkness seep into her. She wrapped her arms around herself, a sudden surge of relief, sadness, loneliness, happiness, and fear all exploding within her stomach and spreading out into her body.

The tears came easily, streaming across her rain- and sweat-soaked face. The emotions grew stronger and stronger, and she couldn't hold them back, no matter how hard she clutched at her stomach.

It was over, wasn't it? She would never have to deal with him again, never have to look at him again. She should be happy! And she was. But the sadness was greater, and everything hitting her all at once just made her cry harder, and she felt ready to collapse inside of herself and explode all at once.

Time became an endless stream in the darkness. After what felt like hours of sobbing, the emotions finally began to subside, and the tears slowed. Her thoughts wandered, to the past few years, to the time she had spent with Uric, the time she had wasted with him, letting him make her think she was just barely worthy of love...

A soft, green glow surrounded her, and she spun around, ready to draw her sword. Only to see Nia, approaching her very carefully. "Amaya," she whispered. "I did not mean to startle you."

Amaya could only imagine how she looked, her eyes red and puffy, and who knew what streaming from her nostrils...

But Nia did not seem to notice, and somehow it was comforting that the young Wizard did not care about such things. Then, much to Amaya's surprise, Nia jabbed her staff into the soft ground, leaving it to illuminate the area, and then she knelt down in the mud next to Amaya.

Too stunned to react, Amaya allowed Nia, the same socially oblivious Wizard that her team poked fun at, to pull her into a warm embrace. Before Amaya could think to control her emotions, they escaped her control, and she wept into her friend's arms.

***

By the time the sun had set, Arkad had found and rallied over two dozen of his darksteel brothers. They encountered a few enemy Warriors, but beyond that they were fortunate enough not to run into further opposition. The wall of fire that Arkad unintentionally created seemed to keep the enemy at bay.

However, panic set in when he could not find Kilack. He asked his troops if they had seen his lieutenant, but none had spotted him since he and Arkad had burst into the clearing together and rushed the Keeper of the Sword.

Had Kilack not made it through the enemy line, as small as it was? Or was he trapped by Arkad's fires?

With his soldiers in tow, he began to backtrack, even knowing it was a grave mistake.

The forest was ablaze and smoke filled the air, threatening to choke them out. The General noticed that the same storm he had seen near the To'kar camp was fast approaching from the south, bright flashes in the sky giving an eerie reminder of the chaos that surrounded them. The fire, smoke, and the storm would make it all but impossible to find any additional darksteel orcs.

There should have been well over one hundred darksteel orcs still present! So many were lost to him now, and he feared that any left behind, including Kilack, would not survive the rest of the war.

After only a few minutes of back-tracking, they reached the wall of fire, quickly spreading their way. Arkad gripped his axe tightly, trying not to let his fears cloud his mind. Yet he could not help it, and he shouted into the blaze, "Kilack!"

No response came through the roar, and the dry underbrush allowed the flames to spread like a stampeding herd of qrishags. "Kilack," he shouted again, tempted to rush into the flames, confident that his armor would protect him long enough to find his friend.

But no. His loyalty to the greater whole overrode his sense of panic and impending loss. His forces here, and back at the camp, needed him. He was still their General.

The heat grew ever more intense, blasting his face with warmth that he had not felt since home. It was comforting, but very quickly became too hot.

His spirits sank, and he turned back to the rest of his troops waiting behind him. They stared at him with mixed looks of sadness and fear. He knew better than to let his emotions show in front of them, but too much had been lost. Too much...

Arkad wanted to find more darksteel orcs, to find Kilack, to make this tragedy somehow seem less wretched, but that was impossible. The fire would either overtake them as it spread faster, or the storm would force them to scatter, lost in the darkness of the woods once the rains suffocated the fires.

Less than thirty of his brothers. It would have to do.

He walked through the center of the troops, each looking to him for guidance. All he could do was pull out the portal vial, examining the tiny potion as he moved. When he was on the other side of his soldiers, he looked back at them.

"I am your General," he shouted above the roar of the approaching fire, resisting the urge to cough. He held up the vial for all to see and continued, "And I could order you all to follow me through this portal. However, you should know that this will not take us back to the fortress. It will take us somewhere else, somewhere far away, where another shaman waits to welcome us into her tribe."

The stir of shock was like a bolt of lightning shooting through the gathered troops, and he waited for someone to object. When no one did, he said what he hoped that everyone thought, "Our shaman has acted without honor, sending us into a hopeless and unnecessary war." He did not admit, and never would, that he felt like the war could have been won, if only he had been a better leader. "Now she demands that we stand our ground to be slaughtered by the humans, while sending my unit off to find other orcs to murder.

"I will no longer serve her. You may choose to remain here and find your way back to the Fortress, or you may follow me. Together with our new shaman, we may yet have a chance to rebuild our people. Our race may yet survive."

Turning on the spot, he found the nearest stone and threw the vial at it with all of his might, shattering it. There was a blinding flash of light, and in an instant, a lilac-colored wall of light appeared before them, lighter and darker colors swirling around each other in a mesmerizing pattern.

He turned back to the gathered troops and opened his arms. "If you will follow me, pass through now and await me on the other side."

Feeling his stomach twist into a knot, he waited apprehensively. There was no time for him to explain further, not with the wall of flames growing dangerously close. He could not explain to them how their shaman's powers had waned in the brightness of Tana's light. Could not explain Tana's vision. Could not explain why this was their best hope. All he could do was wait and hope.

The soldiers looked to one another, uncertainty in their eyes at first. However, as each one looked to the other, something changed in their eyes, and they looked at him. Then, without a word, they all surged forward, and to his greatest relief, they streamed around him and into the portal.

Every single one of them.

His heart soared, elation filling him with an energy he had not felt in such a long time. He clasped the shoulders of the some of the orcs as they passed by, and they each in turn nodded to him, saying respectfully, "General."

After so long of enduring defeats, at the hands of not one but two enemy forces, it was his first true victory. He still felt guilty about leaving behind so many, but the ones he had found still thought of him as their leader.

The last one passed through, the fire now close enough that his armor began to feel like an oven. He watched as the flames grew closer, felt the heat growing to an almost unbearable intensity and the smoke choked him.

A fleeting though crossed his mind, the hope that some of the enemy soldiers were caught in those flames and burned. Tana would not have approved, but it was the least they deserved for how they had treated his kin for the last three thousand years.

Now…now Tana wanted to make peace with them. Asked him to fight side by side with them in the future. He knew it was the only hope they had, but that didn't mean he had to like it.

Turning to the glowing, shimmering portal, he took in a deep breath, but then immediately started coughing.

He covered his mouth with his left hand, his battle axe gripped tightly in the right, and made for the portal.

A flash of motion distracted him, and before he knew what was happening, a tiny blur of mottled grey-white and black flew at him.

Twin daggers flashed in the firelight, and it was reflex alone that saved him when he smacked the figure away. The attacker still managed to gash a deep gouge into his left cheek, gushing thick, black-red blood from his face.

Roaring a curse, he turned towards the tiny figure, only to be shocked by whom he saw. A woman he had hoped to never see again.

"Orinda?"

The small orc woman had tucked into a roll when she landed, and now crouched several feet away from him, twin daggers he had never seen before clutched in both of her hands. Then she leapt at him, displaying a nimbleness he did not expect.

Arkad tried to bring his axe up to deflect her assault, but even with his strength, the weapon as too heavy and big, and she latched onto his arm with one of her arms, trying to slash at him with her free hand.

The first slash missed his nose by a hair, the second barely cut into his chin, and he had to flick her off of his arm. Rage flared within, and he let loose that anger with a barrage of fire from his axe right at where he had flung her, but she was too fast and dodged his attack.

When she leapt at him again, he punched with his left hand as hard as he could, connecting at the base of her rib cage, sending her flying backwards again. The points on his armor should have cut into her, but her leather armor, burnt long ago in an attempt to make it look like darksteel armor, protected her.

In a wild craze, she screamed and attacked again, and again, and again. Each time he would bat her away, and it was all he could do to keep her from cutting him again.

What he didn't realize until the heat was unbearable was that she was drawing him away from the portal and closer to the fires, the ones he had just started together with the incoming blaze and cutting him off from the rest of the world, leaving only the portal as an escape.

The creaking, cracking of a tree falling distracted him, and he had to leap away as the flame-engulfed top landed inches away, embers pelting him. He shielded his face, but that momentary distraction was all Orinda needed. She darted away from him, towards the portal.

Seeing her run, he very nearly sent a stream of fire at her, but then realized it would have cut off his only remaining escape. In a snap-decision, he arched back, and then lobbed his axe at her. It spun through the air in a lazy loop.

Without even waiting to see what happened, he charged after her, watching, waiting, hoping as the axe seemed to move in slow motion. She could not be allowed through the portal!

The axe missed, sailing over her head, but it made her stop short in surprise. His axe planted itself into the ground not two feet in front of her. Just as she looked back towards him, he was on top of her, tackling her to the ground and, he hoped, crushing her with his weight.

The impact made her drop one of her daggers, but the other was still in hand, and flashed in front of his face, barley missing his mouth. She scrambled under him, somehow squirming out, but he grabbed at her ankle before she could get any further.

Arkad reached forward with another hand to grab her torso, but she lashed back at him. The blade went right between two of his fingers, finding one of the few weaknesses in his armor, and sank a good inch into the flesh between his middle and ring finger.

Roaring in pain, he reeled back, her grip tight enough that the blade slid out, cutting further through the thin glove beneath his gauntlets. He was on his knees, and she jumped up, now having the obvious advantage, and tried to jab at his face. He slapped her jab away, but she just used that opportunity to come in closer, and tried to stab into his neck above his armor.

Not knowing what else to do with such a little fury, he opened his arms wide, and then closed them around her, trying to restrict her movement by cinching off her arms. She kicked at him, and even tried to bite at him, so he reflexively released his grip just a little.

Too much.

The dagger flashed before him, and pain exploded around his right eye, the firelight suddenly going dark on one side. He released her and clutched at his eye, roaring in pain, wiping at the fresh black-red blood streaming forth. Had she pierced his eye, or was he simply blinded by blood?

Arkad opened his left eye just in time to see her jabbing for him again, intent on taking his sight from him completely. He was just quick enough to deflect up, but just barely, the dagger cutting his eyebrow and skating up along his flesh, opening up another wound on his forehead.

More blood streamed forth into his only good eye, and now he was completely blinded! He wiped at the blood, the salty liquid burning his left eye, but there was little he could do to clear it up, and he realized he was at her mercy…

Until he felt a sudden burst of cold right in front of him, and he heard Orinda cry out in pain and surprise.

He panicked, and tore his left gauntlet off so that he could wipe the blood away, or as best as he could, and then held his hand above his left eye to keep more blood from streaming in. His vision was still blurred, but a figure clad in darkened armor stood before him, holding a mace. Could…could it be?

"General," Kilack's voice came to him, relief washing over his entire body.

But Orinda was not out of the fight yet. She launched herself at Kilack, intent on doing to him what she had done to Arkad. However, her battle with Arkad had fatigued her. Kilack threw her off, and then just as she leapt at him again, he swung his mace and caught her in mid-air, the hard, pointed, enchanted weapon slamming into her body with a sickening thud.

She fell to the ground next to Arkad and did not move again.

He stared at her, and she at him, blood already trickling from her mouth. She no longer breathed, and moments later, she stopped bleeding.

Arkad was too stunned at first to do anything, but the heat quickly reminded him that he had no time to gawk. Another tree fell nearby, and the flames had spread all around them. The fire he had started only moments ago was inches from the portal, and their time was up.

Looking to his trusted lieutenant, he saw Kilack staring back stoically, the barest hint of horror on his face as he looked upon his wounded, deformed General. Grunting as he went, Arkad pushed himself up with is free hand and stared back.

Arkad shook his head, and then looked through his blurred eye at the portal. The fire had reached it, and was beginning to surround it. The larger fire behind them was only a few feet away.

Without another word, Arkad took two steps forward and reached down to pull his axe out of the ground. It did not come as easily as he'd hoped, and he cursed his sudden weakness. He cursed his failure.

When he looked again at Kilack, his lieutenant did his best to give a smile, and nodded. "You fought well, General. I will tell the men as much."

Relief filled his chest, and he nodded. Without another word, Kilack turned to the portal. They could not simply walk through it now. So his lieutenant got a running start and leapt in, the flames licking at his boots as he did.

As fatigued as he was, Arkad managed to get his own running start, but his muscles gave out just before he should have leapt, and he stumbled, stomping through the ash and flames. He started to fall forward, but he just barely kept himself upright long enough to fall through the portal, and to safety.

Like every portal he had ever been through, it was like passing through a door, and in one instant, the unbearable heat gave way to shocking cold, taking his breath away as a torrential downpour instantly cooled him, and made his armor creak and pop. He lay face-down in the mud, and could feel embarrassment overtake him.

Embarrassment because he knew that his men now saw him broken and bleeding.

The mud had sloshed up into his wounds, and his left eye was blinded by the mix of blood, rain, and mud. He pushed up slowly and wiped away as much of it as he could, but his vision would not completely clear.

Stand up, you weak fool, he thought to himself. *Don't let them see how broken you really are...*

He pushed, as hard as he could, his muscles protesting every inch of the way. His head spun, and he knew he was dehydrated and beyond fatigued. But he wouldn't give up. He couldn't.

After what felt like an eternity, he finally managed to stand. It was almost pitch black, and he only caught glimpses of his men from the flashes of lightning arching across the sky every two or three seconds. Thunder boomed, setting his teeth chattering.

His men...they stared at him every moment of his struggle. But once he was upright, his knees locked to prevent them from giving out, they cheered.

It was then that he knew it was okay. They closed in around him, and he feared that they would knock him over in their triumphant roars, but instead, they only wanted to help him. They held him up, and as he motioned in the direction he knew the camp was, they pulled him along.

They would not let their general fall again.

Never again.

***

Zerek's heart thundered in his ears. The cold night air whipped by him as he leapt across a small gap between buildings, landing on the low-pitched roof of yet another shop, and taking them one building closer to the Castle District.

It was a section of the city that he was very familiar with, having used the same location every time he snuck out of and back into the Castle District. He could have done it in his sleep.

He marveled at how far he had come, realizing that it had only been a few short months since his first terrifying attempt to leap across the streets.

Tonight, however, he was terrified for an entirely different reason.

At least I'm not alone, he thought to himself. He was accompanied by Sorin and Laira, and he knew that they had to be careful. If anyone saw or heard them, their mission into the castle would be over before it began.

His heart raced, but not because he was running. In fact, he was quite fit now, after months of running after Laira, and he barely worked up a sweat. No, his heart was pounding against his rib cage because he was terrified.

Zerek continued to wrestle with his decision, wondering if he was doing the right thing, or if backing out now would be the right thing. He was convinced that it was the Prince hiding the kingdom's situation from the King, and this was their chance to make things right. But he still felt like he was betraying his oath to defend the city and the castle, to defend the throne.

And then his time ran out. They leapt onto the last rooftop, and the wall separating the Castle District was before them. He crouched at the peak of the roof and knelt down, resting his hands on the ridge. Sorin came up on his left, Laira on his right, and they stared over the pitch at the wall.

To his surprise, he watched cautiously as a guard idly strolled along the battlements, slowly making his way to their left. Zerek knew patrols had increased since the orc incursion by the river, but he was under the impression that all of those extra patrols were deployed to the outer wall. This was something new.

"So that's why you took us around the long way," Laira whispered to him, reaching out and gently caressing his back. "You knew there were more guards out."

He felt his skin tingle in excitement at her touch, but he didn't admit that he hadn't known about the guard.

Zerek looked to the right to watch for another patrol, but no other soldiers were in sight. There were torches all along the battlements, so Zerek hoped that if anyone else was nearby, they would have been visible.

"Looks clear," Sorin whispered.

Zerek nodded and said, "Yeah. Hopefully it stays that way. The stairs we'll go down are a few hundred feet to the right." He looked at Sorin with a frown and asked, "Are you sure Endel got the message? It wasn't intercepted?"

Sorin frowned at him, as if offended. "I trust my people. And even if it was intercepted, it wouldn't mean anything to anyone else."

He didn't feel particularly inspired with confidence by Sorin's response, but it was the best they could hope for. They needed Endel for his plan to work.

Drawing in a deep breath, Zerek held it for a moment and stared at the wall before he released it. "Okay, then. Follow me."

Without hesitation, he stood up, positioned himself on the other side of the pitch, and then took a running start before leaping across the gap. It was second nature to him by now, and he barely felt his stomach lurch from the act, until he was solidly on the other side, where he instantly ducked down. Laira came next, followed by Sorin.

There was no turning back now.

Knowing they would not have much time on the wall, he crouch-walked past Laira and led them towards the stairs. Thankfully it was still unguarded, and they climbed down into the courtyard without incident. Ahead of them was a stretch of darkness over what he knew was a flat grassy area, leading up to the garden of a three story, wealthy house.

He wasn't particularly keen on taking his party through that garden, even though it was the path he was most familiar with. It provided cover, but there was hardly a sliver of one of the moons out tonight, so he felt safer traversing the darkness of the open grassy area, even though the dead grass crunched more. It would also be easier to get behind the castle and into the stables that way, where they would meet Endel.

About halfway to the stables, they were stopped by an unexpected guard patrolling the grassy area with a torch. Zerek instantly dropped to his belly and lay as flat as he could, thankful for the black cloak Sorin had provided him, and hoping they wouldn't be noticed. The guard passed within a couple dozen feet of them, but he never looked down at them, and seemed instead to be intent on looking up at the wall. *Thank the gods he didn't see us leap up onto the wall,* Zerek thought.

Once the guard passed and they could no longer hear footsteps, Zerek cautiously pushed up and looked towards where the guard had gone, waiting until he disappeared into the garden of the very house Zerek often passed by when sneaking in and out.

Sighing in relief, they started moving again, keeping low and as far away from any torches as they could.

When they finally reached the stables, Zerek told the others to remain outside, and he tip-toed in. Endel wasn't the only stable boy, and there was every possibility that someone else might have come out to tend to the horses late at night. You never knew when a messenger had to leave for another city, even in the middle of the night.

There wasn't a single source of light inside of the stables, and he didn't even get three steps inside before he realized he had no idea where to go. The last thing he needed to do was to spook the horses and draw the attention of the guards. So where was Endel?

A sudden tug on his right sleeve startled him, and a small squeak escaped his throat. When he turned to the source, he was relieved to see Endel, barely visible from the little light coming in through the stable entrance.

The young boy nearly doubled over trying to hold back his laughter, and it took every ounce of control Zerek had not to shove the boy away. After he gave himself a moment to slow his heart, Zerek motioned angrily for Endel to follow him out, where they joined the others.

There was only a few torches lit outside of the stables, but they were still exposed, and he didn't much like the idea of holding a meeting where a guard could stumble across them. So they retreated back outside of the training grounds, and knelt in the grass.

The night was getting colder, and clouds were building in the south. Would tonight be the first snowfall? It *was* that time of year...

Once they were sure no one was nearby, Endel turned to Sorin and Laira, and even though Zerek couldn't see his friend's face, he knew the boy blushed. "Uh, hello," he whispered.

Sorin said nothing, but Laira reached out a hand and touched Endel's shoulder. "It's good to see you again. We've missed you."

No doubt Endel's face grew warmer, and Zerek couldn't help but smile at Laira's encouraging welcome. "Thanks," Endel said, shifting nervously. "I'm, umm...I'm sorry." He looked to Sorin, the sorrow in his eyes visible even in darkness. "For failing before."

Sorin didn't reply at first, but then he nodded once, a little too coldly for Zerek's comfort. "It's okay, kid. What's important is that you're here, now. You could have easily turned away and not helped us tonight."

Endel's head popped up, and he asked, "Tonight? So we're going in now?" Though still whispering, his voice grew a little louder and they had to wave downwards to make him stop. He practically bounced up and down in excitement. "I thought that was the case, that's why I found my kit again." From a pouch on his belt, Endel produced a rolled up cloth that appeared to have several metal implements inside of it.

It took Zerek a moment to realize what it was, but when he did, he smiled. "A lock picking kit?"

"Yeah," Endel beamed. "It was right where I hid it back when I first came to the castle. I'm pretty good at hiding things."

"Good job," Laira grinned and reached out to scruff up Endel's hair. "I'm glad you came prepared."

"Indeed," Sorin replied, a little less critical. "We can get started right away. What's the best way into the castle?"

"There's six small entrances all around, almost all of them guarded," Endel shrugged. "But the guards are spread pretty thin right now, so they don't keep guards standing at a single door all the time, they rotate."

"So we should be able to get into one of them when it's unguarded," Laira nodded.

"What about the one by the gardens," Zerek suggested. "Even

with all of the fallen leaves, the bushes should provide us with more cover."

"Yeah," Endel nodded in agreement. "And they actually sweep the leaves every day. We should go in there."

Zerek looked around for any nearby guards, and then was about to stand up and lead the way, but then he stopped himself and looked again at Endel. "The guard rotation's changed since I left. Are you more familiar with it?"

With a confident smirk, Endel didn't even answer, he just rose up and led them towards the castle gardens. They did not take a direct route, and in fact it took them twice as long to get to the gardens than he expected, but he trusted in his young friend's knowledge and abilities.

When they finally reached the gardens, Zerek was surprised that almost all of the leaves on the bushes and trees were gone. When he had left only a few days ago, the gardens were alive with vibrant oranges, reds and golds, and only a few had fallen. Now, everything was barren, ready for the first snowfall. He'd heard that winter came earlier for Archanon than much of the rest of the kingdom, because it was nuzzled up against the mountains, but he still wasn't prepared for just how fast everything changed.

A single guard stood at the door, an entrance that Zerek had only used a couple of times during his service to the castle. They stood at the outer edge of the garden, a peaceful sanctuary laden with stones surrounding flower beds, bushes, and trees in grassy patches. Warm, yellow-white everlasting torches lit up the entire garden, making it beautiful even at night. It was idyllic and serene, and he suddenly realized how much he was going to miss the garden, now that he no longer worked at the castle.

Then again, I might find myself in the dungeon after tonight, he suddenly thought. His heartbeat suddenly doubled, and he felt warm and sweaty despite the cool breeze.

The castle guard visibly shivered and wrapped his arms around himself. After another few minutes of waiting and watching, they heard the guard curse the gods. He looked around, and then marched away from the door, cursing just loud enough for them to hear, but not so loud that they could understand what he said.

At first Zerek panicked, since the guard headed in their direction. However, only a few dozen feet to their left was an entrance and a path that led towards the guard shack, and that was the path the guard took.

Once the guard was out of earshot, Sorin noticeably relaxed. "We're in luck," Sorin whispered. "I think tonight's going to be the first snowfall. This wretched cold may have just saved us a longer wait."

Shivering even under his black cloak, Zerek wasn't sure about the use of the word luck, but never-the-less, he was tired of waiting, and of imagining what would happen if they were caught.

Endel edged up to peak over the bushes, but no one else was in sight. He motioned for everyone to follow, and led them to the same path the guard had just used. Once inside of the gardens, they stuck to the outer edges, hiding in as much of the shadows as they could, until they finally reached the door.

When Endel tried to pull the latch, it quietly clicked against the lock. He immediately pulled out his kit and unrolled it on the ground, finding the appropriate tools with practiced ease, and began working on the door.

"Hurry," Sorin suddenly whispered urgently. The door was in a recess in the wall and they were covered by the bushes nearby, but a quick glance through the bushes revealed movement against the backdrop of a torch in the opposite direction of the guard shack. Another guard was coming.

Endel seemed to ignore Sorin's urgency, slowly and methodically working his craft, his tongue sticking out just a little. Suddenly there was another quiet click, and a broad smile washed over Endel's face. He pulled the tools out of the keyhole and pulled the latch, and the door quietly and gracefully opened inward.

As Sorin and Laira rushed in past him, Endel rushed to put away his tools and roll up his kit, with Zerek resting a hand on his shoulder to remind him of the urgency. He could hear the new guard's boots clicking on the stone, and feared that they were moments away from being caught.

Finally Endel finished and they rushed in, Sorin closing the door quietly behind them. They all exhaled in relief, and remained a moment to allow their heartbeats to slow.

When his heart no longer thundered in his ears, Zerek looked around to get his bearings. He had a general idea of where they were in the castle, but there had been so many additions over the centuries, so many rebuilds, that it was a maze, and the only path he knew was to the Allied Council Chambers. They definitely didn't want to go there, even if it was empty at this hour.

It was up to Endel to lead. The boy stowed his kit in his belt, and then led them down the corridor, Sorin right behind him.

Fearing that someone would see and recognize him, Zerek began to pull up the hood of his cloak as he followed, but Laira stopped him with a firm hand. She leaned over and whispered, "It'll block your peripheral, and you might miss something. Leave it down until you really need it."

Feeling himself blush, Zerek nodded and let the hood fall back down. She stayed beside him for a little ways, but as they had to line up at the first intersection with a planned and practiced routine, they had to go single-file and one at a time, each person checking around the corner before proceeding across the intersection.

They passed further into the castle before they came to a turn, and that's when Zerek realized they were headed for a set of stairs. Was the treasury up or down? He had never asked Endel. *Don't be down,* he thought anxiously, thinking that if they had to climb to a higher floor, there was a potential to find a window to escape if they were spotted. Below ground, they might be trapped easier...

And of course, Endel led them downwards, the steel, spiral staircase creaking.

He heard Sorin whisper a complaint about Endel not finding a stone staircase to go down, but Zerek wasn't aware of any stone staircases, except for those at the main entrance. Any staircase that led up or down were either made of wood or metal, either of which would make noise.

Laira nudged Zerek forward to follow behind Sorin, her alert eyes darting back down the corridor and up the stairwell to ensure they would not be caught unawares. Thankfully they made it down to the bottom, which was surprisingly only one floor down, and began to enter into a part of the castle Zerek didn't even know existed.

The ceiling was much lower, the walls closer, and they were forced to go single-file. How were they supposed to evade guards? Thankfully, they never encountered one. As they slowly moved further along, pausing at each intersection and corner to carefully peak around, Zerek felt more and more relaxed.

Maybe, just maybe, they would make it through this.

They came to a stop in front of an old wooden door with a metal handle, Endel raising his hand up for them to be quiet. Slowly, he tried the latch, and it opened with ease. It was in that moment that Zerek saw the taut, worried looks on Sorin and Laira's faces. Whereas Zerek was feeling better about their intrusion into the castle, they looked far worse, to the point that Laira's hands shook a little.

They followed Endel into what appeared to be an unlit, unoccupied office, with a desk at the opposite end and several unlit candles.

After they were all inside, Endel only partly closed the door, leaving just enough of a crack to let in torchlight from the corridor. Zerek felt his anxiety build again, the shadows in the room giving the worry on Laira's face a sharper voice.

"This doesn't feel right," Sorin suddenly whispered.

Endel turned to face them, but with the only light source at his back, Zerek could not make out his expression. "What doesn't feel right," the boy asked quietly.

"Where are all of the guards," Laira asked. "Even this close to midnight, there should be more patrolling the castle."

Endel glanced over his shoulder, and then back at them. "Huh…you're right," he nodded. "Every time I've ever come down here…" His voice suddenly fell silent, and he looked out into the hallway. A moment later, Zerek heard them too, distant voices.

Zerek felt terrified to move even an inch, while Endel closed the door to just a sliver. They waited, listening intently, but the voices never grew closer, and after a few minutes, they stopped.

When his lungs began to burn, Zerek realized he held his breath in, so he let it out as quietly as he could, and gulped in another breath. Endel opened the door just a little bit more, peering out into the hallway, before he shook his head.

"I think that was the guards by the treasury," he whispered without looking at them.

When Endel turned back to them, Zerek looked at Laira, a sliver of light from the door piercing over her right eye. Her expression was very dark, and the foreboding sense he felt inside twisted his stomach into a knot.

When she noticed Zerek staring at her, she shook her head, the column of light dancing across her facial features. "This doesn't feel right," she whispered.

"Agreed," Sorin replied, edging closer to the door to peer out over Endel's head. "But what can we do? We're so close, Laira." He looked at her, tilting his head to one side. "Closer than we'll probably ever get again. We have to do this."

"And if it's a trap," she asked.

The idea of a trap induced another panic in Zerek, and his heart raced yet again as sweat beaded on his forehead. He'd lost everything once, and if they were caught now, he would lose it all again. He imagined being imprisoned in a dungeon, the close walls, the low ceiling, and the stale, cold air. It would be like being in the mines again, only this time with no escape.

Yet even as he thought about that, he realized something else, and voiced it in a whisper. "Then it's too late already, and we may as well try."

Everyone paused and stared at him, their eyes wide. He nodded to Laira, hating himself for saying this, dreading the reality that it meant. "If they know we are coming, then it's too late. We've broken into the castle, they can already send us to jail for that. If they know we're here, then they'll be guarding the exits anyway." He shrugged, forcing the welling lump in his throat back down into his stomach. "So why not go for it?"

Even in the shadows, he could see the smile draw across Sorin's face. "Huh...sounds like something I would have said years ago."

Laira smirked and added, "Or something I'd say now." She looked at Zerek and reached for his hand. Her hand was cold and clammy, just like his, and he realized just how terrified she was. He could feel the quick, hard pulse through her palm, almost matching his.

The fear began to melt away, and he felt exhilarated for what came next. The moment he had dreaded was upon them, and as he looked at Endel, waiting for the young boy to say whether or not he was in, Zerek felt something he had not felt in such a long time.

Freedom.

Whatever happened next, it was because of his choice.

After a moment, Endel nodded. "Okay, I'm in. Let's do it." Looking to Laira and Sorin, he asked, "Do you think you can find your way out?"

Sorin shrugged, and replied, "It won't be easy, this place is a maze. But I'll figure it out."

"We'll be fine," Laira smiled at Endel, but squeezed Zerek's hand.

Sorin gently nudged Endel aside and opened the door a little more, listening. "We should go now."

Suddenly the excitement was replaced with fear, but a different kind of fear. Not for his own well being or his own future, but for the woman standing beside him. Without thinking about what he was doing, he suddenly threw his arms around her, and held on as tight as he could. She returned the embrace, her arms under his, clutching at his lower back, grabbing his shirt and trying to pull him closer, if that was possible.

"I love you," she whispered into his ear. "And I *will* see you again."

"I love you too," he replied, his heart ready to burst from his chest.

After lingering a moment longer, Sorin cleared his throat, and Laira released his tunic and stepped out of his embrace. She did not look at him again, despite how desperately he wanted to gaze into her eyes one last time, even if it was through a blanket of darkness.

She lined up behind Sorin and tapped his shoulder. He nodded once, and then opened the door wide enough to peak out. After a moment of looking both ways, he walked left, with Laira following. When they were out of sight, Endel closed the door almost completely behind them, once again allowing only a sliver of light in.

The seconds passed by painfully, and Zerek had to remind himself to breathe. Breathe in, breathe out, counting four seconds during each action, trying not to think about what might happen...

And then the shouts echoed down the corridor. "Hey!"

"Who's that?"

"Get them!"

There was the sound of boots running across the stone floor, and two shadows passed by the door, nearly making Zerek jump out of his skin. Two more shadows passed by a moment later, the sound of boots echoing into silence.

After several agonizing seconds, or minutes, or hours, Endel exhaled slowly. "Okay. Let's go!"

He swung the door open and peeked his head out, looking both ways before smiling back at Zerek. "Clear," he whispered, waving for Zerek to follow.

Swallowing back the lump in his throat, Zerek followed after

Endel, trying not to let his friend get too far away.

It was only a couple hundred feet to the T-intersection, which Endel stopped just short of, leaning up against the left wall. Zerek stopped just beside him, trying desperately to become a part of the wall as they waited a moment and listened. Endel then looked down, and whispered, "Woops." Zerek also looked down, and suddenly realized that the shadows from a torch behind them were being cast into the intersection.

Endel looked at Zerek, shrugged, and then peaked around the corner. Zerek held his breath a moment, but Endel sighed in relief. "No one stayed behind. We're good."

Without hesitation, Endel hurried around the corner, Zerek almost forgetting to follow. They finally reached the door, which was about two hundred feet down an otherwise dead end, and sprawled out his lock pick kit in front of the door. He began to examine the lock, a frown on his face. "Woh, I've not seen a lot of locks like this."

Zerek panicked a moment, glancing over his shoulder. "Can you still pick it?"

When he looked at Endel, the kid frowned back at him and scoffed. "Are you kidding? I can pick anything!" He retrieved two tools from his kit, and immediately set to work. Zerek resisted cracking a joke about Endel and nose picking. "This one just might take me a minute…"

But he never had a chance to finish. Suddenly the lock clicked, and the door was pulled in away from him, wrenching the tools out of his hand. Before them stood three guards, all of whom were armed. In fact, one had a longsword, which Zerek instantly realized meant a Mage.

The others held their shortswords and shields ready, and in a normal combat situation, they would be better suited to fighting in the narrow corridors than the Mage. But the Mage had his own advantage, and simply lowered the tip to point at them.

"You know what I am," she spoke quietly, as if afraid that if she shouted, they would panic and run. She wasn't wrong. "If you run, you won't get two steps."

"It's over, Zerek," another voice spoke from behind. He turned around slowly, and felt his stomach sink into an endless, black pit. It was Torick Alixton. His once-trainer and friend shook his head.

"We know what you were planning. If your friends haven't been caught yet, they soon will be."

He heard Endel whimper beside him, and almost felt like doing the same. He wanted to bolt, but he knew he couldn't make it past Torick, even if he didn't have to worry about the Mage.

They were dead.

There was nothing for them to do but surrender.

The Mage and Torick kept them covered while the other guards came forward and searched the two of them. They found nothing on Endel, but they did pick up his lock-picking kit from the floor and stored it.

For Zerek, however, there was his dagger, and he tried to stop the guard from unlashing it from his belt. The guard, who neither knew Zerek nor appeared to care, shoved him against the wall and pressed his forearm against Zerek's neck.

"Try it, thief, I beg you," the guard growled in his face.

That took the fight right out of Endel. The guard called him a thief, and it was at that moment when he realized that was exactly what he was now. He was caught, and would forever be branded a thief. His life was over.

After the guard secured his dagger, Zerek and Endel were bound by enchanted shackles and marched through the belly of the castle. He was deathly afraid of what was coming, because he knew that dungeons were almost always underground, and he thought they were being taken straight there. Once in, he imagined there would be no possible escape.

But then something unexpected happened. The guards brought them to a wider spiral staircase and marched them back up to the ground floor. At first Zerek was disoriented, the underground level having a completely different layout from the ground floor, but then he realized where they were.

The guards had brought them up near the front of the castle. Near the throne room. Moments later, as they continued their shameful march through the castle, Zerek realized that the throne was in fact their destination.

Was the King still awake?

They were marched in through one of the many side doors to the throne room, but aside from a handful of guards standing between the statues, it was empty. The King was not yet present.

They were brought before the throne, and forced to their knees by two very rough blows to the backs of their legs, but aside from that, nothing happened. No other doors opened, no one else came or went, they were simply left there, the guards that had caught them standing all around them, ready to pounce.

"What's going on," Zerek finally asked.

One of the guards sporting a shield moved as if to backhand Zerek, and he flinched. "Silence, whelp," the guard spat at him.

"Hey," Torick stepped between Zerek and the guard. "There's no need for that!"

When Zerek glanced up at the two, the guard looked ready to retort, but clearly Torick outranked him and he backed down. Zerek felt relieved at Torick's support, but when his former friend turned to look down at him, the disappointment on his face made Zerek's spirits sink right back down into the depths of despair.

"You were followed," Torick spoke quietly, shaking his head. "When you came back here to talk to Endel, you were followed by Chessick, and he overheard your conversation."

A giant frown crossed over Zerek's face, and he had to look at Endel questioningly. It was the look of recognition on Endel's face that somehow sparked his own memory, and he looked back up at Torick. "Wait, the other messenger that you trained," he asked, incredulous.

Torick nodded curtly. "Yes. He came and reported it directly to me." Torick shook his head, looking down at the ground with barely contained anger. "I didn't believe him. I defended you. But I also knew that I had to report his claim to the Captain, who then brought it up to the King."

Torick shook his head. "He didn't believe it either, until he remembered that there was a mysterious woman that helped you fight off the orcs. What were you doing out after dark? What were you doing by the wall? Why didn't you tell anyone? The pieces started to click into place."

As Torick spoke, the pit in Zerek's stomach grew, and he bowed his head. He realized then that from the very start of his time in the castle, he had broken the rules. Going off to look for Laira during his delivery runs, sneaking out of the castle at night, running across roof tops...

He didn't belong in the castle. Maybe he never had. He was just

371

as discontent in the castle as he was in the mines.

Not knowing what else to say, he started to utter out an apology, knowing how insignificant it would be. But at that moment, the doors behind the raised throne clicked and groaned open, and King Beredis strode in, wearing only the bare minimum of regality.

He did not look happy.

In fact, as he walked around the throne's steps, he glared down at Zerek and Endel, both of whom could do nothing more but stare down at the ground and avoid meeting his gaze. When the King stopped before them, Zerek stared at His Majesty's slippers, examining every detail, trying not to think of what he had just done, nor of the punishment ahead of him.

For what felt like ages, and a thousand pounding heartbeats, the King simply stared down at them, his arms folded in front of him. Zerek risked glancing up towards him once, but immediately looked down, feeling his shame weigh his head down.

When King Beredis finally spoke, it was in his booming court voice, echoing in the largely empty throne room. "Is this how you repay the kindness I have shown you?" Zerek didn't know how to reply, and simply kept his head down, waiting for more.

However, more lecture did not come, and that somehow was worse. The disappointment and betrayal in the King's voice was more than enough to make him wish he was a bug that could fly out the window, far away from Archanon.

"Sire," Endel squeaked. "We, umm..."

The King glared down at Endel, and that silenced him after an audible gulp. Then he looked again to Zerek and asked, "Why?"

Zerek stuttered for a moment, trying to find the words to answer, but having difficulty even forming coherent thoughts. "We had to find proof, my Lord," he shook his head. "I knew the Prince was hiding the kingdom's crisis from you, and I wanted you to know. Wanted everyone to know, he's a..." Zerek stopped short of directly insulting the Prince, realizing that he was already on shaky ground.

After a long pause, the King shook his head slowly. "Do you truly think there is anything that goes on in my castle that I do not know about?"

Feeling his stomach suddenly drop, he looked up at the King, meeting his eyes for the first time. "Sire? You...you knew about the treasury?"

Sighing, the King unfolded his arms and nodded once. "Yes. I knew that my son practically bankrupted us, and that was why he created so many new taxes."

Ones which the King had subsequently repealed upon his recovery, Zerek realized. Which only made the financial crisis worse. But then why had he pushed so hard to rebuild the city, and send aid and support to Daruun?

The answer was self evident, Zerek suddenly realized. To restore faith in the throne. To restore hope. To give people something, *someone* to believe in again.

Could he keep the kingdom from falling into complete financial ruin? Wouldn't the people lose confidence in the throne if they found out its coffers were empty?

Zerek no longer knew if trying to expose the problem was right or wrong. Part of him detested that the King hid it from the kingdom, that he lied to them every day, even if it was a lie of omission. Yet Zerek couldn't help but wonder if there really was a right answer.

Was that even possible? For a situation to not have a right answer, and to not have a solution that was morally true but also served the people?

Unfortunately, Zerek would have a very long time to think about it. The King stepped away, climbing up two steps towards the throne, before he turned around and looked down upon them. "Regardless of your intention, you both have betrayed my trust, and broken multiple laws. I have no choice but to imprison you, until such time that I deem your sentence adequate." A sense of complete emptiness overcame Zerek, and he nearly fell over as the reality suddenly set in. "They are not to be released unless I order it," he added, speaking to his guards. "Where are their friends?"

No one spoke at first, and no other guards had joined them. "I assume the rest of our guards are still attempting to capture them," Torick volunteered.

King Beredis sighed and nodded. "Very well. Take these two to the city dungeon immediately. Once their friends are captured, do the same with them." He shook his head, looking down again at Zerek, before he turned his head to the side. "I do not wish to see them ever again."

The two guards with shields stepped forward and gruffly lifted the prisoners up, then they shoved them towards the entrance they had entered through. Zerek felt the dread and emptiness overcome him, and he realized that he had done the very thing that so many others had done to him in recent days.

It was because of that realization that he tried to stop, and called out, "Your Majesty!"

King Beredis turned his head towards him, but did not actually look at him. The guard behind him stopped shoving just long enough for Zerek to say what he had to say. "I truly am sorry. You took me in when I had nowhere else to go, and for that, I am forever in your debt." He bowed his head and closed his eyes, the burning of tears suddenly blurring his vision. "Thank you…"

While the King still didn't look at him, he did nod his head slightly forward, an acknowledgement of Zerek's words. After that, the guard shoved him forward again, and they were through the door.

Zerek clenched his fists, trying desperately to hold back the flood of anguish he felt and the tears that threatened to overtake him. The reality was setting in like a stone slab, etching forever a mark in his heart.

He walked in a daze, Endel beside him sniffling and moaning. Hearing his friend very nearly broke Zerek with more guilt. Endel, his first and only real friend after the war began, had lost his home and his life, all because Zerek had used their friendship to convince him to help.

His friend deserved better. Even though he had felt truly alive tonight for the first time since…well, ever, it hadn't been worth it to hurt his friend. To betray his King.

While he hadn't paid much attention to where they were going, he suddenly realized that they weren't going to the tiny castle dungeon near the guard shack. They were headed towards the front, no doubt destined for the much larger city dungeon he knew to be in the Red District.

Where the worst criminals were taken.

Once outside, the chill of the winter air nipped at him, and a front of clouds had just moved in, throwing up a strong gust of wind. The first snowfall was coming tonight after all, perhaps at any minute.

Would it be cold in the dungeon? Did they light fires to keep the prisoners warm, or did everyone have to huddle together for warmth? Did the city dungeon even have a communal cell, or were they all tiny, individual cells? What if one of the other prisoners decided to steal his clothes, or simply attack him?

Zerek's mind raced with frightening possibilities as they walked along the central avenue, down the hill through the gate, and left into the rest of the city. It was quiet in the dead of night, well past midnight by now, he wagered. How long had they knelt before the throne?

For that matter, why had the King ordered to be personally awoken? Was it because of the personal interest he had taken in Zerek? Had he just given Zerek a chance to redeem himself, but failed? He realized he could have betrayed the thieves, told the King exactly where to find them. Did the King or the city guard even know about the collection of thieves?

It hadn't even crossed his mind during the audience. Even if it had, he never would have betrayed them. Zerek knew there were criminals that were horrible people and deserved the punishments they received. But the ones Zerek had seen, down in the sanctuary, they weren't horrible people.

However, there were plenty of bad ones out there. Many bandits had attacked the mining camps throughout his life, and they never hesitated to hurt others, even kill others when it suited their purpose. They only cared about themselves.

So how could Zerek tell the good ones from the bad?

Not like it'll ever matter, he thought. *I'll never be released from prison...*

No sooner had that thought crossed his mind, than did he see a brief flash of movement. He looked up at the rooftops to the left, certain he had seen something. His heart fluttered for a moment, realizing that, at this time of night, there was only one thing that was likely up there.

Unless it was just been a bat flying overhead. That was entirely possible.

But...what if Laira and Sorin had escaped? What if they were following them, ready to spree them at the opportune moment?

Zerek looked around, at the two shielded guards, at Torick, and at the Mage. One Mage, three soldiers. Could just Sorin and Laira manage to go up against such experienced soldiers?

If it hadn't been for the breeze, the streets would have been completely silent. The only illumination was from the everlasting torches lining the street. Every single window was dark. Was the breeze enough to conceal his friends' movements?

Zerek looked at the guards again. Most of them didn't pay attention, but Torick noticed him looking, and frowned down at him. Zerek looked away, feeling his face grow warm. *Please don't look up, please don't look up, please don't look up.*

However, if Torick was suspicious, he didn't have time to figure out what Zerek was hiding. All of a sudden, every single torch in their immediate vicinity winked out.

Zerek came to a sudden stop and reached out to grab onto Endel, whose cries had long ago quieted to an occasional sniffle.

"What's going on," one of the guards asked in a panic. What sounded like a small wooden box falling and breaking to pieces caught Zerek's attention, and he imagined that all of the guards looked in that direction, just like he did.

And then the brightest flash he had ever seen lit up the street, leaving a bright afterimage in his vision. The sound of rushing feet and multiple thuds echoed in the empty avenue, and suddenly hands grabbed him and pulled him away. He had lost all sense of direction, and he still couldn't see what was going on.

Panic quickly set in, but then a sweet, beautiful voice spoke to him. "It's okay," Laira said, "just hold my hand and don't let go!"

The familiar shape of her hand was suddenly in his, and he grasped for dear life, trying to blink away the flash. The afterimage faded to orange, and then to brown. Laira tugged him along, and then they ran together.

He stumbled a few times, until the brown spot in his vision faded enough to where he could see Laira clearly. He became more confident in his steps, the rest of the city's everlasting torches still lit. When Laira no longer had to pull him along, she looked back at him, smiled, and then picked up the pace.

Looking behind him, he saw Sorin running after them, with little Endel in his arms.

And not a single guard in pursuit.

He turned ahead again, realizing he needed to pay attention to where they were going. "Please tell me you guys didn't kill…"

A lump formed in his throat when he thought of Torick, a guard just doing his job, dead on the side of the road. But Laira looked at Zerek with an incredulous look. "Are you kidding? Of course not! We don't murder, Zerek. That's one rule we won't break for anything."

Feeling relieved, he squeezed her hand, unsure if she could feel it as they raced through the streets.

Torick was alive, and they were safe now.

At least, as safe as fugitives could be.

***

When dawn came for the To'kar camp, Arkad's wounds were bound, but the pain remained just as strong. Tana and the human, Amaya, had done their best to patch him up, but his right eye was forever blinded. His entire face was a mess from Orinda's assault, but that was not uncommon for orc soldiers.

They were not meant to look pretty.

The only reason Arkad knew the sun had risen was because the pitch black of night had given way to a dull, gray haze. The rain continued to pour down upon the camp, and small rivers had formed and washed away several huts. Lightning still thundered all around them, but with considerably less frequency.

The orcs were already breaking down camp, a difficult task in the weather, but orcs were industrious when they needed to be. It would only take a couple of hours, and then they would begin their journey southeast.

Now, however, there was a different matter to attend to. At the southern end of the camp, in the clearing near the forest, the humans from last night had gathered, along with Tana and Amaya.

It was an unnerving experience, to stand across from human Warriors in peace, not as enemies.

Nor were they allies, he realized. He wasn't sure what to consider them.

While the newcomers were gathered in a cluster, Amaya stood apart from them, facing Tana and Arkad.

She looked at them awkwardly, the rain plastering her black hair to her head, her leather armor soaked. He regarded her curiously with his one good eye, ignoring the pain he felt as best as he could. Never had he considered hair on another species to be attractive, but then orcs rarely interacted with outsiders.

Knowing that this human had saved Tana, had saved the entire To'kar tribe, from another human...suddenly she didn't look so hideous.

Amaya caught him staring and raised an eyebrow. He simply continued to stare, not willing to avert his eyes, not willing to say anything. He had nothing to say to her at the moment.

The human's raised eyebrow slowly lowered, and she shifted uncomfortably at the awkward silence. Finally, she looked to Tana and nodded, before turning to face her people.

She began by stating, "The orcs of the To'kar tribe are not our enemies. Their shaman does not wish to harm humans, but instead wishes to coexist peacefully. Therefore my orders stand, unless rescinded by the King himself. No one is to reveal the existence of this tribe to anyone, nor where this camp is." He noted, with a slight smile on his face, that she did not mention where the To'kar would be going. In fact, she was the one who suggested that. It was the best thing they could do to ensure their safety and their future. She would be the only human to walk away with the knowledge of their destination today.

Amaya nodded to the female Wizard. "Take us home, Nia."

Without a word, the Wizard turned west and planted her staff in the ground, bringing forth a flash of light. A moment later, a blue-white wall stood a dozen feet in front of her. Arkad didn't know where the Wizard was taking them, but he didn't care, as long as it was far away from his people.

As the other humans began to file one by one through the portal, Amaya turned back to them. "Thankfully all but the Wizard are subjects of my Kingdom and are honor bound to follow my orders. I do not think there will be any trouble keeping your existence a secret."

Tana bowed to her, a smile stretched across her face. "Thank you, Amaya. I am glad to have trusted you."

Amaya smiled, a look that Arkad found unusual. He had never seen humans smile before. Not like that, anyway.

"I wish you a fair journey," she nodded. "Or, at least as fair as can be in this weather."

Tana laughed a little. "Indeed. Same to you."

Amaya turned to Arkad and nodded. "General. It…" She searched his face, as if looking for an answer. "Well, it has been an honor."

Arkad's face slackened into surprise, and he found himself not knowing what to say or do. Falling back on old tradition, he raised his fist to his chest and nodded to her. "Thank you, Lieutenant."

Without another word, she turned and walked away. All of the other humans had gone through the portal, which left only Amaya and the Wizard. Amaya stopped by the Wizard and looked at her, pausing just long enough for the Wizard to give her a warm smile. Amaya then preceded the Wizard in, and moments later, the Wizard followed, the portal closing behind her.

Arkad and Tana looked to each other, and then began to walk back to the camp together. They observed the ongoing work as Wastelands and darksteel orcs worked together to bring down the surviving huts and pack the materials for transport. There were no qrishags in the camp, so transporting the materials would mean each and every orc would have to carry something.

Tana turned to Arkad and asked, "How are the ones you brought back handling their new situation?"

Arkad felt a sense of pride grow within him, and he smiled down at her, thankful that she walked on his left side so that he did not have to crane his neck around to see her. "They are my soldiers, and they follow my orders. Furthermore, your speech following our arrival has inspired them. I believe they will follow the two of us without question."

"I am glad to hear that," she nodded. "Though I know some of our future, how we get there is uncertain. There may be very dull times ahead in which soldiers will feel less than useful, but I will be relying upon you to keep them well trained and prepared for the war to come."

Arkad felt a surge of energy inside of him, a hint of the blood rage still buried deep within. If Tana was right, there would come a day when he would be able to avenge his people against the ones who slaughtered his people and drove them from their home.

But there was more to what he wanted than revenge. He wanted answers. Where did Klaralin get the darkened steel armor? Arkad could not imagine even the most powerful Wizard being capable of summoning such weapons and armor in great numbers, so he believed someone else must have crafted them for Klaralin.

As useful as the armor was, it also reminded him a little too much of the invaders of Akaida. He hadn't cared at the time that Klaralin had given it to his people, and he should have. Perhaps it was the old Shaman's power over him that had made him ignore the obvious similarities.

Suddenly he was aware of Tana's stare. He looked down at her, realizing that he had grown completely silent in his introspection. She reached out a hand and grabbed his forearm, bringing them to a stop.

"Will you be okay," she asked, her brow creased in concern. She reached up to gently touch his cheek just below his bandaged right eye.

He felt uncomfortable and uncertain at first by her sudden show of affection, but the touch felt too soothing to ignore, and he allowed her hand to linger. After a moment of staring into her eyes, he nodded. "I will be." He shrugged and added, "I may not be as effective on the battlefield anymore, but I can still lead my soldiers, and I will train around my new weakness. I will not fail you."

Tana chuckled, shaking her head as she withdrew her hand. "You are very much a soldier, Arkad."

"No," he shook his head. When she frowned up at him, he smirked a little. "I am a General. And no wound will ever take that from me." He realized that if he had ever doubted that before, the way his soldiers had reacted to his broken form stumbling through the portal last night assured him. They still looked up to him, even knowing that a scrawny, powerless whelp had wounded him so gravely.

He was still their leader. And he always would be.

She nodded, and began walking again, with him joining her seconds later. Tana asked, "What do you think will happen now that you've killed Orinda?"

Arkad scratched at his chin, just beneath a small cut that Orinda had inflicted. "I gave that a great deal of thought last night." He didn't say what he thought next, *when I wasn't overwhelmed by the pain.* "I think Orinda was influencing the old Shaman. Whispering poison into her ear. That may be why the Shaman led us down such terrible paths."

Tana looked at him with a raised eyebrow. "You feel sympathy for the old Shaman?"

Arkad shook his head vigorously, "No. No, she betrayed our people. She deserves the death that will come to her at the hands of the humans. However, I do believe that without Orinda there to poison her mind anymore, she may face that death with greater honor than she otherwise might have."

After a moment of silence, Tana looked at him curiously. "Is an honorable death really so important?"

He brought them to a stop and looked out over the camp. "When one has not led an honorable life, then yes, it is important. But," he said, pausing to look down at her. Somehow, through all of the pain, he managed to smile at her. "An honorable life is far better."

She stared back at him for a moment, before a broad smile stretched across her face.

He looked again at his people...at *his* people, and nodded. "It's what they deserve..."

***

Amaya fidgeted anxiously, absently rubbing at the pommel of her sword. She stood inside of the throne room, the ancient statues staring down upon her. The King was in session with the Allied Council, along with Draegus Kataar, as they were being briefed on the final outcome of the battle against the orc army. The battle she had missed.

What was she going to tell them? Would she tell them the truth, that she had actually allowed Arkad to live, and that there was a tribe of orcs friendly to them that she wanted to protect? Would the King allow that secret to be kept? Or should she not tell him at all, and tell them that she failed to find the General?

No, she couldn't lie, not to her King.

So she would tell him the truth. And hope that he was the honorable man that she believed him to be.

When the doors behind the throne opened and the King and Draegus stepped in, the look on the King's face was decidedly sour, and she wondered why. Certainly it couldn't be from the battle report.

She and Nia had first reported back to the battle camp, so that she could see her team and make sure they were okay. However, she was happy to hear that they were already evacuated, to Everlin no less, so she would have to go see them later. Amaya was happy to hear that every single member of her team had survived, though almost all of them were wounded.

It was at the battle camp that she had met with General Artula and learned that the battle was considered a complete success. The majority of the orc army was destroyed, with very few prisoners. However, several hundred orcs had escaped, including several of the ones wearing darkened steel armor, and the General suspected that the Allied Council would order the armies to hunt down every last orc.

The General was understandably curious about the result of Amaya's mission, but all she told him was, "He will no longer be a problem."

King Beredis wasted no time in closing the distance between them, and he looked directly at her, anger edging at the corners of his eyes. "I am going to preface my first question with a direct statement to you, Lieutenant," he began, catching her off guard with his harsh tone of voice. "I have dealt with enough betrayal for one day. Do not lie to me."

She almost stepped back, feeling shocked by his opening salvo. After a moment's pause, she bowed to him. "Of course, my King. I would never lie to you." Of course, she wouldn't tell him that she had considered doing so not two minutes ago.

"Did you or did you not kill General Arkad?"

That was it, then. There must have been a report in the briefing about Arkad's presence in that final battle last night.

So she looked at the King with even, emotionless eyes and said, "I did not, Sire."

The King looked surprised by her blunt honesty, and exchanged a curious glance with Draegus. "Then why did the updated report I read only moments ago include you telling General Artula that Arkad *was* dead."

"I never told the General that, Sire," she shook her head. The King was about to say something in response, so she added, "I merely told him that the orc General would no longer be a problem. Which is the truth."

After a moment of stunned silence, Draegus ordered, "Explain yourself, Lieutenant."

Though she felt a small amount of fear at how the King would respond, she launched into her report, trying to be as brief and succinct as she could without leaving anything important out. She told them about tracking the orcs to the destroyed camp, about finding Kilack and communicating with him, about the meeting with

Tana, Amaya's subsequent abduction, and the deal she worked out with Tana. Finally, she told him of her battle against Commander Din, and her decision to banish him.

The King and her Captain let her finish her entire story without interruption, listening attentively. When she finished, they remained silent for a moment, and she felt herself sweating, despite the cold of the castle, and her hands shook.

After what felt like hours of the King staring down at her feet, his arms crossed, his face scrunched in thought, he nodded and looked up at her, unfolding his arms and letting them fall to his sides. "This is all quite unexpected news, Lieutenant. Some might even say that you have taken the liberty of your Guardian status far beyond what you should have." She felt her face turn bright red, and fear gripped her heart. Could she lose her status as a Guardian, despite the King's assurances only a few weeks ago? What did that entail? Would they burn the brand off of her wrist? Cut her wrist entirely off? Or worse?

However, when the King continued, it was not at all what she expected. "However, what you have done is save lives. Possibly more than any of us realize. I do not know if this Tana's supposed visions can be trusted, but whether or not we ever fight side by side with orcs, we already have endured enough casualties, and we cannot afford to pay Sal'fe to resurrect our fallen Warriors indefinitely. This war needs to end soon, so that our kingdom may recover."

There was something in how the King's voice broke a little when he mentioned paying Sal'fe that made her wonder if something else was wrong. She knew that the Wizard King Sal'fe was charging a fee for every single foreign Warrior that he brought back to life with the Staff of Aliz, but was it so expensive that it was drying up the treasury? If that was the case for Tal...what of Erien and Saran? Were they in equally dire circumstances?

"Your orders will stand," the King nodded. He looked over at Draegus and nodded. "Have every Warrior involved brought here so that I may reinforce her orders. This situation will remain an absolute secret for the time being."

Draegus nodded, but then paused and asked, "What of the Wizard, Nia?"

They looked at Amaya, and she smiled reassuringly. "She promises to keep it secret. She sees the value in finding a peaceful end to conflict."

The King nodded, satisfied. Then he did something unexpected and stepped forward, reaching out and resting a warm hand on her shoulder. "I also wish you to know that I fully support your actions against Commander Din." He hesitated and drew in a deep breath, glancing at Draegus. "Although I am certain that General Artula will not be happy about it, Commander Din's banishment will remain in effect." He nodded and squeezed her shoulder. "You did well, Lieutenant. Including in your decision not to kill him."

"Although he is a risk, now," Draegus piped in. "He knows about the orcs, and could tell the other kingdoms about them."

"I will inform the Allied Council of his betrayal and subsequent banishment," the King stepped back, releasing her shoulder. "He will have no credibility with them if he should survive the Wastelands long enough to reach another kingdom."

She smiled, feeling her cheeks turn red at the compliment and support. "Thank you, my King."

"Now," he sighed, shaking his head, "Unfortunately I must return to the Allied Council." He grimaced and added, "On an empty stomach, no less. You may consider yourself on leave until your next assignment. I know you must wish to visit your team."

A broad smile opened up across her face, and she nodded excitedly. "Indeed!"

Without another word, the King turned and left, leaving her and Draegus alone. Once the King was gone, she looked to her Captain and asked, "I know it's none of my business, but what other betrayal was he talking about?"

Draegus grimaced and closed the distance with her, looking around. "Remember that kid that helped you fight off the orcs at the wall? Zerek?"

She frowned and nodded. "Of course."

"He broke into the castle last night to steal something."

Feeling her stomach drop, along with her jaw, she almost stepped back in shock. "What? But, why?"

He shook his head. "It's not my place to say. However, he is now a wanted fugitive."

"My gods," she shook her head. "I can hardly believe it."

For a moment, they stood in silence while she allowed the news to sink in. However, a smile suddenly came across Draegus's face, and he looked at her curiously. "So how does it feel?"

She frowned at him. "Sir?"

"You faced your demons and won, right?" He folded his arms and leaned back a little. "How does it feel?

"Oh," she felt her face grow a little warm. She thought back to last night, to that moment when she stood over Din, ready to plunge her sword into his chest. Absently, she touched the pommel again, somehow feeling reassured by her sword's presence. A reminder of a past that had once consumed her, but now…

"I feel free," she said at length. "And it feels like a great weight has been taken off of my heart."

Draegus's smile broadened, and he clasped her on the shoulder. "I thought so. Listen, I knew Din, knew his skills with a sword. If you defeated him as readily as you say you did…" He shook his head, and finished, "I'm glad you're on our side."

Without another word, he turned and followed the King out, back towards the Allied Council. She stared after him, her heart feeling lighter than it had in so long. The darkness was gone, and she felt like her old self.

She was free!

***

After Zerek and the others had returned to the Thieves' Sanctuary, Sorin produced an enchanted key he had stolen from one of the guards and unshackled Endel and Zerek.

Once they were free and their heart rates had settled, he and Endel told Sorin and Laira what had happened in the throne room, about what the King had told them.

At first, Sorin scoffed and shook his head. "He's leading us towards a crisis that can only end in rebellion or civil war."

Zerek frowned, shaking his head. "Yeah, but getting that book out and making the public aware of just how bad things are could just as easily incite rebellion."

Sorin started to retort, but then stopped. He was silent for a long time, but it was Laira who spoke next. "He's right, Sorin. We can't save the kingdom by destroying what hope people have left."

He slouched then, and nodded in agreement. "I guess that's true."

After that, he stepped away to find his bed and get some rest.

Zerek then tried awkwardly to apologize to Endel, but the kid wouldn't hear of it. "Even though it turned out to be the wrong thing to do, we still had to try. And…I'll miss the castle, I won't lie." He shook his head, and added, "But this is where I belong. This is the only family I've ever known." He smiled at Laira and then launched himself at her, embracing her in a tight hug. "You're like my big sister."

Then, much to Zerek's surprise, Endel turned to him and launched at him, wrapping his arms so tight around him that he could scarcely breathe. How could such a small kid be so strong?

"And you're my big brother."

A giant well of emotion grew in Zerek's chest, and he even felt a little wetness in his eyes. Zerek never had a brother, nor any siblings. Just his Father, and Elina.

Elina… He suddenly realized he hadn't thought about her in weeks.

When Endel left to go find a bed for himself, he and Laira were left alone together. She took him to where she always slept, a small alcove hidden away from everyone else with several blankets laid out on the cold stone floor to act as a mattress. The blankets were torn and shredded and didn't smell very good, but he didn't care.

They snuggled up under several blankets, clutching one another as if they hadn't seen each other in years. He wanted to focus on her, but his thoughts kept straying back to Elina, to his Father, to everyone he had known at the camp.

He didn't know when he fell asleep, or how long he slumbered, but now he lay awake with Laira still in his arms.

As he lay there, feeling her warmth, gently caressing her back, his mind wandered again. He began to draw parallels from life at the camp to his life at the castle.

Under the rule of the Steward, he had been a virtual prisoner, just as he had been at the camp. He also realized that being a soldier would have been no different. He would have been forced to follow orders, living his life at the beck and call of others. Doing what he wanted was rebellious.

And rebel was what he had done ever since he had come to the city. Sneaking off, meeting up with Laira, and now breaking into the castle.

There was one thing and one thing alone that he missed from the mining camp. Family. Not so much his father, for as much as he missed him, it was beyond just that. It was the fact that everyone at the camp took care of each other. Just like Elina had taken care of him.

He looked out of their alcove, out at the random camps of people spread throughout the abandoned underground aqueduct. Most everyone was awake and milling about, and he figured it was well past midday, given how late it was when they had returned to the Sanctuary

They were like a family to him. Just like the mining camp.

Sorin and Laira had no obligation to him or Endel, and yet they had come back to save them. No, not just Sorin and Laira, they had gone back and recruited over a dozen other thieves to help in the ambush, to snuff out the everlasting torches, and to take down the guards without killing them.

This was where he belonged, he realized, looking back to Laira. This was who he belonged with. Laira, the thieves…they were his family.

She stirred, and he was afraid he had drawn her out of the dream world. But then she clutched at him tighter, clearly awake, but not wanting to leave his arms.

"Can we just stay like this forever?" she whispered.

He smiled and wrapped his arms around her tighter. "Why not?" he whispered back. She shifted just enough so that she could look up at him, keeping her cheek on his shoulder. He looked down at her, their noses practically touching. "I'm not going anywhere," he said to her.

The biggest smile he had ever seen drew across Laira's face, and before he knew what was happening, she closed the distance and kissed him.

When she pulled away, she buried her face on his chest.

But he had to say it. Somehow, today, it felt more important, more real.

"I love you, Laira."

ABOUT THE AUTHOR

Jon Wasik has been telling stories since he was a little boy, usually with a cookie and milk at his Great Grandma's kitchen table. It wasn't until 5th grade that he finally put pen to paper, and from that moment on, writing has been his greatest passion.

When he isn't writing, Jon likes to read, play video games, and watch insanely geeky movies with his wife. His Gollum voice impressions are eerie, he quotes Doctor Who like others quote the bible, and he can leap terabytes of data in a single bound!

You can find out more about him by visiting his blog, http://kataar.wordpress.com/

Made in the USA
Middletown, DE
06 February 2019